# Critical Acclaim for
# WHISPERS FROM PROPHECY

Gorgeous cover! (The author) has created a complex and fully imagined world. Descriptions of settings and characters are wonderfully vivid.

—WRITER'S DIGEST REVIEW

Pairing politics, fantasy elements, family ties, and personal relationships is not an easy feat, but author Sandra Valencia brings the same art of balance to this second *Chikondra Trilogy* novel as she did to the first. Sandra and Warnach's bond is more powerful than ever, interspersed with inspiring phrases that elevate their romance beyond the physical into a true spiritual and intellectual connection, which is always refreshing to see. As this intimacy plot weaves in and out of the storyline, the political ideas and new mysteries of the current plot come to the fore, where the excitement really heats up as Sandra makes new connections and reveals some secrets that bring about new characters, alliances, and dangers. *Whispers from Prophecy* continues an already excellent series with new and innovative plot ideas, as well as solid character development.

—5-STAR REVIEW
KC FINN, READERS' FAVORITE

*The Chikondra Trilogy*, 2015 Winner for Published Fiction, Creative Arts Event, Columbus, Ohio.

LCCN: 2019918120

Paperback ISBN 978-1-63337-364-8
Hardback ISBN 978-1-63337-365-5
E-book ISBN 978-1-63337-366-2

Printed in the United States of America

1  3  5  7  9  10  8  6  4  2

# Whispers from Prophecy

## THE CHIKONDRA TRILOGY: LOVE BEAR THE CHALLENGE

*May Love always shine on your path.*
*Sandra Valencia*

### SANDRA VALENCIA

# Dedication

I have been blessed many times over with a family that encourages me to pursue the writing projects that consume so much of my time and energy. My husband continues to support my efforts while cheerfully taking on many household chores to give me more time to write. What a guy!

At the same time, my life is enriched by those whose enthusiasm for my writing keeps me going when my head aches, my eyes blur, and my fingers hurt from long stretches at the computer. These people are friends, new and old, who remind me that all the effort is worthwhile. They have no idea how much they mean to me, but I am proud to share their friendship. My unending gratitude still goes to Jan Thompson and Philippa Ede, but I also feel I must include others who believe in me and keep me going: Angela Bishop, Amy Randall-McSorley, Kathy Hodorowski, Judy Malenick, Ramón and Ana Quiñones.

# Prologue
## From Guardian Redeemed

Idealistic and dreaming of a career in interstellar diplomacy, Sandra Warner reluctantly accepted a special assignment from John Edwards, Under-Secretary of Earth's Dil-Terra Inter-Alliance Services Division. Her assignment was to assist a diplomatic representative from the Dil-Terra Interplanetary Alliance as he delved into the major undertaking of helping the Federation of Earth States prepare its membership application to join the powerful union of planets. Her challenge was to find a way to work with one of the Alliance's most successful diplomats while not yielding to the pressures of his nearly obsessive approach to work.

Notorious for his unrelenting drive and its impact on colleagues, Senior Field Minister Warnach Sirinoya, from the planet of Chikondra, was determined to achieve Earth's acceptance into the Alliance. Events across the galaxy had convinced him that a quiet enemy was actively involved in tactics meant to weaken member planets in order to destabilize and eventually conquer the Alliance. Sirinoya believed Earth's membership would prove essential to strengthening and sustaining the galactic organization and its pursuit of peace. Frustrated by delays and failures in the initial stages of his assignment, he was understandably skeptical when introduced to a specialist he judged far too young and inexperienced to assume responsibilities on a project of such magnitude.

Despite serious misgivings, Minister Sirinoya acknowledged the fact that he had no other alternative but to accept Sandra Warner as his project aide. Following a rocky start as they began work together on Earth's membership project, the two unlikely partners developed mutual respect as they recognized similar work ethics and philosophic approaches. Friendship gradually wound itself into their relationship.

One night, a tragic incident occurred in a run-down neighborhood when Sandra Warner failed to prevent rooftop snipers from murdering a child. The following morning, as Warnach Sirinoya attempted to console her, the respected diplomat and the young Terran were both shocked to discover their friendship had transformed into love.

Determined to protect her from prejudices of her society and differences in their species, Warnach battled his emotions as he decided he could not risk an open relationship with her. Past tragedies in both their lives only heightened the torment of their hidden love. Finally, heartrending events caused Warnach to abruptly end his assignment on Earth to return to his homeworld and leave behind the woman who had captured his heart.

Separation of time and distance would prove no match for startling and inexplicable forces that continued to draw them together. Finally, they faced startling reality. Destiny seemed bent on forcing them to explore their feelings for one another and make decisions destined to impact their future.

Acceptance of their love presented a new series of challenges. To pursue her dreams of a diplomatic career, Sandra prepared to leave Earth to study at the prestigious Chikondran Academy of Diplomatic Sciences. Her first challenge was to build new relationships while beginning a fresh academic career not influenced by the famed diplomat whom she loved. Reluctantly, Warnach acquiesced in her wishes of keeping the personal aspects of their relationship secret.

Arriving on Chikondra, she also immersed herself in the complexities of a modern society coping with the influences of alien cultures while stubbornly clinging to the foundation of its mystical traditions. Patiently guided by

Warnach and his family through a series of complicated rituals, she moved toward the sacred state of unification.

Both accepted faith as integral to their characters and their lives. Warnach, who was more structured in his faith practices, found himself confronted with inexplicable mysteries when elusive and legendary angel spirits began appearing to Sandra. Those mysteries were unfathomable even to his aunt, a woman who had dedicated her entire life to religious service.

Within Guardian Redeemed, two people from dramatically diverse backgrounds balance their growing love with family issues, cultural differences, demanding careers, lofty dreams, and personal sorrows. Those dynamics are woven into a fascinating tapestry of fear and conflict, triumph, and love.

As Whispers from Prophecy begins, Warnach Sirinoya and his bride have just returned home from their eventful honeymoon. Perplexing questions and unexpected conflicts arise almost immediately as she resumes her studies and he returns to work at the Ministry of Field Service Diplomacy.

# Chapter One

"Sandra! Welcome home!" Araman Sirinoya wrapped her son's lifemate in a delightfully warm embrace. Stepping backward, she smiled her approval. "You look absolutely beautiful."

"Thank you, Mamehr. I must admit. I feel beautiful, and it's all because of this wonderful son of yours."

Araman laughed as Warnach bent forward to salute her with cerea-semi'ittá. "If your ki'mirsah looks radiantly happy, I have no words to describe you. Welcome back, my son."

Within minutes of returning home from their honeymoon, Warnach disappeared upstairs with their luggage while Sandra followed Araman to the kitchen. Along the way, the two women chatted about their shared admiration for Cafti and how much John and Angela had enjoyed the beach. Reaching the kitchen, they found Nadana preparing a tray of cheeses and toasted crackers to carry them over until dinner.

"Nadana, I'm so glad you're still here," Sandra greeted, kissing the Simlani's softly wrinkled cheek.

"It's customary, my child, for the entire family to welcome a newly unified couple home. We're also expecting Badrik to arrive at any time."

"And Farisa?"

"Not Farisa, I'm afraid. She'll be on duty at the clinic until late tonight."

"Too bad," Sandra said, pulling out a chair to sit down. Nadana's eyes, though kind and caring, held a piercing look that she could hardly help but notice. Feeling somewhat unsettled, she started to say something when strong arms suddenly surrounded her and dragged her out of the chair.

"Little sister! You've come home!"

Spontaneous laughter was impossible to avoid. "Big brother!" she exclaimed happily, "I missed you! How are you?"

Grasping her shoulders, he pushed her backward and stared into her face with exaggerated seriousness. "Tell me the truth. Has that older brother of mine behaved himself with you?"

She almost choked on laughter. "You have no reason to worry. Your big brother has made me a very happy lady."

"There, dear brother. I told you, but you didn't believe me. Now you have no choice."

Spinning around, Badrik glared suspiciously into his brother's face. "How fortunate for you that she supports your claim," he said before embracing Warnach affectionately.

Evening descended upon the household before anyone realized. Gathering around a candlelit table outside, the Sirinoya family joined hands and prayed before their meal. Smiling but remaining relatively quiet, Sandra enjoyed a sense of contentment while Warnach and Badrik dominated the dinner conversation. She derived so much satisfaction from the affectionate familial exchanges that had been so often missing from her home on Earth.

"I think the ocean is particularly beautiful this time of year," Araman remarked near the end of supper as she spooned a bite of dessert into her mouth. "Perhaps that's why it captivates you so, Sandra."

With delayed realization that Mamehr had spoken to her, Sandra lifted her eyes apologetically. "Perhaps. Perhaps it's also because I have such wonderful memories of the first time you all took me there."

"I can safely say that day was particularly memorable for all of us. I know it was for me," Badrik interjected. "That was the first time I ever knew anything about rules for your game of volleyball."

Reproachfully, Nadana shook her head at him. "Badrik, a day such as that and what you remember is nothing more than a game?"

Noting disapproval in his aunt's eyes, Badrik grinned shamelessly. Looking not the least bit contrite, he said, "My dear Nadana, you have no need for concern. If I rarely speak of our unexpected visitors that day, it's because I remain astounded by something I never expected to see in my lifetime."

"Nor I," added Araman, her expression turning thoughtful. "Sandra, I do hope the day will come when you'll be able to fully appreciate what a blessing you were granted when you saw Quazon. That experience was a singular event likely never to happen again."

Abruptly, Sandra's spoon stopped in front of her mouth. Her eyes darted quickly toward Warnach, whose eyebrows lifted in silent communication. Nadana's sharp eyes observed their swift, wordless exchange, but she withheld any comment.

Later, Sandra excused herself to go upstairs and unpack. When Warnach volunteered to help, she smilingly suggested that he spend some time with his family so that she could get a few things done. She would then rejoin them in time for evening prayers.

While Nadana and Araman disappeared into the kitchen, Warnach and Badrik retired to the family lounge. In a relaxed mood, Warnach walked toward a bar and filled two glasses with after-dinner liqueur. Turning, he offered one to his brother before settling himself at the end of a sofa.

"You do know, my brother, what I intend to ask," Badrik began before taking a seat.

Warnach's eyebrows lifted sharply. "And do you know what it is I intend to ask you?"

Dark eyebrows knit together in question. "I was not the one who canceled half my honeymoon plans for an abrupt escape to the ocean."

"True," Warnach answered with a sideways tilt of his head. "But you might have warned me."

"Warned you? About what?"

Warnach sighed. "I'm not angry, Badrik. At least, not with you. You had no way of knowing."

For a long moment, Badrik stared into his older brother's black eyes. His own eyes began to burn angrily. "Please. Don't tell me my sister heard what that dezhrashth Gazhimna Rihfrajna said."

Grimly, Warnach nodded. "She did. To make matters worse, quite by accident, I encountered Nedthaz Blinsara'á and his lifemate at a restaurant in Zahmichilá. His lovely lifemate made the delightful mistake of telling me how glad she was about my obvious reconciliation with Lashira…just as Sandra walked up and heard everything."

Badrik slowly sipped liqueur from his glass. "I had the feeling your sudden change of plans might be related to Lashira. I warned you…"

"Yes, and you were right, and I was wrong."

"Is Sandra all right?"

"She wasn't, and it was my fault. I am ashamed to admit it, but I exploded."

"I suppose that means Sandra bore the brunt of that infamous temper of yours."

"Badrik, it's over. She knows everything. We discussed it, and it's over."

"I take it that required magnificent effort on your part."

Warnach earnestly studied his brother's stern expression for several moments. "The experience was dreadful. Badrik, you can't possibly know how much I wish I had listened to you. You were right from the beginning."

"I told you she'd understand. What happened with Lashira was too long ago. You should have trusted Sandra."

Exhaling a heavy breath, Warnach nodded. "Your point is a valid one I cannot argue. I made a terrible mistake - one I will not repeat. Now, what about Mirsah Rihfrajna? Were her comments really so bad?"

"Despicable. After you left, I told Mamehr and Nadana. I think they've seen to it that Mirsah Rihfrajna refrains from any future discussion on the subject. If not, I have every intention of informing Dimnazh."

Interrupting their conversation, Araman and Nadana rejoined them. Mamehr sat beside Warnach on the sofa while Nadana took a seat near Badrik. Both men exchanged questioning glances, but Badrik took the lead. "You ladies appear to have something serious on your minds. If it helps, my brother and I already discussed the unfortunate event involving Mirsah Rihfrajna. Regrettably, Sandra did overhear what was said."

Concern clouded Araman's eyes. "Warnach? Is everything all right?"

"Mamehr, she's fine. You saw her. We finally sat down, and I explained everything."

"Everything? Are you certain she's all right?"

His brow creased as he shifted his gaze to Nadana. Something in her tone of voice unsettled him. "Nadana, she knows the whole story behind what happened with Lashira. We discussed it thoroughly, and it finally rests where it should. In the past."

"That is a good thing," she remarked with unmistakable relief. "Now, I have a question for you."

His eyes darted toward Badrik, who only shrugged his shoulders. "I'll answer if I can."

"When Araman mentioned to Sandra about seeing Quazon being a once-in-a-lifetime experience, you both froze. I said nothing in front of your ki'mirsah, but I feel compelled to ask. Was that day last year a solitary encounter?"

Warnach lifted his glass and took a sustaining amount of liqueur. Pensively, he rolled the fiery liquid around his mouth before swallowing.

"I did intend to tell you, Nadana. I was uncertain when or even how to broach the subject."

Chocolate-colored eyes lifted in a prayerful gesture. "Amazing. You've seen them again. Absolutely amazing."

"More than simply amazing, I fear."

"In what way?"

Perplexed by the exchange, Araman and Badrik looked at one another but remained silent.

"Nadana, while we were away, they came to us twice, each time at her request."

Abruptly, Badrik leaned forward. "Warnach, are you telling us you saw Quazon twice while you were at the beach?"

"Saw them. Played with them. Touched them. Talked to them. They came the day after we arrived at the beach house." A lengthy pause ensued. "They returned again this morning."

Mamehr stared at her older son. "Are you serious?"

With an elegant gesture of her hand, Nadana requested silence from her sister and nephew. "You said they came at her request. How is that possible?"

Warnach leaned sideways and set his glass on an occasional table. "Nadana, I'm not certain. When I asked, she told me that they talk to her… that she hears them inside her mind. She said she asked them to come the first time. She then told me she could invite them back. To my total astonishment, they returned just as she said they would. I watched them together. There's no doubt whatsoever that she directly communicates with them. I know how unbelievable it sounds, but I know what I saw."

"Goodness! How serious you all look. I thought you might be enjoying a relaxing family chat."

Raising his face, Warnach smiled warmly and reached for her hand. "Are you finished so soon?"

"Almost." She glanced around at their faces. "Please, tell me I didn't make an embarrassing mistake at the unification ceremony that has brought some terrible shame to the family."

Intending to deflect any possible discomfort, Warnach gestured to her. "Come. Sit beside me. We were actually just discussing how we will ever possibly deal with all the wonderful changes you've brought to this family."

Her eyes reflected uncertainty, but she felt it inappropriate to challenge his statement, especially when those black eyes flashed such affectionate humor. Casting another look around the room, she slowly smiled at Warnach. "Ah, I think I understand now. Not tonight, my lifemate. If you want me to tell them about Quazon, it must wait until tomorrow. I think it's time for night prayers, and I need you to show me where I'm supposed to put a few things before we can go to bed."

Certain that Sandra could not have overheard the family's discussion, Nadana slowly smiled. "Tomorrow, then?"

Sandra allowed her eyes to meet the Simlani's. "Tomorrow."

With morning came cooler temperatures than at the beach. Pulling on a sweater, Sandra left Warnach asleep to go outside for a walk. Just as she opened the patio door, a voice stopped her.

"If you intend to walk and don't mind the company of an old woman, I would be honored to join you."

Turning, Sandra smiled. "Good morning, Nadana. Actually, a peaceful walk was exactly what I had in mind. Your company would make it so much better."

For nearly fifteen minutes, they chatted about various subjects as they strolled along winding paths. After Nadana grew suddenly quiet, Sandra quietly said, "I know how strange this must sound, but, last night, when I was sleeping, they told me yours is a spirit I can always trust. They also told me to expect you early this morning."

Nadana stopped and looked up at the face so fair compared to typical Chikondran faces. "They? Quazon?" Receiving an affirming nod in reply, she smiled. "Grasping this is so difficult. Do you have any idea why they speak to you?"

Continuing along the path, Sandra scanned treetops swaying in gentle breezes. "Warnach asked me the same question. I honestly don't understand at all. Nadana, my heart tells me just to accept without questions. It really makes no sense. However, because I trust them, I'm comfortable not asking. I owe them so much."

"You are wise, child, if you can listen to such wisdom from your heart. Even more so than Chikondrans, you Terrans are famed for your driving curiosity and desire to know. The greatest secrets of Yahvanta's universe are discerned through trust, not analysis."

"Nadana, why do you think they speak to me?"

The Simlani stopped again and gazed upward into green eyes filled with questions. "I have no answer for you, child. When I return to Tichtika, I intend to research ancient archives for some clue. Perhaps there's no other reason than they are pleased by your special love for my world and for your ki'medsah. That is what you wished last year that brought them, isn't it?"

Her smile trembled. "I wanted us always to be able to love one another the way we did that day."

"And now, with the blessing of Quazon, your wish has become reality."

Crunching sounded on the path behind them. Both women turned and smiled as they watched Warnach approach at a leisurely jog.

"Good morning, my lovely Terran." He greeted Sandra with a kiss before turning to his aunt. Embracing her slight form, he kissed her forehead. "And a good morning to you, Respected Simlani. I trust you've enjoyed an interesting talk with my lifemate."

A wide smile crossed Nadana's aging features. "Very interesting. I've decided that your lifemate is a fascinating lady and that you're more fortunate than you know to have won her love."

Warnach's eyes met and held Sandra's as he answered, "Not fortunate, my dear aunt. To be loved by my Shi'níyah can only mean that I am blessed by the Great Spirit."

～

Returning to the academy a week after their honeymoon ended, Sandra launched herself into classes with renewed vigor and purpose. Since she and Warnach had unified, her goals for the future appeared more attainable than ever. No longer was she merely dreaming of a career. Instead, she was taking deliberate, concrete steps toward a vocation she knew would fulfill her dreams of helping improve life within the Alliance.

Happily, the prediction Sandra had made before leaving Earth came true faster than anyone had expected. Three SFSD students, including Nempten Dalinya, had elected to leave the demanding curriculum. Both Peter and Emilio were slotted into the prestigious diplomatic school. Observing his lifemate's excitement over the announcement, Warnach had humorously quipped that the Chikondran Academy of Diplomatic Sciences might not survive the onslaught of the three Terran students in the SFSD. Privately, he had already thanked Farsuk Edsaka for trusting his intuition and authorizing the transfers.

While his lifemate applied her efforts to the demands of CADS studies, Warnach worked hard at adapting to ministry responsibilities on Chikondra. Accustomed to years of constant travel and the undeniable excitement of field missions, he encountered daily challenges to his patience. Administrative activities failed to satisfy his own truest vocation, meeting head-on with parties in conflict for the purpose of negotiating peace.

At the same time, he comprehended that his new assignment held intrinsic value in and of itself. Hectic planning, rushed departures, and life on-mission had driven from his mind the critical importance of accomplishments made by support staff, ministry coordinators, and home ministers. Following a lengthy conversation with Sandra, he found himself comparing the entire process to a symphonic performance. The roles of musicians and conductors could be perceived as difficult to define. What he finally recognized was that the two functions were so integrally entwined that there was no possibility of separating one from the other.

At the end of a day he had found less than stimulating or challenging, she returned home after a late study session with Druska and Ziaman. Meeting her at the door, he received a smile that reminded him why he had decided to observe Karmía in the first place. Listening attentively as she expressed opinions related to current assignments, he understood how valuable an advocate she would become based on the strengths of her expanding knowledge and developing capabilities. After retiring to the privacy of their suite that night, the intimacy they shared successfully reinforced his wisdom in taking the sabbatical.

~

Four weeks after the Sirinoya family hosted a celebration for Sandra's first birthday on Chikondra, she returned home late one evening. On break from the academy, she had spent the entire day on a shopping excursion with Druska and Ziaman. Ruefully, she stared down at an embarrassing number of parcels on the floor at the base of a staircase leading up to the master suite.

Several times throughout the day, she had cheerfully commented to her friends that Warnach might faint from shock once he discovered the extent of her purchases. Laughing, she had also pointed out that her frivolous spree had come at a most inappropriate time, especially considering that her salary from Earth was nearing an end and that she would need to rely on her stipend and her lifemate's generosity for support.

Comical remarks echoed happily inside her mind as she wandered through the house. Reaching the kitchen, she smiled brightly. "Mamehr! I didn't expect you back until tomorrow!"

After embracing Araman, Sandra noted strained features and shifted her gaze to Warnach. Stepping to where he leaned back against a long bank of cabinets, she reached upward to stroke his cheek. "I apologize. I didn't mean to intrude. I'll come back after you finish your discussion."

Immediately, Warnach reached out and grasped her arm. Stormy eyes clearly indicated that he was very upset. "No, Sandra. Stay. You must excuse me. I have a com-link conference in ten minutes. In the meantime, I believe Mamehr has something to tell you." Briskly, he left the kitchen.

Turning puzzled eyes toward his mother, Sandra saw uncomfortable reluctance to speak. "Mamehr?"

Pressing her lips together, Araman said nothing at first. Instead, she removed a second cup from a cabinet and poured two cups of freshly brewed tea. Turning, she went to the table, set down the cups of steaming liquid, and sat. "Please. Sit with me."

Quietly, Sandra stirred a honey-like sweetener into her tea while simultaneously studying Araman's severe expression. Long minutes passed before she finally broke the silence. "I obviously have no idea what's wrong, but I'm more than willing to help if I can."

Araman's mouth twitched nervously. "Child, there's nothing you can do. Warnach isn't happy with me right now. I have no doubt he'll recover."

"What happened? I can't imagine him getting so upset for no reason."

Araman drank from her cup. Then, setting it down, she met Sandra's waiting gaze. "I asked him to go with me to Tichtika to look at some property I found."

"Property? As in something you plan to buy?"

Araman nodded. "Yes. Actually, I found a lovely little house. I thought it would make a perfect place for Nadana and me to spend time together in Tichtika instead of my staying at a hotel while she stays at the Brisa'machtai."

Confusion was obvious in the shake of Sandra's head. "Why would that upset him? It doesn't seem at all strange to me that you would want a private place that's all your own when you visit Tichtika."

Inhaling deeply, Araman forced a smile. "The problem is that it wouldn't be exclusively for visits. I plan to move there. Permanently."

Unconsciously, Sandra's mouth dropped open, and her eyes widened. "Move? Why?"

Stretching her arm across the table, Araman took Sandra's hand. Finally, she smiled. "This house now belongs to you and to Warnach. I should have moved out immediately after you returned from your honeymoon trip. If I tarried, it was because I wanted to be absolutely certain that you were comfortably adjusted. Now, it's time for me to observe the old ways. That way, you can have the freedom to make this house your own."

"Old ways," Sandra repeated. Suddenly, she shook her head sharply. "Mamehr, that makes no sense whatsoever. This is your house as much as it is ours."

Intense brown eyes stared into Sandra's. "Child, even on Chikondra, no house needs two mistresses. You and I enjoy such a close relationship. I have no desire to risk that closeness by staying and creating friction."

"Friction? What kind of friction?"

"Sandra," Araman replied patiently, "the time will come when you'll want to make changes or do things differently than I have. I want you to do that with confidence. I don't want you to be concerned or reluctant about what I might think or for you to worry that I might disagree. This is your home now."

"Mamehr, this is your home, too. I mean, how long have you lived here? How can you even think about just walking away from all the memories this house holds for you? Worse than that, how can you think I would even want you to leave?"

The response prompted an affectionate smile. "Please, trust my judgment. I've watched other families. Especially in the early years, it really is better this way. Later, you'll understand."

Standing, Sandra walked over to rinse her cup. When she spun around, her expression revealed total dismay. "I'm not like other women. Mamehr, this family isn't like those other families, either. Please, think about this. I know Warnach doesn't want you to leave. Neither do I."

Rising, Araman went to her and kissed her cheek. "Daughter, I love your heart. I also know what I must do. As a favor, I ask you to convince Warnach to go with me. Right now, I'm quite tired. I'm going to say my prayers and get ready for bed. Goodnight."

Upstairs, Sandra stared at the pile of packages she had just dumped on the bed. She would certainly have to put things away before she and Warnach could go to sleep. Deciding that task could wait, she hurried back downstairs. Peeking around the open door of his office, she saw that he was still on his call. Sensing her presence, he glanced up and stretched out his hand, wordlessly inviting her to his side.

Crossing the office, she walked around behind his chair. As he conferred with ministers on-mission to Bederand, she stood behind him and slipped her hands beneath his hair. Combing her fingers through long, waving locks eased her anxiety regarding Araman.

Leaning backward, he listened carefully to distant colleagues while savoring her touch that soothed nerves jarred by Mamehr's unexpected announcement. For a moment, it seemed the call would continue most of the night. Growing fatigued and impatient, Warnach finally suggested that the field ministers attempt to utilize some of the tactics he had recommended and consult with him again the following evening.

When the call ended, he closed his eyes and escaped into unique sensations created by loving hands. Slow, rhythmic strokes through his hair produced a soothing, tranquilizing effect. Her hands raised until her fingertips could massage circles of relief against his temples. Breathing in deeply, he expelled some of his stress.

"Warnach?" The softness of her voice interrupted the silence. "Why? Why is she really planning to leave?"

Reluctantly, he pushed himself from his chair. Turning, he pulled her closer. "She honestly believes it will be best for our happiness."

"I don't want her to go. Especially not for a reason like that."

Tilting his forehead, he lightly touched cerea-nervos to her forehead for mere seconds. His face then drew into serious lines. "Shi'níyah, I also want her to stay. However, I think it will be better if we discuss the matter tomorrow. We should say night prayers and get some sleep. Perhaps we can then reason through this in the morning and devise a solution." Then, with his arm around her shoulders, he led her to the Brisajai.

Upstairs, standing inside her enormous, half-empty closet, he attempted to alleviate her unabated distress that he clearly felt. "It appears this break from school may finally fill your closet."

Her rueful smile failed to chase shadows from her eyes. "I think I went overboard. I really don't need all these things. On the other hand, I really like them."

"From what I see, you made lovely choices. I shall be very happy to see you model them for me."

"I'm thinking of returning some," she said distractedly.

"You shouldn't. One thing I've noticed is that you buy very few clothes. I'm glad you finally treated yourself. You quite deserve them."

Lifting solemn eyes, she looked thoughtful. "I feel guilty. My salary ends soon, and, until after graduation, the only income I'll have is my stipend."

Wryly, he grinned and shook his head. "Are you worried that your ki'medsah cannot manage to provide for us both?"

Turning, she hung an elegantly styled nashavri. Still preoccupied, she ran nervous fingers along the magenta sleeves without looking at him. "I have no doubt you can support us. It's just that I've been independent for so long. I've grown accustomed to taking care of myself."

As he did so often, Warnach found himself wrapping his arms around her from behind and holding her against him while he rested his chin on her shoulder. "Sandra, you're no longer alone in life. There will likely be many times in the future when you and I will need to rely solely on one another.

For now, there's no reason at all for you to worry about such matters. Besides, your real concerns have nothing to do with the state of your finances."

Moving from his embrace, she returned to their bedroom and folded back the silk spread and blankets. Without any comment, she undressed and tugged a warm nightgown over her head. Not bothering to pick up the pile of clothes she had dropped on the floor, she sat on the edge of the bed. "If only I could understand why she feels so compelled to leave."

Saying nothing else, she got up and went to the bathroom. Returning to find everything cleared from the floor, she forced a grin. "Honestly. I really was going to pick them up and put them away."

Without a word, he led her to the upholstered seat at the foot of their enormous bed. "First me, then you," he told her as he sat down.

At last, her eyes reflected a soft gleam. Carefully, she removed his Kitak, kissed the metal band, and placed it in the case resting on the dresser. When she exchanged places with him, he knelt on the floor and gazed up into her face. "Shi'níyah, we're both worried, but it will do neither of us any good if we get no rest tonight." Receiving a nod in response, he lightly kissed her lips and proceeded to remove her Kitak and join it with its other half.

Moments later, extinguishing lights and sliding beneath warm blankets, he lay on his side. Reaching behind him, he pulled her arm over his side. Flattening her palm against his stomach, he covered her hand with his. "I love you. Goodnight, sweet Shi'níyah," he murmured as he felt her face nuzzle against his back.

～

Dark, sleep-heavy eyes squinted to focus on the lighted display on the nightstand. Too early to get up on a weekend morning following a tense week. After rolling onto his back, wakefulness insidiously invaded his resisting brain. "Sandra?" No answer sounded in semi-darkness. Realizing he was alone, he squeezed his eyes tightly shut and groaned. She always described herself as a morning person. If only he could comprehend why her mornings came so often at dawn's first light.

Entering the marble-walled bath, he splashed cold water on his face. Deciding to shower later, he wrapped himself in a warm robe and went downstairs to look for her. She had remained at home the day before to give him time alone with Mamehr for the trip to Tichtika. Hopeful eyes had greeted him upon his return. How he had hated to disappoint her by telling her that Mamehr had already agreed to purchase the house.

Coming to bed late after a follow-up com-link conference with colleagues on Bederand, he had lain awake for a long time. Although asleep, she had tossed and turned constantly. Finally, he had raised up to quiet her with cerea-semi'ittá. Forcing from his mind Mamehr's intentions and the frustrating lack of progress on Bederand, he fell asleep.

Sandra had entered the solitude of the Brisajai just after five o'clock. With rosary beads in hand, she prayed traditional prayers that had granted great comfort throughout what had often seemed an unrelenting parade of troubled events. Sometimes, she wondered about the mix of faith practices in her life. Cafti's words echoed in her mind. Yes, there would be confusion and challenge. However, to acknowledge faith in God, she should always remind herself that God had created the universe in its entirety. She must also learn to trust that God would always show her when she was in the presence of true faith, even when that faith was revealed in different ways.

Early that morning, she had awakened with a heart that felt heavy. As much as she loved the beauty of Warnach's religious practices, she craved consolation from the faith she had discovered on Earth. Spiritually, she reached out to home for reassurance and strength to face current sadness.

Later, inside the kitchen, she brewed a pot of fresh coffee. Even the aroma reminded her of home. Despite all the difficulties of her youth, she had successfully built some lasting memories. Sitting down with a china mug filled with steaming coffee, she stared into creamy brown depths and realized how those fond thoughts of home brought more troubling questions to her spirit on Chikondra.

Carefully sipping from her cup, Sandra wondered if there was any way to comprehend the extensive memories Mamehr must have that were directly related to this house. More than fifty years earlier, as a new bride, she had come to build her life with Morcai Sirinoya. In this house, they had shared their love, their dreams - their reality. In this house, they had watched two healthy boys grow into men. Following Morcai's unexpected death, Araman had sought solace in memories forever linked to this house.

More recently, this home had witnessed Araman's wisdom. Here, she had guided Warnach as he decided whether or not to return to Earth to discuss possibilities for a life together with the woman he loved. He had then brought Sandra into this home, where Mamehr patiently taught her son's future lifemate the many nuances and complexities of life on Chikondra. The Sirinoya manor had since become the stage for life celebrations of holy days, birthdays, and unification.

Pushing her mug toward the center of the table, Sandra dropped her head onto her arms. Bitterly, she wept. How could this possibly be fair? She had come to Chikondra as a stranger, and she now found her very presence the reason behind Araman Sirinoya's decision to leave the home she had loved for half a century.

"Sandra, child, please. Don't cry. You mustn't cry so. You're going to make yourself sick."

Lifting her tear-streaked face, Sandra noted both sympathy and worry drawing Araman's features. Still, sobs threatened to choke her, and her body shook. "Mamehr," she struggled to speak, "I can't help it. I feel so guilty. I don't want you to go away because of me."

Araman's petite body drew in a huge breath. Momentarily unable to utter a word, she pulled a towel from a drawer and, wetting it with cold water, gently wiped Sandra's face. Then, sitting with her at the table, Araman reached for her daughter's hand. The forlorn expression across from her was heartrending. "You'll see that my leaving is for the best."

"No!" Sandra exclaimed, unsuccessfully attempting some semblance of calm. "It isn't! Mamehr, I know it isn't for the best! I've heard all your reasons for leaving, but they don't feel right to me. Tell me honestly. Do you really want to move away?"

Araman tried valiantly to conceal her grief over leaving the home she loved. "Daughter, I'll be closer to my sister. She and I can enjoy more time together without having to arrange special lodging or worrying about picking Nadana up and returning her to the Abnilal. At the same time, you and Warnach will have more privacy…"

"Privacy!" Sandra exclaimed again. "Mamehr, this house is enormous! There are dozens of rooms where we can go for privacy. My God, we have a whole wing to ourselves as it is!"

"Sandra…"

"Mamehr, listen to me. Please. This is your home. You belong here. You lived all of your unified life here with Warnach's badehr. You raised your family here. How can you simply walk away from all the memories? I know all the psychological arguments about home being a state of mind and not a place. That's not entirely true. Yes, a home is a place, but it's also a part of your heart. Scratches made by small children crashing into walls. Pictures hung by two people who loved each other and admired the same art. Voices from the past. A million and one life events, all captured within these walls. If I can feel those things here, I know you must. I have to ask again. Do you really and truly want to leave that all behind?"

Reflecting on her daughter's words, Araman felt tears prickling her eyes. Looking into Sandra's flushed face, she felt a momentary invasion of energy that puzzled her. "I've already agreed to purchase the house. Moving won't be that difficult. Besides, as I said, it will be for the best."

"Mamehr, I won't let you run from me that easily. I asked you a question twice, and you still haven't answered. Do you really want to move out of this house?"

Tears finally eased down Araman's cheeks. She dropped her gaze. "No, I don't. You're right about how much I love it here. However, moving is the right thing to do."

Sandra expelled a breath of frustration. "Tell me something else, then. What have I done that makes you feel you have to leave?"

Looking surprised, Araman responded, "Child, this isn't your fault. Why would you think you've done something wrong?"

Raising her right hand, Sandra massaged her forehead. She felt undressed without Kitak. The thought intruded and swiftly fled. "Why?" she choked out. "Because it seems my father was right. He told me that things always go wrong because I'm so stubborn about having my own way! Is that it? Because I wanted so much to be with Warnach, I succeeded in driving you out of your own home? Or, have I said something that upset you? Mamehr, if I did, I swear. I never had any intention of hurting you. I swear it, Mamehr. I love you too much to ever hurt you. You have to believe me." Suddenly, sobs again wracked her body.

Jumping to her feet, Araman wrapped her arms around Sandra's shaking shoulders. Pressing her daughter's soaked face against her own breast, Araman cooed gently. She had never expected such a seemingly simple decision to spawn such an anguished reaction.

Finally, as Sandra calmed, tearful hiccups replaced ebbing sobs. Pulling free of Araman's embrace, she roughly dragged the sleeve of her robe across her face. With evergreen irises locked onto Araman's face, Sandra gazed upward. "Mamehr, I apologize. With all my heart, I apologize for whatever wrong I've done. Please, don't leave me. I love you, and I need you. You can't possibly know how much you mean to me. My own mother wouldn't come to my unification, but you were always there. Every time I needed you. When I call you Mamehr, I really feel that you are a mother to me."

With emotions churning, Araman swayed slightly before sitting again. Pulling her chair closer, she pushed back wet strands of hair clinging to Sandra's cheek. She then held her hands. "Child, you've never said or done anything to hurt me. To the contrary, you are a joy to me. You've become the daughter I never had."

"Then, stay. Please."

"I already committed to buying that house…"

"Buy the house, Mamehr. You always stay in a hotel when you go to Tichtika. If you have your own house, you can make it suit your tastes when you go there. Use it whenever you visit Nadana, but keep this as your real home."

"I just don't know…" Araman's voice faded.

"I know you're worried that having two women in one household will lead to conflict. I don't think it will because we respect each other so much. Besides, it's only a matter of months before I graduate from the academy. Warnach will resume field missions, and I plan to be with him. That will certainly reduce time and potential for any arguments. I'm not saying we'll always agree on everything, but I am positive we can discuss any problems and work them out. Mamehr, why don't we do this? Buy the house, but don't move yet. Stay here for, say, six months. We can sit down and discuss this whole thing again. Then, if you decide you still want to move, I won't object."

"Does it really matter so much that I stay?"

Swollen eyelids slid closed as rose-colored lips pressed together in a tense line. "Warnach loves you and doesn't want you to move. We both love you, Mamehr." Opening red, swollen eyes, she stared intently into Araman's. "You're the only mother I have here, and I need you. Mamehr, I really do want you to stay here with us."

That woeful face looked at her so pleadingly. Araman recalled so many conversations regarding Sandra's strained relationship with her parents. She also remembered when she had also questioned how parents could ever treat their child so callously. Knowing she could not be so brutal in the face of such entreaties, Araman summoned a weak smile. "All right. I agree to your suggestion of six months as a trial period. After that, we shall sit down and discuss my future in this household."

Emotionally exhausted, Sandra's shoulders slumped with relief. Her face, puffy and blotched red from crying, broke into a marvelous smile. Leaning over the table, she kissed Araman's slender hands. "Thank you, Mamehr. You'll see. Everything will be fine."

Outside the kitchen, Warnach leaned against the wall with his eyes closed. He had remained silent while listening to nearly the entire conversation. His heart offered gratitude to the Great Spirit. His ki'mirsah had just accomplished what was surely a miracle. Hearing positive transition in the conversation between the two women in his life, Warnach chose not to reveal his presence. Returning to the upstairs master suite, he closed the door.

"My beautiful Shi'níyah," he whispered into the seclusion of their rooms. "How much I do love you."

# Chapter Two

Although far from being as cold or severe as winters at home on Earth, Sandra was glad for the likelihood of an early end to winter. At least, that's what she told herself. Having been born a summer baby, she had always loved picnic celebrations for birthdays and wishing for early snows for Thanksgiving. Her first birthday on Chikondra had been cold and blustery while Thanksgiving would soon arrive with the promise of bright sunshine and gradually moderating temperatures.

Reaching Warnach's office suite after a late lunch with Zara, Sandra immediately set about reviewing an extensive agenda for the Frehataran delegation scheduled to arrive on-world in two days. Not quite trusting that every detail had been properly addressed, she consulted with Zara before finalizing the program. After brief discussion, they agreed to a couple of minor adjustments before approving the final itinerary for distribution.

Glancing up when Warnach entered the office, both women exchanged surreptitious looks. His face held frustration despite his smile. After pausing to inquire on progress of the agenda and other presentation materials, he quickly disappeared into the privacy of his office.

Within Zara's experienced eyes showed concern. "That was an expression I haven't seen in quite some time."

"Although I may be wrong, I think it has nothing to do with the Frehatarans or the summit."

Zara's calm features showed no indication of her appreciation for Sandra's keen intuition where Warnach was involved. "What do you think the problem is?"

"Bederand. It's no secret that the situation there is deteriorating. The mission team is constantly consulting him. I think it's been nearly two weeks since he got to bed before one-thirty."

"You may be right. However, you mustn't forget the extreme difficulties he and Minister Khalijar encountered on Frehatar. Some unexpected issue might have arisen that complicates the summit."

Thoughtfully, Sandra tilted her head and breathed out a sigh. "Possibly, but I don't think so. He's really worried about the crisis on Bederand. The ministers there are facing factions that have been in opposition for decades. The Bederandans are much more experienced at antagonizing one another than the ministers are at negotiating."

"Did Minister Sirinoya tell you that?"

"No," Sandra said. "Actually, he says very little about it. However, I took time to research archives on how Bederand initially implemented a treaty eleven years ago. Tensions never completely disappeared, but they certainly diminished substantially. Then – suddenly – bang! Hostilities flared again for no obvious reasons. Current leaders are the same ones who fought for years before they were persuaded to give peace a chance. As far as the ministry team currently there on-mission is concerned, only one has any substantive experience in negotiations with such hostile parties. My personal evaluation is that conditions are quickly escalating beyond their capabilities."

Zara smiled her approval. "The original treaty was a major accomplishment for the Alliance. It also remains a shining example of how forceful and persuasive Minister Sirinoya can be. His integrity and determination won respect, and that proved to be the decisive factor."

Sandra nodded thoughtfully. "On Earth, I was fascinated whenever I watched him deal with various leaders. He's masterful when it comes to building confidence and gaining trust."

Zara leaned forward and lowered her voice. "Judging from the expression on his face, perhaps he could use a little encouragement to bolster his own confidence."

Grinning, Sandra nodded and got up. Knocking lightly at his door, she waited. Receiving no response, she quietly entered. He sat with his elbows propped on his desk and his face between his hands. "Warnach, I think what my ki'medsah needs most is a good night's sleep."

A long moment passed before he lifted his head and looked at her. "I think my ki'mirsah could very well be right."

Relieved that he wasn't in the mood to be alone, she crossed his office and perched beside him on the edge of the desk. "Let's go home. We've submitted the agenda, and presentations are all ready. You need some rest if you're going to be effective when the Frehatarans arrive."

"Sandra…"

"Warnach," she cut off his intended protest, "I know how dedicated you are. However, you can do no good for either side if you don't take a break."

A heavy sigh escaped. "I know you're right."

"With that in mind and knowing how stubborn your lifemate can be, are you sure you're willing to risk the consequences of not following her advice?"

Slowing dragging himself out of his seat, he placed his arms around her. "I have faced dangers on many worlds, me'u Shi'níyah, but facing your anger is far too daunting a prospect."

Smiling, she kissed him lightly and teased, "I suppose that isn't proper behavior from a CADS intern; however, this intern is taking her minister home."

Fatigue etched weary lines into his face. "I think your behavior is utterly befitting a future advocate whose responsibilities are to ensure the success and protect the welfare of her minister."

Offering her arm, she laughed. "Never forget that, my dear Minister Sirinoya."

Late that evening, she was studying for exams when his office com sounded. Heaving an exasperated sigh, she got up and answered the call. Hearing a ministry communications officer announce that Minister Meblarak was hailing from Bederand, she advised that Minister Sirinoya was unavailable for consultations. The surprised comm officer conveyed Minister Meblarak's insistence on talking with Minister Sirinoya and proceeded to connect the call.

Irritation was evident in the beleaguered minister's voice as he demanded to speak with Warnach. Unfazed, Sandra held firm. "Sir, as I already stated, Minister Sirinoya is attending another critical issue at the moment. If your call is an emergency, I recommend that you contact Chancellor Edsaka immediately." She then pressed disconnect on the button pad, covered the com unit with cushions from the sofa in Warnach's office, and closed the doors.

As quietly as possible, she slid into bed that night. For a while, she listened to the sound of his breathing. She wondered what repercussions might result from the abrupt end she had given to Minister Meblarak's call. Smiling into the darkness, she wondered if anyone who dared rebuke her could possibly be prepared for her reaction.

When she woke up the next morning, she hated the idea of disturbing him. Relieved that he had gotten at least one night of restful sleep, she sat up in bed. Gently, her fingertips stroked feathery light caresses across his cerea-nervos. With obvious reluctance, sleepy eyes opened. "Good morning, my good minister."

His right brow lifted sharply, and a drowsy smile spread his mouth. "Are you certain it's really morning?" he mumbled.

Grinning, she rose above him and turned, straddling his waist and gazing down into his face. "Positive, my dear lifemate."

Placing his hands firmly at her hips, he pressed her down to sit on him. "Such a lovely way to awaken."

What had been intended as a humorous, playful gesture suddenly assumed a powerfully sensual nature. Even after months together, color suffused her cheeks when he arched his hips, revealing sudden, heated hardness. Tousled locks concealed her face when she dropped her head forward.

"Sandra," he whispered huskily, "between my coming late to bed and your leaving early for classes, we've had little time together. I've been missing you."

Leaning forward, she nuzzled her face into the warm curve at his neck and shoulder. "I've missed you, too."

Quickly, he guided her back onto the bed and rolled over her. Whispering a string of endearments into her ear, he immersed himself within the oceans of her love. The silken feel of her skin beneath his hands. Her fingers creating shivers of delight along his body. Desperate whispers begging for more of him. The inspiration she created was matched only by the tremendous heights of pleasure he received from her.

Later, on the way to the academy, her mind turned back to the morning's passionate interlude. Her body still quivered and trembled inside from the powerful union with her lifemate. With a sigh and a self-conscious grin, she decided it would be impossible to conceal the sparkling eyes and satisfied smile of an exceptionally well-loved woman.

Days later, she wondered if the whirlwind surrounding them would ever ease. The Frehatarans had arrived in Kadranas with a delegation nearly a hundred strong. Under normal conditions, balancing classes and studies with internship responsibilities often proved demanding enough. Those challenges multiplied with the flurry of activities associated with the summit.

On her scheduled internship days at the ministry, Sandra provided welcome administrative support throughout hectic mornings and afternoons. Her added assistance gave Zara and Drajash more flexibility to respond quickly to changing requests related to the negotiations. Intending to solidify personal relationships, she launched herself into social events throughout several evenings and two weekends. Fortunately, academy instructors proved sympathetic to her plight and helped her work around ministry demands to which she was not yet accustomed.

By the time the Frehatarans departed, Warnach and Rodan had combined their considerable diplomatic acumen to achieve an expanded working agreement with the alien leadership. Their accomplishment exceeded any expectations either had imagined possible. Discussing the matter over dinner at the Khalijar home, both men expressed optimism that Frehatar had poised itself to move toward peace and full Alliance membership.

Rodan praised the support both men had received from their lifemates. Both Mirah and Sandra had contributed time and energy to female members of the delegation, some who held political positions and others who had accompanied their husbands. Warnach readily agreed that the success of the summit had been undoubtedly influenced by two women who deserved recognition for charming some of the most stubborn politicians he had ever encountered.

Mirah noted Sandra's swift glance at Warnach. The two then looked at each other. Simultaneously, they burst into gales of laughter that quickly had them mopping up rivers of tears from their faces.

Perplexed, Warnach looked toward Rodan. "Have I missed something here?"

Rodan shrugged his shoulders. "I believe so, my friend, as have I."

"Oh my, Sandra! I believe you've gotten both of us in trouble this time," Mirah squeaked out between bursts of laughter.

"Mirah, I do apologize," Sandra sputtered and coughed as she continued laughing. "I just couldn't help myself!"

Rodan's black brows lifted in question. "What are you two talking about? Neither of you said a word! Would one of you kindly explain?"

Once again, Sandra and Mirah gazed at one another. Just as before, hilarity overcame them until both covered their faces with their hands. Unfortunately, every attempt to recover sane expressions proved impossible.

Finally, Warnach turned sideways in his chair and grasped Sandra's hands, pulling them toward him. Amusement mixed with piqued curiosity. "Would you please enlighten us as to the reason behind this outburst?"

Shaking her head, Sandra licked her lips. "I'm not quite sure how to explain." Desperately, she looked toward her hostess who offered absolutely no help at all. Meeting Warnach's gaze again, she grinned and stifled a fresh wave of laughter. "My ki'medsah, it's difficult to explain to men when women communicate on an intuitive plane."

"Intuitive? Are you going to share with us unfortunate, unintuitive men what's so funny?"

Drawing her features into an almost serious expression, Sandra gazed at him with glittering eyes. "You might get angry."

"Angry?" Shifting a bewildered gaze toward his best friend, Warnach shrugged. "Did you note anything at this table that might anger me?" When Rodan responded with a shrug and a perplexed shake of his head, Warnach leveled a mock glare at his young lifemate. "I think we men deserve to have our curiosity tamed here. I promise I won't be angry. Now, what is this mystery communication that has you and Mirah so amused?"

Biting the inside of her cheeks, Sandra avoided Mirah's laughing eyes and stared directly at Warnach. "Remember that I love you as you are when I tell you this." Pausing, she breathed in deeply. "My ki'medsah, when you referred to the Frehatarans as stubborn, the thought crossed my mind that you might well have been describing the Alliance diplomat I admire most in the galaxy."

Warnach's mouth opened and closed. Glancing sideways, he grimaced as Rodan nearly choked while attempting to control his own urge to laugh. "Mirah, is she telling the truth?"

"For the sake of personal sanity, I think I hear Kaliyah. Excuse me. Sandra? Would you like to help?"

"Absolutely!"

~

Reluctantly rising from the table with a sincere apology, Warnach left the dining room. Sandra swallowed concern and gave her friends a warm smile. "Shall we have coffee and dessert in the lounge?"

Sandra and Araman carried serving trays holding an urn of fresh coffee, cups, dessert plates, and pie. Araman then excused herself and left her daughter to entertain holiday guests. Druska, Emilio, and Peter then launched into a round of good-natured teasing about Thanksgiving dinner served without traditional turkey. Acting insulted, Sandra defended the dinner that otherwise had been completely authentic from cranberry relish to pumpkin pie.

Knowing her well, Peter and Emilio could not help but notice Sandra's distraction. Her humorous quips could not disguise eyes that constantly shifted, and they sensed her worry that Minister Sirinoya had not yet returned. Both wondered about the stresses facing her now that she was sharing life with one of the most sought-after diplomats in the known galaxy.

When Warnach finally reappeared after half an hour, he lowered himself onto the chair next to where Sandra was sitting on the floor. Both young men noted the brief, tense look he gave her before raising solemn eyes to his guests. "I sincerely apologize for interrupting your holiday feast." He paused and sighed. "The call I took was quite serious in nature. Bederand just announced the expulsion of the Alliance ministry team on-mission there."

Slowly, Sandra got up and sat on the arm of the chair beside her lifemate. "I thought Minister Meblarak reported progress only yesterday."

The curt shake of his head clearly revealed aggravation. "Apparently, he was either overly optimistic or totally misinformed. However," Warnach smiled for his guests, "we can leave that matter in the capable hands of the Field Service Ministry. Today is your Thanksgiving, and I must agree that there is much for which we can be thankful."

∾

"They demanded what?"

"Badrik, please, lower your voice. I don't want Sandra to overhear. There's no reason for her to know. She has more than enough right now with her current studies and trying to catch up on assignments delayed when she assisted me during the Frehatar summit."

"Tell me one thing. Do you intend to honor your commitment to Karmía?"

Warnach's smile held reassurance. "I do. I owe that to Sandra and to myself."

Badrik released a sigh heavy with relief. "I thank the Great Spirit for that. How do you plan to proceed?"

"I'll meet with Baadihm tomorrow morning. We'll concentrate on trying to develop changes in strategy, but I fear great difficulties lie ahead. Reasoning with the Bederandans via com-link presents all sorts of complications. The time difference alone will be hard enough to overcome. Add to the equation seasonal changes in planetary alignments that will affect communications..."

Badrik helped himself to a drink and sipped the fiery gold liquid. His expression was grim. "You were the driving force behind the first treaty. Are you sure you can convince them to enter negotiations again?"

Warnach stared blankly past his brother's shoulder as his mind regressed to a time in his career that had exposed him to danger day after day. Finally, persistent efforts had culminated in a treaty that had garnered him great professional acclaim and notoriety. None of the accolades began to match the personal satisfaction he derived from knowledge that thousands upon thousands of lives had been saved when war had ended.

"My brother?"

Shaking his head, Warnach apologized. "Badrik, forgive me. I cannot avoid thinking that war on Bederand will likely spill over to Nelsiua and possibly even into the Garolian System. Bederand could drag that entire sector into interplanetary war."

"Even so, you must not place undue pressure on yourself. Others can and should step in to help. Even if wide-scale war does erupt, you cannot blame yourself. How many assassination attempts did you escape the last time you were there? No one could ever doubt your courage or your determination after everything you experienced on Bederand."

"It's so hard not to wonder what minute detail I left untouched that led to this crisis."

"Stop it. You confronted what dozens of diplomats across the Alliance were terrified to attempt. Bederand's leadership is responsible for not dealing with their own internal strife." Badrik continued in a lower, more insistent tone. "As for you, dear brother, it's time to concentrate on yourself and this new life you're beginning to build with Sandra. Karmía isn't just some antiquated idea dreamed up by our ancestral tribal leaders. It is a wise and sensible concept, especially today. Besides, tell me when in your life you've ever been happier."

A thoughtful smile twitched at the corner of Warnach's wide, sensitively curved mouth. "Badrik, when you're right, you are absolutely right." He breathed out a sigh. "Sandra has given my life meaning and fulfillment beyond anything I ever expected."

Badrik strode across the lounge and firmly grasped his brother's shoulder. "Remember that, and don't let Baadihm prey on your dedication or that overdeveloped sense of duty of yours. My sister needs you. So does your brother."

～

Three weeks later, Druska joined Sandra in the kitchen to help bake Christmas cookies. An array of Christmas carols filled the background.

Araman occasionally popped her head inside to inquire on progress. Sweet, rich aromas wafted from the kitchen and perfumed much of the downstairs.

While Sandra concentrated on decorating Warnach's favorite shortbread, the man himself strode into the kitchen and embraced her from behind. "Ah, I see that my bride prepares her magic to sweeten my disposition and fatten my waistline."

Giggling, she leaned back against him. "My dear Minister Sirinoya, I doubt that you'll take sufficient time to eat enough cookies to do either."

Glancing at Druska, Warnach grimaced. "Am I mistaken, or have I just been sweetly rebuked?"

Grinning, Druska shrugged her shoulders. "Well, if you really want my opinion, I would say you just received an extremely diplomatic scolding."

"So I thought."

That evening, while turning back sheets and blankets on the bed, Sandra looked up when the door suddenly opened. Eyebrows arched above green eyes that reflected surprise. "I thought you left to meet Baadihm in Kadranas."

Unfastening the wide mehshtra around his waist and undoing a long row of buttons, he removed his coat and took it to his closet. When he emerged a few minutes later, he wore only satiny, black pajama bottoms. Reaching for her, he placed his right palm against the coolness of her cheek. Even his voice held fatigue when he finally responded to her earlier remark. "Shi'níyah, I called Baadihm. We're making so little progress that one night away will make no difference with the crisis on Bederand."

Lingering concern marked her expression as her hand covered his that still pressed so tenderly against her face. "I'm glad you decided to stay. I've really been worrying about you."

Minutes later, they snuggled close together in bed. Sensitive fingers stroked across cerea-nervos that too often over the past weeks had throbbed in uneven rhythm. "I want you to rest."

"I will, Shi'níyah. That's why I decided to stay home tonight. I also want you to know that I told Baadihm he must do without my services tomorrow, too."

"Tomorrow? You mean you actually plan to spend some time at home?"

Affectionately, he kissed her nose. "That is exactly my meaning. It's your weekend. If I recall correctly, it's also time for us to look for a Christmas tree."

Reaching behind her, she managed to press the button that turned out the lights. "You didn't forget," she whispered.

"Christmas and Meichasa come close together. Both hold precious memories, especially now that we're together. How could I possibly forget?"

Soon, as she hummed *Silent Night,* her gentle caresses coaxed him into a deep sleep.

Morning brought with it time to spend precious hours together. When they awoke, their need for one another had been expressed in terms of indulgent kisses, lavish caresses, and the lovemaking that bound them together so completely. Prayers and breakfast were followed by an unhurried trek through the woods that provided ample opportunity for leisurely conversation and moments of unity belonging only to those deeply in love.

Deciding on a small evergreen, then following an old Chikondran custom, they joined hands and bowed to the tree. Thanking the Great Spirit for the gift of nature, they cut the tree down and carried it back to the house. Soon after their return, Warnach tried to help her decorate but found himself much more interested in teasing her with nonsensical suggestions while he sipped hot coffee and munched buttery shortbread.

Late afternoon was interrupted when the chancellor stopped at the house. His attempt to convince Warnach to reconsider attending a com-link conference call was firmly rejected. Farsuk's pleas met an immoveable wall. Rarely did Warnach disagree with Farsuk. However, he sternly reminded his godfather that, no matter the circumstances, no other minister was expected to make such constant sacrifices of private time. Warnach had reached the stage where he needed to give priority to his personal life, a point he made very clear.

Farsuk's reliance on Warnach's unique sense of duty had relieved the chancellery of many burdens. His godson's exceptional talents at dealing with parties in conflict had fostered peace on many worlds and strongly enhanced the careers of both men. As the chancellor departed the Sirinoya home alone, he mulled over Warnach's decision to unify and observe Karmía. Personally, his beloved godson had lost his dark, gloomy demeanor and admittedly deserved the respite. Professionally, Farsuk worried about the loss of such a valuable diplomatic resource for even the short span of a year. So many lives could be destroyed in a single day, not to mention a full year. He feared that Warnach's departure from field service diplomacy for any significant length of time could have long-lasting repercussions for individual worlds and the Alliance overall.

Christmas. Again, Warnach resisted Farsuk's demands and insisted on keeping his promise to spend Christmas holidays with Sandra. On Christmas Day, he happily helped his lifemate entertain homesick friends for one of Earth's most revered celebrations. The Sirinoya home had reverberated with laughter and spontaneous song. For him, the truest spirit of Christmas had been reflected within her eyes as she prayed together with some of her closest friends who shared her faith tradition. Mentally dismissing Farsuk's ceaseless arguments, Warnach felt neither regrets nor remorse for making time for himself and his lifemate.

Days later, the Sirinoya family gathered together for the Chikondran holy day of Meichasa. Inside the kitchen, Sandra bravely took charge of the culabanta. She hoped that she could either duplicate the success of her first effort on Earth or find out if Warnach had been too polite to tell her that her variation tasted awful. In the meantime, Nadana and Araman prepared other classic holiday fare. Affectionate and amiable chatter abounded, and happy voices brought Warnach mellow satisfaction as he set the table and prepared the Brisajai for communal meditation.

Because Farisa had been on duty at the hospital clinic where she practiced medicine, she arrived with Badrik only half an hour before dinner.

Badrik first embraced Mamehr and Nadana. Afterward, he performed his usual ritual of picking Sandra up from the floor and swinging her around in a giant, rollicking hug. Once Badrik set her down, Farisa laughed and quickly steadied her by holding onto her arm.

Dinner was soon on the table. Connecting hands, the family created a circle. Silent, Sandra listened as the Chikondrans who were now her family chanted an ancient prayer offering gratitude to the Great Spirit for all blessings, large and small. The ebb and flow of their chanting voices seemed to invade her with an unfathomable effect that left her swaying in place until the final words faded.

The dinner presentation was a spectacular affair of brightly colored, lavishly garnished foods that yielded savory aromas, sparked appetites, and caused mouths to water. Delicately flavored side dishes prepared by Mamehr and Nadana were perfect with the heavier, more savory culabanta Sandra had assembled and baked. With blushes and smiles, she accepted sincere compliments for her culinary triumph.

Dinner ended, and, once dishes were cleared and leftovers put away, everyone got together for a leisurely stroll outside. Light breezes carried fresh scents of budding trees and waking grasses. With his arm tucked around her shoulders, Sandra leaned against her tall, handsome lifemate as the entire family relished their togetherness.

After they returned, jackets and sweaters were hung up before everyone gathered inside the Brisajai. Nadana lit candles while Badrik started several cones of ceremonial Efobé before seating himself comfortably next to Farisa. Warnach twisted his head and gazed for a moment at his ki'mirsah. This would be their first celebration of Meichasa since she had become part of him. Quiet joy shone from within the dark depths of his eyes.

In a low voice, he initiated the chant she had heard first on Earth. As Badrik's voice joined in, she closed her eyes. She understood words asking for protection as those present opened their souls to Yahvanta's universe.

Continuing chants carried prayers that they might all be swept back through waving rivers of time to when their Great Spirit had first dispatched angel spirits, embodied as Quazon, to dwell upon Chikondra.

Opening her eyes, she saw only shadows. No longer did she smell the intoxicating fragrance of Efobé. Candles cast no more dancing lights. Increasing awareness encompassed so many tiny details. Regular beats of her heart. Tingling in fingers and toes. A stray curl tickling her forehead. Profound tranquility in her soul.

"Sandra?" Warnach's face hovered above her.

Her hand resisted moving upward to caress his Kitak. "My ki'medsah."

A deep breath emptied from his lungs. "You finally return to us."

"Return?" she murmured. "I never left you, my lifemate."

Glancing around, he nodded, and Nadana adjusted a lamp so that it cast light across the lounge. Returning his attention to Sandra, he managed a shaky smile. "You don't remember?"

Turning her head sideways, she realized that she was lying on one of the lounge sofas. "I remember the fragrance of Efobé and candlelight. I remember listening to you and Badrik." His hands on her shoulders prevented her from rising. "Why do you look so worried? Did something happen?"

Placing a gentle hand on Warnach's shoulder, Nadana silently requested to sit beside Sandra. "Dear child, a very long time has passed since we began our meditation in the Brisajai."

Curious and still somewhat confused, Sandra's expression held questions. "How long?

"Our meditative journeys all ended about an hour after we entered the Brisajai. That was three hours ago."

The smile that crossed Sandra's face could only have been described as mysterious. "That long? It seems only seconds ago that I heard Warnach and Badrik start the prayers."

"How do you feel?"

Sandra breathed in and out several times. How did she feel? Certainly not normal. On the other hand, she felt no pain, no discomfort, no anxiety - no nothing except profound love and tranquility. Again, she smiled into Nadana's perplexed features. "A little tired, I think. Mostly, just very, very happy. You have no idea how wonderful I feel, just knowing that all of you love me so much."

Thoroughly mystified, Badrik turned black eyes to meet his brother's. Earlier, with the realization that Sandra's meditation had delivered her into an unusually deep trance, they had carried her to the sofa. Always the physician, Farisa had quickly extracted a handheld diagnostic scanner from her attaché. Results were frightening. Scans showed that Sandra's breathing and heartbeat had slowed substantially while vital functions had reached a virtual standstill.

Nadana had grasped Sandra's cool hands. With closed eyes, the wise Simlani had felt mystic currents swirling around the young Terran. There existed no sign of distress. What the highly experienced spirit guide had sensed left her thoroughly mystified. Sandra's personal connection to Quazon had simply intensified and lengthened her meditative journey. Without comprehension of how or why but accepting the reality, Nadana had advised patience.

Trusting his aunt, Warnach had first reassured Farisa. Then, he had leaned over and touched Kitak to Kitak. For mere seconds, he felt awash in the seas of his lifemate's meditation. Instinct drove away worry. His soul knew she was safe, so he had seated himself on the floor by her side to begin his vigil and await her return.

Slowly, as Sandra regained sufficient strength to sit up unassisted, Farisa again utilized the scanner. Vital signs were quickly returning to normal, functional levels. Almost as strange as the readings after that horrible headache. She avoided phrasing aloud the thought that had suddenly intruded upon her mind.

As the week progressed, for Sandra, the only lingering effect from the incident at Meichasa was a heightened sense of inner calm. Among themselves, away from her presence, members of the family questioned Nadana. What had happened? Why had her meditation lasted so long? Could something be wrong? Although undeniably curious, Warnach followed Nadana's lead. Patiently, he would wait in the hope that revelation from the Great Spirit would be soon forthcoming.

# Chapter Three

Professor Dehmerah excused herself to respond to an unusual knock at her classroom door. Grateful for the interruption, Sandra reviewed notes from classes held earlier in the week. This course was challenging her like no other during her entire academic career. However, she recognized in Dehmerah genius combined with compassion. More than any others, with the exception of Professor Bizhanda, this teacher comprehended on a distinctive level that, through students whose careers were being developed, her personal efforts could have direct and lasting impact across the Alliance.

Returning to class, Dehmerah cast light brown eyes on Sandra Sirinoya. Concern showed on the still beautiful face of a woman who had just turned eighty. Her smile held kindness for this student who had sought assistance after missing several classes during the Frehataran summit. Alibrah Dehmerah had been more than glad to offer help and encouragement. The summit had provided a very rare opportunity, and she had known that, in the long run, Sandra would gain great benefit.

Seeing her student totally absorbed in her review, Professor Dehmerah smiled. "Mirsah Sirinoya?"

Surprised, Sandra looked up. "Professor, I apologize. I didn't realize…"

Quietly, Dehmerah interrupted the apology. "You're being summoned to Ministry Headquarters. An escort is waiting outside."

Sandra's eyebrows knit together in question. "Professor, we're in the middle of class. Can it wait?"

"I think not," the professor replied. "I'll be in my office later. Stop by, and we'll arrange a time to review today's discourse."

More worried than puzzled, Sandra gathered her things into her attaché and left. Outside waited a man she recognized as one of Chancellor Edsaka's personal security officers. Swallowing hard, she gave him a terse nod and followed without comment.

Ten minutes later, she walked through the corridors of the chancellery. Never before had she entered this part of Ministry Headquarters. Fine woods, antique light fixtures, and solid furnishings stopped short of being opulent but successfully created an ambiance of stability, comfort, and continuity.

Finally, she reached the enormous reception area just outside Farsuk Edsaka's office. The attendant got up without smiling to open one of the double doors to the chancellor's office. "Mirsah Sirinoya, His Excellency is anxiously awaiting you."

Sandra's mind fleetingly reviewed the past two weeks. Warnach's irritation with his godfather had ballooned into outright fury. As great as his anger had been, his resentment was even stronger. Edsaka's continued pressure on Warnach to relent and leave on-mission to Bederand had met with more than obstinate refusal. She wondered if her lifemate would ever regain the same level of respect for Baadihm Farsuk that he had possessed prior to the current crisis on Bederand.

With back straight, shoulders squared, and head high, Sandra walked past the aide and entered the chancellor's inner sanctum. Focusing her mind on the intentions behind Farsuk's summons, she was completely unaware of the confident aura she exuded. Neither was she intimidated by the fact that the office she had just entered had sheltered centuries of decisions that would forever influence the futures of worlds across the entire Alliance. Unconsciously, she braced herself for the unexpected meeting.

"Sandra!" With a broad smile, Farsuk Edsaka met her just inside the doors with a warm, welcoming hug. "You look lovely today. How are you, my dear?"

"Baadihm, I am well," she answered, ignoring the compliment. "You look tired."

Still smiling, he guided her to a seat in front of his desk before going to sit in his own chair. "The past few months have been unusually trying. Enough of that for the moment. Tell me. How are your studies?"

She breathed in and out. Make your quarry feel comfortable, she thought cynically. "Quite well, as a matter of fact. Despite interruptions caused by the summit, my evaluations remain high."

The smile he gave her was genuine. "So I've been made to understand. Your professors have written very strong reports complimenting your progress. Many are convinced that you will advance quickly through diplomatic ranks. You've succeeded in impressing some very exacting people with your talents."

She nodded her thanks. "My professors have been very generous. My performance is due more to hard work than to any innate talent."

Edsaka chuckled. "My dear, if the worlds could only understand that diplomacy relies on ninety-five percent hard work and only five percent talent and inspiration, the diplomatic field would crumble altogether, and the galaxy would likely fall into total anarchy. I'm encouraged that we still have young people willing to undertake the trying labors required for this profession."

Noting the gleam of assessment in his eyes, she boldly changed direction. "Baadihm, if you'll forgive me, there are times when flowery words and complimentary phrases might be necessary to establish a tone for a meeting. However, I really don't think this is one of those times. I'm quite certain you summoned me for something much more specific and much more important than banal discussion of the state of my studies."

Respect sparked anew in his eyes. "My dear Sandra, the first time I met you, you impressed me with your confidence to identify and directly address points that would have intimidated others into shrinking away into silent oblivion. This ministry has too many ministers who could learn from your example."

Consciously, Sandra held her gaze steady. "Baadihm, I cannot imagine you would summon me from class for anything other than a matter of serious import. Your time is far too valuable."

His eyes darkened as the tone of his voice lowered. "You are, of course, absolutely correct. However, my dear, that doesn't make my observations about you any less accurate — or less sincere."

The line of her mouth softened without forming a smile. "What is it that you needed to discuss so urgently?"

Farsuk Edsaka's broad chest rose and fell several times. Well aware of the risk he was taking, he felt he had no other viable alternatives. Leaning forward, he clasped his hands together on his desk. "Sandra, what has Warnach told you about the crisis on Bederand?"

"Actually, relatively little until last weekend."

Pursing thin lips together, Edsaka sighed. "Then you know about our disagreement?"

"Disagreement?" she asked as her eyebrows sharply arched. "Your choice of words hardly begins to describe Warnach's mood when he stormed into the house."

Irony showed in Farsuk's smile. Knowing he had to win her support, he continued cautiously. "My heart aches over the argument we had. Sandra, my unification came very late in life. Warnach and Badrik have eased the emptiness of having no children. I know he was angry. I also understand why."

"Exactly what do you understand about his anger?"

Perfect eyes, he thought. Around friends and family, those eyes shone with affection. With Warnach, those mirrors to her soul reflected astounding love. At the moment, they were cool and observant. Even with his highly

44

developed intuition, he could not clearly grasp thoughts lurking behind those sharply intelligent eyes.

"When Warnach informed me of his intent to observe Karmía, I gave him my blessing. I knew I would encounter difficulties in filling his void. I give you my oath. I never anticipated anything so potentially cataclysmic as the Bederandan conflict."

When his pause grew too long, she broke the tense silence. "That doesn't explain what you understand about my lifemate's anger."

He did not dare grow impatient. Besides, she had every right to hold her ground. "Sandra, as you know, my godson is a man who truly reveres tradition. He grasps the concepts that gave birth to those traditions, so he harbors no resentment toward them. To the contrary. He cherishes them even as he clings to them. Under even extreme circumstances, the observation of Karmía makes perfectly logical sense. However, circumstances on Bederand far surpass our normal understanding of extreme.

"Leaders on both sides of Bederand's war trust Warnach's integrity and wisdom as they trust no one else in the entire galaxy. They understand and respect his dedication to peace with justice and fairness to all involved. They have offered to suspend hostilities if I agree to dispatch Warnach to mediate the dispute."

For a moment, Sandra digested his words. "You just referred to the conflict as a dispute, but you started out by saying the factions are at war. Which is correct?"

Enlisting her help might be far more difficult than he had expected. No wonder academy professors were singing her praises. She was as sharp and analytical as her ki'medsah. "This will soon be common knowledge. War is rapidly escalating on Bederand. Reports indicate that deaths already exceed twenty thousand. Judging based on intelligence at hand, I estimate that Nelsiua will be drawn into the violence in less than four weeks. After that, it's difficult to say how long before hostilities spill into the Garolian System. Sandra, war is no longer imminent. On Bederand, war is already stark reality."

Her attention was fixed when he continued. "I know how much it means to Warnach to meet his commitment to spend this first year of unification with you here on Chikondra. I know his concerns. I also know his commitment to his responsibilities as the most accomplished and respected minister in the Alliance's entire diplomatic corps. He realizes that, solely through the force of his character, a truce can be implemented, and he can redirect Bederand toward peace. You know him. Sooner or later, he will shoulder personal guilt for the deaths and the spread of war."

Uncomfortable, long moments passed. Not once did she drop her gaze. "I understand now. You want me to convince Warnach to relinquish his promise to observe Karmía. That way, he can leave on-mission to Bederand."

Unbelievable. Her voice was as calm and steady as if they were discussing the weather. Had he not known better, he might have considered her extremely cold and uncaring. "Yes, Sandra. He'll listen to you. You know, I suddenly realize how wrong I was about one thing."

"And that would be?"

He answered with a grimace. "Before I sent for you, I believed Warnach was the key to ending the war on Bederand. The truth is that you are that key. You're the only one with sufficient influence to convince him to go."

For the first time since the discussion began, he observed emotion in her expression. Damn it, he thought, if only he could penetrate her mind to read that emotion. Quietly, he waited for her to speak.

Rising unexpectedly, Sandra took several steps toward the left and paused. She appeared to study an old oil painting. In actuality, her eyes were sightless. Her mind replayed images of her new life with Warnach. She suddenly pivoted and faced Edsaka. "Excellency, what you ask of me is something I cannot do."

Impatience finally crept into his voice. "Why not? His love for you won't change. Eventually, he'll thank you for giving your blessing to do what he does better than anyone else alive. If you don't convince him to go, millions will surely die. How can you say no?"

"Excellency, I don't reject your request without serious consideration. I have to ask. What would you do if Warnach were physically impaired in some way so as to be unable to travel? What would you do if he were sick? Would you not be obligated to seek some other solution? The problem is that you and the entire Alliance have relied on his skill to the extent that you nearly destroyed him.

"Warnach has a right to this time. He has earned it time and time again. He isn't just observing Karmía. He's restoring his whole being - re-energizing the very strengths and courage that made him such an effective and formidable negotiator all those years. He needs this time as much for himself as for our unification. He needs this break to prepare for a future that we all know to be in jeopardy."

"Sandra, listen to me. I recognize the truth in what you say. I also know that people are dying every hour on Bederand. I'm asking… No! I'm begging for your help."

Her breathing quickened. Her posture stiffened. She dispensed with any familiarities. "Chancellor Edsaka, you forget something far too important to disregard. Warnach's unparalleled successes in field ministry were accomplished not just because of acute intelligence and exceptional work ethic. Warnach excelled because of the power of his faith and his uncompromising integrity. You're not simply asking me to convince him to turn his back on promises he made to me. You're asking me to persuade him to set aside his honor and his beliefs to accept the mission to Bederand. His personal convictions make him the man I love and respect. Those same convictions are the basis for his own self-respect. I cannot ask him to turn his back on who he is or on the faith and honor in which he believes."

One last effort, Farsuk thought. "Sandra, honor lies in sacrifice that saves lives and brings peace. No one understands that better than Warnach Sirinoya. With your approval, he can go on this critical mission with a clear conscience. The truth is that he's afraid."

"Afraid?" Her expression grew puzzled. "I don't understand. He's been on dangerous missions in the past. I can't see how our unification has diminished his courage."

Hoping for an opening, no matter how slight, he pressed ahead. "Sandra, he's afraid to leave you behind during this time."

"Why?"

"For some irrational reason, he fears you might enter Ku'saá."

"Warnach wouldn't hold such an irrational fear," she defended.

"Sandra, of all Chikondrans unified in Nivela, I would say no more than ten percent ever experience Ku'saá. Our faith has evolved to the extent that Ku'saá is almost unheard of nowadays. That's for Chikondrans. My dear, when I say what I'm going to say, please, understand that I in no way mean it as a disparaging remark. However, facts are facts. The fact that you're Terran almost completely negates any risk of your entering Ku'saá. I cannot get that through to him."

"What you're saying is that, not only would you risk Warnach's integrity, you would even risk my life."

"Your plan to accept a ministry advocacy position will immediately place your life at risk. This is really no different."

Her pause lingered too long. "Well?"

"Respectfully, sir, I disagree. By assuming ministry responsibilities on-mission, I proceed with full awareness of potential dangers. There will also be safeguards in place to protect me from many of those risks. In other words, the dangers are subject to some control and the possibility of avoidance. As I understand Ku'saá, there is no warning, no control, no mercy."

"Sandra, you're almost as stubborn as your lifemate."

"Excuse me for stating a contradictory opinion, but, as I see things, you're being more stubborn than both of us combined."

"All right," he said, impatiently throwing his hands into the air. "Just remember. Every time you hear death count reports from Bederand, you might have prevented that loss of life."

The only outward signs of the struggle with her temper were the rising flush in her cheeks and the clenching of her fists. "Excellency, Warnach nor I will have drawn weapons. At some point in time, those who perpetrate violence must be held responsible for their deeds."

Mastering his irritation, Edsaka called her name just as she started to leave. "Sandra, I will ask of you a final favor."

Twisting her head, she aimed a pointed stare in his direction. "And that would be?"

He shook his head in aggravation. "There's no need to inform Warnach of our discussion."

Her jaw moved back and forth several times. "Chancellor Edsaka, Warnach is my ki'medsah. We share Kitak. Sooner or later, he would know anyway. You've already asked me to convince him to forsake his personal ethics. Now, you ask me to deceive him."

"Child, there is no deception in saying nothing of things best left unsaid."

"Excellency, from my perspective on this matter, the truth you would have me conceal from my lifemate remains as dishonest as any openly stated lie. Goodbye."

Touching his communication console, Farsuk spoke wearily to his assistant. "Gamahnj, I wish not to be disturbed."

Leaning back in his chair, he contemplated the conversation that had just taken place. He had fully expected to gain her sympathies. Never had he anticipated such complete personal control and restraint from someone so young. He could not doubt for a moment her devotion to Warnach. Neither could he doubt the accuracy of her understanding of his godson's character. Reluctantly, Farsuk admitted to himself that even he had not foreseen the strength of her character. Grimly smiling, he acknowledged that he had unwittingly undertaken a sparring match with the one person who might actually exceed Warnach's renowned tenacious resolve.

～

Two days later, desperation once again prompted Farsuk to summon Sandra to his office. Warnach had remained adamant about not undertaking a mission to Bederand. As before, Sandra refused to participate in any effort to change her lifemate's mind. By the time she abruptly stalked from his office in disgust, he stared at the closed door. If he could not convince Warnach to accept the assignment to Bederand, Farsuk Edsaka believed that, beyond failure to stop this war, he would have to prepare to lose his post as chancellor to the Dil-Terra Interplanetary Alliance.

～

Instead of studying for exams, Sandra sought solace in nature. Finding a large flat stone near the stream, she sat and watched clear waters tumbling over rocks. Glinting from the water's surface were sparkles of silver and gold. Chattering birds called from greening trees. Quietly, she fingered crystal beads as she prayed her rosary, seeking comfort, wisdom, and divine guidance.

Watching her from the path above, Warnach stood very still. For days, her mood had been noticeably reserved. Several times, he had come upon her without her noticing. She had looked almost as distant as she did at that moment with her rosary rhythmically moving through her fingers. Earlier in the morning, when she had placed Kitak upon his head, he had sensed her troubled spirit. Although she had smiled and kissed him, her eyes had held a haunted look.

For a moment, he thought to leave, to let her reconcile whatever weighed on her mind. When he saw her lift her right hand, he watched as her fingers moved in tiny circles against her Kitak. As if in direct response, he felt unusual vibrations in the band he wore. Those circles created by her fingertips transmitted through Kitak her need for his presence.

He would have reached her side without her noticing had loose pebbles not tumbled down the embankment. Twisting around, she didn't look at all surprised to see him. The faintest of smiles looked almost sad.

Crouching low, he placed a lingering kiss over the spot on her Kitak that she had been touching. "Me'u Shi'níyah, it seems you were calling me."

This time, her smile brought light to darkened evergreen eyes. "I'm glad you heard me."

Sitting down beside her, he watched flowing waters. "Shi'níyah, your heart is heavy. Will you not share your burden with your ki'medsah?"

Long eyelashes fell into a feathered fringe. A glistening tear found its way onto her cheek. "My ki'medsah already carries too many of his own burdens. I can manage mine."

His voice gentled even more. He stretched out his hand until his fingers could caress the taut line of her jaw. "Sandra, I have strength enough to share whatever makes you look so sad."

Her face dropped and then lifted, turning toward him. "Do you have any idea how much I really love you?"

"I sometimes think I do."

"Will you take me back to the house?"

Perplexed, he stood and brushed dust from his trousers. He then offered his hand to help her. Rising to her feet, she paused before catching him in a desperate embrace. Shocked, he wrapped his arms tightly around her and dropped kiss after kiss onto her hair. "Shi'níyah," he whispered, "tell me. What's wrong?"

With her eyes closed, she pressed the side of her face against his chest. The sound of his heartbeat penetrated the farthest reaches of her soul. Nothing could be wrong, she thought distractedly…not so long as she could remain in her perfect place to be.

Finally, tilting his head backward, he gazed down into her face. "Tell me."

"Not now. I just want to be close to you. What I really want is for you to hold me."

Without reservation, he tightened his embrace. He would persuade her to confide in him later. For now, he needed their embrace as much as she.

∾

After prayers and breakfast, she excused herself and went to her office to study. Exams were a week away. Already losing a day of study to moody contemplation, she consciously resolved to clear her mind and focus on one task at a time.

Five hours later, Warnach peered around the door connecting their offices. Her abilities to concentrate always impressed him. He called out her name. Slowly, she looked up with eyelids blinking and an almost blank look on her features. "Warnach, I'm sorry. What time is it?"

"Time, I think, for you to take a break. I could be mistaken, but I suspect you know that material as well as, if not better than, your professors."

A smile lit her face. "If that were the case, I wouldn't need classes at all."

Grinning in response, he reached out to her. "Mamehr fixed us a light lunch. Let's go eat and take a brief walk. All right?"

"How could I possibly turn down lunch and a walk with my handsome ki'medsah?"

During the meal, he unsuccessfully tried to draw her into conversation. Brief answers to his questions were the most he could manage. After clearing the table, he led her outside. Tucking her arm beneath his, he started along their favorite path.

Only a few minutes had passed when she stopped and gazed up at passing clouds. "Warnach, are things really as dire on Bederand as they say?"

Releasing her, he turned and caught her gaze. "I take it you've been checking news reports."

She nodded. "The subject is getting a lot of discussion at the academy. Professors are explaining the history, and a lot of people are asking why Alliance leadership isn't taking a stronger, more active stance. You were there, and you've also devoted most of your time lately to the com-link conferences. I just wondered about your perspective."

Studying her face, he sensed currents far deeper than the little she had just voiced. "The situation is likely the most critical the Alliance has faced in the past three decades."

"Including the crisis you averted on Frehatar?"

"Including Frehatar."

She started walking again. "If I live a thousand years, I'll never comprehend why people find it so necessary to fight and kill. When I see those reports...the photographs of the dead... Warnach, I remember when Derek and Diana died." Her voice choked into a forced whisper. "I remember holding that little boy and then watching him die in his mother's arms. The concept of willfully killing another person paralyzes my brain."

"Shi'níyah, you've witnessed violent deaths in ways far too personal. Because of that, you value life for the very sake of life. Whether or not you realize it, that same pain provides you with a source of great strength."

She swallowed hard. "I can't help but think of the innocent who always suffer. Men and women who choose to fight one another make the choice that could freeze their destinies within a moment of violence. Some of us choose options of peaceful resistance, but still, there are risks. Derek and Diana knew those risks. We all did. None of us shied away from them because we believed in the ultimate goal. We exposed ourselves to violence without participating in it. Children don't have the power to make such choices."

He clasped his hands behind his back as they walked. "That's why the work I've chosen is so important to me. When a man's work can save a single life, then his life becomes more than worthwhile."

"Warnach, I am so proud of you. Considering your career, there's no question that you've been instrumental in saving millions of lives."

"I receive credit for accomplishments that required the efforts of many."

"My ki'medsah, who you are as a man was the driving force that made the difference. I know that. Professors at the academy teach that. Dignitaries across the Alliance openly acknowledge that."

Their walk grew silent for a while. Changing direction, she left the path to walk onto a broad meadow and dropped to the ground. Drawing her legs up, she locked her hands around them and looked up into his face as he joined her.

"What?" he asked, seeing something indefinable in her expression.

Her breasts rose with a deep breath. "Can anything be done to alleviate the Bederand crisis?"

"Can anything be done?" Regret crossed his features as he shook his head. "No. Nothing at all until the Bederandans agree to cease their hostilities and enter negotiations aimed at ending the bloodshed."

"I read an editorial from Earth questioning why the eminent Senior Field Minister Sirinoya wasn't responding to Bederand's repeated requests for his intervention."

Instinct told him she was finally opening her thoughts to him. Cautiously, he proceeded. "Shi'níyah, your society doesn't understand the nuances of Chikondran culture. Explaining Karmía would be nearly impossible."

"If it weren't for me and our period of Karmía, you would have gone weeks ago." Her voice sounded flat as she made an indisputable statement.

Worried by perceptions he could not express in words, he quickly dismissed caution. "Sandra, what are you really thinking?"

Her eyelids fell. Her expression grew more somber. Finally, she directed her gaze back to him. "Warnach, people are dying. Thousands every day. I just want you to know that, if you feel you could go and make a difference, I would never try to stop you."

How to answer? Drawing air into the depths of his lungs, he heard truth in her words. "Shi'níyah, I already know that because I know you. Yes, the Bederandans have refused to enter negotiations if I'm not present to lead them. That is their decision to make, whether it is responsible or not. I have my own decisions to make, and you are the most important consideration in my life. I made promises to you. I also vowed to the Great Spirit that I would watch over you and protect you to the best of my ability. Karmía is part of that commitment."

"When you talk about protecting me, is it because of Ku'saá?"

Several moments passed before the significance of her question penetrated his brain. "Why do you ask that?"

"Because I need to know."

"The answer to that question is an obvious yes. I cannot risk being so far away if you should enter Ku'saá. I would lose you."

"Warnach, isn't it really more than improbable that a Terran would enter Ku'saá?"

Cold fury instantly flowed like ice through Warnach's veins. He experienced an abrupt invasion of certainty. That question had been planted by a man who had surely preyed on her sensitivities. "Sandra, I want you to tell me the truth. Has Farsuk approached you about this matter?"

Her eyes studied his face. "Twice. Don't be angry with me, Warnach. I really wanted to tell you, but, in all reality, I've seen you so little over the past few weeks. When we did find a few minutes together, I didn't know how to broach the subject."

His hand extended, and he pressed his open palm against her cheek. "Shi'níyah, whatever he told you doesn't matter. You are more important to me than anything else in my life, and that includes my career."

"Warnach, to you, your career isn't just the work you do. It's part of who you are. The results of what you do can't be measured by signatures on treaties or how much history is written. What you do can be measured in the lives of men, women, and children who don't have to face the consequences of war. You make a real difference in lives that are saved."

"I don't doubt the sincerity in what you say. On the other hand, I made a decision based on my commitment to you. How can I simply disregard that?"

Her eyes shone with fresh intensity. "Warnach, you mustn't see this as showing disregard for your commitments to me. You and I both know the risks inherent in field diplomacy. It won't be so long before I'll be out there with you, facing those very same challenges and dangers. Nothing is cast in stone. Either one of us could lose our lives in an instant. I don't see this as failure on your part to fulfill the promises you made. What I see is that we are a couple, unified by our love and our values, discussing a process in which we both believe."

Blood rushed to his face as cerea-nervos began to throb painfully. "Shi'níyah, I do appreciate your support. More than you know. However, I will not risk your life this way. I will also never forgive Farsuk for dragging you into this. He had no right to interfere."

"Warnach, he only did what he felt was necessary. I'm really not sure what is right or wrong here. Tell me the truth about one thing. Honestly. How likely is it that I would enter Ku'saá?"

"Sandra…"

"My ki'medsah, I calculated the risks. They're about one in a trillion. Not bad odds. Much better than I'll face when I accompany you on-mission."

"That really isn't the point, and you know it." Warnach rose and watched her unfold herself and stand. He saw a hint of a smile cross her face.

"My ki'medsah, I'm not trying to convince you to go. I have absolutely no wish for you to leave me and go so far away. Neither do I want you to feel torn between your commitment to me and a decision to go to Bederand.

I want you to know that you have my blessing to do whatever you think is necessary. No matter what."

Pulling her into his arms, he clutched her tightly. He knew she meant every word. Holding her, he subdued furious desire to confront Farsuk. That could wait. For the moment, her presence alone served as balm to the weariness permeating his being.

That evening, although he would have preferred otherwise, they found themselves again discussing news broadcasts they had watched together. Several heavily populated cities on Bederand had been leveled. Casualties were mounting rapidly. Only restricted access to the most modern weapons had prevented more widespread destruction.

Nelsiuan tactical forces had also begun to assemble. Inflammatory rhetoric incited the masses to rally in support of the Bederandan Pifanamars, whose ancestors had fled to Nelsiua to avoid widespread persecution by the Bederandan majority called Cosomonds. Three planets in the Garolian System were bracing already, anxiously awaiting the arrival of Alliance defenses to protect their peaceful planets that were rich in resources capable of sustaining years of their neighbors' appetites for war.

Prayers in the Sirinoya Brisajai reached a new level of intensity. Warnach's chanted entreaties were raised in a quivering voice. As his hand gripped Sandra's almost painfully, his senses soaked in her feelings. Within his heart, he did not want to leave her. However, he understood that the consequence of his decision translated to massive loss of life. He beseeched the Great Spirit to provide him guidance and wisdom. He pleaded for peace.

Before dawn, she sat up in the darkness of their bedroom. He had been restless, tossing and turning constantly. Finally, he had left the bed. Sensing his presence, she looked around and barely made out his dejected silhouette as he sat on a loveseat and stared out a window overlooking dense woods. Making no sound, she slid out of bed and went to him. Leaning over from behind, she encircled tense shoulders.

"Sandra, you should rest. You have class in the morning."

"And you should sleep. You torment yourself too much. You're not to blame."

"A great many people around the Alliance seem to think I am."

"Only because the truth is beyond their understanding."

"Shi'níyah, what should I do? I keep asking myself, and each time I come back to the same conclusion. Honor the commitment I already made to us. Yet, in the meantime, people are dying."

Rounding the end of the loveseat, she knelt in front of him. "What you must do is search your soul. Decide what to do, and then do it with the full knowledge that, whatever your decision, whatever the consequences, I'll understand and give you my complete backing."

Trembling fingers stroked her face. "Shi'níyah, I'm truly afraid. Not of being on-mission to Bederand. What I fear is leaving you. I'm the one who promised to support you as you approach the final phase of your studies. Sandra, I want to be here. I don't want to go and face weeks or months without you."

Swallowing and suppressing tears, she laid her head on his lap. His fingers gently moved through her hair. "My ki'medsah, if you should choose to go, you'll have Kitak to remind you that I go with you, and, wherever you are, my love will be with you. If you choose to stay, I'll stand with you against any criticism. I wish I could free you from this dilemma, but I can't."

"In my place, how would you decide?"

Created by his touch, tremulous sensations raced down along her neck. With eyes closed, she considered his question and her painful response. "My ki'medsah, you've dedicated so much of your life to the pursuit of peace.

"I look forward to joining you soon in working for that noble goal. Warnach, it breaks my heart to say this, but, for now, you're the only one who can bear the torch for us both."

Barely able to swallow back sobs, she finally stood and tightly gripped his hands. Pulling him to his feet, she led him back to bed. There, they lay in each other's arms until morning's light filtered into their room.

# Chapter Four

Reluctantly, Sandra left home in the transport Warnach had bought for her shortly after their unification. He had walked her outside, kissed her, and watched her leave. His tension had been palpable, and she couldn't help but worry. By the time she engaged her vehicle's auto-guidance system, her thoughts were redirected toward classes. Unless she graduated from the academy, she could never hope to relieve the excessive burdens he had carried so frequently throughout the years.

When Warnach returned inside, he strode directly to his office. Drawing in a deep breath, he pressed in a pre-programmed com code. Half an hour later, he stalked out of the house, entered his transport, and, leaving the garage, streaked toward Kadranas.

Fury marked Badrik's impressive image in full officer's uniform as he preceded Warnach through the entry carousel to the Alliance Chancellery. Long legs rapidly carried him toward the elevator tube rising to the floor housing Chancellor Edsaka's office. Neither brother spoke as they abruptly emerged from the elevator, causing waiting passengers to either scatter or be bowled over.

Upon their arrival at the chancellery reception office, the aide stood. "Excuse me. Chancellor Edsaka is meeting with Master Barishta. He does not wish to be disturbed."

Before Warnach could utter a word, Badrik snarled at the young man.

"I don't give a damn what the chancellor does or does not want. Move aside, or I will gladly move you myself."

Startled, the attendant froze as Badrik passed so closely that he almost knocked the man over anyway. Grabbing brass handles, he shoved them downward and flung open the doors. As both Master Barishta and Farsuk Edsaka looked up in shock, Warnach launched himself past Badrik. Then, grabbing Farsuk's jacket, he roughly jerked him from his chair.

Within seconds, two security guards appeared at the door. Met by the daunting presence of Captain Badrik Sirinoya, neither was certain what to do. Pivoting sharply, Badrik spoke to Warnach. "Release him, brother." Then, calmly, he said to Master Barishta, "You may leave. My brother has urgent need to speak with our illustrious baadihm."

Barishta shot a worried glance toward the chancellor. Stern-faced, Edsaka waved him off. "Go. This is a personal matter. We can manage well enough on our own."

After Master Barishta reluctantly departed with the guards, Badrik secured the doors and turned around. Rage was etched into the face that family and friends normally associated with broad, brilliant smiles. His expression could only be described as fearsome when he coldly stared into his godfather's eyes.

Assembling his wits, Farsuk tugged his long coat back into place. "You must excuse me if I have no appreciation for such abruptly rude entrances. I'm quite certain your badehr would be appalled if he were still alive."

"You can be quite certain that my badehr's spirit is already aghast that his best friend could commit such horrific treachery against the family he entrusted to you."

Feigning calm, Farsuk retreated behind the barrier of his desk. "Am I to deduce that Sandra chose to disregard my advice about not discussing our meetings?"

"Meetings?" Warnach snapped. "Unlike you, my esteemed baadihm, Sandra respects me."

"And what respect have you shown me? Or to the Alliance to which you pledged your service? You turn your back on millions of people who face death because you would place higher priority on your personal life rather than on trying to avert interstellar war!"

Warnach's face flushed scarlet. "You disgust me. I've given more and risked more for this Alliance than most of your precious field ministers combined! For the first time in over twenty years, in full accordance with our laws, I have chosen to be on Chikondra to honor sacred traditions…traditions that you have publicly advocated for the continuing good of our world. Then, you sneak behind my back and prey on the compassionate conscience of my ki'mirsah in hope that I will do as you and turn my back on those very same traditions. I always admired and respected you as an honorable man of faith and integrity. No longer. You have proven yourself to be little more than an abominable, cheating hypocrite."

Stunned, Edsaka glared at his godson. Though he dared not admit it, he could not possibly defend himself against Warnach's vile description. If their roles were reversed, he would have made exactly the same assessment. Swallowing hard, he dropped his face but maintained the stridency in his voice. "My responsibilities to worlds that comprise this Alliance required desperate actions. Warnach, I will not stand here and argue your description of me. In some ways, it is apt. However, I chose to risk myself and even your opinion of me if it meant having any chance at all to halt the spread of this war."

"And so you would risk the life of my ki'mirsah when she hasn't the faintest idea of what could happen to her."

"Damn it, Warnach! I love her in my own way, but I would risk my own lifemate if it meant saving millions of lives! Why do you not see that?"

"If it means so much to you, why not offer your own services? Why do you not go and negotiate a cease-fire?"

"If I thought they would listen to me, I would be there already. Even if I knew I would die there! However, for reasons of their own, they trust only you," Farsuk ground out. "You may be the most difficult and obstinate minister in the Alliance, but no one can deny that you're also the best. If I had even the faintest glimmer of an alternative, do you really think I would ask such a sacrifice of you? Do you?"

Warnach swallowed the flood of insults that burst into his mind. For brief seconds, he heard Sandra's tearful words echoing inside his mind. Recognizing that duty and the souls of the dead cried out to his conscience, her advice had been for him to go. He had heard her fear and her hurt, but he had seen something more - her courage and her love.

"I will go only on my conditions," he finally announced.

"Which are?"

"Captain Tibrab will command the mission from onboard the Curasalah. I expect free and ready access to com-link so I can stay in close communication with Sandra and my family. I will do my best, but, if no tangible progress is accomplished within four weeks, I will end the mission and return to Chikondra."

Relieved, Edsaka nodded. "I will inform Tibrab to ready his ship. When will you leave?"

"In five days. I need time to organize for the mission and prepare my family for my absence." Warnach stepped backward, then paused. "I also expect every possible safeguard to be implemented to protect my family."

Farsuk's voice softened. "Warnach, she'll be fine. She knows how much you love her. Besides, until you return, she'll be surrounded by people who love her. You know as well as I that you worry for naught. Nothing will happen to her."

Unable to utter another word in response, Warnach spun around and stalked out through doors that Badrik quickly opened and closed.

Seeing that Badrik remained in the office, Farsuk's eyebrows lifted. "Yours has been an ominous silence. Do you also have something to say?"

Long strides carried Badrik across the office and around his godfather's desk. Even more roughly than Warnach had done earlier, he clutched the fabric of his baadihm's coat and lifted him completely off his feet. When he spoke, his voice held bone-chilling menace. "Hear me now, Farsuk. I chose to say nothing in Warnach's presence. However, as Badehr's spirit is my witness, if something happens to either my brother or my sister, you will answer to me."

Then, in total disgust, he gruffly released the older man and departed.

Days passed much too rapidly as Warnach galvanized his office staff to prepare for the emergency mission to Bederand. Zara and Drajash hastily consolidated research data and reference material for transfer into the private database the minister would carry with him. Whenever possible, Sandra went to the office to provide additional assistance. Her outwardly poised and efficient façade lent confidence to a process undertaken with utter urgency.

Availing himself of one of Sandra's strongest assets, Warnach consulted with her extensively on planning the itinerary for use after his arrival at the embattled planet. Several times, he stopped to review the recommendations she developed from his stated objectives only to marvel over her uncanny ability to logically sort priorities, schedule sufficient time for various meetings, and allow flexibility for unexpected events or rapid changes. Her superior planning skills would free him to concentrate on studying the substance of the conflict. He could then project probable reactions and strategize maneuvers to deal with whatever might arise.

During the evenings, he severely restricted all work-related communications. Anguished by his impending departure, he jealously guarded every minute he had to spend at home with his family. With careful management, he made time for his mother while concentrating mostly on his lifemate.

Having lived through years of such comings and goings, Araman deeply empathized with the emotional plight facing her daughter. Unlike Sandra, she had stayed behind with her own family on her own world. Despite natural concerns about Warnach leaving on-mission to a world so embroiled in hostilities, she controlled maternal desires for every available moment with her son. Instead, she encouraged him to devote more time to his ki'mirsah.

Music soothed some of the distress related to their imminent parting. Each evening, they set aside time to listen to some of the musical compositions both loved most. Reclining close together on his special lounge, they said little but touched constantly. Each evening, they joined Araman for night prayers. Each night, they clung to one another with desperate, consuming passion.

Lighthearted banter seemed almost out of place. However, at dinner on the night before the Curasalah's departure, Sandra gently teased and joked as the family gathered for supper. Only Nadana, who had gone away on retreat, was absent. Food prepared by Araman represented the finest cuisine normally reserved for high holy days. Excellent wines flowed generously, and conversation tilted away from politics and war.

Badrik and Farisa stayed late enough to join in the family's night prayers. By the time they left, neither could quite believe how exceptionally calm and poised Sandra had seemed. Indication of any underlying anxiety came only from the way she constantly sought to touch Warnach or from occasionally woeful glances that were quickly concealed behind wide smiles.

Entering their suite that evening, Warnach noted that their bed had already been turned down. Swiftly, she had disappeared into the bathroom. When she emerged wearing a shimmering, filmy robe, her face glowed. With shaking hands, she undressed him. Quickly folding his clothes, she laid them aside. After letting him remove her robe, she embraced him tightly.

How incredibly warm did that impressive male body feel next to hers. Smiling, she kissed olive skin. When his hands began to slide down toward her hips, she shuddered. Pressing closer, her face lifted as her lips parted and begged for his kisses. Her hands flattened and swept up and down along the smoothness of his muscular back.

His body responded instantly to the unspoken demands of hers. His long hands spanned her waist, pulling her firmly against swiftly rising evidence of desire evoked by her caresses. His mouth welded to hers, seeking sweetness beyond description. Her velvety soft skin tantalized every inch of him that it touched. His rapidly pounding heart forcefully pumped enflamed blood throughout his body.

Before he realized, they lay together on the bed. His hands feverishly sought each curve of her body as if determined to memorize every inch that responded so completely to his touch. His ears captured every nuance of sound, every whisper holding his name, every whimper conveying her need. With sudden overwhelming power, he impelled himself to the deepest core of the woman he loved.

Frantically, they loved one another. Careers, fears, and wars were exiled from their consciousness. Any concept of past or future dissipated. Impending separation drove them. Merged physically as well as emotionally, they gloried in their unification while seeking escape from the dread of separation. When at last they parted, they refused to release one another. Exhausted by the absolute satisfaction created within their total unity, they finally surrendered to sleep.

~

With the backs of his fingers, he caressed her cheek. "Are you certain you'll have no problem missing this morning's class?"

Her smile held reserve. "I spoke with Professor Dehmerah. She understood completely." Pausing, Sandra glanced around. "What happened to Badrik?"

"Likely checking final security details." He could not bear to shift his gaze from her face. "Are you certain you can manage?"

She grinned and sighed. "I can manage, although I certainly won't promise how well."

Swallowing against the rising lump in his throat, he drew her close. Touching his forehead to hers, energy from his cerea-nervos created a gentle sensual invasion. "Ci'ittá mi'ittá, me'u Shi'níyah," he murmured. As he withdrew, his gaze revealed how deeply he worried about leaving.

Oblivious to the arrival of those who would pilot the shuttle to the orbiting Curasalah, she whispered his name. Her insides quivered as she resisted fleeting nausea. Hollow emptiness ached within her chest. Already knowing how lost she'd feel after his departure, she felt no shame at remaining in his arms until the last possible second.

Finally, Badrik returned. "All is cleared. The shuttle departs in ten minutes."

Reluctantly, Sandra moved from her lifemate's embrace. The two Sirinoya brothers hugged each other tightly. Warnach's voice cracked. "I fear so much that I'll regret this mission. Badrik, I entrust my Shi'níyah to your care."

Badrik's black eyes met his brother's anguished gaze. "You mustn't worry. You know that we'll watch over her."

Nodding, Warnach twisted slightly and reached one last time for Sandra. His eyes caressed the face that held such a sweet smile. "Shi'níyah, you must make a promise before I leave." Receiving her solemn nod, his hands rose to cradle her face, and his voice trembled. "You must promise that you'll wait for me to return."

A little puzzled, her eyebrows knit together. "How could I not wait for you to come home?"

"Sandra," he said insistently, "I leave on this mission with too many uncertainties. I must know beyond all doubt that you'll be here when I come back. Please, Shi'níyah, promise me."

Not quite understanding the desperation lurking in his plea, but remembering what he had shared about Lashira, she lifted her face and lightly kissed him. "Warnach, I love you. I promise. I'll wait as long as it takes until you're back home with me."

Suddenly, he grasped her upper arms so tightly that he hurt her. "No matter what, Shi'níyah. Promise me that you'll be here waiting for me. No matter what."

"Warnach," she responded, her own voice beginning to shake, "I swear. No matter what, I'll wait for you. I need you too much. I love you. Ci'ittá mi'ittá, me'u Warnach. Ci'ittá mi'ittá."

His mouth claimed from her a lingering kiss. Despite their previous partings, this one was the most difficult ever. Forcing himself to walk toward a waiting escort, he paused for a final look at her beloved face. Then, resolutely, he disappeared into the embarkation corridor.

Sandra ran toward a wall of windows and watched until the shuttle lifted, hovered a moment, and then disappeared into cloudy skies. Turning around, she stared into Badrik's face that was so like Warnach's. Admirably, she had stayed calm and controlled her emotions. Such need no longer existed. Bursting into tears, she launched herself into her brother's arms and wept.

Over the years, out of the need for self-preservation, she had honed extraordinary concentration skills as her primary method of escaping emotional difficulties. Those abilities had never been more valuable than after Warnach's departure for Bederand. She felt so alone without him. Distraction came only by immersing herself in assignments and final projects due at school.

The two-week break following term had been especially difficult. When she was with Mamehr, their conversation invariably shifted toward reports from Bederand. Captain Tibrab and the Curasalah had delivered Warnach and his mission team safely to the war-torn planet. After initial com conferences from on board, he had decided to shuttle to the planet's surface. Once there, he undertook personal consultations and established a format for formal talks.

Three times during the journey and twice since his arrival, he had contacted her at home via com-link. Concerned that guilt might hamper his concentration, she had kept relatively brief conversations positive and encouraging. He had expressed pleasure upon hearing of her continuing success at the academy. He had also questioned her about how she was feeling. Not once did he fail to touch his Kitak and remind her how much he loved her. Once the com-links ended, she invariably found herself near tears. His image from so far away sliced into a heart longing for his presence.

Enlisting the support of Professors Bizhanda and Dehmerah, Sandra completed last-minute changes to her class schedule just in time for the new term. Initially, she had planned to complete the bulk of major course requirements during earlier sessions so her final term would be less hectic. Concerned about her ability to maintain concentration, she chose to take only two major subjects and the required S&D course covering security and defense techniques. The change would require a demanding final term with three majors and a minor, but, confident that Warnach would be home by then, she was convinced hers had been the most logical decision.

Two weeks into the new term, she sat at lunch while poring over notes in her electronic portfolio. Looking up, she grinned. "Need a place to sit?"

Blue eyes questioned her. "You won't be ashamed to be seen with a lower-level classmate?"

Shaking her head, she snapped the slim notebook closed. "When was I ever ashamed to be seen with you for any reason?"

Quickly, he placed his lunch tray on the table and sat down across from her. "Have you eaten already?"

"Yes, I did, and I already put my tray away. Thought I'd take advantage of today's longer break between classes to work in some study time."

Starting to eat, he studied her carefully. "You look great considering the circumstances. I shouldn't say it, but Emilio and I were kind of worried about how you would do with the separation."

She gave him a wry smile. "What you see on the outside is a far cry from what's on the inside."

"Do you really think I don't know that already?"

Sighing, she shook her head. "Peter, it's been a lot harder than I expected."

"I noticed. Don't worry, though. The rest of the world doesn't know you well enough to figure that out. I am glad that Emilio and I got slotted into S&D with you. We can at least keep an eye on you part of the time."

"Thanks," she replied. "So, what did you think about the security part?"

"Mind-boggling," he said after swallowing a bite. "Codes and regulations and procedures. As if stressed, overworked advocates won't have enough on their plates tending to the demands of various ministers and their assignments."

"I agree," she said, humor creeping into her voice. "I'm trying to figure out how I could possibly remember all those codes and procedures, especially if I've been swamped with work on-mission and find myself caught in a crisis to protect my minister."

Peter unexpectedly snorted his laughter.

"What's so funny?"

"Sorry," he answered sheepishly as he dabbed his mouth with a napkin. "I just got this visual of the poor devil who would dare threaten your particular minister and be forced to face your wrath."

Finally, she joined his laughter. "Good point. I suppose my minister couldn't have planned for a more motivated advocate slash bodyguard, could he?"

"If only he knew!"

Later, they met Emilio and walked all together to the building reserved for S&D training. Ziaman and Bejil were also part of a class that enjoyed a reputation for leaving its students exhausted and very often sore and bruised. Due to the course's nature, classes were kept small and lasted the duration of the afternoon. After changing into appropriate clothing, everyone gathered inside a large, dimly lit room with padded walls and thickly cushioned floor mats.

"Students, I promise that you will find this course filled with difficulties. Physically, you will be challenged. You will be shocked and surprised as we condition you to face potentially life-threatening circumstances that endanger ministry personnel on-mission. At times, you are likely to curse me. However, I will remind you that there are those who would attack you and your ministers with every intent to kill without mercy. My goal is to teach you techniques that will help you save lives, including your own."

By the time the class ended, not one of twelve students doubted their instructor's warning. Physical conditioning bordered on brutal. Obstacle courses and weight training began as preparation for instruction in defensive techniques. Sharp commands from tough trainers sliced through the air and students' nerves. Exhausted by the end of the day, they understood exactly the reasons for it being conducted only during afternoons.

By the beginning of the following week, most students complained that their defensive arts class could prove deadly. They had been warned to stay alert and never hesitate to defend themselves in whatever way possible. Instruction strategy would begin with observation of students' reflexes and reactions. After that, specific techniques would be introduced.

Emdroh Barmihn, the lead instructor, led students into a specially constructed classroom. Low lights revealed sturdy dividers set up to simulate corridors and rooms complete with obstacles that, in a real setting, might have been furniture. Students were then challenged to see how far they could get through the course.

Bejil was the first to go. Less than halfway through, he met his demise at the hands of a surprise adversary. Students who followed fared no better. Attackers were strong and adept at subduing their hapless victims.

When only Peter and Sandra remained, they exchanged curious grins. Medsah Barmihn asked who would go first. Speaking up quickly, Peter answered, "Ladies first."

Sandra responded with a scowl, "Why do I always have to show you how to get things done?"

Conspiratorially, Peter winked at their instructor. Barmihn's grin showed complete misunderstanding of the meaning behind Peter's gesture. Eight minutes later, leaving four attackers flat on their backs, Sandra emerged from the course.

Next, Peter shrugged his shoulders and started his run. When he rejoined her, she gloated. "Nine minutes to my eight. What took you so long?"

"Tripped over one of your victims," Peter responded glibly.

Fellow students laughed and applauded. As far as anyone knew, the two Terrans were the first ever to negotiate the complete course on an initial attempt. Trainers quickly joined their pupils and praised the efforts of all.

After class, Medsah Barmihn asked Peter and Sandra to remain behind. Curiosity shone from hazel eyes as he questioned them about their unique accomplishment. Having already conspired to withhold details of their experiences with the group at home, they only admitted some training in Earth's martial arts. Leaving class, they exchanged laughing glances. It wouldn't take long for him to learn the extent of their capabilities. When that time came, they would remind him of the day he had told them that surprised enemies were always more easily subdued.

～

Exhausted, Warnach slumped into the corner of the sofa inside his quarters. Reaching for the console on the table beside him, he pressed the programming pad. Leaning back, he closed his eyes. Intricate chords played on a grand piano from Earth. How soothing the flow of that sweeping melody. How right she had been about the mysterious way it seeped into one's very soul.

He smiled as her image floated before his mind's eye. How young and lovely she looked. Images had been captured forever within his memory. That first day they had gone to the beach. The night they had entered Shi'firah. Their unification day and the night that had followed. Memories. Hundreds upon hundreds of them, tucked away to be retrieved whenever his heart ached for consolation and encouragement.

Five weeks had elapsed since his departure from Chikondra. In that time, he had traversed empty space and crowded solar systems to place him light-years from home. He had embarked on establishing agenda and guidelines necessary to organize and conduct meetings with officials from Bederand. With the foundation set, he had proceeded to revive old relationships and to determine what had failed and how to move beyond failure in the hope of stimulating negotiations. Cautiously, he had begun to erect framework upon which peace could be reconstructed.

Intellectually, he recognized that what he had accomplished thus far could nearly be considered a phenomenon. His labors had accomplished in weeks what frequently took months. Still, he knew better than to grow overly confident. Despite absolute certainty of commitment from leadership of both the Pifanamars and the Cosomonds, he harbored no doubt. Hidden in the background, other forces performed sinister deeds aimed at perpetuating the violence.

Frowning, he sensed the tactics of Zeteron instigators. Sooner or later, they would be forced to abandon their destabilization strategy. They would have to decide either to retreat and find other more vulnerable prey or to spring into open challenge against the Alliance. How long, he wondered. How long could he and other dedicated ministers desert homes and loved ones in order to fend off war? Could they maintain the grueling pace long enough for the Zeterons to abandon the chase and seek easier targets?

Tones at the door heralded the arrival of a visitor. Rising, he crossed the sitting area and pressed the keypad. When the door slid open, Captain Tibrab waited outside. "Forsij, please, come in."

The two men passed nearly an hour together as they discussed plans, schedules, and security. Throughout the conversation, Tibrab studied his best friend's older brother. Over the years, he had come to admire Warnach and had later come to consider him a friend. On duty at the far end of the Alliance, he had missed Warnach's unification to the young Terran who had traveled to Chikondra aboard the Curasalah little more than a year earlier.

Thoughtfully, he redirected their conversation away from mission work. "So, my friend, I'm glad to know you've forgiven me for my inability to attend your unification. From what I understand, you've turned much of our conservative society upside down."

Lightly touching his Kitak, Warnach smiled. "Perhaps. Most people who meet her find it practically impossible to resist her charm. I know I did."

Tibrab chuckled. "I must agree with you. Even I was quite taken by her."

Warnach grinned and drained a glass of spirits. "She is special."

"You miss her. I can hardly believe you actually left her. Badrik told me that you had intended to observe Karmía. Are you not worried?"

Warnach sighed and got up to fix himself a second drink. "Worry is unavoidable. Logic alone should allay my concerns. I remind myself how few Chikondrans rise into Ku'saá. Chances are essentially nil that a Terran should do so. The problem is that my Sandra has already astonished me and others."

Curious at the distant look that crept into Warnach's eyes, Forsij asked, "In what way has she astonished you?"

Warnach's eyebrows lifted. Long hair swayed as he shook his head. "I assume I can trust you to hold any confidences."

Tibrab grinned mischievously. "If only you knew how many secrets I've kept about Badrik over the years."

"I can only imagine," came the amused reply. Gradually, a more serious expression overtook Warnach's face. "Forsij, have you ever seen Quazon?"

The captain's eyes sparked anew with curiosity. "Me? Quazon? Not once. Other than one or two spirit guides, I think I know of no one who has ever actually seen Quazon. Why? Have you?"

For a moment, Warnach's mind regressed in time. Then, his gaze locked on Forsij's. "I have. Three times. All beginning with Sandra's first visit to Chikondra."

Intense surprise draped over Forsij's face as he leaned forward. "Three times? Unbelievable!"

"Do you want to know something even more incredible?" Receiving an astounded nod in response, he continued, "Sandra was in the water each time. They came so close. They even allowed both of us to touch them. Forsij, she communicates with them. Telepathically."

Captain Tibrab collapsed back into his chair. He held no doubt about the truthfulness of Warnach's revelation. "Does anyone else know?"

"Mamehr, Nadana, Badrik, and Farisa were all at the beach with us the first time. They each witnessed an event that still has me in a quandary. Only Farisa doesn't know about the times they came when Sandra and I were at the beach after our unification. Forsij, that time, they came because she asked them."

Minutes passed in contemplative silence. Completely dumbfounded, Forsij shook his head. "My friend, that day I escorted her for a tour of the ship, I sensed something extremely unusual in her. Since then, I've occasionally wondered about that feeling. I wish I could explain. Warnach, trust me. You need to be with her. Not necessarily because of Ku'saá. I think that, for Quazon to accept her, there must be purpose far beyond what we imagine."

Pensive, Warnach leaned forward and placed his empty glass on the table. "I tell myself that. I also know that she and I both have lives to live, goals to pursue."

"My friend, live your life with her and pursue your goals. That you must do. What you must not do is to leave her long out of your care. Remember. Quazon have obviously accepted you, too. I believe their message is that your purpose must be one united." Pausing thoughtfully, he added, "Trust me, Warnach. We must expedite resolution of Bederand's crisis in order to hasten your reunion with your ki'mirsah."

~

"Back away! Everyone! If you don't, I'll kill her!"

Instructor Barmihn had grabbed Sandra from behind and pointed a weapon toward her face. Fellow students, caught off guard, stared in shock. Except, of course, Emilio and Peter. Neither moved. Peter cast a sidelong glance toward his friend. Both shrugged as, suddenly, Sandra went totally limp in her captor's arms.

As he struggled to hold up dead weight, disbelief crept over Barmihn's face. In all his years as an instructor, never had a student fainted in class. Realizing he had no other choice, he eased her down to the floor. Straightening slightly, he shot an irritated look at one of the trainers. "Quick. Summon a paramedic."

Abruptly, the instructor found himself pitching backward as his legs were jerked out from under him. Before he could catch his breath, she stood over him with her foot above his throat.

She seriously studied the stunned look in his eyes. "I forgot to tell you. I hate being grabbed from behind." Then, with a mischievous glint in her eyes, she bent her knees and offered to help him up. Just as she had suspected, he attempted to drag her down. However, with her stance fixed, she had firmly grasped his wrists. Swiftly, she gave a solid heave, jerking him upwards and hitting his head as if it were a soccer ball.

"Mirsah Sirinoya," he addressed her a little later as he rubbed the small bump showing next to his cerea-nervos, "do you not think the maneuvers you demonstrated today were somewhat unorthodox?"

Smiling despite the swelling lump on her own forehead, she said, "Perhaps, sir. However, if someone's going to succeed in killing me, I have no intention of making it an easy task."

The next day, the class appeared to be embroiled in an all-out brawl. One of the trainers, who had been absent the previous afternoon, repeated Barmihn's move. Just as Sandra began the special focus technique Derek had once taught her, she glanced toward the door. Badrik had entered the training center and, wearing a grave expression, was speaking to one of the trainers while nodding toward Sandra.

Adrenalin instantly shafted through her body. "Let me go!" she demanded. "Let me go!" A third time, she shouted so loudly that everyone stopped to look at her. "I said let me go! Now!"

Her instructor tightened his arms around her. As if in a real-life confrontation, he ordered her to be still. In a blinding flash, her head forcefully shot backward into his face, and, within the span of a heartbeat, she had broken his hold on her. With blinding speed, she whirled him around and sent him crashing to the mat. When he grabbed for her leg, she pivoted and smashed her foot onto his wrist.

Furiously, she snarled, "When I say let go, I mean let go!" Then, spinning, she ran to Badrik.

Breathless and fearful, she took no notice of his brief glance toward the injured trainer. "Badrik," she gasped, reacting to the tension on his face. "Warnach? What's happened? Badrik! Is Warnach all right?"

Badrik firmly grasped her shoulders while his black eyes stared down into her frightened features. He shook his head. "We don't know yet, sister. A surprise attack has been launched, apparently from Nelsiua. The diplomatic team is trapped on Bederand. Forsij is organizing a rescue mission. I came to take you to Alliance headquarters."

Running up in time to hear Badrik, Peter and Emilio flanked her and put their arms around her. Her body trembled, but there was also strength in her posture.

"Chica," Emilio said softly, "I'll get your things for you. Then you can go."

Nodding shakily, she turned glazed eyes to Peter. "I...I think I broke the trainer's arm. I didn't mean to..."

Peter grimaced. "You did, but it was an accident. Besides, it's nothing an HAU can't fix."

Emilio quickly reappeared with her dress clothes and her attaché. "If there's anything we can do to help…"

She turned to Badrik. "Can you hold these for me?" Then, turning back to her friends and restraining the threat of tears, she dropped to her knees and looked up. "Pray with me?"

Both Peter and Emilio joined her on the floor. In unison, the three of them formed the sign of the cross, symbol of their shared faith. Oblivious to onlookers, close friends joined hands and repeated a beloved prayer before Sandra's voice pleaded for the safety of diplomatic personnel on Bederand and the minister who led them.

# Chapter Five

Fired by marauding fighters emblazoned with Nelsiuan insignia, laser cannons pierced the skies with fiery surges. Stone chunks erupted from exploding buildings and created deadly hail that pummeled streets below, crushing men and machines. Thick dust and flying debris swirled through the air. Some attack craft were armed with SVCs. Sonic vibrations rattled weakened, already damaged structures, causing supports to fail. One after one, city edifices collapsed to the ground.

"Agaman! Run!" The shouted warning was drowned out by a nearby SVC strike. Agile and swift, Warnach raced forward and lunged toward one of two deputy ministers who had accompanied him to Bederand. As he threw his arms around his younger colleague, desperate momentum carried them barely a meter beyond the point where a stone cornice came hurtling down from twelve stories above.

Jagged bits of broken stone and concrete spat into the air from the small crater plowed into the street. Several sharp chips flew into the exposed side of his face. Ignoring the burning sting, Warnach dragged the stunned Agaman to his feet. Percussion rocked the streets, causing them to stagger and stumble as they raced toward the entry of an underground shelter.

"Minister Sirinoya! Faster!"

The frantic shout came from an aide to the governor of Bederand's Pifanamar Territories. Glancing upward, Warnach groaned and shoved

Deputy Minister Agaman forward just as a smaller assault craft dived and took aim at them. Dropping and rolling sideways, Warnach successfully dodged fire from the craft. The governor's aide had collapsed on the street.

Choking on dust-laden air, Warnach groaned again and ran back toward the fallen Bederandan. "Where are you hurt?"

The young man's face contorted with pain. "My leg! I can't feel it! Sir, go! Get to the shelter! Forget about me!"

Ignoring the injured man's words, Warnach hoisted the aide's body over his shoulder and headed toward the shelter. With the assault craft slicing through the air on a second run, his legs pumped with every bit of strength he had. Suddenly, clouds of dirt and stone exploded on the street, darkening the entrance behind him.

Together, Deputy Minister Agaman and Warnach carried the injured aide through a short corridor dimly illuminated by banks of emergency lights. When they reached a heavily reinforced chamber, others immediately stepped forward to guide them through the crowded bunker. A side room equipped for medical emergencies was already staffed by three doctors. Carefully, the Chikondran ministers laid the man on a cot.

Smiling down into a dirty face that seemed far too young, Warnach smiled. "Mr. Partizia, you likely saved our lives. Thank you."

The courageous aide flinched against searing pain and forced a grim smile. "Any favor was admirably returned, sir. You risked your life for mine."

Nodding once, Warnach looked up at the doctor who had begun assessing Partizia's injuries. "You will have my personal appreciation if you take especially good care of this young man." He then turned around and joined others who had escaped the chaos that continued outside.

"Minister Sirinoya, may I speak with you?"

"Governor Maijarus," Warnach replied with an assenting cock of his head. He then stepped toward a less crowded area where they could speak more privately.

The elderly governor's gray eyes held anger and dismay. "I saw those aircraft and their markings. Despite what you may think, I had nothing to do with this attack. Bederand's Pifanamars are peaceful people."

"With all due respect, Governor, if your people were so peaceful, there would have been no need for my presence here."

Bushy gray eyebrows met together over the governor's bulbous nose. "My people have found it necessary to protect themselves. No matter what the Cosomonds say, we have been long persecuted. You know from before that proof exists to support that claim. However, too many remember the last war and all we lost. My people pressure me to find ways to restore peace. I cannot begin to explain why Nelsiuan forces would strike now. They knew we were hopeful about moving forward into meaningful negotiations."

Astute and intuitive, Warnach detected truth in the man's words. Heavily, he sighed. "I'm sure you understand that my most pressing concern is getting a report on the condition of my mission team. Then, I need to determine how best to get us all out of here safely. Right now, I suggest you give some encouragement to that young aide of yours. His warning saved my life."

"I have a suggestion for you as well. Your face is bleeding. Have one of the doctors check it."

Raising his hand to the side of his face, he drew away dirty fingers streaked with blood. Heeding the governor's advice, he returned to the busy infirmary. A medical technician quickly plucked slivered stone and glass from Warnach's left cheek. Once the minor wounds were cleansed, he rejoined the large group assembled in the primary chamber.

Solemn-faced, Deputy Minister Agaman approached him. "Minister Sirinoya, all but two of the mission team safely reached the shelter."

"Who is missing?"

Debris particles dropped in a flurry from Agaman's long hair when he shook his head. "Technical Officer Gelfinmah." He paused uncomfortably. "Deputy Minister Delzianahl. Both are confirmed dead."

Little emotion showed on Warnach's face. He knew that surviving team members would look to him for stability in crisis. "Where are their bodies?"

"Near the conference headquarters. One of the technical officers was nearby when they were killed. He ordered them left behind to get wounded to safety."

"What about other mission staff?"

"Minor injuries only. Everyone was fortunate to get themselves as well as several injured Bederandans here to the shelter."

Warnach's chest rose and fell with a frustrated breath. He felt revolted by the idea that his colleagues' bodies had been left behind in dark destruction on a strange world. Setting aside personal feelings, he glanced around. "Defenses. How much protection do we have here?"

A Bederandan military officer, head wrapped in gauze bandages, heard the question and stood. "Tunnels from the conference center collapsed before most of our security forces could get here. We have on-site no more than twenty armed soldiers."

"Twenty?" Warnach repeated. "Not many should some of those assault craft discharge land soldiers. Excuse me. You are?"

Despite his grimy appearance, the officer performed an elegant bow. "I am Lieutenant Mirzanzi."

"You are Cosomond, are you not?" Warnach asked, observing an embroidered patch on the man's jacket sleeve.

"I am. Eleven of the soldiers guarding the remaining two entrances that are operational are also Cosomond. They stand side by side with Pifanamar soldiers. We will defend your mission team to the last."

Shaking his head, Warnach could hardly believe that he and most of his mission team were now sharing emergency quarters with citizens from both sides of Bederand's bitter conflict. How ironic, he thought abstractedly. Outside the walls of this bunker, these soldiers were sworn enemies. Inside, they cooperated to guard refugees from both sides and the alien mission team that had hoped to end hostilities on their world. The thought boggled his mind.

After a lengthy delay, he inquired, "Are you seriously wounded?"

"No, sir. Chipped bone in the skull. Mild concussion. Pounding headache." His head inclined toward the bustling infirmary. "Others need medical care much more than I."

Despite the presence of Governor Maijarus, Warnach assumed leadership of the survivors as easily as if he had been a lifelong military officer. Quickly, he organized activities to shift chaotic conditions to a more quiet level of efficiency. Tasks were assigned to distribute food and water from well-stocked supply pantries. Blankets were passed out. Soldiers on duty in the corridors were provided relief by ministry security personnel.

Hours later, Warnach went to a corner and lowered himself onto a folded blanket on the floor. Gratefully, he accepted bottled water and a food pack from his senior communications officer. Grimacing, he noted the contents of the square included shredded meat.

"I apologize, sir. The selection is limited. Protein on Bederand equates to meat."

Involuntarily, his nose turned up. Tentatively, he took a bite. The flavor was far too strong and rich for his tastes. Suddenly, he gave the worried officer a smile. "I suppose I should be less particular and more grateful. You have no idea how many times on Earth I watched friends consume meat." He took another bite. "This really shouldn't bother me so much. After all, I'm the one unified with a Terran omnivore."

Between bites, Warnach spoke quietly with the com officer. "Are your emergency communication devices still functional?"

About thirty and exuding calm, the female officer confirmed her equipment was in perfect condition. All attempts to establish communications had proven futile. Thick, reinforced walls protecting the inner chambers caused enough difficulties. Sonic wave weaponry created impenetrable interference. Without any show of emotion, she informed the worried minister that, unless they could get closer to the surface or out in the open altogether, they would be unable to inform the Curasalah of their location.

Finishing little more than half of his food ration, Warnach leaned back against the cold wall. He thanked the com officer and instructed her to await further instructions. In the meantime, he needed to isolate himself and concentrate. Through the bunker's solid masonry, he felt telltale vibrations in the floor and walls. Explosions were still rocking areas close to the shelter.

Closing his eyes, he raised his hands to his temples. Sensitive fingertips drew small circles atop the rafizhaq ring circling his head. In his mind, he could have sworn he heard her voice. Straining, he tried to distinguish her words. Something about not letting him do something. Wishing for silence while again touching Kitak, he mouthed words that he prayed he might live long enough to say to her again. "Ci'ittá mi'ittá, me'u Shi'níyah. Ci'ittá mi'ittá."

～

Gently, Badrik shook her shoulder. "Sandra, wake up."

Mumbling incoherently, she stiffly lifted her face from her arms. Her neck ached almost as badly as her head. Looking around, she saw busy communications officers everywhere. She had fallen asleep at a conference table in full view of banks of computer screens monitoring communications across Alliance territories and interests.

"Sister, it's two in the morning. I'm taking you home to get some rest."

Determinedly, she shook off drowsiness. "No word yet?"

Grimly, Badrik said, "Nothing. Baadihm has authorized Forsij to utilize whatever means necessary to rescue the mission team. I have complete confidence in Forsij."

Memory carried Sandra back to her voyage on the Curasalah. Captain Forsij Tibrab. More than competent, she thought. Dedicated. Intelligent. For a moment, she wondered how resourceful he would be under such extenuating circumstances. Gazing back into Badrik's tired eyes, she took heart. Within the fatigue, she noted confidence in his friend.

"What if they find them?"

"They will advise us immediately. Come now."

The night following Warnach's departure, Sandra had moved his pillow into his closet and placed another on the bed. Several evenings, she had come upstairs after prayers and gone straight to the closet. Hugging his pillow tightly, she could smell faint traces of the masculine scent of the soap he used. Comforted, she would tuck it away again and go to bed.

After Badrik brought her home from the communication command center, she had gone to bed with that pillow, clutching it desperately. Still lying awake in bed just before dawn, she turned onto her side and wrapped her arms even more tightly around her ki'medsah's pillow. Knowing he had slept on it somehow drew him physically closer.

Adjusting her own pillow, she fidgeted, trying to find a comfortable position. Unable to bear removing her Kitak, she had decided she would rather deal with the discomfort than total separation from him. Despite troubled restlessness, she finally fell asleep.

Bleary-eyed a few hours later, she hauled herself out of bed and into the shower. Despite her weariness, she dressed quickly and hurried downstairs. She wanted to call Zara to tell her she wouldn't make it into the office for her intern assignment.

Arriving at the bottom of the staircase, she heard voices from the lounge. Two ministry officials sat inside with Araman. Both had been friends of Morcai Sirinoya and had worked with his son. They had come to offer encouragement to the family of their colleague. Her heart sank. What she heard of the conversation indicated no news, no known change in the situation.

"Mamehr," she greeted as she knelt in front of Araman and kissed both her cheeks. Smiling wanly, Araman leaned forward and touched her cerea-nervos briefly against Sandra's forehead.

"Daughter, you do remember Masters Yoshanda and Siliriahn, do you not?"

Rising, Sandra turned and greeted each master with the formal Chikondran bow. "As I recall, your last visit to my home was under much happier circumstances."

"Mirsah Sirinoya, I pray that you may someday extend a new invitation under circumstances just as happy as your unification."

So morning began. Calls of support. Visitors offering encouragement. At one point, she excused herself and rushed outside. Gulping in huge breaths of fresh air, she fought back nearly uncontrollable nausea. A horrible thought had sprung into her mind. She had suddenly felt like a widow receiving courtesy calls from acquaintances of a highly respected, recently deceased husband. The thought had panicked her.

Within moments, Nadana was at her side. "Calm yourself, child. Calm. Calm. Think calm."

Exercising taut control over her breathing, she managed to quell the acidic rise from her stomach that scorched the back of her throat. She turned a weak but grateful smile to Nadana. "Thank you," she murmured.

A little later, a lull occurred in the stream of callers. Bending forward, she picked up the remote control from a table and increased the volume of a news broadcast. A photojournalist had managed to transmit scenes from the continuing battle on Bederand.

For a moment, she did nothing more than stare blankly at images arriving from the faraway world. Although the condition of top government leaders and the status of an Alliance diplomatic team remained undetermined, the journalist reported, both Bederand territories had condemned the mysterious and unwarranted attack by Nelsiuan fighters. Agreeing to a temporary suspension of domestic hostilities, military units had organized and joined forces to repulse the marauders. However, Bederandan pilots were making little headway against exceptionally skilled attackers.

Other shots showed widespread destruction in Mijirina, the acknowledged, traditionally neutral capital of Bederand. Whether by courage or insanity, the journalist had dashed through besieged streets to tell his story. During one quick pan, she glimpsed bodies on the street. Although distant, dirty, and rumpled, there could be no doubt. The attire belonged to Chikondrans.

Araman gasped just as the camera focused on another angle. Sandra quickly pivoted and rushed to her. Tears filled Araman's dark eyes. Nadana sat on the arm of the sofa and rubbed her sister's shoulders.

"Not my son. Please, please. Not my son."

Sandra firmly grasped Araman's hands and brought them up to trembling lips. "No, Mamehr. Not your son. Not my Warnach."

Chocolate-colored eyes filled with sorrow and gazed back at her. "If he were alive, he would have communicated with the Curasalah by now."

Without conscious thought, Sandra lifted her hand. Resting her fingertips against Kitak, she closed her eyes and breathed in and out. It must be the middle of the night in Mijirina. He must have sought a place to wait out the attack.

Rising to her feet, she released Araman's hands. Her posture straightened noticeably. Her features assumed a totally obstinate expression. "Mamehr, I want you to trust me. You must believe me. I'm going into the Brisajai to pray. I promise. Warnach is in danger, but he will not die. I refuse to let that happen. I will not let Warnach die."

Spinning around, she ran through the house until she flung herself through the doorway of the Brisajai. Stumbling and falling to her knees, she reached out with her heart and her spirit. Clinging tenaciously to faith, she prayed as she had never prayed before. All the while, an echo sounded inside her mind. "I will not let you die, my ki'medsah. I will not let you die."

~

Quietly, to avoid disturbing those who had fallen into uneasy sleep, Warnach placed his hand on the shoulder of the communications officer. With a quick tilt of his head, he directed her toward the passageway through which he had arrived. Inside the darkened corridor, his voice was hushed. "It is imperative that we establish communications with the Curasalah."

"Have you any idea how?"

His expression reflected grim resolution. "Instruct me on the use of your device and your emergency protocol. I will go outside and try to contact Captain Tibrab."

"No, sir," the young woman responded.

"Excuse me? I am in charge of this mission…"

"Minister Sirinoya," she interrupted, "communications out there will be difficult, if possible at all. Even if I show you basic operations, you aren't trained to scan for emergency frequencies that may be accessible. I am. I'll go."

Reluctantly accepting the validity of her point, he nodded. "I shall accompany you. You'll need someone who can watch for approaching danger."

"Approaching danger, sir? Vibrations beneath my feet tell me that danger is all around outside."

"I suppose we'll just have to do our best to avoid it."

On the way out of the tunnel, three Pifanamar guards insisted on going with them. Grudgingly, Warnach agreed as he peered through a dusty observation portal. For all he knew, there could be troops on the ground. Armed soldiers might prove valuable.

Opening security doors while other soldiers stood at the ready, everyone released a collective sigh of relief. The outer doors had not been damaged. Peering through another portal, Warnach saw brilliant flashes across the night sky. Fighting above them continued.

A Bederand soldier quickly poked his head out the door. Swiftly looking from side to side, he saw no signs of ground troops. The only inhabitants appeared to be dead bodies scattered amongst piles of mangled transports and building debris. Otherwise, the street was deserted.

Rapidly, they moved outside. Keeping close together, they hurried toward an open area where the com officer hoped to obtain clear frequencies. Everyone dropped to the street when a laser bolt collided with a building one street away. When they dared exchange looks, the same thought passed through every mind. The attackers seemed intent on obliterating Mijirina from the face of Bederand.

Scrambling along several eerily dark blocks, they finally came to a spot that was relatively sheltered but open enough to provide hope of piercing continuing interference. Huddling behind the decorative stone wall of what had been a government archive center, the Chikondran com officer concentrated on the lighted screen of her emergency communicator. Normal frequencies were jammed, likely the result of resonating SVC waves. Patiently, she tapped in additional codes to broaden the frequency sweep.

"Have we come on a fool's mission?" Warnach whispered.

Intently watching her readout, she lifted only her eyebrows. "Only a fool would not try, sir. It is but a matter of time before someone discovers the location of the shelter. My preference is for that someone to be part of a MERR team."

Suddenly, an attack craft hurtled low above their heads. Another craft followed in rapid pursuit, and both ships screamed as they angled sharply upward. High altitude acrobatics left fiery trails blazing across black skies. One of the pilots made an error. Within seconds, the com officer found herself pinned beneath Minister Sirinoya, who protected her with his own body.

Rolling sideways until his back flattened against the brick wall, Warnach's shocked eyes swept the chaotic scene. The attack craft had crashed into the street behind the ruined archive center. The explosion at impact had impelled a hellish fireball into the sky. Soldiers with him stared in amazement. All had watched as the ship, spinning out of control, had made an impossible veer from a trajectory that had seemingly targeted their position.

Warnach's voice conveyed the urgency in his assessment of the situation. "It's useless! Hurry! Let's get back! It's getting worse out here!"

"One minute, sir. Just one more minute," the com officer answered calmly, although her cerea-nervos pulsated a rapid rhythm. Suddenly, she leaned closer to the device. "Mission team reporting to Curasalah." Triumphantly, she passed the device to Warnach.

Urgently, he reported their status to Captain Tibrab and described their location. Almost immediately, the Curasalah's powerful scanners locked onto their signal and calculated their coordinates. Alliance fighters had arrived from the nearby Garolian System and would immediately enter Bederand air space. A Mission Emergency Rescue and Recovery team was launching right behind them. The mission team should prepare immediately for a dangerous evacuation.

Within minutes, they were on their way back to the shelter. Focusing on the entrance, not one of them spared a glance at lights streaking across the heavens. The shriek of weapons, spitting deadly venom through the night, pierced their brains and hurt their ears. Intermediate safety was merely yards away. Reaching the entrance first, Warnach heaved open a door and urged the brave band inside. Glancing outside just before dragging the door closed, he breathed a prayer of thanks. Another fighter had crashed and was careening along the street in a blazing path of fire.

~

Clouds blocked all light from moons and stars. Raindrops fell from the skies in a steady shower. Standing in an open doorway, Sandra wondered if

Chikondra's heavens might be crying for their world's lost children. With a heavy sigh, she turned and went back to the lounge.

Araman sat quietly next to Nadana and Mirah. Talking softly, they looked through photographs that had captured events in the lives of the Sirinoya family. Lifting her gaze to her daughter, she attempted a smile. "Memories bring comfort."

Sandra smiled back, determined that Araman not witness her wavering confidence. "Reunions bring joy. He will come home, Mamehr."

Conversing with Rodan, Badrik paused. "Mamehr, it's too soon. You must not give up on Warnach."

Again, Sandra needed a moment to herself. "If you will all excuse me, I need to check something in my office. I'll be back in a few minutes."

Watching her disappear, Rodan turned back to Badrik. "She handles the stress better than I would have expected."

"She holds her hurt and fear inside. However, my brother would be more proud of her than ever."

Inside the office Warnach had designed for her, Sandra stopped and picked up a photo from her desk. Tracing her fingertip along the outline of his face, she studied his features. His eyes were so dark and shining. His brilliant smile was framed by the blackness of his beard. And that mouth. How much she longed to kiss that sensuously shaped mouth.

Raising her head, she turned and listened. The tone sounded again. Sighing, she put the photo down and walked through the door connecting her office to his. Pressing buttons on his console pad, she answered the call.

"Minister Sirinoya's office. May I help you?"

"Is this Mirsah Sirinoya?"

"Yes."

"Mirsah Sirinoya, this is Lieutenant Doma'anjoh at Alliance Communications Central in Kadranas. Please stand by for deep-space com-link. The two-way link will complete in sixty seconds."

Instantly, her heart swelled, and her stomach pitched. "Standing by."

As she tensely leaned across Warnach's desk and stared at the monitor, sixty seconds seemed more like sixty centuries. Gradually, the broadcast image cleared. "Captain Tibrab?"

"Mirsah Sirinoya, we finally have news. Several hours ago, we received a message from the mission team on Bederand. I immediately dispatched a MERR team. They…"

When he stopped and looked quickly away, she feared for a moment that she might faint.

Turning his face back so that she could see him, he smiled kindly. "I apologize. As I started to say, the MERR team executed an evacuation. I thought that you might wish to speak with one of the survivors who just arrived on board."

Suddenly, Warnach's dirty and disheveled image appeared on the monitor. "Shi'níyah, I know how worried you must be…"

Choking on a sob, she gasped. "Warnach! My God! You're alive! How are you? Are you hurt? Warnach?"

The sight of her anxious, relieved face prompted a weak smile. "You mustn't worry. I'm exhausted but uninjured."

Tears spilled from her eyes as her entire jaw quivered. "We've been praying constantly for you and all the others. Oh, Warnach…I was so afraid."

"Me'u Shi'níyah, don't cry. I need to see your smile."

Struggling to breathe and calm herself, she accomplished a wobbly smile. "You look so tired, my ki'medsah. You need to get some rest."

His expression was serious as he nodded. "I will. Mamehr? Is she all right?"

"Oh, Warnach, I'm so sorry. Let me call her."

"No, Shi'níyah, you can tell her. You were right. I do need to rest. I'm quite certain I can convince the good captain here to let me contact you all again. Perhaps around seven in the morning, your time?"

"Seven," she agreed in a tremulous voice. "Warnach, I love you. I love you so much."

"I know, Sandra. When I come home, we'll discuss that. I'm convinced your love saved me."

"Warnach, you don't know how much I've wanted to be with you. If they'd only let me, I would leave right now. I swear, I'd come to you. I want to hold you."

Inhaling a deep breath, he gave her a wan smile. "I know that, Shi'níyah."

Resisting overwhelming desire just to keep talking with him, she smiled again. "Go. Get some sleep. I'll wait for your call in the morning, but I do want to speak with Captain Tibrab before the link is disconnected." She smiled. "Ci'ittá mi'ittá, me'u Warnach."

By the time the captain's image reappeared on her monitor, she had almost regained her composure. Still, her voice shook. "Captain, I hope you'll allow me to ask a favor of you."

"And that is?" he asked in a kind voice.

"I know it probably sounds silly, but I love him so much. Promise you'll take care of him and keep him safe."

"You have my promise. I shall do everything in my power to deliver him safely home to you."

By the time she returned to the lounge, long-suppressed emotions surfaced. Halting when everyone suddenly looked up at her, she couldn't stop herself from bursting into tears. Rodan, who was closest, quickly rose from his chair and went to her. Unable to regain any semblance of self-control, she moved into his arms and pressed her face against his chest and wept uncontrollably.

"Sandra?"

Stepping back only slightly, she looked up into his worried face before casting a teary glance around the room. Overcome, she struggled for intelligible speech. "They...the com-link. Captain Tibrab..."

Araman's hand covered her mouth as Mirah and Nadana both instantly put their arms around her. Badrik jumped to his feet and rushed to Sandra. Determinedly, he maintained his calm. "Sister... Forsij...did you talk to Forsij?"

Freeing herself from Rodan's fearful grasp, she tossed her hands in shaky waves in front of her, frustrated by her inability to speak. Closing her eyes, she drew in a short, shallow breath and nodded. "I did. Oh, Badrik. Warnach." Her voice broke on a sob. "I...I didn't lose him. I talked to him, too. He's safe."

An incredible rush of relief inundated Badrik as he reached out and pulled her into his arms. Smiling through a glaze of tears, he listened as she repeated over and over again, "I didn't lose him. I didn't lose him."

The following morning, Badrik and Araman both spoke to Warnach via com-link. Laughter and tears reflected their close bond and the fears all three had shared throughout the ordeal. Then, reluctantly, mother and son left Sandra to speak privately with her lifemate.

Their conversation was necessarily brief despite all they wanted so much to discuss. Thoughts and feelings were too numerous for expression via com-link. Learning that she was planning to attend classes that day, Warnach promised he would have a VM waiting for her by the time she returned home. Smiling through a veil of tears, Sandra reminded him how much she missed him and how much she looked forward to his homecoming.

When the com-link closed, Warnach sat back, closed his eyes, and sighed. Glancing at Forsij, he nodded appreciatively. "I thank you, my friend, for allowing me the privacy of your quarters for that call."

Forsij offered him a drink mixed from juices of exotic Chikondran fruits. "I'm glad I could share one of the benefits of being captain of this ship." Forsij sat down across the table from Warnach. "I hope you plan to go back to your quarters for some real rest."

Warnach sipped his drink. "Five hours of sleep hardly make up for the past few days. Believe me. I'm quite ready."

A thoughtful expression draped Forsij's features. "Your ki'mirsah is quite a remarkable young woman."

Reflective thoughts carried Warnach back to home as he considered Forsij's comment. With a slight shake of his head, he breathed a sigh. "More than remarkable. She is intelligent, strong, and spirited. And, perhaps, a little stubborn. But, at the same time, she's so loyal and loving."

"I'm nearly jealous of your good fortune. I heard what she told you yesterday. Most women would have been begging or demanding that you come home immediately. Your Sandra spoke only of wanting to come to you. I hope you appreciate the significance of that difference."

Pensively, Warnach stared into his half-empty glass. "Even though that's typical of her reactions, I still find myself surprised."

"A piece of advice. Never take her attitude for granted. Now, help me keep a promise I made to your ki'mirsah. Go back to your quarters and get some sleep."

Half an hour later, Warnach lay quietly in bed. His body ached, and his face felt faintly sore. His heart, however, savored feelings she had created from far away. Forsij had been right. His ki'mirsah had granted him confidence and freedom to pursue what he felt was necessary without inflicting any pangs of guilt.

Turning onto his side and nestling the uninjured side of his face into his pillow, he sighed and closed his eyes. He continued to grapple with a terrible sense of guilt. More than ever, he regretted having left her behind so soon after their unification. A comforting thought crept into his mind as he fell asleep. She had promised him that, no matter what, she would wait for his return.

# Chapter Six

Arriving at the academy, Sandra was nearly late reaching her first class. Peter and Emilio had seen her and literally run through the corridors to wrap her in a huge, affectionate hug. She had also received almost identical greetings from Druska and Ziaman. Even professors, some of whom she barely knew, had stopped her to express their relief upon hearing news that Minister Sirinoya had been rescued with so few losses to his mission team.

Two days later, she sat in front of the monitor in her office at home. For the third time, she watched and listened to the VM he had sent while she was still sleeping.

"Shi'níyah, please forgive me for being such a coward. I think I could not have faced you via com-link. Governor Maijarus and Governor Lodarius both boarded the Curasalah with a number of their respective cabinet members. So much divides them. However, more than ever, they are willing to work at developing a viable plan to end hostilities. With confirmation that the attack was launched by unidentified forces from a Bederandan moon, it becomes even more imperative that we seek a solution to their problems since they now must unite against an unknown enemy.

"Sandra, please, I beg your understanding. I want so much to come home, but I cannot forget what you said about so many lives being lost here. Shi'níyah, I must try one last time. I need your support more than ever.

Please. Send me a reply letting me know that you understand. I love you. Ci'ittá mi'ittá."

By the next day, she still hadn't responded when Araman found her in the kitchen. "Sandra, there's a call for you. They're connecting a com-link from the Curasalah."

Glancing upward with sad eyes, Sandra forced a smile and got up. "Thank you, Mamehr."

For a brief moment, Araman stopped her just as she was leaving the kitchen. "Child, you must be honest with him. Tell him how you really feel. He needs to know."

Tension etched into weary features. "Mamehr, I don't know how. I'm so mixed up that even I'm not sure exactly what I feel."

Reaching his office, she confirmed to the waiting com officer that she was ready for the com-link. When Warnach's face appeared, she noted lines of intense worry around his eyes and mouth. Somehow, she found the ability to smile. "My lifemate, I was planning to send you a message."

Quietly, he regarded the image transmitted via technology so complicated that it seemed to defy natural law. "I expected to hear from you yesterday."

Swallowing uncomfortably, she nodded. "I know. Warnach, please, don't be angry with me. I...I didn't know what to say."

"Sandra, how could I possibly be angry with you? I constantly find myself asking more of you than is right or fair. Tell me, Shi'níyah. What are you thinking?"

She was almost grateful for the thick, heavy blockage lying somewhere between her heart and her throat. It served well as a dam to hold back sobs. She swallowed hard before she could answer. "I wish I could. I feel so confused, Warnach. So torn. I know how critical things are on Bederand. I also comprehend the repercussions if peace can't be achieved. At the same time, I'm hurting. So much. I've been so afraid. I want you back. I want to hold you. I want..."

"Sandra, talk to me…" he pleaded when it seemed she couldn't say another word.

Finally, she forced herself to go on. "I do understand why you feel the need to stay. I'll try to manage. I…I'll do my best."

"Sandra, give me two weeks. If I see no substantial progress in two weeks, I will terminate negotiations."

"Two weeks?" Words failed her. Somehow, two weeks sounded more like eternity. Frightened without knowing why, she rubbed her fingers nervously against her Kitak. "Two weeks. Then?"

"Two weeks. One way or the other, I come home."

Sighing, she gazed at his image. "I love you."

Finally, he smiled. "Just remember that promise you made."

Three days later, she sat inside a quiet restaurant in Kadranas. She stared into the bowl of soup she had ordered. Having eaten less than half, she already felt as if she couldn't take another bite.

"Chica, you can't go on this way."

Evergreen eyes lifted. "Emilio, I can't remember feeling so tired. I'm even having trouble focusing on my studies."

"You're hardly eating. You say you're not sleeping well. It's no wonder you've had a headache. You need to pull yourself together. That husband or lifemate or whatever you call him is going to come home to a frumpy, grumpy, skinny skeleton."

Grinning, she stuck out her tongue. "Thanks for the compliment."

Later that evening, she sat in the academy's main library. Squinting and blinking, she tried to clear her vision to make sense of words and charts displayed on a study monitor. Her body felt strangely hollow. Unconsciously, she nervously rubbed her Kitak. Blowing out a heavy breath, she shook her head and immediately regretted the action. Sharp, blinding pain shot through her brain.

Frustrated, she got up without closing the document she had been reviewing. When she walked outside, fresh air did nothing to revive her.

Grimacing at the thought of how she couldn't stand wearing units fitted to the ear, she sat down on a step and fumbled inside her attaché for her cell-com. Praying it wasn't too late, she entered a pre-programmed code.

"Central Security. May I help you?" sounded the crisp response.

"I hope so. Has Captain Sirinoya left yet?"

"No. May I advise him who's calling?"

Less than ten minutes later, Badrik's private transport stopped in front of the library steps where she still sat. Stepping out, he hurried to her. "Sister, whatever is wrong?"

Her eyes were watery when she looked up at him. Her voice quivered. "I'm so sorry for disturbing you. I feel so awful, Badrik. I didn't want to risk piloting myself home."

Leaning over, he picked up her things before offering her his hand. "There's no reason to apologize. Big brothers are always on duty to rescue their little sisters."

Inside his transport, she leaned backward with her eyes closed. Glancing sideways several times, he realized that she appeared excessively tired and pale. "Do you think we should stop by the clinic?"

Her head rolled from side to side against the padded headrest. "No," she answered very quietly. "I just want to go home."

"If you're sick, you should see a physician."

After a long pause, she answered him. "You're right. I'll call in the morning and make an appointment. For now, just take me home."

Firmly, he supported her as they entered the house. His concern was mushrooming. She had hardly spoken on the way home. Stepping out of the transport, she had stumbled. When he had reached out to steady her, he had been surprised by how weak and shaky she really was.

Hearing their arrival, Araman came into the foyer to greet them. Her smile quickly faded. "Sandra? What's wrong?"

"Mamehr, I think I'm getting sick. If you don't mind, I think I'm just going straight up to bed."

Watching her walk slowly toward the staircase, Badrik lowered his voice. "Mamehr, I'm really worried about her. Why don't you go upstairs, so she's not alone? Farisa should be home by now. I think I'll call and ask her to come."

"Of course. Nadana should be back any minute. Let her know that I'm up with Sandra."

Smiling several minutes later, as he talked with Farisa, Badrik leaned forward to greet Nadana's arrival with a kiss to her cheek. Suddenly, he almost dropped the cell-com before whirling around. Bloodcurdling shrieks sounded from upstairs.

"Farisa! Hurry!" Dropping the cell-com to the floor, he broke into a run. Practically flying up the staircase, he ran through the corridor and into the master suite.

"Badrik! Help me!" Araman desperately cried out.

Running toward Sandra, Badrik grabbed her upper arms. Her body jerked and twisted violently as shrill screams continued one after the other. Swiftly glancing around, he saw Nadana drag his mamehr out of the way to give him more space.

Holding Sandra by the arms accomplished nothing. Her eyes rolled wildly as her head tossed from side to side. Sweat glistened on her face. Strong as he was, the powerful jolting of her body required every bit of his strength just to hold onto her. Moving quickly, he wrapped his arms around her and bound her as tightly as he could.

"Sandra!" He shouted her name. "Sandra! Listen to me! It's Badrik! Sandra, you're going to be all right! Listen to me! Sandra!"

Gradually, the horrible jerking slowed and eased into a rhythmic twitching. He felt her arms tighten around him.

"Badrik." Her voice was hushed and hoarse. "Help me, Badrik. Oh, dear God, help me."

"Shsh, little sister. Don't be afraid. You know I'll take care of you. Let me get you into bed."

Stunned, Araman could hardly move. Nadana hurriedly pulled back the covers on the bed so Badrik could lower Sandra onto the mattress. "Sister, get some wet washcloths so we can clean her face."

Snapping back to reality, Araman rushed past them both and disappeared inside the bathroom. When she returned, Sandra lay limply against her pillows with Badrik sitting by her side. Her right hand clutched his. Hurrying around the bed, Araman climbed in beside Sandra and gently washed away tears and perspiration.

"What happened?" Farisa asked when she strode into the room.

Badrik glanced up and moved aside. "I would say a seizure, but I think she was completely aware of her surroundings. She was jerking uncontrollably and screaming like nothing I've ever heard in my life."

Briskly, Farisa took his place and started to take readings on her scanner. Her forehead wrinkled as she studied the output. "Her blood pressure is dangerously high. Her heart rate is rapid, and her temperature is elevated. What I don't understand is the indication of brain waves. Badrik, something is terribly wrong. We need to transport her immediately to hospital."

Unexpectedly, Sandra's eyelids flew open. Her head rolled on the pillow, and her hand shot out to grasp Farisa's. "No! Don't move me. You can't! Don't!"

Leaning over her, Farisa smiled reassuringly and stroked her cheek. "Sandra," she began soothingly, "you need to be in hospital. We can identify what's making you sick and take care of you."

Sandra began to cry softly. "No, no, no, no. You don't…understand."

"What don't I understand?"

Her throat constricted. Her breathing labored. "Here. I…I can feel him here. If you take me away, I can't fight it. Farisa, I'll die."

Farisa glanced around. "Does anyone have any idea what she's talking about?"

Nadana signaled Farisa to move and sat down in her place. "Child, look into my eyes."

Blinking rapidly against brutal pain, Sandra managed to hold her eyes open for several seconds.

"Child, can you tell me when your pain began?"

Her answer was a weak murmur. "Last week. In th…the Brisajai. When I went that afternoon to pray."

"Can you tell me anything about how you feel?"

"Nadana," she started to cry anew, "my head hurts so badly. My entire body feels heavy on the outside but empty inside. I feel like… Nadana, it makes no sense, but I feel like I'm dying. I…"

Abruptly, her head jerked back into her pillow. Her hands flew up to her temples and pushed from both sides against her Kitak. Suddenly, Warnach's name carried throughout the upstairs upon scream after scream as her body writhed and her legs kicked against the bed.

"Badrik!" Farisa cried. "Get on the bed! Hold her down!"

Quickly, Nadana jumped away to give Farisa the chance to administer a sedative. Piercing screams grew further apart until they stopped altogether. Between her hands, Farisa held Sandra's face. "Sandra, you need to go to hospital. Now. We must get treatment for you."

Glassy-eyed but aware despite swiftly invading effects of the sedative, Sandra begged pitifully. "No. You don't understand. I'll die. Mamehr? You believe me, don't you? Mamehr, please, don't let them take me."

Seeing that she had quieted, Badrik moved toward the end of the bed so that Araman could get close to Sandra. Tenderly, Araman smiled and took Sandra's hand. "Child, you need care. You know something is terribly wrong."

She whimpered as she fought against the effects of the tranquilizer, and fresh tears wet pale cheeks. "I can't go. I promised Warnach I'd wait. No ma…no matter what. Mamehr, I can't keep my promise if they take me away from home."

Firmly, Nadana placed her hand on Farisa's shoulder. Sitting again by Sandra's side, she looked first into Araman's eyes. Seeing that her sister did not yet understand but would back her completely, Nadana smiled reassuringly into Sandra's terrified face. "Child, I want you to rest. I'll be honest. You fight for your life. I swear to you, though. I will die before I let anyone take you from this house."

"And I will stand by my sister."

A faint smile crossed Sandra's face. "Nadana?" she whispered.

"Yes, child, tell me."

"Don't let anyone take my Kitak."

Araman forced back the rising knot in her throat. "Child, we'll watch over you the best we can. We won't let anyone remove Kitak."

A weak sob was the last sound Sandra made as Farisa's injection finally accomplished its work. Noting that she was resting, at least for the moment, Nadana signaled with a curt lift of her head that everyone should leave the room.

Outside in the hallway, Farisa turned furiously snapping eyes toward Badrik's aunt. "Have you lost your mind? How could you possibly make such a dangerous promise? She needs to be in hospital! We need to diagnose what's causing this problem!"

Sternly, Nadana responded, "I know exactly what's making her sick, and she will not be moved from this house."

Araman, fearing the growing suspicion in her mind, backed her sister. "This is her home. She will stay here, even if it means she dies here."

Turning slightly, Farisa spoke to her mate. "This is absurd! Badrik, please! Help me reason with them! Sandra needs urgent medical care!"

Perplexed, he said to his aunt, "Farisa is an exceptional physician. You know that. Her examination and scans revealed severe problems but no cause. How can you know when she does not?"

Sadly, Nadana smiled. "Farisa, I know that you're a fine doctor. However, you've separated yourself from something just as real as your medical science and your technological gadgets. You avoid acknowledgement or acceptance of unseen forces of mind and spirit. That does not make those forces less real than your science."

Impatient, Farisa responded, "That makes no sense. You're likely condemning Sandra to death. I want to know why."

"Nadana, please, you must explain."

Araman placed her hand on Badrik's arm. Her voice trembled. "Badrik, Sandra crosses the boundary. She enters Ku'saá."

Stunned, he raised his hand and pushed long hair back from his face. "Ku'saá? How can you be certain?"

Nadana shook her head. "Did you not hear what she said? Did you not hear those screams? Her soul is in agony. It cries out for her ki'medsah. There is one way only to save her from losing her life and her soul. Warnach must reach her side before she loses strength to cling to the spirit that will surely be lost trying to find him."

"Ridiculous superstition!" Farisa spat out furiously. "She needs medical care, not mystical fantasies."

Araman spoke out. "Farisa, you're entitled not to believe. That is your right. However, I believe Nadana is absolutely correct. Judging by Sandra's request, she instinctively understands that she may be dying already. We can stand here and waste precious time arguing, or we can do what must be done."

Sickened by the comprehension seeping into his being, Badrik placed a hand on each of Farisa's shoulders and turned her to face him. "Dear one, I understand how difficult this is for you, but I'm pleading with you. Help us. We must try to keep her alive long enough for us to bring Warnach home."

Farisa's eyes stared into his. "Are you saying you actually believe this, too?"

"I do. Farisa, we need to organize medical care here. At the house. Whatever equipment you think you need. Nurses. Anything at all. You know I ask little of you when it comes to my family's beliefs. Just this time. Please?"

"This is insanity." Her jaw clenched, and her cerea-nervos visibly throbbed. "All right. Just know that this goes completely against my professional recommendations. I take no responsibility if she dies."

Ever-so-briefly, Badrik touched his cerea-nervos to hers. "Thank you, dear one." Then, he spoke to Nadana. "How long do you think we have?"

Nadana's eyes closed. "Impossible to say. I'm not sure how she's alive now. She says the pain began almost a week ago. Had she been Chikondran, she would be dead already."

Badrik's thoughts raced. If the Curasalah left Bederand immediately, it would need eight days to make the journey. If a qualified pilot could take one of the Curasalah's specially designed crafts reserved for emergency evacuation of the chancellor, the journey could possibly be reduced by maybe two days. Too long. As he formulated possible solutions, his military training surged into command mode.

"Mamehr, stay with Sandra. If she has another attack, call for help and stay back to avoid being hurt. Farisa, contact whoever you think necessary and get equipment and medical staff in to assist. Do whatever it takes. I expect this to be a very difficult and painful ordeal for all of us. We will need outside help."

He paused, his eyes gleaming with fury as he looked at Nadana. "While I contact the Curasalah and make special arrangements, I want you to call Baadihm Farsuk. He needs to come. I want him to see in person what he has done."

~

Captain Forsij Tibrab barked orders at his second-in-command as they raced through the corridors of the vast ship. Impatient for the end to an elevator trip that lasted less than a minute, he emerged at a dead run onto the deck with the secure conference room where Warnach was currently conducting negotiations with Bederandan leaders.

Reaching the guarded entrance, he sharply addressed security personnel with clipped commands and then barged through the doorway. Instantly, he heard loud, angry voices competing for domination of hot disputes. At the head of the table, Warnach's face showed total exasperation. Glancing around, Tibrab realized that not one of the Bederandans had taken notice of his arrival.

In a commanding voice, Tibrab interrupted the unruly group. "Gentlemen! Pardon my intrusion." Irate faces that looked around also appeared indignant. "I must speak to Minister Sirinoya. Alone."

With a curt nod of his head that bordered on sarcasm, Warnach stood. "Excuse me."

Following Forsij from the conference room, Warnach looked puzzled. "Forsij?"

"Come. We must speak privately." Rapidly striding around the corner, Forsij led his friend to a smaller meeting room. Inside, as he faced Warnach, his eyes were filled with dread.

"Forsij, something has happened. What?"

"Warnach, I've ordered the EV-2C prepared for immediate deployment. It will be ready to depart within twenty minutes. I've also taken the liberty of sending one of my officers to your private quarters to assemble some of your belongings to stow on board. I shall leave the Curasalah under the command of my first officer so that I may personally pilot the EV-2C. You must prepare to leave. Now."

Warnach stared at him. Alarm suddenly flooded his insides, and he felt faintly sick at his stomach. "Tell me. What happened?"

For only a moment, Forsij closed his eyes. Swallowing against tightness in his throat, he said, "I just spoke with Badrik via com-link. Warnach, it's about Sandra. She has entered initial phases of Ku'saá."

Staggering, Warnach grabbed the chair in front of him. Blood turned to ice in his veins. Terror gushed throughout his entire being. Sandra was Terran. It wasn't possible. The thought screamed at him. Neither was it possible for her, a Terran, to communicate telepathically with Quazon. Panic filled the eyes that looked back at Forsij.

"Quickly, Warnach," Forsij said, grasping his arm. "Inform the

Bederandans that you're leaving. We may already be too late, but we must try. You must try."

Hardly able to breathe, Warnach stared at Forsij. "Where do we meet?"

"One of my officers will escort you to the launch deck. Hurry. I'll have a com-link connected before we depart."

Swiftly, Warnach returned to the conference room to find the Bederandans arguing again. "That's enough! Stop it!"

Shouting stopped as all faces turned toward the door. Exploding fear had completely depleted Warnach's final reserves of patience. "I am sickened by constant bickering that allows no one to express a clear thought that anyone else can hear, let alone understand! I came to announce that, if you care to continue discussions, you may do so here on board the Curasalah, but you will need to rely on the assistance and advice of Deputy Minister Agaman."

Governor Maijarus stood and addressed Warnach in a gruff voice. "Exactly what does that mean?"

Sharply, Warnach answered, "It means I'm departing from the Curasalah immediately."

"Leaving? How can you leave now? I thought you were committed to achieving a resolution to this problem!"

Sick inside, Warnach barely croaked a civil response. "Governor, my negotiation team and I risked our lives seeking resolution to your world's problems. Two of my colleagues even died for the benefit of Bederand. Sacrifice enough has been made. The time has come when you, Governor Maijarus, and you, Governor Lodarius, must decide among yourselves whether or not you place as much value on your own world and your own people as we have. Perhaps you would benefit from taking a good, long look at your families to see if their lives are incentive enough to inspire you to enter honest negotiations. I wish you well."

Turning to leave, Warnach heard the snide voice of the Cosomond governor. "How dare you bring our families into this?"

Pivoting abruptly, Warnach could not hide the raw emotion burning on his face, and he virtually snarled his response. "How dare I? Your families remain safe. I cannot say the same for mine. Merely because I chose to come to Bederand, my lifemate lies dying on Chikondra. That is how I dare. Your unending argumentative attitudes sicken me. Considering your appalling lack of cooperation, I curse myself for coming at all. I knew that doing so might jeopardize the life of the one person I value more than any other in the universe." Furious, he paused to catch his breath. "Goodbye."

Breathless after running to the launch deck, Warnach rushed over to a grim-faced Forsij. The captain moved from his chair and let Warnach sit down. "You have five minutes before we board."

His brother's solemn expression frightened him more than ever. "Badrik! Tell me! What happened? Where is she?"

"Warnach, she's upstairs, in bed. Farisa sedated her. Mamehr is with her. My brother, it's more dreadful than I can begin to tell you. We can talk more once you're underway. Technicians are coming to install com-link equipment in your suite now. Nadana thinks that if Sandra can communicate with you, she might be able to fight longer against the effects of Ku'saá. We don't know. We're trying, Warnach. I swear to you. We are trying."

Involuntary tears coursed down Warnach's cheeks. Thickened by emotion, his voice sounded low. "I know you are, Badrik. I know. This is my fault. Had I only listened to my instincts…"

"There's no time for guilt or blame. We can only exert our best efforts to save her. Go, Warnach, and pray. Turn your heart and thoughts completely to Sandra. She needs you."

Just as they were ready to terminate the call, the sound of horrific screams caught Badrik's attention. "Warnach, it's Sandra again. I must go. They'll need my help."

Badrik must have left the household intercom open in case of emergency. Staring at the suddenly blank monitor, Warnach could hardly believe what he had heard. Cold sweat beaded on his face, and his hands turned clammy. His insides quaked with unadulterated fear. That tormented scream had come from his beloved Shi'níyah. Panic collapsed in the wake of horrendous, gut-wrenching guilt.

# Chapter Seven

Wearily, Nadana got up from the sofa when chimes signaled the arrival of visitors. She said nothing upon seeing Farsuk Edsaka waiting outside. Opening the door wider, she invited him into the house.

"Nadana, Ifta interrupted a late meeting and insisted that I come here immediately. Has something happened to Araman? Is she all right?"

"Araman is fine. Please, come in. We need to talk."

Coldness in Nadana's attitude irritated the chancellor. "If nothing is wrong with Araman, then I fail to understand the urgency for me to drop everything and come here."

Abruptly, Nadana stopped and turned to face him. Fierce anger burned in her eyes. "I assure you. There is urgency in the need for your presence."

"Look, if this concerns the crisis last week on Bederand, I personally authorized every available resource to rescue that team. No one regrets more than I that two lives were lost. However, Warnach is safe."

"Is he?" Nadana demanded in a cutting tone. "Are you really so certain?"

Farsuk's voice assumed an impatient, sharp edge. "Yes, I'm certain. He's conducting negotiations right now on the Curasalah. What's wrong with you, Nadana? Where is Araman?"

"What's wrong is that you broadcast your sympathetic messages reminding our people to cling to our faith practices to deliver us through these tragedies. What's wrong is the hypocrisy you hide behind your speeches.

What's wrong is the fact that you have failed to keep sacred promises you made to the Great Spirit and to Morcai to protect his children in every way possible."

"You make no sense. Where is Araman?"

"Mamehr is upstairs," Badrik brusquely informed him as he quickly trotted down the staircase. "She's with Farisa and Sandra."

"And?"

Just as the annoyed question was uttered, shrill screams echoed from upstairs. Closing his eyes, Badrik dragged in a breath and paused for only a moment. Reaching for Nadana's hand, he gave her a reassuring smile. "Remember. Dr. Barrett is there with another attendant. They'll help." Cold fury in Badrik's eyes then caused Farsuk to take several steps backward.

"Wh…what was that?" Farsuk demanded, shaken by the intensity of the screams that had carried through the house.

"That, my esteemed baadihm, would be the result of your failure to honor the very same faith you so highly extol. I thought you should experience it for yourself."

Farsuk cursed. "I grow tired of all these mysterious accusations. What were those screams, and why is it that you blame me?"

Badrik responded, "That, Baadihm, was the scream of a tortured soul. Sandra has entered Ku'saá."

Stunned, Farsuk Edsaka swayed. "You're lying. No, I cannot believe that! She's Terran."

Nadana said, "Terran she may be, but she has entered Ku'saá. Warnach told you how he feared for her. After all these years, you should know he would never have been so insistent without good cause. You betrayed him when you went to Sandra behind his back. You played on her emotions to create a sense of guilt so that you could satisfy your own ambitions."

"Ambition? You call wanting to save millions of people from interstellar war being ambitious?"

"When it could have detrimental effects on upcoming elections? Without any doubt."

Farsuk ground his teeth together. "I was trying to save lives."

Nadana's piercing gaze did not falter. "Once you lose vision of the value a single life, Farsuk, especially one which you are bound by sacred oath to protect, no longer can you properly value any life at all."

Glaring at his godfather, Badrik seethed but knew how necessary it was to contain his anger. Carefully, he maintained an even tone of demand in his voice. "Forsij has already departed the Curasalah with Warnach on board the EV-2C. We're certain there's no possibility that they can arrive in time. I want authorization to pilot the Cuseht 1T. I'll meet them en route and perform an emergency docking long enough for Warnach to transfer. Then, we'll return to Chikondra. Instead of eight or nine days, we have a chance to make the trip in five."

"What? Are you out of your mind? You haven't flown a mission in years! The Cuseht isn't even fully tested! You could be flying a death trap! I will not hear of it!"

"You will hear of it, and you will authorize it! You know very well that I've maintained all of my flight certifications despite my transfer to home duty. You also know as well as I that initial tests on the Cuseht have yielded astonishing successes. Further, I know Dr. Efrehriahn quite well. I have complete confidence in his assessment of the ship's flight readiness."

Farsuk crossed the room in nervous agitation. With the sound of agonized screams still ringing in his ears, he knew there would be no escaping his role leading to Sandra's condition. Adding to guilt and burgeoning remorse was abject fear. Badrik was fully willing to risk his life in the slim hope of bringing Warnach home in time to save Sandra from a torturous death. In the end, Farsuk could find himself forced to accept responsibility for her death as well as the deaths of both of his godsons.

When he faced Badrik again, dark eyes were indisputably anguished. In a strangled voice, he pleaded, "Badrik, please, do not ask this of me. I cannot bear

to risk both your life and Warnach's. You must believe me. I never would have
sent Warnach to Bederand if I'd honestly thought there could be any danger
to Sandra. I love all three of you. Don't ask me to authorize use of the Cuseht."

Badrik showed no sympathy. "My brother tried to warn you. You did
far worse than ignore him. You betrayed him. In doing so, you also betrayed
Badehr's memory as well as the trust he placed in you. Your regrets come
far too late. I will not sit back and do nothing while there's a chance to
save my sister."

"Badrik, no. Think of Araman… She could lose all of you. She could
not bear the sorrow."

"Farsuk, I will never bear the sorrow in the eyes of my son if his ki'mirsah
dies this way."

Farsuk spun in the direction of the firm voice that addressed him. His
jaw clamped tightly shut, and he swallowed multiple times as his head moved
back and forth. "Araman, we could lose them all too easily."

Despite her petite stature, Araman exuded a formidable presence.
"My sons are my life, Farsuk. I take no joy in Badrik's decision. In fact,
his intentions terrify me. However, his courage honors the heritage of the
Sirinoya. His devotion to his family also honors the integrity of the man
who was his badehr. You know as well as I. Losing Sandra like this will finally
destroy Warnach. He will die a man emptied of spirit and purpose. Badrik
understands this about his brother. If I do lose my sons, I shall have the
comfort of knowing they died living the lives Morcai and I taught them to
live. Authorize deployment of the Cuseht."

"Araman…"

Reaching out, she grasped his hand tightly. "Come. Follow me."

When they entered the master suite, Dr. Barrett looked up. The fact that
the chancellor of the Alliance had joined them made no impression on the tall,
gray-haired, Terran physician. Sympathy showed clearly on his face. "Mirsah
Sirinoya, there's no physical cause we can treat. The screaming coincides with

spikes in the pace of her heartbeat and blood pressure. However, we can discern nothing treatable."

Araman gave the doctor a faint smile. "We understand, Dr. Barrett. Thank you for coming."

Hesitantly, Farsuk approached the large bed. His heart swelled into his throat. The dynamic young woman who had come to Chikondra with his blessing had changed suddenly and dramatically. Gone was the natural blush of a healthy complexion. Instead, ashen pallor lay beneath features blotched and wet with sweat. Neatly styled hair that usually gleamed with golden highlights had separated into straggling, soggy strands straying at wild angles against her face and pillow. Her hands twitched uncontrollably, and her body shook beneath the covers.

Deep affection was evident as Araman leaned forward and whispered into Sandra's ear. "I love you, daughter. Fight, child. You must not leave us. Your ki'medsah is coming."

Completely oblivious to Farsuk's presence, Sandra's eyelids lifted slightly. "Mamehr, are you sure?"

"I'm sure, child. You must wait for him."

Sandra's face rolled to one side. "I'm trying, Mamehr. The pain. I…I'm trying."

Seeing that she again fell quiet under the effects of heavy sedation, Araman turned back to Farsuk. "You see now with your own eyes. Your actions have done this to her. Only you have the power to give her any chance for survival."

With jaw quivering, he looked away. "I never meant for this to happen," he choked out. "How could I have possibly known?"

"The greater question is how you could have so callously disregarded Warnach's judgment on a matter rooted in faith and his understanding of his ki'mirsah."

Suddenly afraid those horrific screams would begin again, Farsuk swiftly fled the room. In the hallway outside, he tightly clutched a carved wooden handrail with both hands. His head dropped forward. His posture conveyed an image of despair. "Tell Badrik to get what rest he can. I shall authorize preparation of the Cuseht for immediate launch."

Sunrise brought no cheer to the Sirinoya household. Awaking to fresh waves of screams, family members ran to the master suite. Medical technicians from the main hospital in Kadranas had spent the night watching over a patient who pitched and rolled in the bed. One had approached her with a syringe ready to infuse a fresh dose of sedative. Shocked by her strength, he found himself sprawled on the floor several feet away from the bed.

"No!" she shrieked. "No more sedative! Get away! No more!"

As the other technician grabbed her to control flailing arms, Nadana hurried to the bedside. "Child, they don't dare use neuro-sedation. Take the medicine. It will help keep you calm."

"No! I can't hear them! They're trying to help, but the medicine doesn't let me hear them! Nadana, please! Make them stop!"

Tying the belt on her robe as she hurried into the room, Farisa stopped suddenly. "She's suffering delusions. Here," she said, snatching the syringe from the technician's hand.

Nadana's arm shot out and prevented Farisa from approaching. "Wait!" she commanded. "Child," she said, her voice gentling as Sandra began to still. "You know the medicine is intended to help. Farisa would never hurt you."

Piteously, Sandra began sobbing. "I know. Medicine…lose control. Can't hold…it pulls away. They're trying to help, but the medicine… Can't hear them. No strength to fight."

For the first time, tears rolled freely down Nadana's cheeks. "Child, the pain. What about the pain?"

Some part of Sandra's mind fought the frenetically swirling and twisting currents that sucked at the fabric of her soul. "Pain. Must cope with pain. Focus on pain. Nadana." She sobbed again. "No more medicine. If they can, they'll help me."

Quivering lips placed a kiss against Sandra's burning cheek. "No more sedatives."

Downstairs, Farisa raged. "Why am I here if you counter everything I try to do for her?"

"Farisa, please, calm yourself and listen. Sandra possesses a powerful sense of concentration. The sedatives prevent her from concentrating against a force that draws away the very spirit that gives her life. She does need help, but I think you must look at something besides a sedative. Something to ease the physical pain without clouding her ability to use her mind."

Farisa rubbed her cerea-nervos. "I don't understand this. I just don't understand."

Nadana went to her and put an arm around her. "Neither should you have to. None of us should have to face this. If Warnach were here, this would be a time of incredible beauty and harmony for them. Since he's not... Farisa, during ancient times, this is the reason why wise elders decreed the period of Karmía."

"Nadana, who was she referring to as trying to help her?"

Nadana gave Farisa a faint smile. "Quazon."

"What? Quazon?"

"Farisa, you've already learned that Quazon are not superstition. What you do not know is that, somehow, she communicates telepathically with them."

"No. That cannot be possible."

"Yesterday morning, you would have said that Ku'saá is impossible."

Perplexed and frustrated, Farisa stared blankly across the room. "I'll discuss the matter with Dr. Barrett when he returns. Perhaps we can devise an alternative treatment." She paused. "In the meantime, I want to spend some time with Badrik before..."

"Go, my dear. I'm glad he slept in the other wing. He'll need every moment of rest...and encouragement from the woman he loves."

Entering the bedroom, she pensively gazed as he turned over and smiled. Quickly, she moved toward muscular arms reaching out for her. Drawn onto the bed beside him, she closed her eyes and lost herself in passionate sensations awakened by his cerea-semi'ittá. Their lovemaking assumed an intensity new to her. Pushing everything from her mind except Badrik, Farisa immersed herself completely in the compelling union he created with her.

Later, after they showered together, she helped him dress in the fresh uniform he always kept at Warnach's house. Anxiety prompted renewed awareness of how handsome Badrik truly was. Slightly taller than Warnach, the younger of the Sirinoya brothers had the same dark eyes and waving hair. Fearful as she was of the mission he would soon undertake, she couldn't help but respect and admire his courage. A finer man she could not have dreamed of finding. Rising onto her tiptoes to kiss him, she made a silent vow. If only he survives, she thought.

"Dear one," he said softly as he looked into troubled eyes, "whatever happens, you must know that I do love you."

Professional practice aided her in holding tears at bay. "I know that, Badrik. I shall do everything possible to help Sandra. I know how much she means to Warnach and you."

Gently, with fingers beneath her chin, he tilted her face upward. "Do you know how much you mean to me?"

Delicate features tensed before she stretched her arms around him. "I love you, Badrik. I...I... Badrik, I cannot deal with life if I lose you. Be careful. Please. You have to come back. I need you."

Badrik's arms contracted around her. Hardly ever did she speak aloud her feelings. Moved by words rarely heard in the life they shared, he clung to her more tightly. His voice shook as he whispered against smooth, straight hair, "I have every intention of coming back. More so now than ever before."

Within two hours, Badrik settled into the pilot's seat of the Cuseht 1T. The ship had been readied for take-off a full hour earlier than expected. Engaging system after system, Badrik breathed prayer after prayer. Just as Dr. Efrehriahn had promised, the sleekly designed spaceship appeared perfectly ready for its maiden mission.

Chancellor Farsuk Edsaka watched as the powerful craft lifted from the ground, adjusted trajectory, and fired powerful engines that propelled it from sight within a matter of seconds. He found little consolation in the knowledge that Badrik's flight skills had once exceeded even those of Forsij Tibrab. Forlorn and alone, Farsuk searched his soul. Warnach and Badrik were the sons never born to him. If only they could know that he would have preferred his own death rather than place their lives in the jeopardy both now faced.

～

"Shi'níyah? Sandra, can you hear me now?" The deep ache in Warnach's heart grew evermore profound as he looked upon changes in her image transmitted by com-link. Seeing her so still and quiet compounded his fears. Only a few short hours earlier, he had connected the link. Horrified, he had watched as medical assistants physically restrained her during a seizure-like episode accompanied by anguished screams that had crossed space to pierce the very core of his being.

Labored movements evidenced excruciating levels of pain. "Warnach?"

Helplessly, he watched as she reached toward the com-link system from where she had heard his voice. "Shi'níyah, I'm coming. As fast as possible, I am coming. Shi'níyah, I know how strong you are. You must resist the force that draws at you. Wait for me."

Weakly, she began to weep. Farisa adjusted volume controls to allow him to hear muffled words. "I'm trying, my ki'medsah. You don't know how hard…Warnach, the pain…so bad…worse than before. So much worse."

For just a moment, he choked. Before. How often had he had wondered about the headache that had felled her before their unification? He should have known. Signs had been present from the very beginning. He forced himself to continue. "Shi'níyah, you can do this. You can fight a little longer. You must not surrender to the pain."

"Warn..." His name caught in her throat as a new fit overtook her. Tensing first, her body then launched into violent flailing of arms and legs. Frenzied twisting made restraint difficult and required the efforts of three male assistants to hold her to prevent her from injuring herself.

Ineffectually jumping from his seat, Warnach's frightened voice carried into his suite from millions of miles away. "Sandra! Shi'níyah!"

"Warnach!" She shrieked as she desperately stretched hands and fingers toward the sound of his voice, almost as if she could reach him through the com-link. "Help me! Help me, Warnach! Oh, God, help me! Warnach!"

"Shi'níyah! Fight, Sandra! You can fight it! Sandra!"

Abruptly, her body went limp. Dr. Barrett and Farisa were instantly at her side. Scanners revealed rapidly worsening symptoms. Dr. Barrett administered a drug to slow her racing heart. He questioned aloud how she had not suffered a stroke or heart attack already. Farisa gently stroked tears from Sandra's perspiration soaked face. Relieved, she noted the slowing of erratic, rapid breathing. "Shsh, Sandra. It has passed for now."

Glassy eyes stared back at her. "Warnach? Is he still connected?"

Moving aside so Sandra could again see the monitor, Farisa glanced toward Warnach's image. Her heart went out to him. Tears rolled down his face, and he trembled violently. She could only imagine the complete helplessness he must feel.

"Warnach?"

Almost strangling, he answered her. "I'm still with you, Shi'níyah."

"I love you, Warnach. You must promise me something."

"Anything, Sandra. Just ask."

"If I...if I can't do this. I want you to go on. Do what you do for both of us..."

"Sandra…Shi'níyah, you will join me in field ministry. You have no choice."

"Warnach, I don't think…"

"Shi'níyah, listen to me. Listen carefully." Desperation saturated his voice. "At the shuttleport. The day I left. You promised. You swore you would wait for me to come home. No matter what. Shi'níyah, I will die if I lose you. You must keep your promise. Sandra, please, remember your promise. Wait for me."

"Warnach…" She sounded weaker. "Ci'ittá mi'ittá, my Warnach. Ci'ittá mi'ittá." Quiet filled the room as her eyes closed.

"Farisa?"

"She's exhausted, Warnach, but she's still with us. You look as if you need some rest. May I speak with Forsij?"

Warnach disappeared from the monitor, and Forsij's image came into view. "He left the cabin for the moment. Farisa, how much longer?"

Farisa shook her head. "I can hardly believe we haven't lost her already. Have you heard from Badrik?"

Forsij's smile reassured her. "I believe he pushes the Cuseht to its performance limits. So far, the ship has shown no signs of strain or malfunction, and he's far closer than originally projected. We expect to rendezvous and initiate docking procedures in about five hours."

"My Badrik is a fine pilot," she said softly.

"Badrik is an excellent pilot, Farisa, and an even better man. Trust him."

She fought tears. "I do, Forsij. I just can't help being afraid. For all of you."

Captain Forsij Tibrab methodically reviewed computer sequencing lights signaling that all was ready to begin the docking procedure. "Stand by, Cuseht. Docking anchors opening. Initiate docking…now."

Only the slightest bump indicated that the Cuseht had come into contact with the EV-2C. Warnach watched as the captain continued rapid manipulation of the computerized controls commanding the ship's equipment. Calmly, Forsij leaned closer to the display pad. "Anchor one not secured. Releasing all anchors. Ease away."

Warnach closed his eyes and prayed fervently. She was still alive. A mechanical malfunction could destroy all hope of saving her. Daring to look again, he watched as Forsij's fingers continued to dance across the padded control console.

"Cuseht, initiate new approach. Stand by. Docking anchors open. Initiate docking approach." Another bump. "Anchors closing. Seals locked. Docking tunnel secure and airtight." Forsij and Warnach simultaneously sighed audibly in relief. "Opening hatches."

Within minutes, Badrik embraced his brother, then Forsij. "You need to check anchor one, my friend. When I pulled away, the connectors were still partially closed."

Forsij grinned. "And here I thought I could blame the rusty skills of the pilot."

"Hardly. This pilot has too much at stake." He paused. "What's the latest news?"

Warnach's face was a mask of gloom. "The seizures grow longer apart. Farisa says she's struggling for consciousness. Her vital signs are quickly weakening."

Grim-faced, Badrik nodded. "Then I suppose we shall need to find out if the Cuseht 1T is all Dr. Efrehriahn says it is." Shifting slightly, he placed his hands on Forsij's shoulders. "I apologize for the short visit. We shall make up for it when you bring the Curasalah back to Chikondra."

Just before climbing through the passage to the Cuseht, Warnach aimed a grateful gaze at Forsij. "I don't know how to thank you for the risks you've taken."

Forsij smiled encouragingly. "Save your ki'mirsah. There will be time later for thanks."

Entering the Cuseht, Warnach noted tighter quarters than on the EV-2C. However, the design provided sufficient comfort and functionality for pilot and one crewmember. Settling in, he leaned back in the ergonomic seat that would serve as both chair and bed until their return to Chikondra. Needing distraction, he focused on his brother's quick, efficient handling of the ship as he prepared to pull away from the EV-2C.

Badrik's furious curse startled him. "Damn that anchor! It isn't releasing!"

"Badrik, ease back toward me! Easy! There! Give us fifteen minutes."

The one officer on board the EV-2C with Tibrab rapidly donned emergency gear that would enable him to enter the short tunnel and anchor himself while Forsij manned the hatch to secure the inside of the transport. Within scant minutes that wracked everyone's nerves, the anchor joint was adjusted. Working frantically, Tibrab checked all sensors a final time, and his officer safely reentered the cabin of the EV-2C.

Back at the main controls, Forsij again initiated the release sequence. "Badrik, prepare to leave docking position. Initiating docking release sequence. Begin separation on my signal…now."

Long, tense seconds found men on both ships holding their breaths. Cautiously, Badrik guided the Cuseht away from the EV-2C. Checking critical readouts, Badrik then shut his eyes for a brief moment, almost as if willing the anchor to function correctly. He actually felt the hesitation as the joint stiffly resisted, then opened to free the Cuseht.

Prayerful thanks were heard aboard both vessels. Turning his ship toward Chikondra, Badrik hailed the EV-2C one last time. "Forsij, I'll be waiting for you to return home."

"You leave with our most earnest prayers, my friend."

~

In utter darkness, monstrous claws scraped and jabbed her. Sharp, needle-like points speared into her brain. Pain inside her head throbbed and pounded. Desperately, she pressed her hands against her skull as if trying to contain impending explosion.

All through the night, she had tossed and rolled atop softness that was starkly incongruous with the harsh agony her body endured. Occasionally, strong hands had prevented her from crashing over the sides of steep cliffs. Still, she had sought escape from those invisible hands that imprisoned her. They could not comprehend her soul's desperate need to free itself, to cross the entire universe if necessary. The spirit that could end the pain was lost, and her soul cried out for that spirit so that she might survive and be whole again.

Some part of her clutched through the black void for clarity of thought. Escaping from darkness yet again, she opened glazed eyes. Her voice emerged from a throat raw and sore from screams she no longer recalled. "Mamehr?"

Smiling tenderly, Araman had defied caution and spent the last hour sitting on the bed with Sandra's head in her lap. She made no allowance for tears. There would be time enough later to cry. Her daughter needed comfort and encouragement. "I'm here, child."

In response, she received a weak smile. "Mamehr? Do you believe me now?"

Puzzled, Araman's forehead creased questioningly. "I'm not sure I understand your question."

"You were going to leave us. I — I told you how much I love you. That I needed you. See? I was right, Mamehr."

Exhausted and dying, barely able to speak, this dear child still found it necessary to express love. Araman forced a smile even though her heart was weeping. "We need you, too, Sandra. Try to rest a little."

Coughing, Sandra refused to be quiet. "My parents won't come, will they?"

Araman bit the inside of her cheek. She had pleaded with Lee Warner to leave Earth and come to her daughter. Sandra's mother had trembled and cried. Terror-stricken by the very idea of being on a spaceship so far from Earth, she sobbed that she would be no help to her daughter if she fell apart. Besides, her husband had refused to let her go. He insisted that the Sirinoya family was exaggerating Sandra's condition. Begging pitifully for understanding, she had blessed Araman and her family for tending to her daughter with so much love.

Araman choked, unable to voice an answer. All she could manage was a solemn shake of her head.

Smooth and cool, Sandra's right hand found its way into Araman's left. "It's not Mom's fault. She really is afraid. I know that." Tears crept down pale cheeks. "I worry about her when I die. Daddy might blame her."

"Child," Araman said quietly, "your parents must decide their own way. You must concentrate not on them, neither on your death. You must focus on trying to live. Remember all you have now. Your Chikondran mamehr needs the daughter she finally received. No one wishes to face Badrik if he loses his sister. Your ki'medsah lives for you. He is coming to you."

Eyelids closed for several long moments and opened again. Words carried forth within a scratchy whisper. "Mamehr, I want to live. I want to feel again what it's like when Warnach holds me. You don't know how hard this is or how much it hurts." She paused, breathing heavily. "Mamehr, will you do something for me?"

"If I can."

"If something happens - if I can't do this - tell Warnach that it isn't his fault. He isn't to blame. Tell him - I want him - to follow his heart. Pursue peace the way we both dreamed. Tell Warnach - my love will never leave him. Will you do that?"

Caressing the smoothness of Sandra's forehead without touching Kitak that she still wore, Araman attempted a smile. "I'll tell him."

Pained features relaxed. Eyelids closed, concealing glassy eyes. No sound emerged as dry lips formed simple words. "I love him, Mamehr. I love you all."

～

Farisa supervised the attendants who were gently moving the unresisting body onto the hoverbed they would use to transfer her downstairs. Having seen so much over these past few days, Farisa no longer doubted the mystical factors draining life from her patient. Physically, there was absolutely nothing wrong except the abrupt changes in temperature, heartbeat, and pulse rates when the seizures occurred. The only other notable physical abnormality was the tremendous fluctuation in her brainwave patterns. At times, the brainwaves appearing on medical scanners bore no resemblance at all to patterns in Sandra's previously recorded medical records.

Agreeing to Nadana's request, they would take Sandra downstairs to the Brisajai. Nadana hoped the sanctified space would provide spiritual support to the war Sandra waged for her life. If not, death would come in a holy place. Perhaps her tortured soul might then find the blessing of peace.

After the transfer, Farisa sat on a chair beside her patient. Her ever-present scanner lay in her lap. Her hand wrapped around Sandra's. The coolheaded, efficient physician set aside her well-practiced bedside manner. Tears shone in her eyes. "I wish I knew how to make this easier."

Sandra blinked several times. With her strength waning, she could barely whisper. "I know. Farisa?"

"Yes?"

Swallowing against soreness in her inflamed throat, Sandra struggled to speak. "Don't be afraid, Farisa. Even after this. Don't be afraid. Badrik loves you. Don't hide your love. I didn't. Even now, I have…no regret. Warnach. He gave…me everything. Don't lose that with Badrik."

"Sandra, can it really be worth what you've suffered?"

For several moments, memory's tide held back the nearly irresistible forces sucking away her life. His smile. His touch. The sound of his voice when he called her Shi'níyah. Feelings deeply embedded within Kitak. Faintly smiling, she answered simply, "Absolutely."

Needing some rest, Farisa left Sandra in Dr. Barrett's capable care. Joining Araman in the kitchen, she gratefully accepted a cup of richly fragrant tea. "She grows weaker with each minute that passes."

Araman nodded sadly. "I can hardly believe we still have her."

Sipping steaming liquid from her cup, Farisa nodded agreement. "Her will to live is astonishing."

"I believe her will to live is strengthened by her capacity to love."

Defying her own will, tears slid down Farisa's cheeks. "Araman, I'm so afraid. I overheard Farsuk. He's terribly worried that Badrik is exceeding the capabilities of the Cuseht in his push to get home. He said that even Dr. Efrehriahn grows concerned. Araman…" She stopped, her words interrupted by a quiet sob. "I've never told Badrik how much I truly love him. I'm not sure I realized myself until now."

Not really surprised by the admission, Araman got up. Placing her arms around Farisa's shoulders, she hugged her. "Facing danger such as this often awakens appreciation of what we too often take for granted. If we are blessed with their safe return, my advice is that you tell Badrik. To hide your love does good for neither of you."

"Sandra said almost the same thing."

Gloom permeated the Sirinoya household. Tired and somber, Farisa sat inside the Brisajai. Nadana had gone outside to pray. Farsuk and Ifta Edsaka sat on a sofa with Araman between them. Rodan and Mirah Khalijar had joined the family's sorrowful vigil. Dr. Barrett had left minutes earlier after informing the family that Sandra's organs were gradually ceasing to function and that death should come quickly. Expressing sympathy, he left.

Half an hour later, enormous front doors to the house were flung open. Breathless, Warnach raced inside. "Mamehr! Nadana! Farisa!"

Leaping to his feet, Rodan ran from the family lounge. Halting abruptly, he grabbed his old friend by the shoulders. "Warnach! Eyach'hamá eu Yahvanta! You're safe!"

Terrified eyes met those of Rodan. "Where is she?"

"In the Brisajai."

Shock contorted handsome features. "What? By all that is holy, no! No, Rodan! It cannot be that I've lost her! Tell me it isn't so!"

"Warnach, listen," Rodan told him as he led his staggering, grief-stricken friend by the arm toward the Brisajai. "She's been there since yesterday morning. Hurry. You must go to her while she still lives."

Breaking into a run, Warnach lurched through the house. Pausing only to cast a fleeting look of sorrow at his mamehr, he rushed into the solemn darkness of the Brisajai. Burning candles cast dim light throughout the sanctuary. Rapidly rounding the end of the hoverbed now resting securely on the Brisajai floor, he fell to his knees.

Drawing a chilled hand from beneath the blanket, he placed her palm against his tear-stained cheek. Looking across the bed at Farisa, he begged for encouragement. The bleak expression on her face crushed his hopes.

Quietly, Farisa said, "We tried everything, Warnach. She fought to live. It has been too much. She entered the coma earlier this morning."

"Farisa?" He strangled on a sob.

"Stay with her. Death is near. Perhaps she'll feel your presence. Perhaps it will bring some peace if any part of her soul remains." Then, Farisa silently left Warnach to bid farewell to his beloved ki'mirsah.

Intellectually unable to process the import of Farisa's words, Warnach stared in disbelief at the face he adored so much. Rising and sitting by her side, he surrendered to total panic. With shaking fingers, he quickly removed his Kitak and placed it over her heart. Then, he removed hers and, after saluting it with a kiss, joined it to his. Bending over her, he placed frantically pulsating cerea-nervos against her forehead.

"Sandra," he desperately pleaded as energy from his cerea-nervos charged into her limp body, "don't leave me. I'm so sorry. Please, Shi'níyah, I beg you. Let me prove how much I love you. Shi'níyah, I need you."

Minutes passed. He raised his head. She looked so calm, so peaceful. No more were those fair features distorted by the agony of thwarted Ku'saá. Brokenhearted, he lay down by her side. Reaching across her, he turned her, drawing her tightly against him on the narrow bed. Again, in desperation, he pressed throbbing cerea-nervos against her forehead. Ragged breathing hampered words ripped from his soul. "Ci'ittá mi'ittá, me'u Shi'níyah Sandra. Ci'ittá mi'ittá. Ci'ittá mi'ittá. Ci'ittá mi'ittá."

~

Walking dejectedly through the corridor to the family lounge, Farisa looked up. "Badrik!" Breaking into a run, she flung herself into his arms. "Badrik! Oh! Badrik!"

"Farisa?" he whispered against her hair. Never had he experienced such emotion surging from her as he did at that moment. Except, he thought, when they had made love the morning of his departure on the Cuseht.

Pulling away, she lifted trembling hands to his face. "I love you, Badrik. I was so afraid you might not survive the return trip so I could tell you how much I really love you. Oh, Badrik..."

Holding her again, he wondered in awe. Such a gift in the face of tragic circumstances. Reluctantly drawing away, he gazed into her tearful face. "Dear one, I love you, too. I always have." He paused. "Sandra?"

Sadness chased away her earlier expression of relief. "I left Warnach with her in the Brisajai. She went into a coma this morning. I thought he would want to be alone with her for whatever time she has left. I was going to wait with the others."

Badrik's head sharply twisted away. He closed his eyes against wetness that scorched his eyelids. Momentarily, his voice caught in his throat. "I don't know if Warnach can withstand her passing. Guilt will surely torment him into an early death."

"Come. Later, we can help him through this. For now, we can do nothing more than wait."

Reaching the lounge and halting abruptly, Badrik glared as Farsuk stood and looked at him with a grieving expression. Every shred of self-control evaporated in the face of explosive wrath far too powerful to contain. Flinging himself forward, Badrik spewed a furious stream of vile curses as his fist crashed into Farsuk's face, sending his godfather flying across the room and onto the floor.

"Badrik!" Farisa cried out, rushing toward her mate.

Rodan had been faster and fought hard against the mighty anger that seethed throughout Badrik. "Badrik! Stop! Stop it!"

Fire shot from Badrik's eyes as he twisted against Rodan's restraining arms. Furiously, he shouted, "How dare you defile this home with your presence after what you've done? How dare you! Have you no shame at all?"

Frantically, Farisa clutched Badrik's arm. "Badrik, please. Not now! This isn't the time! Badrik, for me! Please! For Sandra! Not now!"

Gradually, Badrik calmed. Araman rushed past a shocked Ifta and knelt down. Farsuk pressed his hand against his bruised and bleeding face. Glancing into Araman's frightened face, he muttered thickly, "I'm all right. He had every right, Araman. He had every right."

~

Velvet darkness eased the void. Warmth invaded the chill. Calm expelled the chaos. Tension lessened, releasing the pull on tenuous connections. Air filled empty lungs. Blood tingled in fingers and toes. Fragile awareness crept into a waking mind. The pain had fled.

Her body was tightly bound and scarcely able to move. Eyelids fluttered, then opened. Vision blurred in dim light. Although weak, she found sufficient strength to free her hand. Placing her palm against his cheek, she thought about welcome death that had beckoned her. Then, he had come and called her name. Her wandering soul had not completely severed its ties to the vessel within which it dwelled. His voice had summoned her spirit back, away from the brink of oblivion.

Sensing unexpected movement, he resisted opening his eyes. How was it possible he had fallen asleep? Someone had surely discovered his latest transgression against the woman he loved. How could he possibly face whoever had come to take him away from his Shi'níyah? Then, as dry as the crackling leaves of autumn, the sound reached his ears. Almost fearfully, he surrendered and opened his eyes.

"Warnach?"

Stunned, he tightened his arms around her. "Sandra," he gasped on a shuddering breath. "Eyach'hamá eu Yahvanta! Oh! Me'u Sandra, you heard me! You came back. Eyach'hamá eu Yahvanta!"

She felt hot tears touch her fingers. Drained by the mighty battle waged for her very life, she had little strength to comfort the man so close to her. Her throat was so sore that even whispering hurt. Her eyelids fluttered again, and she whispered, "Warnach, my throat. It's so sore. It hurts to talk."

The smile that crossed his face quivered. Gentle lips pressed against her forehead. "I can get you something to drink, but you first must promise to wait for me to go and come back."

His comment prompted a faint smile and another hoarse whisper. "Do you forget? I always keep my promises."

Again, he tightened his arms around her. "By all that I hold holy, Sandra, I will never forget that again."

When he emerged from the Brisajai, he had no idea that he had been with her for more than two hours. Weary steps carried him toward the lounge where he stopped just inside. Dark eyes met those that waited. Overcome by emotions held too long in check and unable to speak, he wept when he saw his mamehr. When he finally reached her, he failed to notice tears on any faces but hers.

"Warnach," Araman murmured brokenly, "we did our best. All of us did."

Nodding, he smiled. "I know, Mamehr. I know. We'll talk later. Right now, I promised to hurry. She needs something to drink."

# Chapter Eight

M otion disturbed her lapse into exhausted slumber. Heavy eyelids slowly lifted. In her mind, despite the tired lines etched into his face, he still looked devastatingly handsome when he gazed at her. A faint smile spread her lips. "Warnach?"

Never had his gestures been more lovingly tender. Tucking a light blanket around her, he caressed her cheek with his fingertips. "I apologize. We tried to be careful so as not to disturb you."

Her head barely moved back and forth. "It's okay." Speech still required great effort. "It feels good to be in my own bed."

Leaning forward, he pressed a lingering kiss against her forehead. "We both had a nice long nap this afternoon. Is there anything I can get for you, or would you prefer to go back to sleep?"

"I am a little hungry," she whispered.

Entering the kitchen downstairs, he was glad to find his aunt adding finishing touches to dinner for a very tired family. Sniffing the fresh aroma of vegetables baked in a shell of smooth, thick mabnatar, he smiled appreciatively. "Your timing is perfect, Nadana. My ki'mirsah is awake and has decided she's up to eating a little."

"Your timing is perfect," she remarked while removing the wide casserole from the oven. "Do you want enough for both of you?"

Nodding, he went to a cabinet and withdrew a large tray. Busying himself getting napkins and utensils while his aunt prepared dishes of food, he sighed thoughtfully. "Sandra will be happy. She says mabnatar is about as close as she gets to mashed potatoes from Earth."

Without looking up, Nadana said, "I hope you fully appreciate your blessing at being able to share this meal with her."

Warnach's hands froze. He knew he deserved so much worse than the gentle reproach contained in her remark. Casting a sideways glance in her direction, he drew in a deep breath. "This meal is a blessing I do not deserve."

Nadana gave him a weary look. "I was not admonishing you."

He paused before uncomfortably meeting her gaze. "But you should. I've made many mistakes in my lifetime, but this has been, by far, the very worst."

Nadana's expression remained steady. "That point I will not argue with you. All I can really do is emphasize what I'm sure you already realize. The fact that she's still alive is no less than a miracle. You must never again let anything like this happen. The Great Spirit has granted you a precious reprieve. You must avoid any repetition."

Carefully, Warnach picked up the heavy tray. "My dear aunt, there is nothing in this entire universe so important that I would ever again subject her life to such risk."

As he turned to leave, she issued a firm reminder. "Honoring commitments you make before the Great Spirit must always be your first allegiance. Never again let anyone convince you otherwise."

Her words echoed throughout his mind as he left the kitchen and walked through the quiet of his home. Climbing the wide staircase, he recognized both truth and warning in her statements. Silently, he promised Sandra that he would prefer death rather than fail her as he had upon leaving for Bederand.

Entering their suite, he felt his chest absorb the heavy lurch of his heart. Still upright and reclining against her pillows, her eyelids were closed.

Dark smudges created half-moons beneath her eyes, and her face seemed almost colorless. Softly, he called her name.

Fluttering lashes lifted, and she looked toward him with a slowly spreading smile. "I was just resting."

Reaching her side, he positioned the large tray over her lap and then uncovered dishes filled with steaming, aromatic food. Looking up at her wide-eyed expression, he grinned. "I hope you don't mind sharing with your ki'medsah."

"Not at all. For a moment, I thought you expected me to eat it all by myself."

Walking around to the opposite side of the bed, he climbed in carefully to avoid upsetting the tray and sat close to her. Glancing downward, he noticed that her wedding rings had twisted halfway around her finger. Adjusting them into place, he grasped her hand. "It's been so long since we prayed together."

After prayerfully offering thanks for the day's multitude of blessings, he handed her a fork and took one of his own. Seeing tired hesitation shadow her face, he hid a fresh rise of guilt. "Do you need help?"

Sighing, she answered, "I'm not sure." Her hands shook as she lifted the first forkful to her mouth. "Mmm. Nadana made this?"

"How did you know?"

"Mamehr uses more cream in the mabnatar."

"She does?"

"Yes," she said, tasting the second bite transported successfully to her mouth. "Nadana uses more jinipiad leaves."

Tasting the food for himself, he shrugged. "If I notice no difference, perhaps it's because I'm so concentrated on the woman sitting in my bed."

A familiar sparkle gleamed in her green eyes. "Then I was mistaken thinking of it as our bed?"

Dropping his face, he picked up her hand and lifted it to his lips. "Not for a moment." Suddenly, he choked. "You cannot imagine how much I feared coming home to find this bed empty forever."

Despite her weakness, she reached up and touched his face. Shame and fear lingered in the eyes he raised to her. "I had to be here. I promised."

Sweeping eyebrows arched, and his jaw clenched. His voice faltered. "Yes, you did, and you kept your promise. However, your ki'medsah failed to fulfill promises he made to you."

A faint chink sounded against the plate when she laid down her fork. Swallowing the bite in her mouth, she stared intently into dark eyes. "Warnach, don't think that way."

"I only state the truth. I nearly killed you."

With her lips pursed together for several moments and her vision unfocused, she breathed a sigh. "If there's blame in what happened, we must share it."

"Share? Sandra, I knew the risk. Still, I let myself be swayed from what I knew to be right."

Coughing to clear an inflamed throat, she tried again. "I also knew there was a risk. In reality, I think I failed you. While you resisted him at every turn, I let Baadihm Farsuk play on my feelings of guilt. I should have trusted your judgment without question. I should have supported your stance completely, without vacillating."

Pausing to rest, she closed her eyes. "Warnach, we had the best intentions, but we both lost sight of commitments that should have taken priority…no matter what. We shared the decision. We suffered the consequences."

"You didn't realize the extent of the dangers. I did. Look at the suffering it caused you. Had I lost you…"

Her fingers lightly stroked his hand. "Warnach, we made the decision together as a unified couple. I say, let us be stronger for the lesson. We can then look ahead."

His left eyebrow cocked at a sharp angle. "Eat while your food is still warm. You need the energy to get better."

"Warnach…"

"I said eat. I don't wish to discuss the matter further." Knowing how imperious he sounded, he gave her a reserved smile. "You must understand. You hold unfair advantage. The fact that you're still so sick gives me no possibility of winning this argument. If you really want to debate the subject, please be kind enough to give me a fair chance by waiting until you're better."

Stuffing a bite into her mouth, she chewed and then swallowed. "My dear Minister Sirinoya, I accept your terms."

Leaning forward, he dabbed the corner of her mouth with his napkin. "Why do I fear I now face more dreadful challenges than ever?"

Half an hour later, as he gathered everything onto the tray to take back to the kitchen, a light knock sounded at the door. With a smile, he said, "Come in."

When the doors opened, Badrik swiftly strode inside with Farisa following close behind him. "Little sister! You're awake!" Quickly, he bent to receive the hug offered by outstretched arms. Holding her snugly, he chuckled as she kissed his cheek before burying her face against his shoulder.

Finally, she settled back against the pillows. A hint of sparkle had returned to dull eyes. "Badrik. My hero."

Teasingly as he reached out to push hair away from her face, he grinned. "Your hero?" His smile broadened upon receiving an affirming nod. "In that case, I declare myself completely successful as a big brother."

"All right, big brother, move over. I need to check my patient."

Casting his mate a mock frown, Badrik winked at Sandra. "My lovely Farisa is not always as serious as she would have you believe." Getting up, he leaned forward to place an affectionate kiss on Farisa's cheek. "Take care of my sister."

Farisa's eyes rolled upward as she sidled past him. Sitting beside Sandra, she smiled approvingly. "How do you feel tonight?"

"My throat hurts. I feel horribly weak and tired. However, I won't complain. No more headache." Quickly, she lifted her eyes to meet Warnach's.

"Better than that, you and I have the Brothers Sirinoya home, safe and sound. I think I'll be fine."

"And we have you back among us. For a while, we were convinced we would lose you."

Her voice quietly tremulous, Sandra murmured, "So was I." Then, she waited as Farisa verified readings from her scanners.

When Farisa spoke again, she smiled her satisfaction. "Your vital functions have improved tremendously. However, readings are far from normal. You have undergone a traumatic experience. I hope you'll accept my advice and go to the clinic tomorrow. I'd like to do a more comprehensive scan. I also think some hours in an HAU might do you a world of good."

Gratitude showed in Sandra's face. "I hate being inside HAU's. However, if you think it best…"

"I shall make the arrangements when I go back downstairs. Now, this doctor orders rest for her patient."

"No arguments from me," Sandra said, stifling a yawn.

Bright moonlight filtered through sheer curtains. Drowsy but still awake, Sandra watched as Warnach loosened the belt of his robe. Removing the garment, he negligently tossed it over carved rails at the foot of their bed. Subdued light and shadow accentuated muscular lines of his torso, while silky pajama bottoms hugged firmly rounded buttocks. Breathing in deeply, she remembered desperate thoughts that she might die without ever again enjoying the simple pleasure of watching him.

Cautiously, not wanting to awaken her, he slid into bed beneath sheets and a lightweight blanket. Turning onto his side, he started to put his arm around her. Suddenly, he stopped. "Shi'níyah, you should be sleeping."

"I was. When I heard you, I just wanted to watch you." She grew quiet for a moment. "I missed you every minute you were gone."

He pressed a loving kiss against her forehead. "I swear that I missed you twice as much."

Snuggling closer, she closed her eyes as sleep beckoned. "Warnach, I'm so glad you came home to me. I love you."

Warm, moist lips whispered against her skin, "Believe me, me'u Shi'níyah. I love you, too."

～

Early the next morning, Warnach helped her shower and get ready for the day. As they resumed their precious ritual of putting Kitak on one another, tears had shimmered in both their eyes. Each realized how close they had come to permanent loss of their treasured daily routine.

After breakfast, Warnach transported her directly to the clinic where Farisa and Dr. Barrett awaited. The physicians had immediately initiated a series of complicated scans that did nothing to dissolve the mystery surrounding her physical reactions to Ku'saá. Both doctors agreed that her survival had been aided by the fact that she was so strong and healthy. Both expressed relief that scans revealed she was already well on the way to complete recovery. Still, each insisted that she spend several hours inside an HAU reserved for Terran patients.

Arriving home late in the afternoon, she settled herself into the corner of one of the sofas in the lounge. What a relief it was to be freed from the tight confines of the HAU. Before she could even kick off her shoes, Warnach walked in from the front of the house. Meeting his gaze, she noted that wonderful smile she loved so much.

"You have visitors. I know you're tired, but I would hate to send them away."

Glancing over his shoulder, she saw worried faces that brought a smile to her face. "Peter. Emilio. Come in."

Araman had already told her son how Sandra's friends had taken time over several evenings to come in from Kadranas. They had brought study materials with them and had taken turns helping watch over her. Warnach would always appreciate their support during such a critical time of need.

Excusing himself to allow them time to converse, he went to his office to tend to another task. Accessing sophisticated equipment permitted to very few, he contacted his ministry's communication center to establish a direct com-link to Earth. Minutes later, the link was complete. An unfamiliar face appeared on his monitor. "May I speak with Mrs. Warner?"

The man's face appeared drawn and tired. "She isn't here right now. She went for a walk and should be back any minute. You're Sirinoya, aren't you?"

Elegantly, Warnach bowed his head. "I am, sir. You're Sandra's father?"

Almost strangling on the words, Dave Warner nodded and asked the question that had haunted him all night. "My daughter. They said she was in a coma yesterday. Is she…is she…?"

So, Warnach thought, he does care about her. "Mr. Warner, she woke from the coma after I arrived home yesterday. We've been at hospital with her for extensive scans and HAU treatment. Right now, she's tired and weak, but her condition is improving. Her doctors have called her recovery miraculous."

Intense relief was quickly masked by a stern expression. "I hope she gets better soon. Her mommy is coming now. You can talk to her." With that, Mr. Warner abruptly disappeared from the monitor's screen.

Once the link was terminated, Warnach leaned back in his chair and closed his eyes. Lee Warner had burst into tears upon hearing that her daughter was still alive and expected to recover. Between sobs, she had pleaded with Warnach to forgive her for being unable to overcome her phobia of traveling above ground and into space. She had also begged him to express her eternal thanks to his family for the way they had cared for Sandra.

Completely contrary to his wife's reaction, David Warner had resisted any real expression of his feelings. Initially, his fears had been obvious. Upon learning of the unexpected improvement in Sandra's condition, he had quickly established distinct, cool distance. Nothing he had said revealed any warmth toward his daughter. Then, Warnach smiled. Perhaps that conclusion wasn't completely correct. Dave Warner's reference to his wife as Sandra's mommy evidenced an emotional inability to accept that his daughter was no longer a little girl.

Evening brought welcome quiet. Badrik and Farisa had stopped in to check on Sandra's progress. Druska, Ziaman, and several professors from the academy had called. John and Angela, who had been notified by Farsuk at the beginning of the crisis, had sent a cheerful VM upon learning she had emerged from the coma. Heartened by so many good wishes, Sandra gazed thoughtfully into the bathroom mirror. How good it felt to know people who sincerely cared about her.

Quietly entering the bedroom, a smile lit her face as she watched Warnach. He had already folded down the silk spread and turned back sheets. Noting her presence, he looked up. "Ready for bed?"

She answered with only a nod. Crossing the room, he took both her hands and lifted them to his lips. He then led her to the upholstered bench at the foot of their bed. Sitting down, he shifted to face her. Affectionately, she caressed long hair before raising her hands to remove his Kitak. Holding it securely in her lap, she closed her eyes as his hands, warm and gentle, removed the symbolic ring from her head. As he so often did, he placed a reverent kiss against the diamond set in her Kitak. Then, he joined the two engraved rings and put them away for the night.

Standing, he pulled her up from the bench. His expression gentled while long, exquisitely shaped fingers traced gentle trails along her cheek. The fullness of his lips appeared startlingly sensuous. "Me'u Shi'níyah, you need to rest."

Wordlessly, she moved closer and rested her cheek against the bare skin of his chest. Wrapped in his arms and his love, she wanted never to move. The pain of the failed Ku'saá had been far more excruciating than anything she had ever imagined possible. His comforting presence instilled newly appreciated peace.

"Sandra?" he murmured into her ear. "Are you ready for bed?"

"Not really," she whispered back. "I feel so perfect right here where I am."

"Come, my dear one. It's time to go to sleep." Capturing her gaze at last, he smiled. "I promised your doctors that you would go to bed early."

Settling comfortably on her side beneath light covers, she impatiently waited for him to join her. Feeling his muscular body close, she kissed a spot just above his beating heart. "Warnach…"

"Yes, me'u Shi'níyah?" His voice held low, velvety soft tones.

"I…I love you." Deeply, she breathed in. Eyelids fluttered and closed. Her lips formed a delicate smile. Full breasts rose and fell in quickening rhythm. Coherent thought wavered as her heart and mind again sought freedom.

Instantly, he sensed swift change in her presence. "Sandra?"

"My ki'medsah, please. Please…don't leave me this time."

Anxiety wedged its way into his mind. "Shi'níyah, I'm here. I won't…S…Sandra?" Permeated by the sudden infusion of her spirit, he gasped. His last conscious thought was to drag her into his arms and hold her body securely next to his.

Clouds as soft as angel's wings swirled around them. Released from the confines of gravity-bound bodies, both their spirits soared through infinite space. Besides the physical torment, he sensed remnants of the horrific agony her soul had known when it had embarked upon its futile search for his. However, that agony had since been replaced with the purest essence of joy. Discarding any reservations, he freely entrusted himself to her care.

Entwining herself within the complex pattern of all that he was aided her in comprehending on a spiritual plane what it was about him that so inspired her. How deep the grief and regrets now dispatched to a safe distance in the past. How finely developed the integrity of his character. From childhood origins based on faith, his spirit's wealth of compassion and sensitivity had sprung. From pain, experience, and love had grown a man filled with depth and hue, shadow and light.

Hours passed. Freely crossing mystical boundaries, they explored their universe. Sciences held no value. History existed as an undefined concept. Words held no significance. Their love beat as the heart of the universe they had discovered. Their spirits loomed the fabric that captured their bonded experience within a shimmering, iridescent mesh. Their souls assumed command and unified heart to spirit.

Her eyes refused to open. With trembling fingers, she traced fiery paths across the firm curves of his body. Conscious thought proved as elusive as windswept dandelion puffs. Her lips pressed against his skin and desperately navigated the expanse of his chest and neck until they reached his mouth. Every inch of her body quivered in supplication for the accomplishment of absolute union with him.

His lungs struggled to fill with the clean, satisfying oxygen of his world. Her touch ignited fires of a new and awesome nature. Enmeshed as their souls were, he desired more. No! Desperately, he required so much more! Powerless against irresistible, compelling need, he felt the formidable rise of flesh as blood hammered through his veins. A fleeting sense of caution fell immediate victim to her body's insistent clamoring for his.

Merging their physical selves demanded reclamation of soaring souls into sacred vessels. Those vessels, warm, vibrant, and alive, craved intimate touch and connection that perpetuated the love and joy they had first discovered the night of their unification. Her entire body conveyed consuming passion as, with touch and motion, she sought to prolong his deepening possession of her being.

Forever locked within Warnach's soul would be the memory of how his recent journey had nearly cost her life. Unconsciously, he plunged himself more desperately, more deeply, into the sensation-rich sheath her body created for him. Bonded to her in such frenzied totality, body and spirit, he immersed himself in simple truth more meaningful than all of life's complexities combined. He was irrevocably bound to her by sacred pledge and, as well, the consummated love of their unification.

Absorbed as he was within vibrant sensations of intense pleasure and desire, thoughts evaporated until nothing remained except awareness of his union with the feminine body so perfectly attuned to his masculinity. Reaching heights of passion never before known to either, an explosion of incomprehensible magnitude carried them upon towering waves of unparalleled satisfaction. Frantic breathing gradually subsided. Racing heartbeats slowed. Sated and completely spent, they clung to one another until a perfect, blissful sleep claimed them.

Awaking unusually early, Warnach sat up in bed. In hazy semi-darkness, he glanced downward. Beautiful features were deeply relaxed, and the smile on her sleeping face revealed the joy he had discovered at the core of her being. Lying back down and easing onto his side, he contented himself with observing her during the early quiet of morning while contemplating their transcendence to Nivela-Ku'saá.

Long ago, he had read dramatic accounts written by some who had dared to attempt descriptions of the rare mystical encounter. Memory led him along a personal tour of the night just ended as he sought his own private definition. Much of the event had occurred with an encompassing spirituality beyond any meditative experiences he had previously known. On an inexplicable level, he had sensed disappointments, secret fears, and sorrows that had affected her life. Revealed, too, had been the amazing strength and resiliency of her character. Reaching an entirely different plane, he had luxuriated in the boundless joy inherent in the love she bore him. Nothing he had ever read or anything he had ever imagined even began to approach the intensity of feelings now residing within him.

Smiling while tentative fingertips traced a feather-light line along her arm, he remembered making love to her with an abandon certainly beyond anything he had ever before known. Such a common, universal act of physical interaction had carried him to a unique frontier. Even now, his body felt lingering lethargy arisen from the aftermath of their lovemaking. Her spontaneous responses had enhanced the confidence of his male ego while providing his body with overwhelming physical fulfillment.

Thickly fringed eyelashes fluttered softly before her eyelids opened. Even in the misty light, he could see curious questions sparking in her eyes. Her lips barely moved, but he clearly made out his own name within her soft whisper.

"Me'u Shi'níyah," he greeted, "welcome to our new day."

Hours later, Araman looked outside at lawns and gardens drenched in sunshine. On the patio, Warnach and Sandra sat over breakfast. Her steps toward the door were halted when a gentle hand quickly grasped hers.

"No, Sister." Although her face showed no sign of a smile, Nadana's expression reflected satisfied peacefulness. "Look closely at them."

A bit puzzled, Araman gazed more attentively toward her son and his lifemate. Although Warnach never failed to demonstrate his feelings for Sandra, his gestures this morning seemed more noticeable, more pronounced. Watching them slowly consume their breakfast, she suddenly realized how their hands seemed magnetically attracted. Several times, Warnach leaned forward, either lightly touching her forehead with cerea-nervos or planting brief kisses against her cheeks or lips. Always generous with her displays of affection, Sandra glowed as she ran fingers lovingly across the sculpted line of his high cheekbones or bent her head to drop kisses on the top of his hand. Indeed, their closeness exuded a marked difference hard to describe.

Realization crept into Araman's brain. Her gaze met Nadana's appraising eyes. "Is it possible?"

Finally, Nadana gave a slight smile. "Obviously so. They need time to explore their thoughts and feelings after all that's happened. Come. I have tea and breakfast waiting in the kitchen."

Sitting down, Araman reached across the table. Picking up a large, slim book that was obviously very old, she thoughtfully studied the cover as she sipped her tea. "This is a story I haven't thought about since I was a little girl."

Nadana joined her sister at the table. "I was doing some research in Tichtika before the incident on Bederand. One afternoon, I felt the need to break away. I wandered into an antique shop where I discovered this book."

Setting aside her porcelain cup, Araman placed the book on the table and turned thick, yellowed pages. Her eyes skimmed over beautifully elaborated text. "I used to know this entire story by heart."

In a quiet voice, she began to read aloud as a little girl's fantasies were rekindled in the mature mind that had relegated the story to a distant, forgotten corner of childhood.

*"And so the Great Spirit, in all His wisdom, looked down upon the beautiful face of Chikondra. Seeing that danger from dark spirits approached the peaceful world He had created, Yahvanta sighed and asked of Himself what He should do. Should He intercede and drive away the dark forces? Or, should He entrust His favored people to protect the beautiful Chikondra He had given them?"*

Pausing, she glanced up at her sister. With eyes closed, it was apparent that Nadana had drifted away. Surprisingly, she quietly prompted Araman to continue.

*"After much contemplation, the Great Spirit reached a decision that troubled His eternal spirit. Still, the all-sacred Yahvanta knew clearly that his people must recall ancient lessons delivered to them through the gifts of Meichasa. Speaking to legions of ageless spirits surrounding Him, the Great Spirit wove His story, telling of the coming of the Mi'yafá Si'imlayaná."*

"Do you remember, Araman, how strikingly simple and lovely this legend is?"

Smiling, Araman tilted her head. "I remember fantasizing and wishing I could be the Mi'yafá Si'imlayaná."

Nadana's eyebrows lifted slightly. "Perhaps the wish held more than mere fantasy."

Shaking her head, Araman laughed lightly. "My dearly Respected Simlani, you always manage to confound your sister."

Smiling almost mysteriously, Nadana nodded. "In truth, I remembered how much you always loved this story. That's why I bought the book."

# Chapter Nine

Twice during the day, Warnach and Sandra took short walks. Still weak, she had not felt up to going far from the house. They returned the second time to a surprise Warnach had arranged by having one of the gardeners hang a broad hammock from trees near the house. After helping her get in first, he quickly joined her. Teasing and touching her gave him such pleasure as they lay side by side in the hammock's supportive curve. With sparkles in her eyes, she started singing a lilting love song from Earth. Soon, both were caught in the magical relaxation of a summer's afternoon nap.

Evening descended upon a peaceful Sirinoya household. Araman and Nadana had spent their day looking through photographs and other memorabilia. Reminiscing refreshed bonds of sisterhood while giving Warnach undisturbed hours with his lifemate. The only interruption, a call from Farsuk, lasted only minutes. Araman had sternly advised him that Sandra was not yet well enough to face him.

Gathering together around a table outside, all four held hands as Warnach offered grace over a simple evening meal. Small, freshly baked loaves of bread were broken in half and spread with creamy nut butter. Sliced mabnatar had been topped with herbs and savory chunks of bifihfnah, an onion-like vegetable, and then broiled. Accompanied by colorful steamed vegetables, the meal satisfied eye, nose, and palate.

When Sandra suggested staying up to listen to music, Warnach had insisted on early prayers. However remarkable her recovery might be, he was determined that she go to bed and rest. He had even put his foot down when she suggested going to Kadranas the next morning for the week's first day of classes. Believing that she needed more time for full recuperation, he had argued that she could surely afford to miss one extra day of class plus the following day of internship duties. Noting that she voiced little disagreement, he realized that even she accepted her limitations.

The next morning, Warnach contacted Zara early. Conceding to Sandra's worries about her classes, he requested Zara to schedule appointments with Sandra's instructors on the following day scheduled for internship duties. They would go to Kadranas so both could meet with her professors. As her sponsor, he knew he should also consult with them. Appointments were coordinated so he could talk with the teachers while allowing her time to discuss plans for filling any gaps created by her absence.

After lunch, they decided to relax and listen to music. A piano virtuoso's performance filled the music room with melodies both complex and moving. Comfortably nestled by his side, she soon fell asleep and did not hear Mamehr's voice.

Swinging long legs off the lounge, Warnach stood and gazed down at his lifemate with grim eyes. Rapidly leaving the music room, he quietly eased the door closed and growled an expletive. "Damn! Why can he not leave us alone for a while?"

Araman answered softly as they walked toward the lounge. "You must give him some credit. He feels extremely guilty over what happened."

"As well he should," Warnach ground out bitterly. "I will never forget the way he went to her behind my back. Neither will I ever forget her screams nor how she nearly died."

Reaching the end of the hallway, Araman paused and held her son's arm. "For me, Warnach, please, try to remain calm. Farsuk wrestles with terrible guilt. A man who did not sincerely care about the consequences of his actions would not be here."

Entering the lounge, Warnach acknowledged his godfather with a sharp nod. "You wish to speak with me?"

Squaring his shoulders, Farsuk stood and stared directly at his godson. "Yes, but I had also hoped to speak with Sandra."

Diffidently cool, Warnach strode to the sofa directly across from Farsuk. "Sandra is sleeping. She tires easily. According to Farisa, she will likely not regain her strength completely for several days yet."

Closing his eyes briefly, Farsuk inclined his head. "Then, I hope you will grant me some of your time."

With a cynical expression, Warnach gestured for Farsuk to resume his seat. Sitting on the sofa beside Araman, he gazed pointedly at his godfather. "Continue."

Uncomfortably, Farsuk swallowed several times. He could face the most dignified and powerful leaders in the Alliance under extremely harrowing circumstances. Facing his godson at this moment, however, struck fear into his heart. Private recollections of recent days made it too easy for him to understand the fury lurking behind Warnach's black eyes and harsh countenance.

Minutes later, Farsuk wondered if he would ever find means to break through the stony wall Warnach had erected between them. Choosing words carefully, he attempted to explain his desperation to seek some resolution to the eruption of hostilities on Bederand. Expressing profound regret for having dragged Sandra into the situation, Farsuk reasoned that too many lives had faced ruin. He swore that he would never have been so demanding had he thought there was any realistic risk that she might enter Ku'saá. Heartfelt laments met unyielding resistance evidenced by Warnach's simple question as to why his judgment had been totally disregarded.

"Warnach?"

Cold, harsh eyes instantly softened as Warnach stood up and went to her. "Shi'níyah…"

"You left me," she murmured.

"My esteemed baadihm insisted on speaking with me."

Sleepy-eyed, she cast her gaze toward the sofas and, for the first time, realized that Farsuk sat there with his back toward her. Lifting darkening green eyes, she grimaced and tilted her face forward. Hiding her face for a moment against Warnach's chest, she nervously breathed in and out several times.

"Shi'níyah, go upstairs and lie down. There's no need for you to trouble yourself with this right now."

Dragging in a deep breath, she finally raised her head. She dreaded facing Edsaka but decided it might be best to address the situation and move on. "My place is beside you. Especially now. We both need to deal with this."

Firmly grasping her hand, he looked directly into her eyes. He had touched her memories during Ku'saá, and those recollections haunted him. Just as he started to say something, Farsuk's voice interrupted.

"Sandra, how good it is to see you. You cannot possibly know how worried I've been."

Only nodding, she clutched Warnach's arm as he led her to the sofa across from Farsuk. Unsure what to say, she leveled an unnerving gaze at Edsaka and waited for him to initiate further conversation.

Recognizing her reluctance to speak, Farsuk focused his attention on her. Of one thing, he was certain. If there were even a single chance to reestablish a decent relationship with Warnach, Sandra would be the key. Besides, he thought sadly, restoring her affection and confidence was just as important. She had delivered renewed optimism and vitality into more than just Warnach's life.

Clearing his throat, Farsuk began what he imagined might be the most important discourse of his life. "Sandra, it's very hard for me to know where to begin. You have no idea how difficult the past weeks have been for me."

When she interrupted him, her subdued voice held more sting than a needle stabbing into his heart. "I suppose you think they were easy for me?"

Pained regret showed in his expression as he shook his head. "I know they were not. I will not be so arrogant as to tell you I know how you feel. All I have to do is close my eyes, and I can…" His words stumbled. Breathing heavily, he swallowed against the swelling lump in his throat. "Sandra, in my heart, I will carry to my grave the sounds of your screams. I have told the same to Warnach as I now tell you. I swear to you. If I had honestly thought Ku'saá a possibility for you, I would never have pushed him into undertaking that mission to Bederand."

The firm tightening of her fingers kept Warnach silent. "You refused to trust him. His loyalty to you and to the Alliance has always been unshakeable. You demanded of him what you would not have dared to ask of any other minister in service. I don't understand that. I can't."

Regrouping his thoughts, Farsuk tried again. "What you say is true. Although I admit that my motives were mixed, my concerns were sincere about the peoples on Bederand and nearby planets. That is no lie, Sandra. I'm even willing to admit that I believed an unaddressed situation would negatively impact elections next month.

"You also know, just as I do, that there is a general consensus that your ki'medsah is the most influential and effective field service minister of our time. I needed that ability, and I relentlessly pursued Warnach through you.

"What I'm going to say is not meant in any way as an insult toward you or any other Terran alive. I simply didn't believe for one minute that you, as a Terran, had any possibility of entering Ku'saá. It should not have happened, and I'm still awed by an occurrence that should have been impossible."

Swiftly, Sandra cast a glance toward Warnach. She felt angry tension stiffening his body. His profile reflected restrained fury. Smiling only inside, she sensed protectiveness as his hand tightened around hers.

Returning her attention to Farsuk, her face remained solemn. "After the attack on Mijirina, I was terrified while waiting for word about the fate of our mission team. I directed every thought and feeling inside of me to Warnach while praying that some shred of that energy would reach him and maybe help him.

"Then, when I entered Ku'saá, I discovered that there really are some things worse than death. To say I suffered isn't merely an understatement. I fought against agony more horrific than you can possibly imagine. During the few respites granted me, I wrestled with the knowledge that Badrik and Warnach and even Captain Tibrab were endangering their very lives to save mine. Tortured body and tormented mind and soul were what you gave me. Can you really expect me to forget that?"

Again, quietly spoken words presented themselves as extremely effective weapons. Looking away, he blinked against unwelcome tears. Cerea-nervos began to throb. His head started to ache. Part of him wanted to run away in disgrace. Love for his godsons refused to allow him such an easy escape.

Drawing in a deep breath, Farsuk gazed back at her. Red blotches no longer marred her ivory complexion. Beads of fevered perspiration no longer shone on her skin. Calm had replaced ragged breathing. Sparkle had been restored to dull, nearly lifeless eyes. He had to continue. He had to try again. If he failed to reach her, he would be forced to abandon all hope of reconciliation with Warnach and Badrik.

"Sandra," he began with a shake in his voice, "I would not be so stupid as to expect you to forget. If I accept that I'm doomed to remember, how could I ever imagine you could forget? What I ask is for you to believe in my regret for actions that hurt you all. I offer apologies from a man forced to analyze his behavior and realize that much of what he publicly professed was no longer manifest in his own life. I made a mistake. Not just one. Several. Dreadful mistakes. Mistakes for which I am truly sorry.

"I also don't expect you simply to smile and tell me all is forgiven. My transgression is far too serious. What I'm pleading for is a chance to earn your forgiveness. I want to prove to you…and to Warnach and Badrik…that I love all of you. I cannot turn back the days or weeks to undo my deeds. I can look only to the present and the future. Sandra, with the Great Spirit as my witness, I am so sorry."

Releasing Warnach's hand, Sandra got up and paced toward ceiling-high windows. She stared outside without seeing summer's finery, and her mind turned inward, seeking to understand familiar voices. Dropping her face, she pressed her forehead against her loosely closed fist. "How can I do it? How?"

Hearing strangled words, Warnach immediately started to go to her. Leaning so far that she practically lay on the sofa, Araman reached for his arm. With his face reflecting rising distress, Warnach turned concerned eyes to his mamehr. A simple shake of her head accompanied Araman's gently worded restraint. "They never once deserted her. Let her listen to them. They will guide her."

Perplexed by the odd exchange, Farsuk's eyebrows met above his nose in a baffled expression. "Araman?"

Stern eyes looked back at him. Her voice rose barely above a whisper. "Warnach's concerns about Sandra entering Ku'saá were not without foundation. Patience."

Momentarily dismissing Farsuk's presence, Warnach anxiously observed his lifemate. From her posture, he discerned growing tension. She paced back and forth. Then, slowly turning, her attention locked directly on her ki'medsah. Starting toward him, she swayed weakly before stumbling and barely catching her balance. Leaping to his feet, Warnach reached her in an instant.

Evergreen eyes were clear and alert but filled with confusion. Welcoming the support of his body, she leaned against her lifemate. "My ki'medsah, I don't know if I can."

Kissing her hair and nuzzling his face into silken softness, he spoke in comforting tones. "Shi'níyah, you must remember. I don't hear them as you do. Help me understand."

Pressing firmly into his embrace, she waited with eyes closed. Their words penetrated her mind with such clarity. She wondered how they understood so much. Then, with the reminder that theirs were angel spirits, fresh comprehension dawned. She owed them already debts that could never be repaid. Her only possible decision was to strive to honor their requests.

Backing away a little, she gazed up into Warnach's darkly handsome features. "They say his heart is sincere. They're encouraging me to extend the chance for him to redeem himself."

Behind them, Farsuk shook his head in bewilderment. The conversation with Warnach sounded senseless. "Araman? Who is she talking about? When she says *they*, who does she mean?"

Crossing to sit beside him, Araman found it impossible to smile at the man who had been her lifemate's closest friend and confidant. Morcai had trusted Farsuk to protect his sons, not to jeopardize their lives unnecessarily. Setting her jaw for a moment, she willed retreat of her anger. "She speaks of the primary reason Warnach believed she might enter Ku'saá. It is a private matter that our family has guarded."

Glancing around, Farsuk noted that Warnach had his arms securely around Sandra and was returning to the sofas. Suddenly, her knees started to buckle, causing her to slump toward the floor. Jumping up, Farsuk rushed to her side and, together with Warnach, helped her back to where she could sit.

Leaning forward with her elbows on her legs, she covered her face with her hands. The unexpected weakness had startled her. Farisa had been right to warn her to expect sudden spells of faintness. Finally, raising her head, she looked directly into the eyes of Farsuk Edsaka. His expression was a mix of fear, guilt, and concern. A sheen of tears glazed his brown eyes.

"Child, are you all right? Can I get you something?" Farsuk asked as he knelt in front of her.

She reached outward, and her fingertips moved along the still healing cut and bruise marring his cheekbone. "You've been hurt."

Eyelids fell shut. How innocently childlike she sounded. What was it about her that made him wish she had been born his daughter? "It's nothing, Sandra. Not even worth an HAU treatment." In actuality, the injury had ached abominably, but he had welcomed the pain as a deserved reminder of misguided deeds.

"I think it will take time. I can't forget what happened, but they told me you really didn't mean to endanger me. They say your heart is filled with grief. I promised them I would try to forgive."

"Sandra, I must apologize. I don't understand."

"Shi'níyah, here. Drink this." Reappearing from a swift trip to the kitchen, Warnach handed her a glass of her favorite mirmaja juice.

Seeing how hard her hands shook, Farsuk swiftly reached out to steady the glass in her grasp while she lifted it to her lips. Patiently, he wrapped his hands around hers and the tumbler. When she was finished, he handed the empty cup to Araman. "Are you sure you're all right, child?"

Sighing shakily, she felt grateful that Warnach was beside her. "I'm sorry. The doctors told me to expect weak periods over the next few days. This one caught me by surprise."

Araman moved, allowing Farsuk to rise stiffly from his knees and sit beside Sandra. Braving possible rejection, he took Sandra's hands. "You must not be sorry."

Pale and trembling, she forced a smile. "Before I ask my ki'medsah to take me upstairs, I'll try to answer your question."

"Shsh, Shi'níyah," Warnach whispered as he wrapped an arm around her and then reclined against the back of the sofa, protectively cradling her cheek against his chest. "Rest. Mamehr and I will explain."

Clenching his jaw, Warnach summoned sufficient willpower to face Farsuk calmly. "She says they told her that you deserve her efforts to forgive you. *They* are Quazon."

Stunned curiosity transformed Farsuk's worried features. "Quazon? You must explain."

Pausing to drop yet another kiss upon Sandra's head, Warnach swallowed hard. "Farsuk, Sandra communicates directly with Quazon."

Shocked doubt reflected in Farsuk's entire countenance. "What does direct communication mean?"

"Telepathy." Warnach's right brow lifted slightly. "They communicate with her telepathically."

Casting a swift glance toward Araman, Farsuk received a confirming nod. "How is that possible? I don't mean to be disrespectful, but Quazon reveal themselves to Chikondrans only on the rarest of occasions. How is it they communicate with a Terran?"

"Farsuk," Araman said, "not one of us understands how or why. We only know that they do."

"What makes you so certain that she communicates with Quazon?"

"We've all seen her with them."

"What?"

"Farsuk, during Sandra's first trip to Chikondra, Mamehr wanted to meet her. We invited her to spend a day at the beach house with us. While there, she and I went into the water." His thoughts drifted back to that magical moment. "A wave carried her away from me, and I watched her change to a solemn mood. Within moments, she was surrounded by four Quazon."

Closing his eyes, Farsuk felt a unique surge inside his chest. What he had felt the first time he met her on Earth suddenly returned. Never in a lifetime would he have connected that sense to Quazon as he did now. Curiosity mushroomed. "You actually saw them, too?"

"We all did," Araman replied. "Nadana, Badrik, Farisa, and I all watched as the Quazon played with both Sandra and Warnach. We were more stunned when we saw Sandra caressing them in the water."

"Amazing. Truly amazing. How can you be so sure their voices are the ones she hears?"

Smiling tenderly as he realized Sandra had drifted off to sleep, Warnach lowered his voice. "Baadihm, when we went to the ocean following our unification, she stood on the beach and talked to them one night. The next morning, I found her in the water with them. It was obvious they were somehow conversing. Later, I told her how I wished I could give them my thanks for a special blessing. She said she would ask them to return. They did."

"Are you telling me that you've now seen Quazon three times?"

Nodding, he answered, "On three separate occasions, I've seen them, played with them, touched them. Now do you understand why I resisted leaving her to go on-mission to Bederand?"

Farsuk did not avoid Warnach's direct stare. "More than ever. This is so much for me to absorb. Warnach, I honestly regret what I did. That's why I felt compelled to come today. The time since Sandra became sick has been the worst of my entire life. No matter what doubts you may have about me, I love you and Badrik as if you were my own sons. I confess that I made miserable mistakes."

Awed once again by Sandra's mystifying words, he paused as his voice cracked. "So great are my shame and my guilt that even Sandra's Quazon feel my sorrow. Still, I am bound to beg forgiveness."

Straightening after a long silence, Sandra gazed into Warnach's ebony eyes. "We can help each other do this," she murmured.

Swallowing hard, Warnach felt the lump push from his throat all the way down until it crashed into the pit of his stomach. Taming anger, resentment, and disappointment would be difficult. In unison with Sandra, he twisted slightly to stare into the hopeful face of his baadihm. "I will be honest. Forgiveness won't come in a day. However, I shall honor my ki'mirsah's counsel, and we shall work toward that goal."

A slight tic twitched at the corner of Farsuk's mouth. Once again, he reached for Sandra's hand. His eyes held earnest sincerity. "Child, my life's greatest goal will be to earn your forgiveness. I begin by telling you what I can say because of my promise made long ago to Morcai. His children are as my children. That makes you my daughter. I promise you now. No man alive could have more pride in his daughter than I have in you."

# Chapter Ten

Summer grasses shone lushly emerald. Turquoise colored skies above. Warm breezes swayed tall-stemmed flowers in beds along park walkways. Clean waters cheerfully splashed in fountains. Laughter and youthful banter filled the air as students crossed brick paths on the way to lunch or afternoon classes.

"I'm trying to figure out who should be most worried about tomorrow," Druska remarked with a grin as she reached for a sandwich on the lunch tray sitting between them on the grass.

"Meaning what?" Sandra asked as she sipped mirmaja from an aseptic container.

"Meaning there's been a lot of chatter about tomorrow's public S&D finals. We're all betting that Barmihn and his trainers are shaking in their shoes about having to face you, Peter, and Emilio. Geez, I wish I hadn't waited until next session for S&D. I hear you three have terrorized the instructors."

"Mmhm," Sandra mumbled as she chewed the bite in her mouth and then swallowed. "I suspect they've been plotting some unorthodox event to catch us unawares."

"From what I hear, I wouldn't be surprised. S&D enjoys a stellar reputation for injuring students. So far, you three have turned the tables on the instructors by dislocating four shoulders, breaking one arm, a wrist, two collarbones, and one nose, all while wreaking general havoc on the lot. I think you guys are in for it. Uh-oh."

"Uh-oh what?" Sandra asked as she popped a handful of fresh berries into her mouth.

"Company's coming."

Twisting around, Sandra watched as Warnach strode toward their shady picnic spot. Flashing him a brilliant smile, she patted the mat beside her. "Minister Sirinoya! Good afternoon! Care to share what's left of your intern's lunch?"

Without regard for his formal attire, he dropped down beside her. How glad his heart felt to see her health and spirits restored. "Have you anything good left?"

Leaning over the tray, she made an exaggerated accounting of remaining food. "Well, my good minister, other than half of a michapia cheese sandwich and some timifi berries, there's only me."

"My dear intern," he countered, "I do believe you were the one who issued the edict against my partaking of the fine flavor of you on campus."

Grimacing, she looked at him with one eye closed. "That was before Ku'saá. I think I deserve to exercise my Terran female prerogative and change my mind. Dessert first?"

"Dessert first," he responded teasingly as he leaned forward and captured lips that tasted of sweet timifi berries. His mouth spread into an indulgent smile. "Utterly delicious."

"Okay, you two. I am still here, you know."

Sandra wrinkled her nose at Druska. "Spoil sport."

"So, ladies," Warnach began as he took the sandwich Sandra offered, "the two of you looked a bit mischievous when I walked up. Are you plotting something?"

"Excuse me, my good minister? Plotting? What kind of question is that?"

Druska couldn't help but laugh at the exaggerated look of innocence on Sandra's face.

"Plotting? Not exactly. More like planning."

Black eyes narrowed suspiciously. "Why do I think your plans relate to S&D finals tomorrow?"

"Minister Sirinoya," Sandra responded formally, "Instructor Barmihn was very clear in his introduction on the first day of class. Students should always be prepared for the most unexpected events."

"Sandra, I don't think I like the way you said that. Do you have any idea of the barrage of commentary I've endured regarding how many instructors have suffered concussions and broken bones at your hands?"

Green eyes grew wide with an innocent expression. "Do you think I've escaped those classes unscathed? My shoulder has ached something terrible since yesterday's class. It was everything I could do to avoid disturbing you last night."

"Why did you not tell me?" he asked, his expression turning serious. "I could have taken you to the clinic."

"I didn't want you to worry more than you already do. Besides, it's probably just a minor strain. It helps when I can reach back far enough to rub it."

Quickly finishing his sandwich, Warnach scooted behind her. "Which shoulder?"

Sandra's eyes glittered merrily as she watched Druska attempting to stifle laughter without strangling on lunch. Sounding suitably pitiful, she said, "My right shoulder."

Gently, Warnach's fingers began to knead the muscles along his lifemate's neck and shoulder. "How does that feel? Any better?"

"Much better," she sighed heavily, her eyes closing as she savored the lusciousness of his gentle massage. "My ki'medsah, you have the perfect touch in those warm Chikondran hands of yours. Just a minute more? Please?"

Moments later, he issued a stern warning about letting him know if the shoulder was no better by evening and then excused himself to return to ministry offices for a meeting.

Barely waiting until he disappeared from sight, Druska burst into laughter. "That was awful! How could you do that to him?"

Giggling shamelessly, Sandra shook her head back and forth. "Girl, do you think I'm completely stupid? I've got training in ten minutes to prepare for tomorrow. That massage was a great way to get these tight muscles loosened up and ready."

～

"Chica, are we ready?" Emilio asked the next day, his face uncharacteristically serious.

"I think so," she replied, checking her demonstration uniform one final time for any loose closures. "Did you drill Peter again in the signals?"

"Sí, sí," Peter replied with a grin. "I think we're ready for whatever they throw at us."

Donning a grave demeanor, she lowered her voice. "My friends, we agree to expect something outlandish. We may be wrong, but I don't think so. Remember. I heard that even Chancellor Edsaka plans to attend today. This is a chance for S&D instructors to shine."

"Chica, how much polishing do you want us to do?"

Staring at him, the broader implication of his question finally struck her. Laughing at his double meaning, she said, "Emilio, they deserve as much as we can give them. We've put them through torture this session. A little more should make a perfect ending."

While other students milled around, Sandra withdrew to a corner. Facing the wall, she cleared her mind of extraneous concerns and focused on every muscle and joint. Running through a well-practiced technique, she charged her body and the functionality of her mind and senses.

The announcement sounded for students to assemble in the open arena. Peter, who had watched her carefully, noticed that the young woman who emerged from the corner had assumed a totally transformed presence. Prepared to face whatever the next three hours might hold, he tightened the band around his left wrist while thinking their instructors simply had no clue about what they might be facing.

With so much of Chikondra's purpose directed toward avenues of diplomacy, dedication to the security and defense of ministry personnel on-mission commanded high priority. Exceptional time and effort were devoted to safety measures and defensive techniques. For many years, interest in the S&D class had evolved into the regular demonstration of skills developed by academy students slated to enter field mission assignments. This session's final event had garnered more interest than usual because of the much-discussed performances of Earth students.

Halfway through the presentation, rhythmic applause signaled approval from onlookers watching the demonstrations. Students clad in snug-fitting gray uniforms met highly skilled instructors dressed in black. Demonstrations of physical strength and agility won loud approval from spectators. Overall, the class performed remarkably well while sparring with their more experienced teachers.

After a brief intermission, Instructor Barmihn announced the exhibition's primary event, the running of the obstacle maze. Students had been permitted to divide into teams of three. As expected, the students from Earth had joined forces. Furthermore, meeting the expectations of classmates and spectators alike, the Terran team had elected to go last.

Midway through the exhibition, it was quite obvious that trainers were in head-on competition with their students. From the first team, of which Bejil was a member, only one student emerged successfully. At every turn, booby traps or instructor-attackers lying in wait had either impeded or halted progress. After the second team fared even worse, Ziaman led the third group. Mindful of secret coaching from the Terrans, her team exited intact. However, one needed medical attention from physicians on duty.

Waiting for the signal to enter the maze, Sandra was surprised when several shrill, piercing noises zinged through the air. Sharply glancing toward Peter, she jerked her head toward the right, and all three Terrans hit the ground. Instructors shouted for students and trainers near the maze to take cover. The high-pitched whine of laser weapons sliced through the air.

"What the hell are they doing?" Peter muttered angrily.

"I don't know!" Sandra hissed as she attempted to assess the situation. "Look at the trainers! They're all scrambling to get students out of the way."

"Chica!" Emilio shouted as he forcefully jerked her toward him. Rolling, they both dodged a shot aimed in her direction.

"Damn it!" Darting eyes caught sight of the reserved section where Chancellor Edsaka and other Chikondran council members had been seated. Warnach was among them. Security guards were surrounding the chancellor and his entourage. Frantic efforts appeared underway to shield Edsaka while preparing to safely evacuate him.

"Do you think this is a test or a real attack?" Emilio huddled close to Sandra.

"Who the hell knows? Those laser shots looked real enough! Let's treat it as if it's real. If it's not, I intend to kick Barmihn's..."

"Sandra!"

"Don't worry! I'm okay!" she shouted, swiftly pushing herself further behind the wall of the maze. "Quick! Look for shooters!"

The attack appeared frontal. Splitting up, Emilio raced the length of the maze's back wall. In Spanish, he called out locations from which fire was originating. In the meantime, Peter had scrambled and leapt inside the end of the maze nearest him. He, too, called out locations that he was able to spot.

"Okay, guys! On my signal of three, head for the center of the maze. Emilio, grab our bags, and be careful! Uno! Dos! Tres!" Tucking herself into a tight ball, she rolled through the entrance where Peter waited for her, barely avoiding a volley of fire aimed in her direction.

Inside, they encountered several classmates huddled together behind cowering trainers. One of the instructors looked up and called out, "Students! Get down where it's safe!"

Irritated, Sandra only scowled. In rapid-fire Spanish, the three Terrans mapped out the results of their reconnaissance and strategy. Just as swiftly, Emilio passed around contents from the knapsack he had left behind the course. As they started toward the end of the maze where Emilio had entered, a teacher jumped up and grabbed Sandra by the arm. "It's too dangerous! You can't go back out there!"

Glaring impatiently at the man whose arm she had broken, she rolled her eyes and switched to English. "Just let go of me."

Crouching low, the three observed apparent pandemonium. Shouts filled the air. Crossfire came from what appeared to be two shooters on the far left and four on the right. Craning their necks to see the main seating area, they had no doubt that Edsaka's party was trapped.

"This looks downright weird to me," Peter groaned. "Sandra, you run behind and try to get the ones on the far side. Emilio and I'll head off the four goons on this side."

"Okay. Just remember. Any shouted communications in Spanish. That way, there's less chance for them to know what we're planning. Be careful!"

Once she reached the end of the wall, she peeked around the corner. The shooters on her side were shifting attention from the demonstration platform to security guards on their knees to protect the chancellor. Reaching into her pocket, she secured her weapon and hoped she could still fire with some semblance of accuracy.

Bolting from her corner, she raced toward the edge of the platform, leapt off the end, and rolled across the grass and underneath a flight of steps. Glimpsing Peter and Emilio, she grinned. They were fast.

"Ouch!" she exclaimed. "Good for you, Peter! One goon down! My turn now!"

Moving quickly against the small arena's sidewall, she lunged behind a large trash receptacle just in time to avoid a laser strike. Grinning, she watched one of the shooters on her side stop and take aim toward Edsaka's security team. Dropping to one knee while simultaneously whipping weapon and ammunition from her pocket, she quickly loaded and fired. "Not bad, girl," she muttered. "That shot should be good for a long-term migraine."

Glancing over her shoulder, she laughed. "Good shot, Emilio! Two more to go for you guys and one for me."

Jumping up, she grabbed sturdy railing and swung herself over the steel barrier and onto the main spectator deck. Dodging another laser round, she dived between two rows of seats. Snaking along concrete decking, she made her way toward the other shooter who was advancing toward Edsaka.

"Bloomin' idiot." The thought shot through her brain as she stopped and took aim. "Direct hit," she silently congratulated herself. "No sitting down for him for a while."

Continuing her advance, she waved toward Edsaka's uniformed guards. "Cover the chancellor!" she shouted in Chikondran.

"Sandra!" Warnach hoarsely called out above noisy commotion.

Knowing the security detachment would prevent him from moving, she ignored him. She had spied what she thought Peter and Emilio had not. Reversing course, she scrambled back toward the maze. Carefully ducking in and out behind seats and various obstacles, she reached the demonstration platform.

Muttering under her breath, she realized she must have jerked her ammunition out of her pocket. Lifting her head upward, her line of vision caught a heaven-bound laser bolt. "Five!"

"Hey, kiddo, goin' for the gusto here?"

"Collins, you're good. Real good."

"Told you that a long time ago. I don't think they know we're here."

"There." She pointed toward an opening in the sheeting surrounding the platform. "Crawl under and come in through the back door."

"Lead the way!"

Frowning, she shook her head. "I always gotta go first."

Following her underneath stiff skirting that scraped their backsides, he hissed, "Ladies always go first."

Peering from beneath the skirting, they saw their way was clear. Stealthily, they crawled out and climbed back onto the platform.

"I need another shot."

Swiftly, he produced one from his pocket. "Last one. Make it count."

Again splitting, they rushed to opposite ends of the maze. Two shooters had appeared on the platform and were pointing laser rifles in the direction of two instructors and several students who had taken cover behind tall equipment cases.

Peter's aim was dead on target, dropping the attacker closest to him. On the other hand, Sandra missed her shot. Tossing her weapon so that it clattered across the floor and drew the attacker's fire, she leapt from her corner with a bloodcurdling war cry and dropkicked the attacker just above his kidneys. Sending him sprawling across the floor, she grabbed his rifle and jumped to her feet just as she saw Emilio take out the last attacker in the stands.

When the other students would have jumped to their feet and cheered, she dropped to the floor and shouted, "Stay down! And be quiet!"

Carefully, her eyes scanned left to right, up and down. All was calm. Catching Peter's gaze, she nodded. She jumped to her feet and sprayed laser fire off the edge of the platform as he raced toward her. Nothing happened. Up in the stands, Emilio waved the all-clear.

Collapsing onto the platform floor, she heaved a relieved sigh. Glancing toward shocked classmates, she shook her head. "You can scream now if you want."

Minutes later, a beaming Emdroh Barminh strode toward Peter and Sandra. Close behind him were officers from the chancellor's personal security detachment accompanied by the chancellor, Warnach, and a fiercely proud aerospace captain.

"Excellent! Excellent, Medsah Collins and Mirsah Sirinoya! Your performance was outstanding."

Growling indignantly, Sandra dragged herself to her feet. "Performance?" she screeched at the instructor. "What the hell do you think I am? A damned circus monkey?"

"Please, Mirsah Sirinoya, no one was ever in any real danger."

"Oh, no? What about your attackers? Tell them that!"

"They were volunteers, and they're already being transported for medical treatment."

Emilio ran up behind her. Breathlessly, he grabbed Sandra's shoulder. "Chica? Cómo estás?"

"Bien. Bien furiosa," she responded.

Warnach and Badrik exchanged glances. The fire spewing from her eyes did not bode well for the instructor who had insisted on letting his best students ever have the opportunity to prove their prowess.

Approaching Sandra, Barmihn paused and bent over, retrieving her discarded weapon. Turning it around curiously, he lifted his gaze. "I'm not sure I've ever seen such a weapon as this. What is it called?"

"It's called a slingshot."

"Shall I demonstrate its use?" Peter called out from a vantage spot at the end of the maze.

"Of course!" Barmihn exclaimed.

"My pleasure!" Peter responded, just as he let go a projectile that hit Barmihn in the upper arm, causing the instructor to spin around and cry out in pain.

Immediately, three Terran students looked at each other and grinned. "Ahora!"

Clutching his injured arm, Barmihn bolted from the three who chased him at a dead run until he collapsed face-first onto the grass. Stumbling to keep from stepping or falling on him, they surrounded him and joined amused spectators in breathless laughter.

Late that night, Sandra lay on the floor of the music room while strains of a Kurulian symphony soothed her jangled nerves. Straddling her thighs, Warnach massaged tired and aching muscles in her hips and lower back. Breathing in and out, she relished the relief delivered by his touch.

"Warnach?" she murmured.

"Yes, Shi'níyah?"

"Are you really sure I can't just strangle him over today?"

Chuckling, Warnach shook his head and kneaded more deeply into the spot she had said ached worst. "I'm certain. He was right. Surprise is the best training, even if it isn't the most pleasant."

"I suppose. However, I refuse to accept the offer from Baadihm's security commander to help train his guards. How am I supposed to teach them street smarts?"

"You cannot. All you can do is take pride in the fact that you and your friends have secured an auspicious place in academy history."

"Yeah, we attacked an instructor and chased him until he couldn't run anymore."

"That you did. However, that same instructor lauded rare achievements from very talented students. He said your team reacted quickly, observed well, and executed your plan. In the end, you made sure everything was secure. Barmihn also congratulated me personally."

"He did? I expected he might warn you that you were unified with a madwoman."

"I distinctly recall that he said I could look forward to having a very effective and courageous bodyguard once you're allowed to accompany me on-mission."

She twisted and slightly tensed as he pressed an especially tender spot. "Minister Sirinoya, I will gladly devote my entire life to guarding your body."

"You did that already, and I can assure you. My body is forever grateful."

She laughed softly. "By the way, is it really true that you never had slingshots on Chikondra?"

~

Except for the previous year when she and Warnach had unified, never had Sandra more welcomed an extended break from classes. Physically and mentally tired, she needed a prolonged respite and appreciated the fact her lifemate recognized that need. Smiling to herself, she finished packing so they could leave for the beach house and a private celebration of their first anniversary.

Arriving around noon, they immediately carried luggage and supplies inside the house. Then, while Warnach opened windows, unpacked, and hung clothes, she put away groceries and prepared a light lunch. He finished just in time to help carry things outside for a calm, relaxing meal at a shaded table where they could watch and listen to the sea. Afterward, she cleaned up as he busied himself with hanging the same wide, colorful hammock they had shared the first time he had brought her to his special retreat.

Dark and tranquil, his eyes beheld the softness of her features as she waited for him to join her in the slowly swaying hammock. Settling himself by her side, he smiled as she unavoidably rolled close against him. Affectionately, he kissed her forehead. "Happy now?"

Closing her eyes, she breathed in the warm, clean fragrance of his body. "With you? Of course, I am."

"Good. I've been worried considering how difficult these past months have been."

Detecting the depth of his concern, she snuggled even closer. "If good comes from the bad, then we're stronger for the trial. That's what Cafti always told me. You survived Bederand, and I survived Ku'saá. Look at what we have now."

Silent moments passed before Warnach realized she had quickly fallen asleep. Smiling to himself, he closed his eyes and listened to her rhythmic breathing accompanied by the rush of waves curling up onto the shore. Reflecting on her comment, he contemplated all he did indeed possess.

With a sigh, his thoughts spanned the short number of years since they had met. Within his embrace rested the woman who had restored vitality to his life. Her fresh perspective had revived waning ability to pursue a career he loved. In loving innocence, she had introduced him to the greatest spiritual wonders of his own world. His already eventful life had taken on a completely new dimension. Fears, when they came, had grown more intense. Private joys and personal satisfaction soared to unimagined heights.

Moving slightly, she briefly tightened her arm around his waist. When she grew still again, his mind settled peacefully. Without conscious intention, he whispered his feelings to her. "Me'u Shi'níyah, despite our sharing Nivela-Ku'saá, you cannot possibly know how much I need you or how much I love you. How I thank the Great Spirit for delivering you into my life."

Again, her embrace momentarily tightened, and her face pressed closer to his chest. Instinctively, he felt that her heart had listened to his thoughts. A smile crossed his face as, just before drifting asleep, he murmured, "Ci'ittá mi'ittá, me'u Sandra. Ci'ittá mi'ittá."

The following morning, Warnach awoke early. Turning over in bed, he reached out to find only her pillow beside him. Lazily lifting one eyelid, he looked across the room. Entering their bedroom, she carried a wide tray laden with brightly colored cups, covered dishes, and thermal carafes filled with juice and fresh coffee.

"Happy anniversary, my ki'medsah." The lilt in her voice and the gleam in her eyes held the sparkle of a completely satisfied woman.

Sitting up, he grinned broadly. "I wish the same for you, my dearest ki'mirsah."

Frowning slightly, she placed the large tray across his lap. "English lesson of the day, my good minister. Dearest makes it sound as if you have more than one ki'mirsah. I hope that doesn't mean you're hiding a nasty surprise from me."

Reaching up, he pulled her down and kissed her cheek. "There can be only one ki'mirsah for me. Ever. Now, I'm hoping she'll help me eat this generous breakfast."

Lightheartedly, they teased and bantered over breakfast. Theirs was a comfortable, confident togetherness beneath which lay fiery passions that had bound them as one for hours the previous night. Glancing at her occasionally when she was pouring coffee or cutting her food, Warnach basked in the glow surrounding her. Just as the day before, he could hardly believe how much he loved her.

Once breakfast was consumed, he helped her clean up before they showered together. Standing beneath running water, he stroked his fingers through mounds of soapy bubbles cascading from her shoulders to her breasts. Dark eyes immediately smoldered as his body endured a powerfully sensual jolt. Merely touching her heightened primal senses, and he found himself making love to her yet again.

Physically sated, he held her hand as she stepped from the shower. Drying each other with thick, fluffy towels seemed more magical than mundane. Heavy sighs, gentle touches, and loving glances communicated what words could not. In silence, they helped each other dress in casual clothes.

When she emerged from the bathroom, her hair was dried and brushed into a curving, shining curtain that framed her face. Meeting her gaze, he smiled but said nothing. In his hands, he held the case where their rejoined Kitak had rested through the night.

Taking his cue, she approached and removed his half of Kitak. Instead of sitting in a chair or on the bed, he knelt before her as if paying her homage. "Ci'ittá mi'ittá, me'u Warnach," she said aloud as she carefully placed the rafizhaq ring on his head.

Still too moved to speak, he encircled her hips with long arms and rested his cheek against her abdomen. Such total contentment, he thought. Rising, he gazed down at her diamond-adorned Kitak. In what had almost become ritual, full lips placed a kiss over the brilliantly faceted, oval diamond that matched the gems in the wedding rings she wore. Then, guiding her onto the bed, he lovingly set the golden crown upon her head.

Kneeling again, his hands caught hers. Lifting his face, he studied expressive features that still reflected the aftermath of their physical love. Tones of profound emotion sounded in the voice that finally banished silence. "Sandra, I wish that I could tell you how much I love you."

With the tips of her fingers, she lightly touched her Kitak and then his. "Me'u ki'medsah, I feel how much you love me."

A slight turn of his head caused a gentle sway of waves in his long hair. "Shi'níyah, I think even Kitak cannot fully convey my love to you."

Placing her hands against his cheeks, she studied his expression. Unsure how to respond, she bent forward and kissed cerea-nervos and then his Kitak.

Hours later, they strolled along sandy shores caressed by sparkling ocean waters. Snowy white mountains of clouds cast shadows across land and sea. Velvety warm breezes caressed their faces. Occasionally, they paused to enjoy nature from a different angle or to share the sweetness of a lover's kiss.

By the time they returned to the house, both their appetites had been stimulated by the long walk. Pausing before going inside to get ready for dinner, Sandra looked far out to sea as a smile crept across her face. Studying her image carefully, Warnach said nothing. He was beginning to recognize those strange moments when her mind wandered into the realm of Quazon. Patiently, he waited. Then, when she turned back to him, he led her inside so they could change and leave on time for dinner reservations at a nearby exclusive restaurant.

Enhanced by candlelight and the complex flavors of fine wines, dinner looked and tasted deliciously exotic. Service had been excellent without intrusiveness. Conversation had been quiet and reflective. Returning to the house, Warnach opened the front door for them to go inside. Feeling her hand gripping his arm, he looked down at her.

Quickly stepping out of elegant sandals, she smiled beautifully and lifted her eyebrows high. Her eyes mirrored silver moonlight. "Hurry. Follow me." She then turned and ran barefoot along the brick walkway leading to the beach.

Nearing the water, she bent forward and slid flowing trousers down her legs before pulling the matching tunic over her head. Clad only in lacy bra and panties, she signaled him to hurry. Shrugging indulgent surrender, he first removed shoes and socks. Discarding tailored trousers and elegant silk shirt, he splashed into glittering waters behind her.

Immersed above the waist and awash in white foam, he laughed heartily as the first mighty slap sent a spray of water into his face. Her laughter carried notes of joy as she pressed her lips to his just as a synchronized series of splashes soaked them. For the next half hour, they frolicked with Quazon beneath the light of Chikondra's moons.

When he realized the playful creatures were ready to leave, he backed away just a little. His heart swelled with both pride and elation as he watched her bid farewell to her sleek friends. Long bodies curved around hers as she wrapped them in affectionate hugs. Once each had received a parting kiss, they disappeared into the oceans as quickly as they had appeared.

Back on warm, dry sand, Warnach fell to his knees, pulling her down with him. Holding her tightly, he kissed her with breathless abandon. When he finally looked into her face, he ran his fingers through damp, curling tresses. "Me'u Shi'níyah, never has there lived a man happier than I am with you."

Months later, Warnach's mind momentarily strayed to retrieve sweet images from that night. Returning his attention to the auditorium stage, he studied her as she sat among nearly fifty students celebrating graduation from the Chikondran Academy of Diplomatic Sciences. Dressed in the dove-gray nashavri traditional for graduating women, she sat with erect, regal posture. With her head high, her attention was fixed on Headmaster Pipachna as he introduced Farsuk Edsaka, the keynote speaker for the ceremony.

Despite the phrasings of lofty-sounding ideals, Farsuk Edsaka had never delivered a more riveting or sincerely motivated speech. Receiving a standing ovation, he stood back to observe the faces of students who had been first on their feet. So many of them aspired to goals upon which he had elaborated. A few would be unable to withstand the unrelenting demands of diplomatic field ministry. Sadly, he knew others would likely perish while in pursuit of noble goals. Most would tenaciously cling to optimistic ideals and doggedly refuse to surrender to the dangers or the sacrifice. They would join the struggle to perpetuate peace.

For a matter of seconds, he permitted his eyes to dwell on Sandra's face. He dismissed the notion that affection and lingering guilt were causing him to deceive himself. He firmly believed that she was one of precious few of these students capable of creating impressive accomplishments. Shifting a quick glance toward Warnach, he remembered another graduation day long ago when a similar thought had occurred to him. Yes, separately, each of them could accomplish significant change. A startling new thought crossed his mind. Together, they might well achieve enduring greatness.

Triumphant music filled the auditorium as a prelude to the procession and awarding of graduate sashes and the highly prized, gold-embossed diplomas bearing the coat of arms of the academy's School of Field Service Diplomacy. Each student's name was announced along with his or her ministry assignment. According to tradition, each graduate's ministry sponsor would meet the newly sashed colleague on center stage to exchange formal Chikondran bows.

Maintaining a sense of decorum proved difficult for Warnach. As pride swelled, so did the urge to draw her into his arms and salute her with a kiss. His glittering eyes and mischievous grin made it even harder for her to avoid outright laughter. Instead, just as she had done on Earth, she bowed and then stretched her arms upward to encircle his neck. Making a small concession this time, she allowed herself the reward of kissing his cheek while surprised onlookers applauded.

That evening, Farsuk Edsaka and his lifemate hosted a private reception in Sandra's honor. In an unusual move, Ifta had decided to stage a lavish buffet at the Edsaka home. She had then invited guests, including dignitaries from Earth, Peter Collins, and Emilio Dominguez. Knowing the circumstances behind the absence of Sandra's family, Farsuk had gladly consented to his lifemate's plans.

Finally, Sandra found time to talk to Director de Castillo and Premier Carlsson without distractions. Both had journeyed to attend ceremonies for Earth's first student awarded a degree from the famed Chikondran Academy of Diplomatic Sciences. Happy, confident, and charming, she delighted them with animated anecdotes regarding her experiences at the academy while simultaneously adapting to her new Chikondran lifestyle.

Both men had brought prestigious pins to add to the official ministry sash she had received at graduation and would continue to wear on special ministry occasions. As they secured Earth's official emblem and an exemplary service award pin to her sash, they humorously insisted upon hearing her version of the hilarious stories told by Emdroh Barmihn about how four S&D honor pins attached to her sash corresponded to four courageous instructors who had been injured by one extremely resourceful student from Earth.

Her recounting of the unfortunate demise of class instructors and volunteers at the S&D finals prompted everyone to laughter. Inviting Emilio and Peter to join in the storytelling only enhanced the entertainment value that caused her to laugh so hard that, in self-defense, Warnach eventually removed a drink from her hand.

Near the end of the celebration, Farsuk called for everyone's attention. His eyes shone with pride as he announced that Sandra's Chikondran family prepared to honor her accomplishments according to her new world's customs. He then invited guests to join the family in a circle around her.

With due pomp and ceremony, the distinguished chancellor and his lifemate presented their openly acknowledged goddaughter with an elegantly braided chain of gold. From the chain hung a star-shaped pendant set with an array of brightly sparkling jewels. As she read the card that accompanied the necklace, she smiled at the blessing written by Farsuk's own hand. Appreciative of the lovely gift, Sandra embraced both of them.

Araman and Nadana had discussed the rare and valuable book found in the Tichtika antique shop. Reading again and again the story of the coming of Mi'yafá Si'imlayaná, they had finally decided that the legend was so wonderful and the book so beautiful that they would give it as their graduation gift. As Sandra admired the elegantly bound tome, Farsuk's eyes met Araman's. Wonder and speculation marked both their expressions.

In his typically boisterous style, Badrik swept Sandra into his arms and off the floor. Slowly turning around in the center of the circle formed by friends and family, he noisily kissed her cheek several times. Setting her down, he stretched his hand out to Farisa. "I must apologize to all of you and ask your forgiveness. The gift Farisa and I have for my little sister is a secret."

The grin that lit her face was infectious as she laughed at his mysterious expression. Sandra found herself sandwiched between the two as Badrik whispered very quietly into her ear. "Little sister, Farisa and I have only a handmade card that bears a very special poem that we composed for you to read later. What we give you now is our unending love and appreciation because..."

When emotion choked him to the point he could not continue, Farisa whispered, "Sandra, you helped me understand how much I love Badrik. Because of your example, we want you to be the first to know that we've decided to leave Nivena behind to unify according to Nivela."

Sandra nearly stumbled as she went weak at the knees. Her mouth dropped open, and her eyes widened. "Oh, my God! Oh, my God!" Unable to say another word, tears brimmed in her eyes as she fiercely hugged them both.

"Excuse my interruption." Warnach's firm voice commanded their attention. Puzzled by expressions on three shining faces, he shook his head. "I can hardly wait to learn what secret brings tears to three sets of eyes on such a day of celebration. Now, with your consent, dear brother, I would appreciate my turn."

With a graceful bow, Badrik saluted his brother and, holding tightly to Farisa's hand, rejoined the ring of family and friends. Left alone with Sandra inside the circle, Warnach lovingly gazed into evergreen eyes that opened her soul to him. Reaching out, he took her hands and kissed each one.

"My beautiful Shi'níyah, I have long awaited this day. I cannot deny fear for potential danger. However, I believe that I could have no better colleague to join me in my diplomatic pursuits. In that respect, I am the one who receives today's greatest gift."

Pausing, he released her. While stretching out one hand to touch her Kitak, he withdrew from his pocket a small box of silver filigree. "This, my precious ki'mirsah, expresses my admiration for all of the hard work that earned you such acclaim at the academy."

Tentatively taking the polished silver case, she carefully lifted the tiny latch and opened the lid. Nestled inside against a bed of black satin lay an intricately detailed brooch studded with diamonds. Her hands shook so much he rescued her by taking the box. Extracting the pin, he attached the glittering pair of Quazon to her sash. "Blessings do I wish upon you, me'u Shi'níyah Sandra."

# Chapter Eleven

Entering their suite, Warnach paused. Cushions were piled between the high, curved arm and his lifemate's back as she sat sideways on the sofa. Cloud-filtered winter sunshine streamed in through ceiling-high windows and cast shadowy light upon her profile. With her knees up, her legs created an easel for the large book she was reading. Totally engrossed, she hadn't noticed his arrival.

Quietly crossing the spacious room, he finally reached out and stroked her hair. "What do you read that's so fascinating?"

Blushing, she glanced upward. "I'm sorry. I didn't hear you come in. Did you just get home?"

Smiling, he bent over and affectionately kissed her. Straightening, he nodded as he unbuttoned his coat. "I was beginning to wonder if that meeting would ever end." Removing the coat, he negligently tossed it across the back of the sofa before coming around to kneel in front of her. "So, you failed to answer my question. What are you reading?"

Delicately, she drew her fingertips across the thick paper of her antique book. "The book Mamehr and Nadana gave me for graduation. It's really too hard for me to read, but what I can make out of the story is enchanting."

"What was the title?" When she lifted the large book so that he could read the embossed cover, he removed it from her hands. Standing, he went to the far end of the sofa and sat down. Turning to the elegantly scripted title page, he read aloud. "*The Coming of Mi'yafá Si'imlayaná.*"

"The book is beautiful, but I think the language format is very old."

Meeting her gaze, he nodded. "This book must be at least four hundred years old. The story itself is positively ancient." Pausing as his eyes traveled over elaborate lettering, he found himself again reading out loud.

"*Cradled by spirits of ground and sky, the voyager sought comfort from Mamehr Chikondra. Cheerless and lonely, discouraged and weary, the defender spirit struggled. Too far from home, too long in darkness, the guardian's soul ached for elusive peace. Strength had waned, yet the saddened defender clung to faith as if to life. Disenchanted yet undefeated, the spirit retreated from tradition lost to send sacred prayers to touch the Great Spirit's heart.*

"*Unto those entreaties did Yahvanta listen. Into the soul of Chikondra's child did He probe. Discovering honor and courage, devotion and purpose, the Great Spirit smiled. This child had stepped forth in faith. This child who had weakened at last returned home.*

"*With greater darkness looming in threat, Yahvanta sighed upon the breast of His precious Chikondra. His champion had she borne. His steadfast warrior had He found.*

"*Infinite wisdom did Yahvanta heed. His champion must no longer struggle alone. Arduous would be the paths to peace. So upon His great universe did the Great Spirit look, seeking kindred spirit to ease journeys difficult for the woe-filled child of Mamehr Chikondra. Great eyes, at last, fell upon the helping spirit. Alike yet different, a perfect match was this other child, and, again, did the Great Spirit smile.*

"*Satisfied, the Great Spirit decreed to His angels. From the warm embrace of a faraway star to Chikondra would journey a new light. Borne by that light to Yahvanta's precious world would be soft rains of sadness and shining rays of hope. Yet, with strength ever-present, that strangely mystic glow would kiss the heart of the world to which it had come. Filled with the essence of the Great Spirit's love, that light would shine upon Yahvanta's chosen, upon Chikondra's great warrior.*"

Warnach lifted his eyes to look over the top of the book. With hers closed, she seemed to have escaped into the pages of the legend. "What do you think so far?"

Eyelids opened, and she gave him a dreamy smile. "I think I wish I'd always had you around to read to me. You have such a wonderful voice. I don't think I ever consciously realized that before."

Closing the cover and setting aside the book, Warnach leaned forward and reached for her hands. "If it makes you so happy, then we must make time again for me to read to you. However, Mamehr probably has dinner ready by now. I expect that Badrik and Farisa have also likely arrived."

Squeezing his hands, she nodded and stood up. "My stomach is growling."

Chuckling, he also stood and linked her arm with his. "Mamehr was quite happy when you decided on a family dinner before you leave."

Matching her step to his, she walked toward the door and then into the hallway. "Since I don't know how long before I'll come back home, it seemed like a good idea. I think I miss them already."

"Did you finish packing?"

"All done. I started yours, too."

"I'm quite certain I shall have time to finish. I expect some sleepless nights until I leave to join you."

Once they reached the top of the broad staircase, voices drifted upward. She turned to gaze into dark, beloved eyes, and her expression reflected comprehension. "I can still change my itinerary."

His mouth spread into a regretful smile. "No, Shi'níyah. Two years is a very long time. Despite everything, I know how much you miss your family and friends."

Dropping her face, she watched as her feet negotiated each marble riser. "I wonder if it isn't a good thing that Baadihm asked you to delay your trip to Earth. If nothing else, I'll have a chance to gauge Daddy's reactions."

Stopping one step above her, he grasped her shoulders, forcing her to turn around. "Sandra, are you certain you don't want to stay with John and Angela until I reach Earth? You know I'd rather be with you when you face your family again."

"Warnach, don't think I'm completely crazy. No matter what, I love them. I want to see them again. I'll be okay."

"Little sister! I thought I heard your voice!" Badrik's jolly greeting prompted laughter as he appeared at the bottom of the staircase with the intention of escorting them to the dining room.

Araman's menu selection consisted of Sandra's favorite Chikondran foods and elicited delighted approval from everyone. Accompanying wines contributed to a congenial, mellow mood. Conversation moved easily from one subject to the next. Farisa had grown more open in her show of affection for Badrik as the two shared plans for their transition to Nivela. Turning upside down the old adage about glowing brides, Badrik's face was alight with newfound happiness and his unique zest for life. Warnach and Sandra participated in the dynamic discussions while contentedly enjoying the closeness of their family.

Hours passed until everyone showed signs of tiring. They all congregated together inside the Brisajai to share night prayers. Candles and fragrant incense created mystical ambiance. Familial love suffused all with a penetrating sense of peace. Warnach, as the elder child, initiated the melodic chant and was quickly joined by Badrik. A vast array of prayers laden with gratitude and hope rose heavenward.

Later, with pillows supporting his back, Warnach thumbed through pages bearing elaborate script and elegantly drawn illustrations. When Sandra returned from the bath, he set the tome aside and reached for her. Drawing her on top of him, he bestowed a possessive kiss. A husky laugh sounded from his throat when he noted the sensual lowering of her eyelids.

"My good minister," she murmured, "do you have any idea how delicious you taste?"

"Another sample, perhaps?" Instantly, his mouth reclaimed hers. Probing the fresh depths waiting just beyond her lips, he gloried in her fiery response. Tightening his arms around her, he turned to cover her body with his. Dragging his lips away, he breathed out heavily. "You, me'u Shi'níyah, taste sweeter with each passing day."

Laughing softly, she laced her fingers into thick hair and pulled his face back toward hers. Greedily welding her mouth to his, she lost herself in the utter sensuality of his kiss.

Knowing that they faced only brief separation held little significance for them. Since entering Nivela-Ku'saá, their unification had assumed an intensity more vital than ever. Anticipating weeks apart proved sufficient to spark frantic need for one another.

Rising above her, Warnach quickly shed his pajamas and then pulled her gown over her head. Diffused light from bedside lamps shone soft highlights upon silky skin. Leaning forward, he placed his hands upon her shoulders and languorously slid them downward until open palms rested over the enticing fullness of her breasts. How beautiful she felt, he thought, as he watched her expression transform. With eyelids closed and mouth slightly open, he noted pure pleasure, sheer desire.

His hands continued to roam across the curving expanse of skin as her body reacted with undulations that grew more rapid and more intense as his touch increased its intimate exploration. Whimpering, she reached upward. Desperately, her fingers tangled into his hair, allowing her a grasp firm enough to pull him back to her.

"Warnach," she whispered into his sensitive ear, "don't tease me. I want you so much. Please…" Driving home her plea, her hands swept along his bare back until she could press her hands against his hips as hers rose in ardent invitation.

Gloriously lost, he found himself totally immersed in her love. Instinctively pacing himself, he drew from her the heated responses that would carry each of them to soaring heights of passion and culminate in a veritable explosion of spectacular sensation.

In the middle of the night, he stirred and awakened. Carefully turning over, he noted the way her body still curved where she slept, tucked near to him. A faint smile crossed his sleepy face. Unable to resist, he adjusted his position on the pillow and approached her. Placing pulsating cerea-nervos against her forehead, he released a muted, contented sigh.

Inside the Kadranas shuttleport the next morning, Warnach's expression was serious as he gazed down at her face. "Promise me again that you'll be careful when you reach Earth."

"You have my most solemn promise." She gave him a gentle smile as shuttle boarding was announced. "I love you."

Oblivious to the presence of others, he pulled her into his arms. "I love you, too, Shi'níyah."

Watching her disappear from sight, he reminded himself that this separation would last less than three weeks. Slowly walking through the shuttleport, he half laughed to himself over how much he had come to rely on her mere presence in his day to day life. His thoughts momentarily drifted back to the years he had traveled from one end of the Alliance to the other. Throughout that time, so focused had he been on work that he had trained himself to ignore most personal concerns. Now, thoroughly accustomed to having her with him, he recognized how much he had needed to create balance between the professional and personal aspects of his life.

Exiting the port facility via sliding doors, he noted enormous expanses of gray clouds beginning to float across what had begun as sunny skies. Appropriate, he thought. Upon departing, she had taken the light that brightened his days. Reaching his transport, he slid in and sat back in the contoured seat. Pursing his lips together, he silently prayed that her journey would be safe and the reunion with her family smooth. Then, he engaged the engine of his transport and headed toward Ministry Headquarters.

That evening, Warnach knelt with his mother inside the Brisajai for night prayers. After she went up to bed, he wandered aimlessly around the downstairs until he finally ended up in Sandra's office. Walking toward the windows, he peered out at cold, steady rain. Smiling ruefully to himself, he wondered if Chikondra was also weeping over her departure. Sighing into night's gloomy darkness, he turned around, switched off the lights, and started to leave.

Suddenly, he stopped. Glancing toward her desk, he noticed a greenish, phosphorescent glow. Turning the lights back on, he curiously crossed her office and sat down in her chair. A polished, emerald-cut crystal shone beneath the ceiling lights. Beneath it was a sheet of blue stationery bearing her handwriting. Smiling thoughtfully, he picked up the heavy crystal and rolled it around in his hand as he slowly read the page.

*Warnach, my ki'medsah, if I'm right, you're reading this mere hours after my departure for Earth. I understand your concerns about my going back alone and facing my family after all that has happened. I wish I could allay those fears, but I know I can't. Please, don't worry. Over the years, I've learned to keep my disappointment in proper perspective.*

*Speaking of perspective, I think you may now know how I felt all those times you had to leave me behind. Some advice, my wonderful lifemate. I reminded myself every day that you really loved me and that you would not fail to come home to me. Saying it each day made it better. (Oh, all right. Not much but a little better!) Things are a bit different this time, but you must still come to me, and, as always, I'll be waiting for you.*

*So, close your eyes and touch Kitak. You will feel my love for you. I also leave with you a second promise meant to endure a lifetime. I promise that no one will ever love you as much as I.*

*Ci'ittá mi'ittá,*

*Sandra*

Closing his eyes, he leaned backward in her chair and lifted the fingers of his right hand to rest against his Kitak. Embedded within the ring were patterns permanently recorded from her innermost thoughts and feelings. In the solitude of her office, his smile broadened. Her note had well reflected her identity. Within her words, he had read concern, encouragement, and humor. She had also given him a new promise. Exhaling a long sigh, he picked up the letter and the crystal, extinguished the lights again, and went upstairs to bed.

~

Five long days later, Sandra finally returned to Earth after a boring, uneventful trip aboard a luxury liner. Setting foot on her home planet for the first time in two years, she was surprised when a security officer noted her Alliance diplomatic status and quickly escorted her to an exclusive, fast-moving line. Landing formalities took only moments. The officer on entry duty respectfully welcomed her home. Rapidly, she strode past crowded entry kiosks and headed toward the arrival concourse to retrieve her luggage. From there, she would transfer to the domestic station and depart for the final leg of her trip.

Reaching the transport station in her hometown, she grinned to herself as she noted curious glances in her direction. Despite the fact she had purposely donned a casual sweater and jeans, her Kitak was a distinctively different accessory that caught people's attention. Collecting her luggage, she turned and ran directly into the excited embrace of her brother, Curt.

"Hey! There's my big sister! Wearing a crown, too, I see!"

"Good grief! You could at least wait until no one's around before you start your tormenting."

Stepping back, Curt grinned humorously. "No insults intended. You look terrific!"

"Thanks," she laughed. "I feel terrific these days."

On the way to her parents' home, a prolonged silence followed questions about how and what everyone was doing. Glancing sideways, Curt turned serious. "I know you've got to be worried about Dad. He's calmed down some ever since you were sick. I think it really scared him."

She stared straight ahead, her eyes seeing little. "I almost died, Curt. They didn't even try to come to me."

"Sis, you know how scared Mom is when it comes to heights and flying. I think she nearly had a breakdown over the whole thing. Dad didn't really believe you were so sick until that physician from Earth sent the VM explaining your condition. By then, I don't think he had any idea what to do. I would have come, but I was in training in the backcountry. I didn't really know until after it was all over."

She smiled grimly. "I know you would have been there." She sighed. "Warnach's family sat with me night and day until he returned from Bederand. Curt, you can't imagine how good they are to me. Badrik, his brother, even risked his life going to get Warnach."

"Mom told me. Did they ever find out what made you so sick?"

Her face dropped, and she stared at her wedding rings. "We knew from the beginning. I told them not to tell Mom and Dad because I didn't want them to blame Warnach. It's really complicated, but it happened because Warnach was so far away on the mission to Bederand."

Frowning, Curt slowed his transport for cross-traffic. "How could his being away nearly kill you?"

She shook her head. "I'll explain some other time. It's something peculiar to Chikondrans and should never have happened to a Terran."

"What you mean is that you managed to do the impossible…again."

She couldn't help but laugh. "Something like that."

When they stopped in front of her childhood home, Lee Warner threw open the door and ran outside. Sandra had barely cleared the transport before she found herself locked in her mother's embrace. Never could she have prepared herself for such a greeting. Tightly hugging her mother, all she could do was look at Curt's unusually serious countenance with stunned eyes.

Over lunch, discussion centered primarily on Lee Warner's lingering concerns about her daughter's health. Later, as they unpacked clothing and an assortment of gifts, questions turned toward Sandra's new life on Chikondra. Mrs. Warner studied every nuance of her daughter's expressions, noting deep-rooted happiness. So quickly did the hours pass that, when an antique grandfather clock rang four chimes, they both stared at each other in surprise. Shrugging, they exchanged private girl talk for the kitchen and dinner preparations.

As Sandra was setting the dinner table, the sound of the front door opening made her freeze. Despite her mother's reassurances that her father welcomed her visit, her heart thudded, and she felt short of breath. Swallowing hard and catching a deep breath, she placed the last glass on the table and straightened before heading toward the living room.

Stopping just beneath the archway leading from the dining room, she looked directly into her father's clear blue eyes. Surprisingly, those eyes held none of the cool disdain to which she was accustomed and certainly none of the anger from their encounter two years earlier. Mustering her courage, she smiled hesitantly. "Daddy. Hi."

Momentarily forgetting their last heated encounter, he reflected on the precocious little girl he had once bounced high above his head. The memory prompted a slight smile. "I see you actually made it."

Her left eyebrow lifted. "I sure did. I was really feeling homesick. With school over, I finally had the chance to come home for a visit. By the way, supper's only about fifteen minutes away if you want to change and wash up."

Pausing uncomfortably as if he wanted to say something, Dave Warner dropped his gaze. "I'll be back down in a few minutes," he said. With that, he turned and disappeared upstairs.

Returning to the kitchen, Sandra looked into her mother's questioning eyes. Smiling, she shrugged. "Well, he didn't yell at me."

With the passing of days, tensions eased, becoming less evident. Although not totally free of reservations, their conversation grew increasingly spontaneous. Avoiding negative incidents, she gave glowing accounts of her experiences at the academy. Slowly gaining greater confidence, she spoke more openly of Araman and Badrik. Carefully choosing responses, she explained to her father that her Kitak was Chikondra's version of a wedding ring. The only subject he clearly preferred to avoid regarded her relationship with Warnach.

～

"How much she does adore you, my friend."

Warnach's eyes sparkled as he nodded. "I cannot believe how beautiful she is," he said, stroking his fingers through the silken tresses of Kaliyah's hair as she dozed with her head against his chest.

Rodan's expression held gentle pride. "She resembles Mirah so much."

"You are a fortunate man, my friend, to be loved so well by two such beautiful ladies."

Pausing, Rodan deposited himself in a chair across from Warnach. "Do I detect a bit of longing in that remark?"

Sweeping black eyebrows lifted momentarily. "I'm certainly glad that Farsuk decided to call for an early vote to end this session of Council. I can hardly wait to leave for Earth tomorrow."

Rodan gave him a wry smile. "Missing her?"

As he continued to pet his sleeping godchild, Warnach nodded again. "Most definitely. I never quite expected such a strong sense of disconnection."

Dark eyes studied his longtime friend. How much Warnach had changed since his unification. His facial muscles had lost the tension that had created an almost constant scowl. Even his body had relaxed, and his movements had regained their fluid grace. Still, years of sharing friendship and confidences allowed Rodan deeper insight that revealed troubled thoughts.

"Am I wrong when I detect a dark note within you?"

Shaking his head, Warnach expelled a heavy breath. "Perhaps our friendship allows you to see more than you should."

"Warnach," Rodan responded quietly, "our friendship allows us to be open and honest with one another. Tell me. What is your concern?"

Thoughtfully, Warnach concentrated for a moment on the feeling of Kaliyah snuggled so closely. "Rodan," he began tentatively, "there are times when I cannot completely dismiss concerns about all Sandra has sacrificed for our unification. Right now, holding this tiny treasure of yours, I also realize how much I would love to have my own child. If I feel that way now, how will she feel in a few years?"

Rodan drew in a deep breath and shook his head. "Do you begin to regret your unification with a Terran?"

Warnach's face transformed. "Not for a moment. I accept her not as a Terran but, instead, as Sandra. Her presence in my life has become completely indispensable."

"As I thought. My friend, you already know that you've undertaken a life fraught with potential difficulties and with sadness that is likely unavoidable. I believe in the integrity of her character. My advice is to rely on the strength of your love. It is the only way either of you will be able to cope with future disappointment."

"What you say is true. I think my problem is that I dread the idea that she may grow sad simply because of ramifications stemming from our unification."

"You too quickly assume fault for a decision you both made together. Just as you made the decision together, so must you face together any consequences. Personally, I hold every confidence that you'll overcome whatever difficulties you might encounter."

Warnach's eyes dropped. Gazing down at the top of Kaliyah's head, he felt a strange surge within him. Never in his adult life had he given such serious thought to having a family of his own. The desire to have children with Sandra had caught him by surprise. The impossibility struck him as so unfair. Setting aside private regrets as Rodan diverted their conversation, Warnach concentrated on discussing details regarding upcoming missions to be undertaken with his new advocate.

≈

"Can you actually say something in Chikondran?"

Sandra grinned broadly at the teenaged boy who questioned her. "Absolutely!" She then recited the oath of commitment she had taken the day she was sworn in as an advocate in service to the Dil-Terra Interplanetary Alliance.

"Okay. What did that mean?"

Good humor showed plainly on her face. "That was the Chikondran version of the oath I took when I was officially accepted into the Dil-Terra Ministry of Field Diplomacy."

A slender, shy looking girl cast an impatient glance toward her classmate before raising her hand. Receiving an acknowledging nod, she straightened in her seat. "Mrs. Sirinoya, I've read quite a bit about Chikondra. Several articles wrote that the people there are distant and aloof. Some stories even described them as unfriendly to outsiders. What is your experience?"

Leaning back against David Simon's desk, Sandra smoothed the fabric of her nashavri before answering. "I think we Terrans have a tendency to judge everyone else based on our own culture. Many of our worst historical blunders occurred when some tried to force culturally based philosophies on other very different societies. My opinion is that we still haven't learned that lesson well enough because we often make no allowances for cultural differences or traditions on other worlds.

"Whoever wrote that Chikondrans are aloof was not totally incorrect. However, I prefer thinking of them as reserved and private. Their language is very complicated to learn and speak, but in learning the language, I began to comprehend many of the nuances of what I would describe as their cultural identity. Although I had devoured every book and article I could find about Chikondra, I never really understood those nuances until after I began to read and speak the language.

"In truth, I find most Chikondrans to be kind, courteous, and with me, very warm and accepting. To be sure, some of them had a hard time adapting to a Terran entering their private homes. That isn't common there. Also, just like with Terrans or any other people in the Alliance, there are good and bad. However, overall, I feel very satisfied with the life I've found there."

Another hand went up. "Sandra, are studies at the Chikondra Academy of Diplomatic Sciences as tough as their reputation?"

Sandra aimed a steady gaze at her brother. "Roy, I won't lie. The classes were brutal. I realized early on that success hinged on two concepts. Hard work, as in really hard work, and attitude. Knowledge that my CADS education would enable me to work for peace kept my attitude focused and positive."

The time came when Mr. Simon interrupted the exchanges. "Advocate Sirinoya, class ends in five minutes. In closing, we all know that acceptance into CADS is extremely competitive and exceptionally difficult to obtain. Beyond that, as Amanda already stated, the expense can be staggering. What advice can you offer students who might be interested in a diplomatic career at Alliance levels?"

Thoughtfully, Sandra assessed the faces of David Simon's students. Some were completing his class as no more than a standard requirement. Others concentrated on her commentary, and she sensed drive and desire to participate in diplomatic activities.

"Every pursuit in life that is worthwhile demands some kind of price. The education I've obtained, along with the career I'm starting, required many tough decisions and sacrifices, both intellectually and personally. The first step to moving ahead with a career in diplomacy is deciding how much you really want it.

"Take time to consider the entire scope of aspects. There will be both positive and negative. Then, look within yourself. If you find that you can't imagine any other path for your life, you will find not only the ability but also ways to reach your goals. Always stay alert because there are many programs and people out there to help you move ahead with your plans. Be willing to work another hour when you think you can't possibly work another minute. Most importantly, no matter how hard the circumstances or how discouraged you feel, never ever surrender your dream."

Melodic tones sounded the end of classes for the day. David Simon's class stood up and applauded. Students who were usually eager to leave school milled around their classmate's older sister. Even more surprising, pupils attending earlier classes returned. Surrounded, Sandra smiled and patiently answered questions and accepted thanks for appearing at the school.

Amanda Barker stood off to the side until everyone else left except Mr. Simon and Roy Warner. Noting the girl's intensity, Sandra smiled warmly. "You asked some very probing questions today."

Earlier shyness faded. "Advocate Sirinoya, I think I appreciated your comments today more than anyone else. I do have one last question, if I may."

"Of course," Sandra responded, noting the compassionate look in David's eyes.

"I don't say very much about my personal life. That's because things aren't easy for me. My dad deserted my mom, my brother, and me when I was little. Mom works really hard, and we do okay. However, I know the best I can look forward to is a government-sponsored standard degree. Attending a specialized school, even on Earth, is unrealistic. Do you honestly believe someone like me could ever get accepted to CADS?"

Memories flooded Sandra's mind, and images of another shy, awkward, and insecure teenager flitted before her mind's eye. "Amanda, you already know that my family earns a modest living. The limitations I faced were much the same as yours. Life never gives us any guarantees. However, I firmly believe that if you want something with all your heart and soul, you can almost create miracles.

"Sometimes, the path we think we want isn't the path we need at all. We have to keep our minds open to detours that might lead us to even greater satisfaction. However, if you have a dream, you'll never live with yourself if you don't give your strongest effort to achieving that dream." Sandra paused. "To directly answer your question, yes, I believe someone in your position has every possibility to get accepted into CADS. I know because, under adverse circumstances, I did."

Outside that evening, Sandra was on her knees, helping her father trim plants for the winter when Lee Warner called her back into the house. Dusting herself off and hurrying inside, she smiled happily. A VM had just arrived from Chikondra. Planting herself in front of the monitor, she touched console controls to start the message. Quickly, the screen revealed Warnach's clear, crisp image.

"Shi'níyah, I wanted to let you know that Council adjourned its meetings early, so my departure has advanced a day. Even better news is that I will travel aboard a diplomatic vessel en route to Harmijulan, enabling me to reach Earth two days earlier than scheduled.

"I hope you continue to enjoy your visit with your family. Mamehr and Badrik asked me to convey their regards and to tell you that they miss you already. I can assure you, however, that I miss you so much more. There is no way to express how much I look forward to joining you."

He paused, and his expression softened. The fingers of his right hand lifted to rest against his Kitak. "Ci'ittá mi'ittá, me'u Shi'níyah. Ci'ittá mi'ittá."

With her own fingertips resting against her Kitak, she whispered back to him as the monitor darkened. From behind, she heard a faint grunt and turned. Her father's eyes met hers. Earlier humor had disappeared from his expression. Cool distance had again set him emotionally apart from her. Still bathed in the loving glow of her lifemate's words, she returned her father's stony glare with a smile.

# Chapter Twelve

Two days after receiving Warnach's video message, Sandra tossed a woolen shawl around her shoulders as protection against a cool autumn evening. Her father glanced up and frowned. "Where are you headed?"

"I'm going to meet David Simon and his wife for dinner."

"I thought you came to visit your family."

She paused, uncertain how to read the expression on his face. "That's what I've been doing. I figured I could work in a little time for friends, too."

"Well, don't stay out too late. Your Mommy wants to get an early start in the morning."

"Don't worry, Daddy. It's only dinner, not an all-night party."

Shaking off his change of mood, she went to her rented transport, entered navigation data, and left. Fifteen minutes later, she nosed the transport into guest docking facilities, got out, and headed toward the Simons' townhouse. The door opened before she even reached the steps, and Patricia Simon's smiling face warmly welcomed her.

Stepping inside, Sandra immediately sensed the inviting friendliness she had noted upon first meeting David Simon. Hugging both in greeting, she handed her shawl to David and accepted Patricia's invitation to follow her into the kitchen.

"Mmm! Smells terrific!"

"I hope you like it. I wasn't certain what to fix at first since I know that meat isn't eaten on Chikondra. Then, when David laughed himself silly describing your expression over a cheeseburger, I figured pepper steak would work out just fine."

Sandra laughed heartily in response. "The vegetarian thing there suits me fine most of the time. However, there are those days when I could almost die for a piece of fried chicken or a thick, tender piece of meat...any kind of meat!"

Patricia laughingly shook her head as she transferred food into serving bowls that Sandra helped carry to the dining room. As they sat over a delicious dinner, conversation naturally turned to Sandra's experiences on Chikondra. Animated descriptions of academy life produced sympathetic grimaces and spontaneous laughter. Discussion on culture was quiet and more intense. Humor returned as she amused them with anecdotes regarding bumbles in various encounters with His Excellency, Chancellor Edsaka, who was now considered her godfather.

Clearing the dinner table and tidying up the kitchen in record time, the three gathered in the cheerfully decorated living room. Bookcases lined one entire wall and boasted stacks of books covering an eclectic variety of subjects. The décor centered on a country theme created by charming, rustic knickknacks, paintings of rural scenes, and overstuffed furniture perfect for lounging.

After more than an hour of exchanging various ideas, Sandra's eyes began to gleam with spirited confidence. Both David and Patricia Simon had received her idea with enthusiasm. Over a very short time, they had compiled an impressive list of points to cover to transform a well-conceived idea into reality. Departing around ten o'clock, Sandra recalled advice offered to her brother's classmates. Grinning to herself by the time she returned to her parents' house, her mind had settled into its familiar can-do, nothing-can-stop-me mode.

~

Staring thoughtfully into her coffee, Sandra failed to conceal swelling anxiety. "Mom, are you really sure?"

"I won't tell you he's happy about the prospect, but he did agree they should meet."

Sandra released a worried sigh. "I talked with Uncle Rob last night. He said that if there's any problem, Warnach and I are welcome to stay with him and Aunt Janet. Mom, you can't possibly know how good Warnach is with me. I don't want him subjected to Daddy if he's in one of his moods."

In striking contrast with her daughter's fair complexion, Lee Warner's tanned features appeared hopeful. "I think he knows how close he came to losing you. My biggest hope is that he is finally ready to make peace with this entire situation."

Later that morning, with the transport secured inside a docking tower, excited footsteps carried her to the station's arrival concourse. Without a shred of guilt, she shamelessly utilized her diplomatic identification to gain entrance to the secure arrival deck. Expectant eyes locked on the display monitor confirming arrival portals. Hurrying, she reached Portal Three just as the first passenger disembarked.

Despite constant entertainment onboard the space liner followed by numerous day trips to visit relatives and shopping ventures with her mother, the past seventeen days had lasted too long to suit her. Impatiently, she waited. Just as she was beginning to wonder if he had missed his transfer, Warnach appeared, flashing that brilliant smile she loved so much. Dodging several arriving passengers, she rushed into arms that instantly opened.

"Shi'níyah!" he gasped breathlessly as her lips pulled away from his. "Such a welcome!"

Delight added sparkling notes to her laughter as her fingers interlocked behind his neck. "I'll be glad to welcome you again if you'd like. I've missed you."

"Mmm, your offer is definitely tempting, but I think I prefer a bit more privacy."

Her head shook back and forth as she laughed again. "My good minister, I reluctantly defer to your judgment. Come. Let's retrieve your luggage and go find that privacy."

Clinging to his lifemate's hand, he followed her through the transport station to collect his luggage. Although attired in black trousers and black turtleneck sweater, Warnach's appearance was anything but inconspicuous. Her hometown was a relatively small city that very rarely received alien visitors. His long locks, cerea-nervos, and Kitak attracted a number of second glances, many of which were less than discreet.

Reaching the transport, they quickly stowed his luggage and then themselves inside. Before starting the engine, Sandra turned in her seat. Lightly shadowed eyelids dropped as he laced his fingers into her hair. Pulling her face closer, he treated them both to a prolonged kiss.

Finally parting, he caressed her face with only his eyes. "Me'u Shi'níyah, how good it feels to touch you again."

"I needed you with me again," she said softly.

His eyes grew serious. "I've worried about how things have been with your father."

Her smile faded. "They've actually been much better than I expected. On the other hand, he seems to have withdrawn some the past few days. I know it's because of your coming."

Twisting in his seat, Warnach stared blankly through the polymer window. "Knowing you, I suppose you have alternative plans in place."

Facing forward, she started the transport and eased out of the docking space. "If things don't go well with Daddy, Uncle Rob invited us to stay at his house."

Warnach's jaw tensed as his eyes shifted to the side. Her profile revealed tension, and he watched as her lips pressed tightly together. "Shi'níyah, I don't want to see you upset."

"Warnach, I can't promise that won't happen. We're just going to have to take matters slowly, as they come. I don't know if I can make things work, but I have to try."

Reaching out, he stroked her cheek. "Then, Shi'níyah, we shall try together. Just remember. Whatever happens, your ki'medsah will stand by your side."

She cast him a fleeting smile. "I wouldn't dare try this if I couldn't depend completely on my ki'medsah."

Arriving at the Warner home, Sandra's mother surprised Warnach with a very warm welcome. A delicious vegetable stew sent plumes of steam upward from a huge tureen placed on an iron trivet on the table. A basket of fresh bread enhanced the inviting, homey atmosphere. Quietly, Lee Warner waited and watched as Warnach took her daughter's hand to say a brief prayer before eating.

Mrs. Warner discovered herself nervous in Warnach's presence. Modest and reserved, she could hardly make herself believe that such a famous, dignified man actually sat at her dining room table. The fact that he was married to her daughter did nothing to lessen her anxiety. Attempting to make him feel comfortable, she constantly offered him more to drink or asked if she could get him anything else.

Finally, Warnach leaned across the table and took her hand. Black-brown eyes commanded her attention. "Mrs. Warner, I very much appreciate your kindness, but I would feel so much better if you would try to relax."

Closing her eyes and drawing in a breath, she cast him a shaky smile. "This is all so different for me. I...I've never had anyone from a different world in my own house."

"Mrs. Warner, I hope you can look beyond my origin to treat me as part of your family. If we can agree on that, then I can ask you if I might have a cup of that coffee you offered."

Feeling suddenly and inexplicably comfortable with him, Lee Warner grinned and teased, "If you want to be treated like part of the family, I might be tempted to say that you're welcome to help yourself."

The spontaneity of Warnach's laugh made it all the more delightful. "In that case, I would ask you to tell me where everything is so that I can get coffee for all three of us."

Late in the afternoon, Sandra sat next to Warnach on the sofa. In his lap, he held an album bulging with family photographs. Several pages in the front revealed the pride young parents felt for their first child. Smiling faces pressed close to plump baby cheeks. Dark curls topped off round, shining features. Several times, his fingertips hovered along the lines of images capturing for him the enchantment of fresh and tender new life. Gentleness filled his voice. "You were such a beautiful baby."

"More like a chubby butterball." Cheerful chuckles halted abruptly.

Instantly, Warnach felt tension stiffen her posture. Glancing upward, he saw the man to whom he had spoken only once. Gently squeezing the shaking hand seeking his, he rose to his feet at the same time Sandra did.

"Daddy." She paused nervously before braving a smile. "Daddy, I want you to meet my lifemate, Warnach Sirinoya. Warnach, this is my father, Dave Warner."

Smoothly releasing Sandra's hand, Warnach extended his arm to shake hands with his father-in-law. Sharp eyes noted both her father's faint grimace and his hesitation. Receiving a handshake so firm that it seemed more like a challenge, Warnach tilted his head. "Mr. Warner, I am glad that we finally have the opportunity to meet."

With a tense nod, Dave Warner said, "It does seem about time."

"I cannot disagree."

Mr. Warner looked toward the sofa, his eyes falling on the album filled with cherished memories of happier times now lost. "I see my daughter has been boring you with old photos."

Warnach's smooth expression remained steady. "Actually, seeing them is quite wonderful. I've thoroughly enjoyed the glimpses into my Sandra's childhood."

Mr. Warner grew stone-faced. "My daughter was something of a handful, even then."

Slight emphasis on the words *my daughter* did not escape Warnach's notice. The comment held understated possessive challenge. Calmly, Warnach inclined his head and smiled. "Your daughter is an impressively dynamic woman." Glancing downward, he smiled reassuringly into anxiety-filled eyes before meeting Mr. Warner's cool gaze. "I can only imagine the many trials faced by parents of such gifted children."

Receiving no immediate response, Warnach again turned to Sandra. "Shi'níyah, perhaps your mother could use some help with dinner. Your father and I can use the time to talk and become better acquainted."

Her eyes darted quickly toward her father and back again to Warnach. Her slight nod was accompanied by a faint smile. "That's not a bad idea. Would either of you like something to drink in the meantime?"

Dave Warner sat down while gesturing for Warnach to do the same. "I'll take a glass of ginger ale."

Warnach noticed that he made no effort to offer anything to his guest. "Nothing for me, Shi'níyah. Thank you."

Lee Warner glanced around when her daughter entered the kitchen. "How did it go in there?"

Sandra shrugged as she removed a clean glass from a cabinet and filled it with bubbling ginger ale. "I'm not sure. Let me take this to Daddy, and I'll come back to help you here."

Almost an hour later, as they were preparing to put dinner on the table, Lee swallowed nervously. "It's been too quiet in there. My nerves are shot."

Sandra responded with a short laugh. "I know exactly what you mean. I'm sure glad Curt and Roy just came in."

Curt's jovial nature prevailed as everyone entered the dining room. Jokingly, he extolled the sensory delights of his mother's recipe for fried chicken and suggested that Warnach might reconsider his vegetarian ways. The two exchanged humorous quips until everyone was seated around the table.

When Warnach covered Sandra's hand with his right one, she smiled quietly at her family. "Please. Excuse us for just a moment."

Warnach whispered a brief prayer and then smiled directly into Dave Warner's staring eyes. "It is our custom to offer thanks for the blessing of a meal."

A muted grunt was the only response as Mr. Warner picked up a platter piled high with pieces of chicken wearing crisp, golden crusts.

Dinner began with Roy and Curt comically demonstrating differing methods of efficiently consuming steaming corn on the cob. Lee Warner offered delicately seasoned green beans while Sandra served Warnach a slice of feshbi, a protein-rich root vegetable native to Chikondra.

With eyebrows lifted high, Warnach glared at her in mock disbelief as she started eating food from the plate in front of her. "You actually prefer chicken over feshbi?"

Biting into the juicy white meat of a chicken breast, Sandra chuckled, and her eyes glittered brightly. Quickly, she chewed and swallowed her bite, then took another. "What do you think?"

Without thinking, Warnach leaned sideways and gave her an affectionate peck on the cheek. "I think I prefer to say nothing."

Abruptly, glasses, dishes, and flatware rattled on the table. Everyone looked up in dismay. Dave Warner's clenched fists rested on either side of his plate. Blue eyes blazed in a face that had suddenly flushed a brilliant shade of scarlet.

"I've had enough of this insanity!" Shoving his chair backward, he rose so quickly that the chair tipped over onto the floor. Within seconds, they heard the slamming of the back door.

Curt's eyes instantly met those of his mother while Roy stared in embarrassment toward Warnach. Lee Warner's features were frozen, and glistening tears visibly brimmed in her eyes.

Fearfully, Warnach reached out and turned Sandra's face toward him. He had expected to see hurt. Instead, the steely glint in her eyes caught him by surprise. "Shi'níyah?"

Silently, she placed her napkin beside her plate and stood up. "Excuse me, everyone."

Her mother practically jumped from her chair and clutched Sandra by the arm. "Sweetheart, don't. You don't need this. Don't go out there. You know how he can be."

Sandra swallowed hard, and her eyes gentled. "I'm so sorry, Mom. I have to face him. Once and for all. There's no other choice."

As she started to turn, Warnach's voice called her. "Shi'níyah..."

"Wait for me, my ki'medsah." Then, clenching her jaw, she turned and strode from the dining room.

Outside, Dave Warner paced around a small, neatly kept backyard. Bending over, he picked up several branches that wind had broken off the yard's single shade tree. Angrily, he tossed the bits of wood toward a corner compost container.

"Daddy?"

Sharply, he pivoted. His handsome face had transformed into an ugly mask of anger. "Go away."

"I will, Daddy. When I'm ready." Her stance widened, and her hands rested on her hips. "There was so sense in what you just did in there."

"It's my house, and I do as I please."

"Yes, it is your house. It's also home for Mom and Curt and Roy. You had no right to subject them to that disgusting, ill-mannered display of temper."

Blue eyes coldly assessed his daughter. "You are stubborn and disobedient. You bring that alien into my house and then expect me to treat him like family. What did you expect?"

She felt her heart pounding and her pulse racing. "I thought I could expect you to behave like a gentleman. I tried to talk to you about it. You refused to talk to me, but Mom said you agreed that you should meet him. She didn't lie, did she?"

Grinding his teeth, he spat out, "Your mother doesn't lie, and you know it."

"Then, why? Why let me bring Warnach into this house for you to insult him and the rest of this family?"

"Because," he nearly shouted, "I wanted to see for myself what kind of degenerate had convinced a girl half his age to turn her back on her family and run off to some alien planet."

"Degenerate? How dare..."

"How dare I?" Her father interrupted her with venom saturating his voice. "That damned alien is older than I am! He saw in you a young piece of flesh and convinced you to disobey me so you'd marry him."

Invading hurt joined her wrath. The volume of her voice dropped sharply. "First of all, I am an adult and legally empowered to make my own decisions. You have no right, legally or morally, to dictate to me. Therefore, I disobeyed no one. Secondly, and most importantly, Warnach is no degenerate. He has the strongest morals and finest integrity of any person I've ever met. You think what you want, and you do what you want. Never again speak of him in my presence in those terms."

Dave Warner stared at his daughter. While they had often argued, never had he seen in her such fury as now emanated from her entire body. Carefully, he ground out a reply. "You're too young and too inexperienced to see the truth. When it's too late and he tosses you aside for the next pretty face to come along, you'll come running home. You can tell me then about how you can make all those great decisions for yourself."

Even her anger couldn't prevent the flood of tears that involuntarily poured down her cheeks. Still, she refused to give an inch. "Daddy, I love you, but I won't let you ruin my life the way you've ruined Mom's. She may choose to live her life under a dictator, but I don't. You have no idea how good Warnach is to me. You could never conceive of a finer man. I love him, and he also loves me, probably more than you're capable of comprehending. Nothing you ever say or do will change that."

He glared bitterly at her as he responded in a louder voice intended to intimidate and provoke her. "You're just like your sister."

"That's an absolute lie, and you know it. I'm nothing like her, and I never will be. You've always loved her enough to bail her out of trouble for years." Suddenly, a heartbroken sob wrenched from her. "Why is it you can't love me enough to want me to be happy? Why, Daddy? Why?"

He started to issue a scalding retort but, instead, watched mutely as she spun around and stormed back toward the house. "Stubborn child," he hissed. He then went to sit on the ground with his back against the tree.

By the time she reached the living room, even her blouse was soaked with tears. Warnach stood across the room, engaged in serious conversation with Curt and Roy. Her brothers looked up. Their faces reflected both concern and sympathy.

Without uttering a word, Warnach rushed to her and pulled her into his arms. "Shi'níyah, you should not have gone outside alone."

Burying her face against his shoulder, she sobbed. "I'm so sorry, Warnach. I thought it would be all right. I really did."

Curt's large hand came to rest on her shoulder. "Sis, Warnach knows that. We all thought Dad was finally coming around. It's not your fault."

Lifting her tear-stained face, she sought guidance from the man upon whose strength and wisdom she now relied. "What now? I really tried, but I can't do it anymore."

For brief seconds, Warnach lowered his face to hers, transferring calming vibrations from his cerea-nervos into her shaking body. Breaking the connection, he said gently, "Sandra, your mother is upstairs. I want you to go and get your things ready. Then, we shall leave."

Drawing from his calmness, she gazed at him. She wasn't certain she had ever seen such an expression on his face. "And you? What if Daddy comes in and starts again?"

"He will not. It is time that I go to speak with him."

Fresh fear flared in her eyes. "Warnach, no! You don't know him!"

"Trust me, Shi'níyah. Now, go upstairs and gather your belongings. We shall leave when I return."

Gritting his teeth, Warnach grimly waited for her to turn and disappear up the stairs. When he turned around, resolute eyes briefly met those of Curt and Roy. Saying nothing, his face assumed the daunting scowl that had intimidated many warlike factions into seriously addressing peace negotiations.

Reaching a spot only a few feet away from Sandra's father, Warnach silently waited for several moments. When Mr. Warner either failed to notice or stubbornly ignored his presence, Warnach spoke in a clear, strong voice. "I wish to speak with you, Mr. Warner."

"I have nothing to say to you," Dave Warner growled.

"I shall consider that a good thing. It means there will be no excuse for you not to hear and understand what I will say to you."

Twisting around sharply, Mr. Warner glared at Warnach with icy regard. "Don't tell me you're as stubborn as my daughter."

Smiling grimly, Warnach tilted his head to one side. "Not stubborn, Mr. Warner. Determined. She has been determined to reconcile differences that create such friction between the two of you. She loves you more than you can possibly appreciate."

"If she loves me so much, why doesn't she obey me?" Finally, Dave Warner stood and faced his adversary. For the first time, he realized how young and strong his daughter's husband appeared.

Drawing in a deep breath, Warnach slowly expelled it. "Your daughter is no longer a child. The time has long since passed for you or anyone else to issue commands about how she should live her life. She is an intelligent woman, wise beyond her years, and quite capable of making her own decisions."

"She's *my* daughter."

"Yes, Mr. Warner, Sandra is *your* daughter. She's also *my* lifemate."

"Lifemate," Mr. Warner ground out sarcastically. "What kind of stupid word is that?"

"Stupid, you think? The Chikondran word *kimirsah* translates to lifemate. Unlike your Terran words *husband* and *wife*, lifemate means to us that there is no concept of divorce or dissolution. We are bound by faith and pledge to honor one another for so long as we live. I believe that is far from stupid."

"And I think it's stupid alien bullshit."

Again, Warnach breathed deeply in and out, barely willing himself to maintain control. "Mr. Warner, right now, I care little about what you think, especially about me or what you call alien bullshit. What I do care about right now is that Sandra is inside, crying her heart out because of how much you just hurt her.

"When I go back inside, I intend to take her away from this house and never let her return. I will never prevent her from seeing her mother, or her brothers, or anyone else in her family. In fact, I'll make certain that she has time to visit them whenever possible. However, when I walk out of this house with her, you can look forward to not seeing her again for a very long time. I will not stand quietly by while you subject her to your vile attitude and temper."

Mr. Warner's eyes narrowed. Evening security lights automatically switched on, casting shadowy illumination across Warnach's ominous features. There could be no doubt that the man meant every word of his threat. "That's exactly what I thought. You intended from the very beginning to take her away from me."

"Take her away…?" Warnach paused for only a moment. "Mr. Warner, Sandra may be your daughter, but she is not a thing in your possession.

She may be my lifemate, but never once have I considered her a slave or a belonging. As my ki'mirsah, she shares my life and the decisions that affect both our lives."

"Yeah, I suppose you expect me to believe all that diplomatic garbage."

Losing patience, Warnach said, "To be perfectly honest, I don't give a damn whether you believe or not. However, I do think you should know a few things about the daughter whom you scorn. Your daughter has worked hard and earned recognition from the highest levels of your Earth government and the Alliance Council. Brilliant and experienced officials have noted her talents and her potential to excel in the career she's chosen. Many are honorable men and women who would give anything to have a daughter like Sandra."

"You think I don't know all that? What I want to know is what a man your age sees in a woman young enough to be your daughter. A fling? A toy to play with and then throw away like a discarded whore when a younger, prettier plaything comes along?"

Suddenly, Warnach's cerea-nervos began to throb so violently that even Dave Warner noticed and stepped backward. Warnach advanced with a matching number of paces. At the same time, his body took on a menacing stance that finally intimidated Mr. Warner into wary silence.

"Mr. Warner, right now, because I would never intentionally hurt Sandra, you force me to remind myself that I am not a man of violence. Otherwise, I would gladly rip your tongue out for what you just said. If it were not for Sandra, I would grant you neither time nor breath to justify such crude, sickening comments.

"I do want you to know that I've traveled for many years to worlds with names you've likely never heard. I've met many people and, yes, many women. Never in all those years did I meet a single person who compares with my Sandra.

"Beyond her intelligence and capabilities, she's the finest, most sensitive, and most caring woman I've ever known. A challenge she is, but in the finest ways possible. Beyond that, if you would ever relinquish that bitter stubbornness of yours and visit my planet just once, you would find yourself and your family honored by my people simply because of your daughter's impeccable character."

Daring to speak at last, Mr. Warner scoffed, "You really expect me to believe that?"

Warnach's fists clenched at his side. "As I said before, I don't care what you believe, but you will hear the truth at least once. Sandra brought light, love, and joy into my life when I had grown miserably trapped by my own cynicism. She alone restored meaning to my life.

"With regard to her character, your daughter possesses unique integrity and deep faith. She even entered sacred unification with me as a virgin."

Despite growing darkness, Warnach saw the tense blanching of his father-in-law's face. The mere thought of the intimacies his daughter now shared in marriage sickened Dave Warner in a way that plainly showed in his expression. Warnach, however, continued without mercy or sympathy. "Yes, Sandra came to me as a virgin in a time and age when precious few men and women comprehend the value of such virtue. Every time I address her as Shi'níyah, I openly acknowledge my respect for that virtue.

"That is also why the Kitak she wears around her head bears a perfect diamond. According to the faith and traditions of my people, that diamond signifies that she walks in a permanent state of honor which reflects upon both our families and me. Because she merits such esteem on my world, I would subject myself and my entire family to unending shame should I ever break my oath of fidelity to her. That is something I would never do. Your daughter gives me every reason to cherish her. I would rather die than fail her.

"Now? I will go inside. In one way, I leave you with a sad triumph tonight. I will always regret the sorrow she must bear because of her inability to touch your heart. However, I will take my lifemate from your house. I will hold her, and I will comfort her. I will dry her tears. With time, I will make her happy again. I will love her and protect her in every way necessary to prevent you from ever hurting her again."

In anger, he turned and started to walk away. Slowly, he stopped and faced Dave Warner a final time. "What a tragedy that you discard like common trash such a fine daughter who would give you so much love."

Entering the kitchen, Warnach was met by Lee Warner. Dark eyes that had earlier blazed with anger reflected compassion. "Mrs. Warner, where is Sandra. Is she all right?"

Mrs. Warner's features were pinched from stress. "She's more upset than I can ever remember. She's packing the last of her things to leave." Sighing heavily, Mrs. Warner struggled not to cry. "Please, don't keep my daughter away from me because of this."

Tenderly, Warnach grasped his mother-in-law's hands. "Mrs. Warner, I could never do that to you or to Sandra. You have my promise. Just as we planned, we'll stay nearby so you can continue to see one another until we leave. I'll also see that she visits you regularly."

"Her father?"

Warnach's hair swept back and forth as he shook his head. "Your husband is a man beyond my comprehension."

"He isn't always this way. He really isn't."

Warnach's voice held a soothing tone as he attempted to console her. "Mrs. Warner, I believe you. Neither my lifemate nor you could love a man who was always like the one outside. You must excuse me. I must go to her."

A broad wedge of light shone from an open bedroom door. Peering inside, Warnach watched as she wiped her face before zipping up a small tote. Quietly, he entered and wrapped his arms around her from behind. "Shi'níyah, you're shaking all over."

Turning within the circle of his arms, she rested a damp cheek against his chest. Quietly, she murmured, "I thought he had begun to mellow. I really did. I never would have brought you here if…"

"Shsh, me'u Shi'níyah, shsh." Lifting her face, he looked with regret at red, swollen eyes and trembling lips. Touching his mouth lightly to hers, he managed a smile that she could feel but not see. "Dry your face and come. We must go."

Picking up the larger pieces of luggage, he waited while she gathered her smaller bags. He then followed her through the short hall and downstairs. Depositing everything in front of the door, he put his arm around her waist and led her from the small entrance into the living room to say goodbye to her mother and brothers. Stopping abruptly, Warnach pulled Sandra protectively close.

Across the room, Dave Warner waited. Tension was apparent in his tall body's jerky movements. Blood flushed his face. Angry disdain in his blue eyes had been replaced by what looked strangely like fear. Huge hands visibly shook.

Instinctively, Sandra shrank backward against Warnach. Nervously, she glanced toward her mother, who stood between her brothers. Both Curt and Roy had their arms around Lee Warner. Exhausted and upset, Sandra didn't know if she could possibly walk across the room to hug them. Unable to speak, she waited in wary silence.

"Well?" It was Lee Warner's voice that sliced through the silence.

Dave Warner cast his eyes toward the unusual tone of demand in his wife's voice.

When Mr. Warner remained broodingly silent, Warnach assumed quiet control. "Mrs. Warner, Sandra wished to say goodnight to you and her brothers. We're leaving now."

She had cried so hard that she could barely speak. "Mom? I...I'll talk to you tomorrow."

Frustrated, Lee Warner shot an angry look in her husband's direction. Leaving the protective guardians her sons had become, she went to her daughter and held her tightly. Stepping away, she stroked untidy streaks of wet hair clinging to her daughter's cheek. "I know I haven't said it often enough, sweetheart, but your mother loves you. She really does."

Fresh tears brimmed in Sandra's eyes as she hugged her mother again. "I love you, too, Mom."

"Sandra?" Warnach's voice gently pronounced her name as he once again placed his hand at her waist. "It grows late, Shi'níyah. We must go."

Giving her mother a brave smile, Sandra turned, and Warnach started with her toward the door.

"You don't have to go."

Both Warnach and Sandra stopped. Very slowly, they turned around. Staring at her father, Sandra was sure it could not have been his voice she had heard. The firmness in her own voice surprised her even more. "We do have to go. It's late, and we have to get settled for the night."

"You can stay here."

The feel of Warnach's hands firmly at her waist gave her courage. "No, Daddy, I can't. I go where Warnach goes. He's my lifemate."

Mr. Warner's square jaw jerked sharply from side to side. His eyes closed, and his head tilted backward for a quick moment. When he looked at his daughter again, he couldn't believe how sorrowful she appeared. He wanted to reach out to her, but he was terrified of rejection. For a moment, he almost strangled on his words. Finally, he said, "He can stay, too."

Swollen eyes narrowed. "Daddy, *he* has a name. His name is Warnach."

Dave Warner's blue eyes darted to meet those of his son-in-law. "Sandra…" He paused, swallowing uncomfortably. "Warnach may also stay."

Dropping her face, Sandra stared at shadows drawn across light brown carpeting. She wasn't sure if she dared take the risk she had taken earlier that evening. Her thoughts jumbled in dread of another confrontation.

"Sandra?"

Her father's voice startled her, and she quickly looked back at him. Still, she remained wordless.

"Please. I want you to stay. Both of you." He struggled for words. Every time he found the need to say Warnach's name, Dave Warner thought he might choke, but he forced himself to go on. "Outside… Warnach said something that made me start to think. You've been away at school for so long that I guess I really don't know you anymore. No matter what, you're still my daughter. Please, don't go."

Nervously, she took one tentative step forward. "Daddy? Are you sure? Are you really sure? I…I can't do this again. I can't."

Dave Warner sighed and sucked in a shuddering breath. "I know. And, yes, I'm positive. Will you stay?"

Her jaw trembled, and she hesitated. Warnach's presence gave her courage. Swiftly, she rushed across the living room and into her father's arms. Tearfully, she hugged him tightly. "Oh, Daddy, only if you're really sure. You don't know how awful this has been for me. I love you, Daddy. Really, I do."

"I know, honey. I can't say how this will all turn out, but I promise to try as long as you stay. I…I love you, too." Dave Warner's gaze locked on black eyes staring at him from the opposite side of the living room. Warnach communicated wary acceptance and sincere gratitude with an elegant bow of his head. Mr. Warner's expression acknowledged the unspoken message before he turned full attention to the daughter he had nearly lost.

# Chapter Thirteen

Following the clash with Sandra's father, Warnach finally felt able to relax. Rob and Janet Warner had organized a family gathering at the small farmhouse where they lived, and he appreciated the opportunity for a long walk with her uncle. Fresh autumn air filled his lungs as he walked along a path through a densely wooded area. Stopping, he peered between trees in the direction Rob pointed. Gracefully, a doe hurtled fallen timbers and hurried into the brush and out of sight.

"We have quite a few deer around here. They can sometimes be a nuisance."

"Seeing them in their natural habitat is still remarkable. They are beautiful creatures."

Rob smiled and then braved the question uppermost on his mind. "I hope you'll forgive me for asking. How are things going with my brother?"

Warnach's eyebrows lifted thoughtfully as the two men resumed their walk. "Since the initial confrontation, things have been relatively calm. I believe your brother tolerates my presence only because he knows that doing otherwise will drive Sandra away permanently."

Rob huffed out an impatient breath and shook his head. "Dave's biggest problem is you. Nothing more. Nothing less. Believe it or not, none of my family was raised to be bigoted."

Warnach leaned forward to help Rob lift a large branch and move it off to the side of the path. Brushing bits of dirt and bark from his hands, he looked into Rob's eyes that were even brighter blue than Mr. Warner's. "I'm glad I got to know you first. Otherwise, your brother's example would make that difficult to believe. He has made several clearly derogatory comments about alien peoples."

Rob nodded and listened as he peered upward into sparse foliage. Pointing, he noted several branches that appeared diseased and made a comment about having to remove the tree the following spring.

"Sorry. I wasn't ignoring you," he said. "Dave is an odd person. I never understood why, but he has this tendency to think that what is his is always his. According to his way of thinking, you've taken his daughter away, and I don't think he'll ever forgive you for that. It would have been no different regardless of where you came from. He's like that. When he loses control, he becomes totally irrational. All he seems capable of doing is striking out to hurt any way he can. He'll hit at every possible detail that he thinks will drive home his point. I'm surprised he's only focusing on the alien angle."

Warnach stared thoughtfully ahead at trees still heavily laden with leaves colored brilliant shades of ruby and lemon yellow. "How well you know him. He was also quick to point out my age in comparison to Sandra's."

"Is it that big of a difference?"

Wryly, Warnach grinned. "Chronologically speaking, I am older than your brother."

Rob's eyes gleamed with humor. "Now, I'm mad…and jealous. You look ten years younger than I am."

"Metabolic processes of Chikondrans go through various changes that do not occur in humans. In comparison, we age more slowly. As time progresses, however, my body will change so that Sandra and I will actually be able to grow old together."

"I didn't know that, but I'm still jealous. However, going back to my brother, I wish I could give you some advice that would help. Maybe he'll change with time. I really don't know."

"My concern isn't how he feels about me. I worry about Sandra. Family is so important to her."

Rob directed a warm smile toward Warnach. "Judging by the way she talks, she's found a marvelous family on Chikondra."

Gleaming brown eyes held a thoughtful gaze. "My family adores her."

"And she obviously adores them."

"I suppose time alone will either serve to reconcile her father to our unification or…"

Rob picked up the conversation after Warnach's words lapsed into silence. "Warnach, I wish I could tell you he'll get used to the idea. I honestly doubt it, but, as we say on Earth, stranger things have happened. My only real advice is that you stand your ground. As long as Dave is convinced you'll take her out of his life, he'll likely avoid further open conflict."

By late morning, aunts, uncles, and cousins had turned the Warner farm into a noisy, happy melee. Children ran and shouted everywhere. Balls rolled across wide lawns, and motorbikes zipped around a rough, figure-eight shaped track. Men admitted curiosity about the alien who had joined the family, but, to Dave Warner's consternation, they talked and joked with Warnach as if they had known him their entire lives. Inside, past arguments seemed forgotten as Sandra's aunts amiably chattered while preparing side dishes for a big family feast.

Late lunch was a boisterous affair. Warnach accepted good-natured teasing with witty retorts that quickly ingratiated him with Sandra's extended family. Happily munching his way through a variety of typical foods, he answered questions and redirected some of the more humorous remarks toward his lifemate.

Children were especially curious about his cerea-nervos. One of Sandra's younger cousins boldly came forward and asked if it was safe to touch them. When an embarrassed mother scolded the little girl, Warnach smiled and gave a slight shake of his head. "There is no problem. She's only curious."

Picking the chagrined little girl up and settling her on his lap, he gently grasped the index finger of her right hand. "Now, you must not touch my Kitak."

"Kitak? Is that the ring around your head?"

"Yes, it is. The rules on my world say that, besides me, only Sandra may touch my Kitak. Now, hold very still." Slowly, watching her eyes grow wide, he lifted her hand until her index finger rested against his cerea-nervos.

"Ooooh! Ooooh!" The little girl squealed in excited delight. "That tickles! Do it again!"

Within seconds, the remainder of his lunch grew cold as all the other children surrounded him for their own chance to touch his cerea-nervos. In the meantime, Sandra's lunch got pushed aside while she laughed until she cried.

Children with full stomachs brought a brief period of welcome quiet after lunch. Shooed from the house, Sandra and Warnach headed outside for a walk through a broad pumpkin field. Huge orange orbs were almost ready for harvest. Kneeling down, Sandra ran her fingers along one particularly large specimen. Grinning, she glanced upward. "This one would make a perfect jack-o-lantern."

"Jack-o-what?"

"Jack-o-lantern. An old tradition. I'll explain later." She laughed and stood up.

Suddenly, Warnach realized how much more relaxed she now looked beneath golden sunshine. Grasping her hands, he drew her closer. "Me'u Shi'níyah, I do believe the sparkle has returned to your eyes."

For only a moment, she looked away. Gazing back at him, she smiled. "So many of them used to criticize me constantly. The change is so hard to believe. It's almost like when I was young - before I wanted to leave for school in Washington."

"It is a good thing to see."

Her eyes pensively beheld his expression. "Warnach, I know this has been really hard for you. Daddy hasn't been exactly congenial."

"Neither has he been abusive since that first evening. He has also been more calm and communicative with you."

"I do appreciate all your efforts. I want so much to believe things will get better. I hope this is a start."

"So do I." Gently, he embraced her. Giving in to need for a little reassurance of his own, he brought his forehead to rest against hers. As he claimed her in cerea-semi'ittá, her tiny, soft moans pleased him as her body melted against his. How perfectly she reacted to cerea-semi'ittá. As he backed away, his eyes filled with love. "Ci'ittá mi'ittá, me'u Shi'níyah."

Briefly, she touched her lips to his and then whispered, "I love you, too, my ki'medsah. Ci'ittá mi'ittá, Warnach."

From the door of a storage shed, Dave Warner watched as the two embraced again. Seething with anger, Mr. Warner thought of Warnach Sirinoya as little more than a cradle-robbing thief who had charmed and seduced his daughter. Turning in disgust, he disappeared inside the shed. His heart was breaking. He had lost his little girl.

At early dusk, Warnach stood outside and gazed toward graying heavens. Nearly everyone was gone, and the quiet was unbelievably welcome. He started at the gruff sound of his name. Pivoting, he saw Sandra's father approaching. Nodding his head in recognition, Warnach responded, "Mr. Warner."

Dave Warner was nearly as tall as Warnach, but his build was slightly heavier and much less athletic. Blue eyes were as icy as ever. "Before everyone else comes out, I want to tell you something."

"I'm listening."

"Don't get any wrong ideas. Everyone else may seem to accept you, but that makes no difference in how I feel. I don't trust you, and I never will. I'm only tolerating you right now because I know that, sooner or later, my daughter will have to face the truth. When that time comes, I want her to come home to her mommy and me instead of running off to some other strange planet."

Warnach leveled a steely gaze toward his father-in-law. "Mr. Warner, I have no intention of arguing with you. All I will say is that there is nothing in my life more important than Sandra. I love her beyond what you can possibly comprehend, so, for the moment, we're at an impasse until time proves how wrong you are."

"Hey!" Sandra's cheery voice called out. "What are you two doing out here? It's getting cold, and it's almost dark!"

Quickly masking his feelings, Warnach responded with a brilliant smile. "We were only discussing how friendly your family was today."

Shaken at hearing Sirinoya echo Sandra's exact words from days earlier, Dave Warner quickly recovered. "I wondered how Warnach wasn't scared off by all those wild heathens running around here today."

Neither man failed to smile, but she sensed undercurrents better left unchallenged. Linking arms with Warnach, she gazed up into darkly shadowed features. "I think Mom's ready to go home. How about you?"

Warnach smiled down at her and then looked toward Mr. Warner. "You, sir?"

~

The next afternoon, Warnach sat in the living room at David Simon's house. The mischievous grin on Sandra's face was refreshing. For the moment at least. Clearly, she had some clever plan in mind. He could only wonder what.

Accepting a glass of wine from David Simon, Warnach grinned. "May I assume the wine is to help me survive whatever mischief my dear lifemate so poorly hides?"

Patricia and Sandra exchanged looks, and both chortled in amusement before quickly donning exaggeratedly innocent expressions. David shook his head. "Once you've been with Sandra as long as Patricia and I've been married, you'll discover that feminine plotting can be exasperating. The consolation is that it is often divine torture."

Thoughtfully, Warnach sipped his wine while staring at his lifemate. "All right. I'm as ready as I shall ever be."

"You make it sound so awful." Her petulant expression was laughable.

"When you have that expression on your face, I cannot help but remember the way you, Emilio, and Peter looked the morning of the S&D finals. Personally, I prefer to avoid such punishment as you inflicted on those unsuspecting volunteers."

David turned curious eyes to Warnach. "Sounds like an interesting story there."

"As long as you weren't among the victims who were taken to hospital." Warnach grinned and drank a little more wine. "Now, Shi'níyah, what sort of scheme do you have in mind this time?"

"It really isn't as bad as all that. I've discussed my idea thoroughly with David and Patricia. We've compiled a list, and I've since had some other ideas that I think can really bring this all together."

Leaning back in his chair and holding his glass in front of him, Warnach smiled. "Tell me."

Forty-five minutes later, he leaned forward, intently perusing the list that had grown a little longer since their discussion had begun. Nodding approval, he admired both the Simons and his lifemate. Their plan would require long-term commitment and creativity, but success promised many possibilities for young lives.

"Sandra, you do understand that approval from the directorate level will be needed to move forward. That may be the most difficult task in your plan."

"Actually, I expect that will be the easiest part."

"Why so?"

"Because a certain director owes me big time, and he promised he would always do anything possible to help me."

Warnach's grin curved sideways, and his hair bounced with the shake of his head. "You actually intend to hold Farsuk to his word?"

David's brow furrowed. "Farsuk? As in Chancellor Edsaka? Sandra? Are you actually planning to go to the chancellor?"

Negligently, she shrugged her shoulders. "Why not?"

"Sandra," Patricia interjected seriously, "this is all about secondary students from Earth. The chancellor has much broader concerns than a few teenagers."

"One of those students might well be able to use this opportunity to launch a career as future chancellor. The plan could even expand if other planets choose to get involved. Besides, I don't intend to pull him into the details of the plan. I only need approval for the workshops. He can give that."

David's expression grew more dubious. "But, Sandra, the chancellor? Do you really think he'll listen to you?"

Her gaze held steady. "He will listen, and he will approve. Right now, my biggest concern is establishing the foundation and making sure the investments work. Also, I need to find ways to attract bigger sponsors who aren't going to expect favors down the road except for philanthropic recognition."

Patricia leaned forward. "Are you sure we aren't undertaking an impossible task? I just don't see how you can be so sure about getting Chancellor Edsaka's go-ahead, let alone sufficient funding."

Warnach rose from his seat. "As far as the chancellor, my lifemate is right. He will likely consent to anything she asks of him. Funding presents more difficulties. Sandra's initial pledge of sixty thousand credits from her incentives is an excellent beginning, but we will certainly need more to make this work."

"I was also thinking about plowing a percentage of my salary into the foundation."

Warnach studied her expression and thought he could almost see the ideas developing inside her mind. "Shi'níyah, are you certain?"

Standing, she went to him and placed her hand on his arm. "My personal needs are simple. While we're on-mission, all our expenses are covered. I saved most of the year's salary I received when I was on Chikondra. That can serve as my personal financial base. After reviewing all the details, I think I can easily contribute a quarter of my earnings on an annual basis."

For a moment, he wondered which was greater: her generosity, her creative thinking, or her determination. "All right. If you can establish satisfactory supervision for this little venture, I shall add my pledge. I think a quarter-million credits should start you off quite well."

Stunned, she stepped backward. "What?" she squeaked. "Are you serious?"

"Shi'níyah, I am as serious as you are."

"Minister Sirinoya," David Simon blurted out.

"Excuse me?" Warnach asked. "I thought we had dispensed with titles in exchange for first names."

"W…Warnach," he stammered, "that is an incredible sum of money. We never intended…"

Warnach smiled. "You intended to find ways on your own to make this work. It is a noble venture on its own merit." He then glanced affectionately toward his lifemate. "Someone was once generous enough with time and support to give my Sandra the chance that eventually led her to me. I shall think of this as a measure of expressing my gratitude."

That evening, she lay in bed beside him and stared into the darkness. "I never meant for you to contribute to this cause. I just wanted to help some of those kids I met at Roy's school. Even if only one or two gain long-term benefit, it would make the effort worthwhile."

Turning on his side, Warnach undid the top button of her gown. Pressing hot lips against sensitive skin, he savored silken smoothness. After a few moments, he shifted his position and rested his face against the fullness of her breasts. "Shi'níyah, I know you never once planned to ask me for money. I consider it an honor to offer my support."

"Warnach, you don't understand." Shaky fingers began to stroke through the thickness of his hair.

"What do I not understand?"

"I want to do this for the students. That really is my primary interest. After I thought about it, I also thought it would be a way…"

"A way for what?"

"Warnach…"

"Shi'níyah, you may as well tell me what you have in mind."

For several moments, she lay very still. "I don't know if you will really understand."

Sighing, he sat up. "How am I to understand without explanation?"

"The foundation. Overseeing financial investments, expenses, and actively recruiting other sponsors. I was thinking of talking with Michael McKenzie. His firm specializes in investment trusts and the like." Drawing herself into a sitting position, she reached for Warnach's hands. "I was thinking to name the foundation in honor of Diana and Derek."

Warnach swallowed hard. "You never will forget him, will you?"

"I'll never forget either of them. That doesn't mean I live in the past with them. I was blessed to escape with my life. Then, my blessings compounded thousands of times when I met you. I found my most perfect dream in you. I just can't bear thinking that their deaths marked the end of their dreams."

Faint light filtered through a window. Leaning forward, she stroked his tensed jawline and then drew a fingertip across his full lower lip. "You know that I've never loved anyone as much as I love you. Try to understand."

"I think, me'u Shi'níyah, I shall never understand you." He paused and then moved toward her. With faint pressure, his teeth gently caught one nipple beneath filmy fabric. "You always succeed in leaving your ki'medsah totally perplexed and completely in awe."

Her short sigh of relief was followed by an abrupt gasp. Wrapping her arms around him, she fell back on her pillow. Lacing her fingers into his hair, she pressed his face tightly against her swelling breast. Closing her eyes, she allowed her hands, lips, and body to reveal the truth about how much she truly loved him.

Making love with her never failed to rekindle his confidence. As he lay awake, thoughts bombarded him from so many directions as he pondered strange concepts. During her childhood, this room had been hers. While sweet, little-girl dreams still filled her nights, he had already embarked on his diplomatic career. When she returned home to this room as a teenager visiting her parents, he had been occupied with historic negotiations while wondering if life would ever reveal deeper meaning. Now, as a vital and sensual woman, she slept beside him, the man who loved her beyond anything the entire universe might offer.

Gently, he placed a kiss on the head that rested on his bare shoulder. He then changed positions and eased her head onto her pillow. Resting on his side, he stroked the softness of her cheek. Despite her undeniable strength and fortitude, Warnach dwelled on the sweetness, kindness, and vulnerability that were such ingrained facets of her character. As he kissed her forehead again, his heart bade her silent goodnight. Falling asleep, he could almost understand her father's irrational protectiveness.

∾

The day before their departure for Washington, Minister Warnach Sirinoya and his new advocate stood at the far end of the stage. The auditorium at

Roy's school was rapidly filling with students. At the podium on the opposite end of the stage, David Simon checked lighted indicators that showed the sound system was properly operating. Finally, the hubbub of hundreds of energetic teens subsided.

Miriam Koppel, the school's director, strode to the podium. "Ladies and gentlemen, I know this assembly comes as a surprise. However, I promise bigger surprises yet. Although small and humble compared with many in our district, our school has students who have always impressed me with their talents and capabilities."

For a moment, her voice broke. "Over the years, I've dedicated many hours, inside and outside this building, to searching for ways to help our best pupils enter more than standard degree programs. This has not been an easy task. Today, circumstances are different. For once, I have not had to plead on behalf of worthy students deserving only a chance to prove themselves."

Leaning forward, she smiled. "Today, Tamarack Secondary Academy has the extremely rare opportunity of hosting an illustrious member of the Dil-Terra Interplanetary Alliance's Ministry of Diplomatic Field Service. Teachers and students, I ask you all to stand and join me as I welcome Senior Field Minister Warnach Sirinoya."

Elegantly attired in formal coat that fell to his knees, Warnach strode across the stage and saluted Director Koppel with the ceremonial bow typical on Chikondra. Then, with a broad smile, he faced his audience and saluted them as well. Pleasure showed on his face when many of them spontaneously attempted to copy his bow.

Grasping the sides of the podium, he winked conspiratorially. "Impressive since I imagine that was the first time most of you attempted such a bow. I can tell you that my father and mother used to make me practice ten minutes every single day until I perfected the technique. You cannot imagine my sense of triumph when I finally did it correctly. I started practicing when I was three. I finally mastered the bow when I was eight."

The lighthearted anecdote and subsequent laughter proved an excellent method of focusing the attention of the student body. Warnach smiled at the quiet. "I find myself quite honored to be here, especially considering I'm not the one responsible for today's announcement. However, from another perspective, I know better than anyone the potential that exists in students your age. Several years ago, I met a woman not much older than any of you. Availing herself of a rare opportunity, she applied all her energies until, by age twenty, she had earned two degrees."

"When I came to Earth, that same young woman was assigned to work with me on the project that culminated in Earth's Alliance membership. There is no way to explain how essential her contributions were to that effort. Later, she earned the distinction of being Earth's first citizen ever accepted into the school for diplomatic field services at the famed Chikondran Academy of Diplomatic Sciences. Upon her recent graduation, she was awarded the academy's gold sash in recognition of the highest levels of achievement."

Warnach's smile broadened. "You must forgive me if I sound excessively proud. Not only will that woman serve in the field as my ministry advocate, she has also accepted the even more difficult role of being my ki'mirsah. The closest translation is actually lifemate, but the more common English word is wife.

"It is her idea that brings us together today. She has already taken concrete steps toward transforming a noble concept into a greater reality. Now, I shall let her explain. Please, allow me to introduce to you my ki'mirsah, Ministry Advocate Sandra Warner Sirinoya."

To the sounds of cheers and applause, Sandra approached Warnach and executed a perfect bow. At the podium, her features were alight with humor. "Just so you know, it only took me two years to perfect that bow." Cupping her hand along one side of her mouth as if sharing a secret, she said, "I only practiced from ten until midnight every weeknight."

After laughter subsided, levity disappeared from her face. "I have promised Director Koppel that I wouldn't take too much valuable class time for this announcement. I would, however, like to start by telling you a true story.

"I had just turned seventeen when I was accepted as a member of what we called *the group*. That group consisted of young, highly motivated adults. No one was older than twenty-four. Our goal was to help others, mainly teens, who were caught in a spiral of violence and destruction that characterizes some lesser developed urban areas.

"One night, I was out with several members of our cell when a violent brotherhood caught us in their sights and attacked. The weapons they used were deadly. Two of my best friends were murdered that night. One died on the street, in my arms, behind a construction bin where I had dragged him. Upon finding the other, wounded and bleeding, I performed rescue breathing and first aid until police and paramedics arrived. She died later in hospital with her parents at her side."

Unusual quiet descended over the auditorium. "I had already worked my way into the now-defunct SPEED program. Accelerated studies demanded much of my time and energy. My lost friends, Diana Edwards and Derek McKenzie, had inspired me to doggedly pursue my dream despite the tragedy of losing them. Before the night they died, they had insisted that I take time to define my dreams in the form of goals. Why? Dreams too often grow elusive. Detailed goals require action that makes them attainable. Adding to that formula were promises we made to one another. No matter what, we would never forget the dream and always pursue the goal.

"I could never have done either without support from people who gave generously of time and money. Now, I have an opportunity to repay that generosity. After talking personally with many of you, I spent hours with one of your teachers and his wife. Together, we developed an idea that rapidly approaches reality.

"Today, I'm excited to announce that a foundation is being established in honor of Diana and Derek. Details are not yet finalized, but we have already secured initial approvals to proceed with our plan. Students here at Tamarack will have the opportunity to compete for eight spots on a team that will travel to Chikondra."

Calmly, she waited for the excited murmuring that followed a loud collective gasp. Once attentive quiet returned, she continued, "The students selected will participate in a youth-oriented workshop designed to help them better understand the scope of work required for diplomatic services. Selection will be based on a combination of scholastic achievement and results of verbal and written exams. Participation will be voluntary, and students must be willing to sacrifice time from their summer holidays for the journey."

She smiled at her stunned audience. "The foundation will work to establish sufficient funding to cover costs for transportation and lodging. As a demonstration of commitment, students will be asked to contribute no more than one hundred credits toward their meal expenses. They also will be expected to cover personal expenditures."

Applause erupted, and Sandra waited patiently. "When I was first accepted into CADS, I received several generous grants for the achievement. I hope the contributors will be pleased to know that I have already pledged sixty thousand credits from those grants to this foundation."

Her expression transformed, and her voice quivered slightly. "No one present can possibly suspect the true significance of the next announcement. Neither can anyone imagine how deep my respect and appreciation. Once this foundation is officially chartered and functioning, Minister Sirinoya has generously pledged an additional contribution of a quarter-million credits."

An enormous gasp escaped the audience as everyone rose and applauded until Warnach joined his ki'mirsah. Ceremoniously bowing, he took her hand and kissed it before stepping in front of the podium for closing remarks that included warm thanks for the valuable involvement of David Simon and his wife. Warnach finished by challenging all students to strive for excellence in whatever careers they might choose to pursue.

That evening, Lee Warner helped her daughter finish packing while Warnach spent final hours with Curt and Roy. Chatting about a variety of subjects from the weather to shoe styles, Mrs. Warner wanted to fill every possible second with the sound of her daughter's voice. Finally, with everything neatly packed away, Lee looked around. "You're sure you haven't forgotten anything?"

Sandra gave a quick shake of her head. "I don't think so. I do think I could use a cup of hot chocolate before the guys get back."

Entering the kitchen downstairs, she gazed out the window. Despite a chilly wind, her dad stood alone outside in the dark. "Mom, do you think he's all right?"

Her mother shook her head. "No. I think he's depressed that you're leaving and worried about you traipsing all over the galaxy. Maybe you could go out and spend a few minutes with him. I'll make enough cocoa for everyone."

Stopping inside a covered porch room, Sandra pulled a heavy jacket down from a wall hook and put it on. Sighing somewhat nervously, she opened the door and went to her father. "You should be wearing a hat. That's a pretty raw wind out here."

Somberly, he twisted his head to look at her. "I hadn't noticed."

Stuffing her hand into a pocket, she withdrew a knit cap and handed it to him. "Here."

Silently, he took it but said nothing.

"Daddy, you can't stand out here all night. It's blustery and getting colder. You'll get sick."

"And you could get killed."

"Is that what you're thinking about?"

At last, he turned to face her. "That and a million other things that could happen to you. I can't believe he's letting you risk your life this way."

Carefully, she considered her response. "Daddy, I had planned to do exactly this long before I ever met him. I would have let nothing get in my way. In one way, you should be relieved that I'll be with one of the most experienced senior field ministers in the Alliance's entire diplomatic corps…and the one who travels with the most security."

"That doesn't eliminate the danger."

Swallowing, she pursed her lips together. "No, Daddy, it doesn't. Nothing eliminates danger anywhere. I learned that the hard way when Derek and Diana died. I can stay right here on Earth and be lulled into an even more dangerous complacency."

"You have an answer for everything."

"No, not an answer. Just a perspective that differs from yours."

"You go inside. I'm going to check the gate, and then I'll be in."

"Daddy, before you do, I just want you to know that I understand that you're worried. With good cause. I'm not blind to the risks ahead of me. All I can say is that I'll do my best to be careful and assure you that Warnach will do everything in his power to protect me from harm."

"If something happens to you out there, I will hold him personally responsible. You just remember that, young lady."

"If only you would really get to know him, you might possibly realize how much he would blame himself." Then, spinning on her heel, she returned to a kitchen filled with the sweet aroma of fresh cocoa and the hearty laughter of her lifemate and her two brothers.

～

Four days later, Warnach knelt with Sandra on his right and John and Angela to his left. Fragrant, smoky haze swirled inside the vast cathedral with its soaring arched ceilings supported by carved columns. From a balcony behind them, a choir filled the chamber with angelic hymns such as he had never heard. The church interior held a wealth of detailed sculptures and beautiful paintings. Penetrating sunshine enhanced the jewel-like colors of stained glass windows as invading light formed soft-edged rays shining upon pews filled with worshippers.

Exchanges between the distinguished priest and the congregation fascinated Warnach. Sandra's thorough explanation of the mass progression had prepared him for the rising, sitting, and kneeling. Although John had indicated it would be acceptable for him to remain seated, Warnach had derived unique satisfaction from being able to share with Sandra some of the rituals of her faith for the very first time.

Shared prayer followed by the exchange of individual wishes for peace struck melodic tones within his soul. When Sandra sidestepped between pews and moved forward with John and Angela to receive communion, he watched with intense interest. Smiling to himself, he thought how reverent she appeared. He also noted how several people smiled warm greetings or reached out to touch her hand as she slowly walked up the aisle. Knowing this had been the church she had attended before her departure to Chikondra, he felt gladdened to see her welcomed with such regard.

By the time the priest pronounced a final blessing and recessed from the altar, Warnach smiled broadly at the crush of people that gathered around his lifemate. Several he remembered as her co-workers from division headquarters. Hugs and compliments abounded, and congratulations, some starkly amazed, were offered to both of them. More elegant and distinguished than ever, Warnach acknowledged each with exceptional courtesy and sincerity.

A little later, over coffee, Monsignor Salinas listened attentively as Warnach described some of the faith practices observed on Chikondra. The two engaged in lively dialogue regarding distinctive differences in rituals and the many similarities in fundamental concepts. Their discussion held Sandra's rapt attention as her personal ideas of God's true universality quickly solidified inside her mind. Still, she remained silent, learning more about her own faith as well as that of her lifemate.

The next morning, after rising early, she went out for a brisk walk before quickly showering and getting dressed. Allowing Warnach the rare treat of sleeping in, she joined Angela and John for a light breakfast and prepared to leave the house.

"John," she said as she pulled on a coat and gathered her purse and portfolio, "thanks for looking after Warnach this morning. Oh! By the way, are we still meeting for lunch?"

John chuckled as he shook his head. "Are you sure you're going to have time?"

She responded with a brilliant smile. "Let's see. Lunch with two of my favorite people in the entire galaxy plus my handsome lifemate? Wouldn't miss it!" Suddenly, she swayed and staggered back a step.

"Mmm," a low voice sounded in her ear. Dark eyes gleamed with mischief as he winked at John and Angela. "Such a fortunate man I am to wake up and hear my lovely lifemate describing me as handsome - just before she sneaks out of the house to leave me behind."

Closing her eyes, she tilted her head back against his shoulder. "You are handsome, my dear Minister Sirinoya, and I thought you wanted to sleep in."

Following a lighthearted round of teasing, Warnach walked her to the front door. "I hope all goes according to your plans today."

Her eyes studied his expression. "I'm confident it will." She reached up and ran her fingertips along his unshaven cheek. "If it doesn't, I'll find another alternative. What matters most is your support. You'll never know how much I admire you for backing me up in this."

Half an hour later, she sat in the reception lounge at McKenzie, Jacobs, and Daniels. Plush carpeting covered the floor, and its dark gray provided luxurious contrast for the sleek lines of contemporary chairs upholstered in fabrics woven in a geometric pattern of white on light gray. Floral arrangements in shades of blue, blush pink, and white enhanced the subdued elegance of the décor.

The slim man who had greeted Sandra upon her arrival looked up suddenly. A door had opened, and a very tall, broad-shouldered man appeared. "Sandra! My heavens! How wonderful it is to see you!"

Rising, she took only a single step before he overtook her in a massive hug. When he released her, she stood back and looked up into freckled features that never seemed to age. "I feel exactly the same way. How are you?"

His smile held affectionate warmth. "Doing well. Please, let's go inside my office where we can talk. Would you like some coffee?" Receiving an affirmative nod, he turned toward the reception desk. "Anthony, would you please bring us a carafe of coffee?"

Avoiding the formalities of his executive desk, he invited her to sit on a sofa beside him. After Anthony left them with cups of fresh coffee, Mr. McKenzie smiled appraisingly. Her mannerisms held what he could only describe as understated confidence. "You look so different."

Smiling back at him, she took a sip of hot coffee. "I suppose that's to be expected. I'm older, and my life has changed completely."

Curiously, he pointed. "That band you wear on your head. It's quite striking. What is it?"

Delicately, she rested her fingertips against it for a moment. "It's called Kitak. You might consider it a wedding ring - Chikondran style."

His mouth tensed for a moment, but he quickly recovered. "You look happy. I must admit. I was pretty shocked when Angela told me about you and Minister Sirinoya."

"I imagine most people were," she said with a wry grin. "Anyway, he's helped me overcome so much. At the same time, he's made me happier than I ever thought I could be."

"I'm glad, Sandra," he replied sincerely. "You've seen much too much tragedy for someone your age. You deserve happiness, and it looks like you've found it." He paused, thinking how quickly his own happiness had started to collapse after the death of his only son. Drawing in a resigned breath, he went on. "Now, when I talked with you, you said you had a business matter to discuss. How can I help you?"

Slowly standing, she paced across the room and looked out the window. Sighing, she faced him again. "Mr. McKenzie, I need your professional help. I want to establish a foundation to promote students who are seriously considering diplomatic careers. I'm going to need administration of all legal aspects, management of investments, and assistance and guidance when it comes to soliciting interested sponsors and contributors.

"I've already drawn up detailed plans for what I'd like to do and how. Most of the grant money I received when I earned entrance to CADS will go toward initial funding. Then, if I can set everything else in motion, Warnach has offered to contribute a quarter-million credits."

Failing to note near disbelief on Michael McKenzie's lightly freckled features, she fell silent. Her eyes grew distant as she listened to voices from the past. "I also want to name the foundation in memory of Derek and Diana."

"Sandra?" Strong hands grasped her shoulders and snapped her from regression to that terrible night when two young lives had ended. "Sandra, did I just hear you correctly?"

Shaking herself back into the present, she looked contemplative. "Mr. McKenzie, I was hoping you'd be willing to help me. I'm not asking you to do this out of the goodness of your heart. Your services would be compensated, of course. Too much work is involved not to pay you. I came to you because I know I can trust you."

Watery film covered blue eyes. His chin quivered slightly. "I have to ask. How can your husband be so willing to support this when…"

"When the foundation is set up in Derek's memory as well as Diana's?" Dropping her face, she breathed in and out. "Mr. McKenzie, Warnach is so good and so wise. He understands that Derek was an integral factor in helping me become who I am today. He's also completely confident in the love he and I share. We've discussed the matter thoroughly, and he has given me his blessing."

For the next hour, the two reviewed her initial plans and outline. Impressed with intent and implementation plans, Michael McKenzie discovered means of diversion from the emptiness that increasingly filled his personal life. His wife had been devastated by Derek's death. Despite all their efforts, both he and Mary, his daughter, had watched helplessly as Stella McKenzie slipped more and more into the past.

Ever since the loss of their son, Mrs. McKenzie had steadily receded into her bottomless well of mourning. She had visited her son's grave nearly every day since the funeral where she had collapsed. Counseling and other treatments for depression had failed miserably. Only when she spoke of her son's heroism and brilliance did she show any spark at all. Her husband and her daughter were regularly subjected to tearful lectures and accusations that they had forsaken Derek's memory.

For years, Stella McKenzie had been able to boast with pride that her son's fiancée had remained faithful to Derek. The news of Sandra's marriage had set the final bars on a personal prison. According to Mrs. McKenzie, Sandra had betrayed the love Derek had given her. Retreating into a reclusive shell, she swore that, although alone, she would never forfeit her son's memory.

Impelling sad thoughts to a far corner of his heart, Mr. McKenzie smiled at Sandra with renewed appreciation and admiration. "Have you thought of a specific name for the trust?"

"Not really. I thought you might help me with that detail."

"Well, I think we should keep it simple. Very simple. My suggestion is that we register it as the Edwards-McKenzie Memorial Foundation. I have some ideas for a very emotional charter and mission statement."

Her smile glowed. "Then, you accept the job?"

This time, he reached out and clutched her hand tightly. "How can I not? Sandra, I've wanted to retire early, but I wasn't sure what I'd do with my time. Now? I know." Standing, he helped her up with the hand he hadn't yet released. "How do I thank you for this?"

Moving into his arms, she rested her face against his broad chest. "I really don't want any thanks as long as you help me keep their dreams alive. That's all I ask."

∼

Glancing at the time displayed by the slim watch on her wrist, she sighed with relief. There should be plenty of time before she had to leave to meet John and Warnach at division headquarters for a late lunch. Descending and then docking her rented transport, she carefully removed two containers from the floor on the passenger side. Lifting her face, she noted the ornate scrollwork of iron gates.

Resolutely, she walked along the brick path. Grasses were still exchanging summer greens for winter browns. Branches on tall trees clung to a few rebellious leaves that resisted the wind-tossed journey to the ground. Benches were conveniently located in front of stone edifices and near clusters of carved monuments.

Sniffing richly fragrant roses, she marched on through the chill of a late autumn day. Her feet knew where to take her as her mind wandered. Finally, she found herself stopping. Perched atop a simple obelisk, a robed angel stared heavenward. Without awareness of cold, hard ground, she knelt. Carefully setting her containers beside her, she crossed herself and recited the Lord's Prayer that had always been her favorite. With a faint smile on her face, she reached out and traced carvings that spelled Diana's name.

As she placed the weighted resin container of roses into an insert in the ledge around the grave marker, she spoke softly. "Hello, my friend. I hope you can forgive me for not visiting for so long. To make up for it, I brought your favorites, red roses. Oh, Diana, there's so much to tell you."

Twenty minutes later, she was again on her knees. Having completed the Lord's Prayer a second time, she picked up a scrap of windblown debris and tucked it into her coat pocket until she could deposit it in a trash receptacle. Then, as before, she carefully secured the second container before arranging an assortment of white and yellow roses.

Settling on prickly grass, she ran her hands from side to side, just above the grassy fringe blanketing Derek's grave. "Derek," she began in a quivering voice, "I hope you still like roses. I know it's been a long time. I needed to talk to you - to tell you. I kept my promises. Just like we always discussed. If you can believe this, I've graduated from the Chikondran Academy of Diplomatic Sciences. It was an indescribable feeling. Even better is that I already have a position as a ministry advocate to a senior field services minister. At the end of this week, I'm leaving on my first mission."

Her hand rose to her face and wiped away a single track of tears. "Derek, there's something else. I want you to know that I've never forgotten you, and I never will. You know how much I loved you, but things have changed for me. I met someone very special. He's Chikondran and... Well, he's the field minister I told you I was working with before we secured Earth's Alliance membership. What I didn't tell you is how much I love him.

"Derek, we've actually unified according to Chikondran traditions, so I guess you could say I'm married now." She laughed nervously. "Falling in love with him caught me by surprise. It really did. The good thing is that he loves me, too. For the very first time in my life, I feel completely happy. Especially after I lost you, I was convinced I'd never find happiness again, but I was wrong. There's no need to worry about me anymore. I've found my way and the right path to the destiny I think was waiting for me all along. Anyway, I - I just wanted you to know. I also wanted to remind you that I still treasure all we shared."

Once again, she ran her hand across the length of the gravesite.

"I'll try to come back from time to time. Just so you know you're not forgotten." Stiffly unfolding chilled legs, she stood up and stared at Derek's image encrusted in the stone marker. "Farewell, Derek."

Turning to leave, she stopped abruptly. With her mouth open, she stared into serious eyes and a sad face. "I...I... How long?"

"A while. I had the feeling I might find you here. Are you okay?"

Letting go of an enormous breath, she closed her eyes for mere seconds and then reached for the gloved hand extended to her. "I hope you don't think I've lost my mind."

Finally, Angela smiled. "Not at all. I still check in on Derek myself. Every time I come for a visit with Diana."

"Not just that."

"I know exactly what you meant. I honestly didn't mean to eavesdrop. However, I am glad you could tell Derek about Warnach. Sometimes, it's almost impossible to really leave the past where it belongs. You just put to rest any lingering concerns I might have had."

Walking hand in hand back toward the cemetery gates, Sandra sighed. "Angela, there's no need to be concerned. Warnach is everything to me. It's like I told Derek back there. I firmly believe Warnach was always the destiny awaiting me."

Conversation was subdued as they approached Sandra's transport. Angela had arrived via public transport, instinctively knowing where she'd find her daughter's friend. Together, they traveled toward Alliance headquarters to join John and Warnach.

While waiting in a luxurious reception area, Sandra's head suddenly lifted upon hearing the jolly greeting from Liz. Hugging tightly, the two both laughed before launching into their usual habit of rapid-fire teases and questions.

"So, I suppose you really expected John to show up on time with Mr. TDH, right?" Lis asked at last.

Laughter chased all traces of shadows from Sandra's eyes. "What disappoints me is that Mr. TDH didn't break away to perpetuate the famed reputation Chikondrans have for punctuality."

Humorously, Angela squinted at her two companions. "Mr. TDH? What's that supposed to mean?"

Trying not to laugh too loud, Sandra said, "It's what I call a Liz-ism. You know. A name with a story? TDH. Tall, dark, and handsome. As in my Warnach."

Suddenly, she felt hands tightly grasping her arms from behind. "Twice in one day, I hear my lovely ki'mirsah describe me as handsome. So fortunate am I that I think I should treat her to a nice lunch."

Looking back over her shoulder, she grinned. "Including steak?"

"Oh!" he groaned while drawing his face into a mask of revulsion. "Forget that offer of lunch. Instead, I think I shall go someplace where I can be sick in private."

Warnach had already invited Liz to join them, so lunch continued along similarly humorous lines. Camaraderie bound close friends in dynamic conversation and spontaneous laughter. Drawn into the small, private circle that had once surrounded Sandra so affectionately and so protectively, Warnach thoroughly enjoyed the spirited company while thinking how fortunate they both were to possess such loyal, vital friendships.

# Chapter Fourteen

"Angela?" John called out. "Is Sandra back yet?"

Setting aside the electronic book on her lap, Angela glanced upward and smiled at her husband, who had just returned home from an errand with Warnach. "She got back a while ago and said she was going over to the park for a walk. I'm glad you two are back. She seemed distant for some reason."

"Distant?" Warnach asked curiously. "In what way?"

Angela frowned slightly. "I'm not sure. Maybe I just worry too much, but she wasn't smiling and really didn't seem to want to talk."

Wondering if her most recent morning meeting with Michael McKenzie had prompted a surge of sad memories, Warnach's brow creased. "Well, if you two will excuse me, I think I'll go look for her."

An odd feeling niggled its way into Warnach's mind as he re-buttoned his light coat to ward off autumn's chill. Outside, his purposeful stride carried him quickly toward the park near the Edwards home. By the time he reached the entrance, stiffening winds prompted him to snuggle deeper into his coat. Several minutes passed as he walked along graveled paths.

Suddenly, he stopped when he spotted her on a park bench. Across a wide expanse of grassy turf, seemingly oblivious to dropping temperatures, she sat sideways with legs bent and her feet on the seat. Her face rested on her right arm that stretched out along the back of the bench. Slowly, he approached her. "Sandra?" he said softly.

She lifted a sad smile in response. Tears stained her cheeks. Wordlessly, she stared at him.

"Shi'níyah? What's wrong?" he asked worriedly.

"Oh, Warnach, Miguel contacted me from Santa Ana. It's Cafti. I've lost her. Sh…she died last night."

"Oh, Sandra, I'm so sorry. She was such a wonderful woman. I know how much you loved her."

"Warnach, she gave me so much. Sitting here, I couldn't help but think of all the ways she changed my life. She did so much more than teach me your language. Had it not been for Cafti, I don't think I could have possibly accomplished half of what I've done. I know it sounds selfish, but it's too hard to accept that I've really lost her."

That evening, Angela insisted that Sandra eat dinner. Sympathetically, friends and lifemate listened as conversation turned to fond memories of a fascinating woman filled with intelligence and wisdom. Even Warnach had not realized the full extent to which Cafti had influenced the life of his ki'mirsah.

As teacher, Cafti had utilized lessons on Chikondran language and culture to inspire Sandra into believing she could accomplish transformation of dreams into defined direction. As friend and mentor, she had been instrumental in guiding her young friend through the traumatic aftermath following the violent deaths of Derek McKenzie and Diana Edwards. Cafti's refusal to meekly surrender to terminal illness had provided continual reminder never to yield to fear, sorrow, or loss.

That evening, John and Angela joined their guests when, following traditional chants, Warnach's voice directed evening prayers to the Great Spirit on Cafti's behalf. Upon ending, he briefly opened his eyes to check on his ki'mirsah. Tears ran unchecked down her cheeks. Her lips moved together, reciting prayers tied to the faith she had accepted here in her own world. As she finished, he noted the touching way she formed her most personal gesture of faith, the sign of the cross.

Late into the night, sensing her restlessness, Warnach sat up in bed and lit a small bedside lamp. "Shi'níyah, you need to sleep."

Stretching wearily, she turned onto her side. "I'm sorry, Warnach. You're not getting any rest. I think I'll go sleep on the sofa." She started to sit up, but a firm hand restrained her.

"You always forget that I share your sadness as well as your happiness. I will not let you leave me. My concern is that you get some rest."

Her jaw tensed. "Warnach." Her voice choked momentarily. "I just can't get her out of my mind."

Thoughtfully, he extinguished the light. Lying back down, he caressed her damp face in the darkness. "Shi'níyah," he began quietly, "her final request was that you celebrate the great friendship you shared instead of mourning her death. Let me offer a suggestion. For tonight, let your mind place thoughts of Cafti into the care of your heart. Rest, me'u Shi'níyah." Then, he placed cerea-nervos against her forehead until electrical pulsations projected the tranquilizing effect that coaxed her to sleep.

The next day, Sandra rose very early and went alone to mass. Very few people were present in the church. Within the peaceful embrace of her faith, confounded thoughts calmed. When she knelt to light a candle in memory of her friend, she felt a gentle swirl of air around her face and shoulders. No longer imprisoned by constant pain, Cafti's spirit had surely been set free. That sweet spirit had just reminded her that her teacher's love would never abandon her.

By the weekend, she began to recover her spirits and her perspective. Like Cafti, Warnach had wisely refused to let her wallow in sorrow. By redirecting her energies toward preparations for their departure from Earth and their first diplomatic mission together, he helped her refocus on the good lying ahead without sacrificing the beauty of precious memories.

~

Collapsing onto a thickly padded mat, Sandra lay flat on her back with arms and legs extended. Perspiration soaked blue workout leotards, and sweat covered her face with a glossy sheen. Closing her eyes against overhead lights, she concentrated on slowing her breathing and flexing muscles that refused to relax after ten minutes of cooling down from a brutal workout.

"My friend, I may be mistaken, but it appears your new advocate may be quite useless tomorrow."

Warnach's wide, arching eyebrows lifted. "Forsij, I fear you may be right."

Drawing in a ragged breath, Sandra kept her eyes closed and rolled her head from side to side. "This is a restricted workout area. Women only. Go away."

Warnach's dark eyes glittered. "Women only? I think the ragdoll I saw in your room on Earth more accurately describes that limp body I see lying there."

Remaining on the floor, she groaned. "Next time we visit my parents, I know one Chikondran who can camp outside under a tree."

"Is your advocate always so vengeful?"

"Only when highly stressed," Warnach answered matter-of-factly.

"Gentlemen," she called out in a warning tone, "might I suggest caution? There's nothing in the universe more dangerous than a stressed Terran female who doesn't want the love of her life or his friend to see her looking her very worst."

Forsij blew out a sharp breath. "A suggestion, my friend. I've heard this species can become quite aggressive when even a single hair is out of place. Perhaps we should evacuate and escape possible attack."

Laughingly, Warnach said, "Perhaps, Forsij, your strategy is the safest course. I think our dinner invitation can wait."

Three-quarters of an hour later, attired in nashavri fashioned from shimmering purple fabric, Sandra appeared in the officers' lounge Warnach had jokingly described as safe shelter. Green eyes roved across the room and swiftly spotted the table where her ki'medsah sat, immersed in conversation with Captain Tibrab. Her entire face expressed mock warning in the hope of discouraging a fresh round of humorous teasing.

Both Forsij Tibrab and Warnach immediately rose to their feet upon noting her approach. Following a deep bow, Forsij spoke first as his eyes shifted toward Warnach. "My friend, it seems your advocate is remarkably revived."

Gleaming eyes approvingly assessed her image from head to toe. "Revived, Forsij, and more beautiful than ever."

Reaching out to take the hands he offered her, Sandra smiled appreciatively at his compliment. "I thank you, my ki'medsah." Shifting her glance, she acknowledged Forsij Tibrab. "Good evening, Captain Tibrab."

Respectfully, he bowed his head. "Good evening, Mirsah Sirinoya."

Her mouth spread into a highly amused grin. "You know you can call me Sandra."

"Ah, Mirsah Sirinoya, just as you know that you may address me as Forsij."

The accusatory gleam in his eyes sparked lighthearted, musical laughter. "All right," she conceded graciously. "Good evening, Forsij."

Over dinner, the three discussed the mission that would begin the next day upon the Curasalah's entry into orbit around Frehatar. Warnach's assignment was to review terms of a treaty tentatively accepted by Frehataran leaders during the summit on Chikondra. Once all was deemed to be in order, he would preside over a formal signing ceremony and extend an invitation for Frehatar to initiate proceedings to join the Alliance.

Despite careful development of guidelines and general accord, such treaties still faced the prospect of collapse before ratification could be finalized. Last-minute disputes could potentially send negotiators scrambling to avoid renewed confrontation to salvage fragile peace. Warnach's primary goal would be to meet with each side of the Frehataran leadership to identify and subsequently mediate any possible points of contention before they could negatively impact treaty implementation.

"With any official ceremony unlikely before another four weeks, I wish I could remain in orbit with the Curasalah. After all that happened here the last time, I worry since the Valiant won't reach Frehatar for another ten days."

"Do you fear the treaty will fall apart so quickly?" Warnach leaned back into his chair and brought a stemmed glass to his lips.

"It wouldn't be the first time. Considering how volatile Frehatar has been over the past several decades…" He paused and noted Sandra's thoughtful expression. "Your advocate will be on her first mission. An uneventful initiation would not be so terrible."

Warnach's eyes strayed to his lifemate's face before returning to meet Forsij's gaze. "You worry almost as much as Badrik. Sandra is prepared quite well to face whatever circumstances we meet. Actually, her presence gives me far greater confidence. While she oversees all the underlying details, I'll be free to concentrate fully on consultations."

Forsij's face assumed a pensive look. "You amaze me, Sandra."

Surprised by his remark, her eyebrows lifted. "How so?"

"I know of no other ministry advocate who would dare to accompany Warnach down to Frehatar tomorrow. A very brave woman you must be to undertake such a crucial mission assignment with the likes of your ki'medsah."

A short laugh escaped as she shook her head. "Not everyone understands him the way I do."

"Is such understanding the key?"

"I think so," she said, aiming a smile at her lifemate. "That - plus sharing his vision and goals. I plan on combining our unique synergy with hard work to give him the support he needs. Add to that the fact that I quickly learned to stay out of his way when he's on a rampage - success is virtually guaranteed."

Choking on the liqueur he had just swallowed, Warnach barely managed to set his glass down without toppling it. At the same time, Sandra covered her mouth with her hand to avoid laughing while Forsij stared at them both with amused assessment.

Finally catching his breath, Warnach fixed glittering black eyes on his ki'mirsah. "Me'u Shi'níyah, your words leave me nearly speechless. Have I ever been so terrible with you?"

With lips pursed tightly together, her features formed a pained grimace. "On a few rare occasions."

Directing a swift glance across the table, Forsij rose from the table. "I think this is an opportune time for the Curasalah's captain to excuse himself for a pre-orbit inspection of his ship. Good evening."

Awkward silence lasted more than a minute as Warnach gazed into her blushing face. Finally, he broke the silence. "Rampage? Was that term really fair?"

Comically, she scrunched her face and asked defensively, "Maybe it's a word that doesn't translate so well?"

"Rampage," he repeated distinctly. "Rampage?"

Luminously shadowed eyelids dropped. "Whatever the right word, you must admit that it's much easier to avoid you whenever you…" Stopping in fear of making things worse, she smiled flirtatiously. "You know, the observation deck is usually deserted at this hour. Looking out at passing constellations strikes me as a very romantic way to spend a few minutes together before our mission begins tomorrow."

Warnach's broad shoulders shook as he laughed. "Shi'níyah, if you utilize those same tactics in negotiation processes, I fear the entire Alliance may triple before you complete ten years of ministry service."

Leaving her chair, she walked behind him and leaned forward, sliding her arms over his shoulders. Pressing her cheek against the side of his face, she whispered softly, "My ki'medsah, I think I need a gallant rescue. Will you not be my hero?"

Pulling her with him, he leaned forward and drank the last of his liqueur. "I believe it's too late. As I recall, Badrik is your hero."

"Mmm," she murmured in a seductive voice. "I did say that, didn't I?"

Coolly, he replied, "Yes, you did."

Sandra Valencia

"Well, since my hero isn't present to rescue me, I suppose I shall have to take myself alone to the observation deck." Sighing heavily into his ear, she moved slightly away. "On second thought, perhaps I need only a simple rescue from my gallant lover."

Grinning crookedly, Warnach conceded defeat. Rising, he turned and looked into her eyes. "Why is it you make it so impossible to be angry with you?"

Reaching for his hand, she smiled provocatively. "Because I love you so much?"

~

The slight sensation of the shuttle landing on solid surface magnified a hundred-fold within the pit of her stomach. Outward calm belied jittery insides. Twice, she breathed in deeply and exhaled. Mental discipline overtook anxiety as her mind swiftly clicked off a review of steps related to both protocol and practicality.

Warnach noted the shift in her expression. Her ability to alter mood and thought mode never failed to impress him. For a moment, his thoughts drifted backward in time to the beginning of his first mission as a ministry advocate. Anxiety had tempered any excitement. He had forced himself to concentrate on instructions from the minister he had served. For months, he could hardly believe he hadn't made a complete fool of himself during that trying mission.

Suddenly, her head tilted as her eyes sought his. The faintest of smiles played at the corners of her mouth. Placing her hand firmly in his, she rose from her seat. Stepping into the aisle, she only nodded before smoothing the fabric of her suit.

"Shi'níyah," he reminded, "our purpose here is to expedite the review of amendments proposed to the treaty and secure agreement to any changes.

256

Hopefully, we can finalize the accord. Considering our success at the summit, I believe your presence as my lifemate may actually exceed the importance of your role as advocate. That's why I want you to disembark by my side, not behind me with other staff."

Nodding seriously, she replied, "Understood."

"Don't worry." A slight grin crossed his face. "I promise more than sufficient work to occupy your time."

Finally, she smiled back at him. "I know. Relationships are even more essential than all the hard work. I'll be fine." She inclined her head forward. "Looks like they're ready for us to exit."

Staring outside through tall, narrow windows a week later, she allowed her gaze to follow Warnach as he strolled across a heavily guarded courtyard. Her mind strayed as she recalled their arrival. The old cliché about pomp and circumstance had applied perfectly. Military bands had performed rousing musical arrangements. Flag bearers had pranced, twisted, and tossed banners, creating colorful choreography high in the air above their heads. Uniformed children formed precisely organized, high-stepping columns that eventually circled arriving diplomats. Several broke the circle and created arrow-straight lines between which leadership from both Frehataran parties had marched forward to greet the famed Minister Sirinoya. In fluid, perfect synchronization, Minister Sirinoya and his ministry advocate had performed the elegant Chikondran bow and personally greeted the Frehataran representatives.

From the moment of their arrival, time had assumed the velocity of a whirlwind. Utilizing the meticulously developed schedule she had planned, Warnach had moved smoothly from one meeting to the next. Managing the time she had allotted with exceptional precision, he had accomplished remarkable progress while addressing concerns and resistance regarding a variety of points incorporated into the treaty draft.

The previous night, for the first time since their arrival on Frehatar, they had returned to their suite before midnight. Sitting with her on a sofa,

Warnach's expression, holding critical appraisal, softened at last when he gave her an admiring smile.

"Sandra," he had begun in a carefully modulated voice, "the last time I was on Frehatar, every day presented one crisis after another. Both Rodan and I wondered if we could ever accomplish a working truce. I honestly began to doubt how much longer I could effectively continue diplomatic service. I even contemplated resigning from the ministry." He paused, and his gaze held steady. "I tell you this now without any consideration for the fact that you're my lifemate. The itinerary you scheduled for this mission has blended complicated agenda items with exceptional time management. I've been able to proceed from meeting to meeting in a way that has permitted a logical, practical flow of ideas. Whether by intention or intuition, your plan has given me the freedom to determine who thought what and why, as well as how I could utilize that foresight."

Stopping and noting only humbled silence, he continued with quiet pride. "I am confident that we face a quicker, more successful completion of this mission than anyone ever expected. Much of that is owed to your organization and the depth of the analyses you prepared. I'm very impressed with your work and very proud to have you as my colleague."

Her thoughts returned to the present. She watched as Warnach shook hands with Kapezi Tiltriam, leader of the most unyielding Frehataran party. Both men were smiling amiably as they turned to stroll back toward the meeting center.

Without conscious realization, she also smiled. The night before, she had earned Warnach's professional esteem. His appraisal had satisfied two dearly held goals. One was to become a productive member of the Alliance's field service corps; the other was to alleviate the constant burdens he had carried so that his diplomatic skills could be applied to consummate peace initiatives.

Sighing, she resumed her review of plans for that evening's state dinner. Despite continuing the complex ballet of diplomacy, she looked forward to an event where she could set aside her role as Ministry Advocate Sirinoya in exchange for her cherished identity as Mirsah Sandra Sirinoya.

Days later, following minor modifications to the Frehataran Accords, the voluminous agreement was completed well ahead of Warnach's original estimate. All parties expressed significant confidence as they gathered for the dignified ceremonial signing of the treaty.

Journalists transmitted details of the historic agreement promising far-reaching benefits for the heavily populated Delatar System. Photographs of the event captured the image of Chikondra's Minister Sirinoya, whose legendary reputation had gained heightened attention. Many of those pictures also included the dedicated advocate who had quickly become essential to the famous field minister's vocation.

～

Warnach literally bounced in shock when, with a spontaneous, nerve-jarring whoop, his lifemate raced past him and leapt onto their bed. Arms and legs sprawled away from her body at awkward angles as she wiggled herself deeper into the softness of the mattress.

"Home!" she cried out ecstatically. "My own room! My own bed!"

Shaking his head as he approached her, Warnach clicked his tongue in mock reproach. "My dear advocate! Such undignified behavior from a ministry professional!"

Her eyes closed, and her mouth formed an impossibly huge smile. "My dear Minister Sirinoya! I don't care about professional! I don't care about dignified! All I care about is sleeping in my own bed for the first time in almost six months!"

Seized by her enthusiasm, he kicked off his shoes and fell backward onto the enormous mattress. For several moments, he lay very still. Suddenly, he surrendered completely and joined her laughter. Within seconds, the bed shook as, laughing together with utter freedom, they turned toward each other for a rowdy, rolling embrace.

At last, lying relaxed and still, they stared upward at the vaulted and beamed ceiling. Quietly, he mused, "In all the years I've lived in this house, I can recall only one other homecoming that compares with this."

Her voice was a quiet murmur. "When was that?"

Expelling a deep breath and turning his head, he gazed at her through mists of memory. "The day I brought you to Chikondra to live."

Contentedly, she scooted closer and rested her head against his shoulder. Twisting slightly, he touched sensitive lips against silken hair. His thoughts entertained mere wisps of lonely memories that reinforced the deep fulfillment now in his possession.

~

By midsummer on Chikondra, they returned from mission yet again. Hostilities on Bederand had flared unexpectedly. Even Bederandan leaders claimed to be perplexed by continual outbursts of violence that, although quickly contained, were gradually diminishing the effectiveness of processes initiated to build lasting peace. Once again, Warnach dedicated hours upon hours to exhaustive discussions while attempting to identify root causes of recurring issues in hopes of devising permanent solutions.

In private, certain that Zeteron tactics lay behind persistent problems, he discussed mounting concerns with his advocate. Analyses based on extensive experience were augmented by intuition. If Bederand should fall victim to all-out war, he was certain that Zeteron incursions would expand with newfound boldness.

Surprised upon learning that his lifemate had once encountered a party of Zeterons supposedly visiting Earth for humanitarian purposes, he questioned her extensively. Her answers left him evermore convinced. Although unable to provide any concrete explanations, she had described her perception of feeling threatened by no more than their presence. He merely nodded pensively, saying nothing aloud. Quickly, he was learning how much her instincts merited respect and trust.

Leaving a more settled Bederand, they had squeezed in a quick visit to Earth. While there, Sandra met with Michael McKenzie, who had joined forces with John and Angela Edwards to quickly establish and promote the Edwards-McKenzie Memorial Foundation. They had already orchestrated the selection process for the pool from which the first group of students would be chosen to visit Chikondra. All that remained was for the Sirinoyas to validate final decisions with interviews and their personal seal of approval.

The couple had then spent several days with Sandra's family. Dave Warner had shown affection toward his daughter, but his conduct with Warnach remained stiff and reserved. Beyond that, the visit had fulfilled her needs for reconnection with her family.

While in her hometown, they personally met finalists for the workshop. Decisions presented more difficulty than ever expected. Students had prepared themselves exceptionally well with enthusiasm that was inspirational. During prolonged afternoon talks with teachers, school administrators, and David Simon, Sandra found the prospect of disappointing any of the eleven finalists, including Roy Warner, nerve-wracking.

In the end, with a grin and a kiss, Warnach resolved the quandary into which his lifemate had sunk. Based on the generosity of additional sponsors attracted by Michael McKenzie, he suggested an increase in the number of grants to ten. To avoid draining funds from the foundation or drawing questions regarding potential favoritism, he would personally finance Roy as the eleventh student.

Amused laughter shook her shoulders as she gazed into her lifemate's smiling face. Then, without warning, she had launched herself into his arms for an extremely noisy kiss that drew rowdy applause and whistles from teachers and school officials who had devoted untold hours of personal time to the project.

Upon returning to Ministry Headquarters in Kadranas two weeks later, reports and briefings regarding conditions on Bederand were completed and delivered. At the same time, Warnach undertook a review of issues before the Chikondra High Council. Interesting but nevertheless tedious research frequently ended hours earlier than normal for him. His lifemate provided double benefit. Her organizational skills dramatically improved workflow. Her presence provided inspiration to complete difficult tasks more quickly.

∾

"Warnach!" she called loudly from the base of the staircase. "We need to leave! The shuttle is due in an hour and a half!"

"Patience, Shi'níyah," he laughed as, adjusting his collar, he appeared at the top of the steps. "We need only forty minutes to reach the shuttleport." His footsteps clicked a quick, even rhythm as he trotted downstairs. Taking her by the shoulders, he stared sternly into merrily glittering eyes. "A bit anxious, are you not?"

Unable to maintain a responding pout, she let go of a short burst of giggles. Affectionately, he hugged her close. "Let's go meet that brother of yours."

Entering the terminal center, Warnach practically ran to keep up with his lifemate. "Sandra! Not so fast! We have to…"

Kicking into faster gear, she turned sharply left, dodging other port pedestrians and agilely sidestepping a robotic cart. "Badrik!" she greeted, propelling herself between two startled groups of travelers. Instantaneously, her arms flew up and around his neck. "Thank you for coming to help!"

Winking mischievously at Warnach, Badrik locked his arms around her. "Careful, little sister! Security might come and carry both of us away if people start toppling over in your wake!"

Blushing, she gave him a jolly, not-too-sincere grin. "Sorry, big brother. I guess I'm feeling a little overly enthusiastic."

"My apologies, dear brother," Warnach added as he joined them. "To my astonishment, my lifemate is more highly charged today than usual."

"So I see. Come." Tucking Sandra's arm beneath his, Badrik led the way through the busy terminal to the concourse receiving arrivals from orbiting spaceships.

Sitting back to wait in a reserved lounge area, both men barely contained amusement while watching her jump up every few minutes to peer out through wide observation windows and then pace back and forth before sitting down again beside Warnach.

By her eighth trip to the window, Badrik's black eyebrows lifted, and a comical expression lit his dark features. "Brother, have you no way to calm your ki'mirsah? I fear her anxiety may cause her to collapse before the shuttle even lands."

Reaching out, Warnach took her hand and pulled her toward the plush seat beside him. "Shi'níyah, ten minutes more. Relax."

Sheepishly, she smiled and settled herself beside him. "Forgive me?"

"For what? Just save that energy for the arrival. There will be much to do."

Twenty minutes later, passengers began to disembark and approach security kiosks. Despite being out of uniform, Badrik's mere presence gained them access past security barriers. David and Patricia Simon, who were both acting as chaperones, were the first of the foundation's visiting party to appear from the arrival tunnel. Instantly, they looked in Sandra's direction with enormous smiles lighting their faces.

Completing arrival formalities and passing the kiosk, both hugged Sandra in greeting. Warnach welcomed each before introducing them to Badrik. All five turned their attention to other chaperones and students who were processing quickly through the receiving lines.

As if deliberately prolonging his sister's anticipation, Roy loitered at the end of the line with his friend, Amanda. Leaning toward each other, the two laughingly shared comments until finally advancing. Before exiting the kiosk, Roy peeked around the edge, grinning directly at Warnach. "Control her, will you?" Finally rounding the corner, he found himself enthusiastically captured within his sister's bone-crunching embrace.

That evening, Warnach began the descent of his transport toward home. Quiet conversation between Sandra and Roy was heavenly relief after an afternoon filled with non-stop chatter and laughter from eleven excited teenagers. Four chaperones, all secondary educators, had earned high respect from an experienced dignitary who secretly vowed that the next time he ran into recalcitrant negotiating parties on some war-bent planet, he would simply subject them to the torture of being locked up with fifty teenagers for ten hours. Still, despite the chaos, he and Badrik had both found the youthful excitement uniquely stimulating.

"Roy," Warnach interrupted with a tilt of his head, "we're nearly home."

Spinning in the front passenger seat, Roy leaned forward and peered through transparent polymer windows. Ornate, twelve-foot high gates stood guard at the traditional entrance to the Sirinoya estate. Lighted windows shone golden within substantial and stately stone walls. Glowing orbs lined walkways and the edges of lush gardens.

Roy's hazel eyes widened. "You actually live there?"

Warnach nodded. "This house has belonged to my family for many generations."

Roy tore his eyes away from the impressive manor. Staring at his sister, he snickered. "Sis, you held back. You never told me you snagged such a rich husband."

Giggling at his teasing comment, she leaned forward in her seat and stroked her fingers through each side of Warnach's hair. "The money doesn't matter. I really married him for this gorgeous hair."

"Unified, Sandra. Unified," Warnach interjected humorously as he resisted torrents of shivers racing along his spine while bringing the transport to ground level.

Later, while Sandra helped him get settled in the guest suite, Roy paused several times to gaze at her. Finally, he said quietly, "Sis, I hope you'll let me know if I do something wrong in front of Warnach or his family. I'd never intentionally insult anyone."

Reaching out, she tousled her brother's neatly combed hair. "Just be more serious with his mother and other older people. Chikondrans tend to be very formal. As far as Warnach, I think he's finally gotten accustomed to Terran humor, although he doesn't always understand, which sometimes gets me in trouble."

"Hmm. Thanks for the info."

Frowning at him with mock ferocity, she growled, "Behave yourself, kiddo. Remember. You're not on Earth anymore."

Despite her life so far away from their family, Roy had always felt close to his older sister. Thoughtfully, he observed her over the next two days, which were scheduled as free time so young visitors could adapt to differences in Chikondra's physical environment. Gone were the sad eyes and anxious lines so typical of her expressions whenever she had visited home. Instead, she appeared poised, confident, and happy. Watching her with Warnach's family, he could hardly avoid a sense of envy. Revealed through respect and genuine affection was the closeness she shared with the Sirinoyas.

On the day before Roy would start his workshops, the family decided to avail themselves of lingering summer-like weather to go to the seashore. A day at the beach, any beach, presented welcome diversion. Mid-morning walks along the shore were marked with lively gestures and conversation between Sandra and her brother. Lunch had been a delicious treat as Roy lent support to his sister while she teased her lifemate and his brother about the many benefits of being omnivorous. Glancing occasionally toward Araman Sirinoya, he had smiled at her cooperative silence. Later, nestled into the curve of a hammock, Roy enjoyed a lazy nap.

Following his afternoon snooze, Roy relaxed while standing knee-deep in lapping ocean waters. Brilliantly blue skies were painted across the horizon. Streamlined and silent, scarlet birds glided overhead on afternoon breezes. Laughing as waves threatened to push him off his feet, he listened to Warnach's description of generations of efforts that had preserved the serenity and ecology of Chikondra's extensive shoreline.

Returning to the bungalow, his sister placed a small bowl of cushuska in front of him. Initially, he wasn't sure about trusting her. At last, he dared a taste. Typical of most growing teenaged boys, he quickly finished his dessert. Then, when his sister looked away to respond to a comment by Mirsah Sirinoya, he deftly stole and devoured her bowl of cushuska.

"Roy!" she exclaimed. "How dare you steal…?" Suddenly, she leapt to her feet as he jumped from his chair and fled. Followed by her lifemate's laughter, she chased even faster after her brother.

Abruptly, Roy felt the shock of quiet. No more laughter. No more mock warnings. No more shouted threats from his sister. Only birds above and the quiet wash of low tides upon the shore. Clumsily stumbling forward as he stopped too fast, he twisted around. Catching his breath, he stared at his sister's motionless figure.

Glancing toward the bungalow, he saw that Araman stood with eyes seaward while both Badrik and Warnach had already hurried onto the sandy beach. Closer to Sandra than they were, Roy's feet kicked up sandy clouds as he scurried toward her. "Sis?" he gasped, reaching her and taking her by the arm. "Sis? Are you okay?"

Silently, she lifted her right hand and placed her index finger against her lips. Her head tilted from side to side. All the while, a faint smile curved her lips. At last, she looked at him. "I haven't seen them for quite a while. They want to meet you."

Roy gave a quick jerk of his head before giving her one of the quirky responses so typical between them. "They want to meet me? And who be they?"

"Friends. Quazon." Glancing around, she smiled mysteriously at

Warnach, who had stopped about ten feet away. "They want Mamehr and Badrik to go in, too."

Roy turned around and said to Warnach, "My sister gets a little weird at times. Do you think maybe we should take her in out of the sun?"

Swift steps carried Warnach to Sandra's side. "Are you certain, Shi'níyah?" Receiving a solemn nod, he slowly pivoted. "Badrik, bring Mamehr."

With everyone gathered at the water's edge, green eyes shifted from face to face. Her hushed voice failed to hide excited anticipation. "Wait for me to signal you. They're almost here." She then entered the ocean and, bouncing to keep her balance against incoming waves, reached deeper water.

Roy worriedly gripped his brother-in-law's upper arm. "Is my sister all right?"

Quietly, Warnach answered reassuringly, "Your sister has some rather unique friends. Apparently, they trust you with their secret. Watch."

Abruptly, with an explosion of water and a series of shrill whistles, a silvery duo hurtled themselves high into the air above Sandra's head. Startled, Roy jerked forward but was firmly restrained by Warnach and Badrik. "My sister!"

Warnach's head tilted back as he maintained a strong grip on his lifemate's brother. "Don't worry. She's safe. Watch."

For several minutes, those on shore observed as four Quazon cavorted around the young woman standing fearlessly in their midst. When one finally nudged her, she spun in the water. Her face beamed joyfully as she called out, "They're ready! Warnach, bring everyone in! Slowly!"

Within minutes, laughter filled the air. Badrik's eyes widened with childlike wonder as the younger Quazon bumped against him, occasionally lifting him off his feet. Doing the same with Roy, the smaller ones indulged in playful taps and splashes. As if mindful of Araman's petite stature and her more fragile maturity, the sacred creatures gently nudged her and glided through the water while permitting their sleek bodies to slide smoothly against her legs. The large male focused primarily on Araman while pausing from time to time to urge better behavior from his youthful charges.

Meanwhile, Warnach and Sandra received nearly undivided attention from the adult female. Her pointed face showed genuine pleasure for the long, firm strokes she received from the warm hands of the couple she obviously adored. Several times, she curved fanned flippers to brush against Warnach's body before turning full focus to her Terran friend.

Noting that his lifemate was once again immersed in unspoken dialogue with her visitor, Warnach exchanged glances with his brother and mamehr. Questions clearly shone from Badrik's astonished eyes. Although thoroughly enchanted, Araman's expression held similar inquiry. No doubt existed. Sandra's innate ability to communicate with Quazon had evolved into a deeply spiritual relationship that, for three faith-filled Chikondrans, must be laden with significance yet to be revealed. Speculation could serve no useful purpose. Only time, patience, and vigilance would expose the mystery of why sacred Quazon had chosen to bond with her and had extended that connection to include her brother and her Chikondran family.

That night, Roy's eyes intently gazed at his sister as she sat cross-legged at the foot of his bed. "Except for Warnach, I think everyone else was more astonished than I was."

"I've stopped trying to understand why they come to me. I figure that if I'm ever supposed to know, I'll find out when the time is right. Until then, I can only love them and respect their privacy."

Roy leaned forward and grasped her hands. "Sis, more than ever, I appreciate the chance to be here. I do promise to keep the secret. You know you can always count on your baby brother."

Lifting her eyes and locking onto his gaze, she nodded. "That's something I've known for a long time."

# Chapter Fifteen

Staring through the window at stars far beyond the gleaming shell of the spaceship speeding through a space warp, Sandra scarcely noticed as Warnach lowered himself onto the seat beside her. Her thoughts had shifted backward in time. She could hardly believe that more than a year had passed since the foundation's first group of students from Earth had come and gone from Chikondra. Even she had been amazed by the success of her venture. Plans were now underway for the second biennial group. Extending the program to other worlds was also under consideration. How stimulating - how utterly satisfying to be able to give something back.

"Sandra?"

Her mouth curved slightly as she turned apologetic eyes to Warnach. "Sorry. I was just thinking."

Detecting the thoughtful nature of her mood, he returned a tentative smile. "Good thoughts, I hope."

Nodding, she reached over to touch his hand. "Good thoughts."

"Then I'm glad."

"How was the conference?"

"The com-link failed. Captain Trifehrian was notified earlier of a solar disturbance emanating from the Metregan System."

"Do they expect the interference to last long?"

"Impossible to predict." Warnach glanced through the observation portal. "We may reach Tarmantrua before any link can be re-established."

Nearly a week later, just as Warnach had suspected, wild fluctuations in solar energy waves continued to impede communications. Entering orbit around the mammoth planet dominating the Briliar-Kadan System, he breathed air deep into his lungs. Already, during a period equivalent to five days, his mission team had been quartered in isolated chambers under gradually increasing pressure simulating conditions on the world below. On a world as large as Tarmantrua, the powerful gravitational pull approached tolerance limits of Terrans and Chikondrans alike. Intensive conditioning would merely delay the onset of unavoidable physical exhaustion.

From a small portal revealing the cloud-covered world below, his attention strayed toward his lifemate. Throughout the conditioning ordeal, instead of making justifiable complaints, she had voiced only one or two jokes about feeling as heavy and immovable as a beached whale on Earth. Watching her eyes move rapidly as she reviewed the detailed mission agenda yet again, his expression revealed pensiveness as he avoided disturbing her concentration.

As he redirected his gaze outside the portal, reflective thoughts invaded his mind. Despite difficulties anticipated on the impending mission, he relished time to focus on objectives. His lifemate's position as mission advocate had done more than alleviate the aching plague of personal loneliness. Her rapidly developing professional expertise delivered vast amounts of historical data condensed into logically organized, relatively simple summaries. Further discussion with her allowed him to voice a variety of possible approaches while eliciting valuable responses based on her remarkable insight. Recent, auspicious successes on Frehatar, Bederand, and Carabriliar gave him cause to wonder what the state of his diplomacy would have been had they not embarked on joined careers.

"My ki'medsah, you've been especially quiet since last night," she told him the next day while adjusting his straight, white collar to stand an equal height above the embroidered neckline of his coat. "Is there something your ki'mirsah can do to ease your mind?"

His mouth drew into a smile rare since their departure from Chikondra. "My ki'mirsah has no idea how much she already relieves the mind of her ki'medsah. For now, he can only ask for her promise to remain patient on Tarmantrua."

"Because of the honorable Pekarim's reluctant acceptance of females in diplomatic service?"

Running the tip of his tongue across his lower lip, he smiled again and nodded. "Because, me'u Shi'níyah, Pekarim Gambray is notorious for his lack of respect for females in any professional role."

Her eyes held a glint of rebelliousness. "Perhaps even the honorable Pekarim can learn new lessons."

"Sandra…"

Grinning, she touched her lips to his and stepped backward. "My esteemed Minister Sirinoya, you mustn't worry. I promise to behave myself." Noting fleeting skepticism in his eyes, she said with a laugh, "In the beginning, anyway."

Two hours later, Pekarim Gambray's steel-gray hair poufed slightly into straight lines combed back from his high forehead. Eyes as gray as his hair gleamed icily from a narrow, angular face. The silhouette of his tall, slim, and tensely erect body created severe lines that were accentuated by the long, straight, unadorned cut of his dove-colored coat. His austere image emanated coldness from a man who had imposed his will on the people of Tarmantrua and neighboring moons for nearly four decades.

Surrounded by dozens of uniformed aides, the Tarmantruan Pekarim displayed no sign of a man whose power had been challenged by lunar communities of three moons orbiting the gargantuan planet. Neither did his expression reveal the seething fury of a ruler who was frankly amazed that people on his own world had followed suit and threatened revolt against his tightly regimented government that had fostered years of peaceful prosperity.

With his lifemate's comical quip forgotten, Minister Sirinoya proceeded toward the leader of a war-weary world finally forced to discuss peaceful solutions already approved by the Carabriliar Union. Reaching the embattled head of state, Warnach brought elegantly long hands together and, pointing them directly from the level of his heart, rotated them upward until his fingertips touched his forehead as he bowed. Behind him, his advocate and support aides performed synchronized bows under the scrutiny of ministry security personnel.

"Minister Sirinoya," Gambray responded, "despite my regret regarding the circumstances accompanying your visit, I bid you welcome to Tarmantrua." The Pekarim's voice contained a haughty tone that conveyed resentment.

Demonstrating no outward reaction, Warnach gravely replied, "Pekarim Gambray, I accept the honor of your welcome. I pray our collaboration during my stay will greatly reduce any regrets you may have."

The strained greeting stood as the presage to trying opening days of meetings. Noting more than just antipathy, Warnach dedicated the first day to private discussions with Gambray. He recognized the necessity of establishing a confident base upon which open dialogue could begin. If the Tarmantruan leader maintained aloofness, there would be little hope of expanding the Carabriliar Accords to encompass the world that had initially provoked hostilities in the Briliar-Kadan System.

Preparing for the second morning of meetings, Warnach maintained his grim demeanor as he dried his face after shaving and trimming his beard. The previous day's talks had ended early. Gambray had forcefully expressed animosity for the leaders of the Tarmantruan moons and open disdain for the agreement that had created the Carabriliar Union, thereby forcing Gambray into peace negotiations. Patiently, Warnach had directed discussions in the hope of gaining better comprehension of reasons behind Gambray's attitude. Unfortunately, he had gleaned little. Sighing, he returned to the bedroom to dress.

"You look pessimistic."

Donning his shirt, Warnach shook his head as he snapped closures together. "Gambray not only looks like a column of steel. He's as cold and unbending as steel." Pausing, he smiled apologetically. "I neglected to ask. How are the facilities provided for my favorite advocate and support aides?"

Handing him his coat, she nodded. "Acceptable. Small. Clean to the point of being antiseptic. Everything was operational and secure when I left."

He expelled a short breath. "Gambray instills little confidence. I want you to be especially vigilant."

Green eyes studied his face closely. "You feel it, too, don't you?"

Uncertainty showed in narrowing eyes. "Feel what?"

"Zeteron influence."

Curious, he firmly gripped her shoulders. "Why do you say that?"

Shrugging beneath his hold, she gazed directly into his eyes. "Despite Gambray's reputation as an iron-fisted ruler, this system erupted into violence too quickly. I did extensive research and found none of the usual long-term buildup that leads to such volatile hostilities. Tarmantrua became embroiled in conflict only six years ago. The parts don't fit."

Warnach shook his head thoughtfully. "Your suggestion?"

"Push to get discussions moving quickly. As you said, stay alert. There is something or someone fomenting the tensions. We need to see more and hear more if there's any hope of figuring out what - or who…"

"Sandra, I cannot tell you how glad I am to have you as my ally." Momentarily, his expression softened. Bending his head, he lightly touched cerea-nervos to her forehead. Breathing in deeply, he lifted his face. "It's time for our Kitak so we can leave."

Two days later, Sandra patiently waited in the stark conference room as security specialists inspected every inch of wall, ceiling, floor, and furniture.

Receiving assurances that all was secure, she tested all monitors and equipment that would facilitate the meeting. Although she had supervised technicians while they performed earlier installation, she still insisted on personally conducting a final set of checks before each day's conference. Thorough advance preparation would minimize risk for interruptions or delays.

Satisfied that all was ready, she left the conference room under the guard of ministry security and four Tarmantruan officers. Reaching the nearby quarters serving as mission operations center, she checked with each support aide. General services were ready. Most importantly, communications with Captain Trifehrian, commanding the orbiting Rahpliknar, had been verified as operational on secure frequencies. Closing her eyes, she quietly sighed.

"Advocate Sirinoya, everything is operating according to plan. Why do you look so concerned?"

The left side of Sandra's mouth curved into what vaguely resembled a smile. Calmly, she responded to the aide, "Miryah Chimihnla, you'll always see me concerned so long as an agreement is not accomplished. Too much can go wrong within the span of a heartbeat. Never let your guard down while on-mission."

As days passed, Sandra struggled to keep aides focused on their duties. Indeed, her own fatigue grated on her nerves. Tarmantrua's gravity felt almost suffocating. With the Pekarim's closest advisors now actively participating in talks, Warnach was growing cautiously optimistic. Not only had he begun to understand points of contention, he felt he was starting to develop insight regarding how Gambray's confidants affected the leader's thinking. Recognizing how much Warnach would need continued support, Sandra refused to give in to environmental factors and constantly encouraged mission staff to do the same.

In consideration of Pekarim Gambray's antiquated concepts toward women, Warnach had not insisted on Sandra's presence during initial conference sessions. However, with physical endurance flagging, his stance changed. He trusted her observational skills and judgment as he trusted no one else's. After eight days yielding minimal progress, he informed Farbry Viskavy, the Pekarim's top assistant, that Advocate Sirinoya would attend all subsequent meetings.

Gambray's reaction was expectedly cold. However, keenly intelligent, he understood that Minister Sirinoya presented the best chance he had to regain sufficient stability necessary to retain control over the Tarmantruan government. Gambray's response to Viskavy's vulgar remarks about Minister Sirinoya's reasons for including his wife in the meetings had been nothing more than a grave, forced smile.

While continuing to impose his image of strength, Gambray privately questioned motives behind Sirinoya's sudden announcement. Women in his world were not exposed to the intricate workings of governing and diplomacy that were best handled by the male character. Personally, he could hardly avoid wondering if there might be some hidden reason for the unexpected inclusion of a female in an official conference for the first time during his long tenure as Pekarim of Tarmantrua.

At the same time he reluctantly agreed to Advocate Sirinoya's attendance of official meetings, the Pekarim also secretly pondered Minister Sirinoya's shrewdness at the negotiating table. One point was indisputable. The Alliance minister deserved his reputation for strategic brilliance in diplomatic stalemate.

On the third day with his advocate at his side during especially difficult conferences, Warnach found a source of encouragement and relief in Sandra's silent presence. Alone, he could not possibly watch every face in that room while simultaneously conducting discussions meant to gain Tarmantrua's agreement to enter peace talks. Confident in her ability to scan and detect fine nuances in those around the table, he concentrated on doggedly pursuing dialogue that would draw Gambray into active negotiations.

Dining that evening in their suite, Warnach gazed at the serious face across the table. She had hardly spoken during their meal. Growing more and more accustomed to the way her mind worked, he waited. He respected her knack for comparing research information to active observation and intuition. Patiently, he allowed time for her thoughts to develop fully.

Curiously, he watched as she suddenly stood up and walked through their suite. Her nose wrinkled as she sniffed around the room. "Do you smell something odd?"

His brow lifted in question, and he drew in several breaths. "No, not really."

Watching her carefully, he saw her eyes close. Stepping around in a circle, she twisted her head from side to side. Abruptly, she strode toward the door and opened it to the corridor outside. Quietly, she spoke to one of the security guards and motioned Warnach to join her in the hallway.

Half an hour later, they reentered the suite following a thorough security sweep. The inspection had exposed no devices, but intense scrutiny had revealed that some personal belongings had been disturbed and several items of little value were missing. No one except supervised cleaning people had been permitted inside the suite.

After instructing the mission's security chief to prepare a confidential report without notifying the Tarmantruans, Warnach led Sandra back to the now-cleared dining table. Gazing into her eyes, he could almost see her brain working. "I'm not worried about petty theft. What does concern me is how you knew something was amiss."

Her eyes glittered. "It wasn't petty theft. I think those items will mysteriously reappear. Whatever you do, don't touch them."

Warnach nodded. "No objection. Now, tell me. How did you know?"

Her head moved from side to side, and her fingers tapped nervously against the tabletop. "I wish I could explain. I'm not sure."

"You said you smelled something. What? Strong soap? Cologne, perhaps?"

Breathing in again, she gritted her teeth together. "If only I could remember. I know I've smelled that scent before."

"Shi'níyah, I know better than argue the point. However, until you figure it out, I think we should say prayers and try to rest. I am utterly exhausted."

The next morning, as they ate breakfast, she seemed more open to discussing her observations from the meetings. Referring to points from her research data, she questioned Warnach's opinions regarding Gambray's various advisors. Most had served the Pekarim for years. Something significant had changed to cause the leader to launch attacks against lunar settlements opposing rigid rule from their home planet.

"Sandra, his closest advisors advocate the same policies as ever."

"As far as you know," she commented. "The one concerning me most is Viskavy."

Warnach's eyes glittered. "Because he's the most open objector to your presence?"

"Actually, no," she responded. "Viskavy is relatively transparent. He's selfish and arrogant but not smart enough to head the government. He is closely related to Gambray, which means he likely has more influence. His aide, Tertago, is the one I really distrust."

"I don't understand. Why?"

"Quite honestly, I don't know."

"That helps very little."

Thoughtfully, she drank the last of a cup of strong Tzitua tea. "I will figure it out. That's a promise."

Later that day, Warnach met with his mission team. Quickly nearing three weeks on Tarmantrua, he was well aware that they all desperately needed a break. Experience made him certain that he had approached a breakthrough several times. Each time, for indeterminate reasons, Gambray had backed away. He needed more time. He felt too close to a possible turning point to suspend talks prematurely. Meeting with exhausted staff, he had expressed pride and respect. All had insisted they could manage a little longer.

Returning with Sandra to their suite that evening, he indulged her insistence on entering first. Just as the night before, she closed her eyes and walked around the suite. "I don't believe you can't smell that!"

Meanwhile, with security personnel again scanning the rooms, she continued her own inspection. Smiling triumphantly, she pointed to the dresser and to a shelf in the bathroom. Not only had things been rearranged in the apparent act of dusting and cleaning, but missing items had also mysteriously returned. Quickly, the items were removed for intensive analysis. Again, Warnach insisted on complete discretion pending further investigation.

~

Fury snapped in Sandra's eyes. "If you had opened that bottle, fumes alone could have killed you!"

Firmly, Warnach faced his ki'mirsah. "Fortunately, my advocate kept me safe."

Ignoring attempts to allay her concerns, she forcefully continued, "Gambray must be informed. Warnach, the man is driven to holding onto power. On the other hand, I don't believe for one second that he would condone murder under these circumstances. He's too smart to risk an Alliance backlash."

"Sandra, we left the meeting yesterday in positive light. Let's see what happens today. If there's no progress, I'll release the security report to Gambray and terminate further talks. Agreed?"

"Today. I will know today." Her eyes glittered stubbornly, and her voice held terse confidence.

"Know what, Shi'níyah?"

"I will know who tried to kill you and why." Jerking around, she stormed out of their suite toward transports waiting to take them to the conference site.

"Advocate Sirinoya, I checked everything three times. Systems diagnoses reveal no sign of malfunction. Security scanned twice and found no explanation for the interference."

Leaning over Chimihnla's shoulder, Sandra's eyes studied rhythmic flashes on the monitor. Straightening, she looked around. "Something is causing this disruption. Concentrate on re-establishing contact with the Rahpliknar."

Slowly, with Chief Mission Officer Taplinchna at her heels, she walked around the room, casting her eyes up and down. Abruptly, she dropped onto her hands and knees. Sharp eyes had noted something highly advanced technology had missed. Running hands just above ribbed carpeting, she noted the slightest indentation and detected faint vibration. Inviting Taplinchna to see, they communicated quietly in Chikondran. Concealed beneath the floor covering was likely a sensor set to detect scans and subsequently close and seal the hatch. When the scans were over, the hatch opened to allow high-frequency transmissions to penetrate the room and disrupt sensitive computers.

Aloud, in English more readily understood, she instructed Taplinchna to order constant scans. That would cause the frequency interrupter to retract.

As she strode purposefully into the conference room, her face no longer showed any sign of fatigue. Meeting her gaze as her index finger traced small circles on the side of Kitak, Warnach instantly perceived her unspoken message. She sensed there was danger. Without conscious intent, his own hand raised to touch Kitak.

Adrenalin heightened her senses as she walked around the conference table on the premise of ensuring everyone was comfortable and ready for the meeting to begin. Silently, she sat in a chair placed slightly behind her lifemate. As discussion commenced, her eyes discreetly roamed.

Tertago coughed several times. Viskavy glanced sideways. Rising, Sandra went to the side table set with refreshments and poured a glass of fresh water. Saying nothing, she offered the glass to Viskavy's assistant. She paused only slightly before returning to her seat. The pause was enough to capture Warnach's attention. Minutes later, he called a break.

Quickly, Sandra directed an on-duty medical attendant to stay near Tertago. In the meantime, Chief Officer Taplinchna entered the conference room for what appeared to be standard security surveillance. While Warnach conversed with Pekarim Gambray, Sandra felt the prickly vibration in the security tab on her bracelet. Taplinchna had discovered a problem.

Smiling graciously, she excused herself under the premise of tending the room before resuming the meeting. Inside, she grimly noted the problem. Adhered to the underside of the table was a small square identical to the disposable hygiene sheets Tertago had used to cover his coughs. A substance scanner had detected the same poison that had been planted in Warnach's toiletries. Embedded in the sheet was a filament designed to disintegrate within a short time after exposure to air. The disintegration process would generate sufficient heat to activate the toxin and release enough fumes to kill everyone inside within seconds.

Exiting the room with a smile, she utilized a covert hand signal to ministry security officers. Secure the area immediately. No one in. No one out. Approaching Warnach, her expression revealed no stress. "Minister Sirinoya, the conference room is ready. You're free to return at your discretion."

"Advocate Sirinoya, Counselor Viskavy has informed me that he must dismiss Aide Tertago due to illness."

Glancing directly into the Counselor's eyes, she nodded regretfully. "I'm afraid that's impossible at the moment."

Bristling, Viskavy glared at her. "Advocate Sirinoya, my aide is quite ill today. He made a supreme effort to extend his services to me. I want an explanation."

"Minister Sirinoya," Gambray interjected, "may I inquire as to what right your advocate invokes on my world to refuse dismissal of a Tarmantruan citizen who has fallen ill?"

Arching his eyebrows, Warnach met Sandra's implacable gaze. "Advocate Sirinoya, will you kindly explain?"

"Honorable Minister, I've ordered a security lockdown. Shall we return to the conference room where I may safely explain?"

"Minister Sirinoya…"

With a wave of his hand, Warnach stopped the Pekarim's angry protest. "With all due respect, Pekarim Gambray, my advocate merits my unwavering trust. Let us return to the conference room."

Inside, steely eyes appraised the erect figure of the woman who waited for everyone to retake his seat. Tertago suddenly leaned forward onto the table in a violent fit of coughing. Refusing to be seated, Pekarim Gambray glared at Sandra Sirinoya. "My colleague is seriously ill. I demand an immediate explanation as to why he cannot leave for medical treatment."

Squaring her shoulders without a single trace of intimidation, she faced Gambray. "Pekarim Gambray, I'm fully aware of your attitude toward me. However, my responsibilities are to ensure the safety of my assigned minister above all else. In that capacity, I also find myself in the position of saving your life and the lives of your advisors."

"You're talking nonsense. This is a closely monitored meeting room. No one can enter and tamper with safety precautions."

Her voice snapped with anger. "Just as no one could tamper with communications in the secure service center occupied by the minister's staff. However, that did not preclude the installation of a sliding panel in the floor that concealed frequency interrupters to disrupt communications with our ship."

Narrowing his eyes suspiciously, he stared at her. "Impossible. The personnel who manage this facility are completely loyal to me. No one would allow such a breach."

"Just as no one would attempt to assassinate Minister Sirinoya?"

"What kind of insane accusation is that?"

Another heavy fit of coughing distracted the Pekarim's attention. "I apologize most humbly, Honorable Pekarim. Please, let me leave so you may settle this."

Angrily, with a jerk of his head, Gambray waved two Tarmantruan guards forward. "This man needs immediate medical attention. Help him out."

Instantly, Sandra sidestepped, placing herself between a startled Warnach and the Tarmantruans across the table.

Ministry guards immediately raised weapons. "No one leaves this room," Chief Taplinchna announced. "In addition to the two security breaches just brought to your attention by Advocate Sirinoya, I just located and isolated the third breach in this very room."

"You lie!" Viskavy spat out. "That's impossible! My own people conducted security checks in this room."

"Did they also scrutinize the people who entered?"

"Advocate Sirinoya," Gambray hissed furiously, "are you suggesting one of my colleagues is a traitor?"

Finally, she leveled her eyes in a cold gaze directed toward those of Tertago. "Not at all, Honorable Pekarim. My suggestion is that a member of your group may not be a colleague at all."

Huffing an exasperated breath, Gambray refused to respond to her. "Minister Sirinoya, I believe your advocate well proves why my world frowns on females in this environment. Lack of logic is too often augmented by emotional histrionics. I demand that you remove her immediately."

Moving to stand by Sandra's side, Warnach struck an adamant posture. "Honorable Pekarim Gambray, my advocate is not disposed to what you describe as emotional histrionics. I respectfully insist that you allow her to continue."

Without so much as glancing at Warnach, Sandra returned Gambray's icy glare. "I would recommend that you ask Mr. Tertago if you want more specific details."

"What?" Gambray asked as he watched Tertago jerk away from the table and cover his face as she released a single hygiene sheet to float and settle on the table. "Mr. Tertago, do you have any idea what this woman is talking about?"

Coughing again, Tertago shook his head in denial.

Responding to Sandra's nod, Taplinchna slid an isolation case into the center of the table. "Actually, I'd prefer an explanation as to why this was attached underneath the table, directly in front of Mr. Tertago's chair." Suddenly, a gaseous cloud appeared within the sealed confines of the isolation case.

Unable to disguise startled eyes, Tertago glared at Taplinchna. Unexpectedly regaining a clear voice, the man demanded, "What game are you trying to play here?"

Taplinchna signaled his guards to remain at the ready. "Zinocamitoxin."

Gambray's gray eyes met those of Taplinchna. "Poison? Zeteron origin, if I am correct."

"Poison. Zeteron origin," Sandra repeated, again assuming control. "The same substance was introduced into some of Minister Sirinoya's personal items that temporarily disappeared from his quarters. Fortunately, the threat was detected before harm was done. The sheet in that isolation unit contained sufficient poison to kill every person in this room."

Clearly shaken, Gambray addressed Taplinchna. "It seems I owe you the debt of my life and the lives of my advisors."

Taplinchna shook his head. "You're mistaken, Honorable Pekarim. Your life was saved by Advocate Sirinoya."

The attention of every person was immediately drawn to Tertago. With a groan and an agonized shudder, the aide stiffened and collapsed onto the floor. Stunned, Gambray and Viskavy jumped backward. Staring, they watched as one of the Pekarim's bodyguards touched the lifeless body.

For the very first time, Gambray addressed Sandra in a civil tone. "You must explain. I do not understand."

Respectfully, she inclined her head. "Honorable Pekarim, because the body contains highly potent poison, any autopsy must be carefully conducted. However, I am certain that the results will confirm that Tertago was actually Zeteron."

That night, Warnach held her tightly. His lips moved tenderly against her forehead. "Will you ever tell me how you knew?"

Tiredly, she whispered her response. "You probably won't believe me."

"Curiosity consumes me. Tell me. I promise never to say a word without your permission."

"Remember when I told you about the Zeterons who came to Earth years ago?"

Backing slightly away, he noted the pensive expression on her face. "I remember."

"Do you also remember when I kept smelling something in this room?"

"Yes. And?"

"Today, when I handed the glass of water to Tertago, I noticed that smell again. The odor is faint but quite distinctive. I finally remembered noticing that same lingering odor around the Zeterons who were on Earth. I think it must be a scent distinctive to their species."

"Are you telling me that the global leadership of Tarmantrua and I owe our lives to your nose?"

"Something like that. Warnach?"

First shaking his head on his pillow, he moved close enough to kiss her lightly on the mouth. "What, my amazing Shi'níyah?"

"How soon can we leave Tarmantrua? I really want to return to normal gravity soon."

"You sound desperate."

"I am. I need to function like a normal human being. After the last few days, what I really need is for you to function like my Chikondran ki'medsah so you can make love to me again."

Laughing softly, he tightened his embrace. "I think Pekarim

Gambray will gladly consent to us taking an extended break without jeopardizing further negotiations. Tomorrow, I shall organize our return to the Rahpliknar."

# Chapter Sixteen

Outside, beaming down from the center of Chikondra's canopy of blue skies, natural sunlight cast its glow over a peaceful afternoon in Kadranas. Light breezes stirred leaves in trees. With worried brown eyes staring through the window at the beautiful afternoon, a heavy sigh accompanied the preoccupied shake of Farsuk's head. "If only they hadn't committed suicide before they could be questioned."

Sitting in a chair across the well-appointed office, Warnach spoke to the chancellor's back. "Tertago's collapse shocked us all. The Tarmantruans were unable to subdue the others before they killed themselves."

Slowly, Farsuk turned around and faced his godson. "I suppose we need to look at positives that have occurred. Gambray is now actively engaged in a peace initiative. We also finally have solid proof of Zeteron involvement in destabilization plots within Alliance territories."

Warnach's right eyebrow lifted high. "The question is how much proof will be necessary to convince all the skeptics in the general council."

Impatience marked the shaking of Farsuk's head. "I think some will not believe until Zeterons actually stand on the floor inside the Chamber of Masters. Changing the subject, I must express how pleased I am with Sandra's performance. Taplinchna rarely writes a report as complimentary as the one he submitted on the Tarmantrua affair."

A brief smile crossed Warnach's face and disappeared. "How close so many of us came to losing our lives."

"Your advocate has certainly proven her worth. I want you to know that Pekarim Gambray submitted a formal letter of appreciation for her actions. I have already authorized the awarding of a Commendation Certificate."

"She certainly deserves it," Warnach commented.

Despite lingering tension, Farsuk smiled at last. "How? That is my question. How did she know?"

Recalling his promise, Warnach shrugged. "All I can say is that she seems to have perceptions far different than any of the rest of us."

"Then, we can only thank the Great Spirit for those perceptions."

Later, Warnach leaned far back in the chair inside his office. He stared blankly at the ceiling, his mind reverting to final days on Tarmantrua. Although still aloof, Pekarim Gambray had no longer appeared so rigid. The thwarted assassination had staggered a man accustomed to strict, orderly control of his entire environment. Despising the very idea of an alien power penetrating his inner circle, he had first acted to establish measures to secure the state of his government. Then, finally, he had consulted with Warnach and agreed to implement direct talks with delegates from the Carabriliar Union.

Warnach's thoughts echoed Farsuk's primary fear. The incident on Tarmantrua heralded change in Zeteron strategy. Apparently, they were growing impatient with tactics intended to weaken Alliance members and relationships. Fully agreeing with his baadihm, he was convinced that Zeterons were verging on more openly aggressive approaches looming in a future that was advancing more quickly than the Dil-Terra Interplanetary Alliance could prepare to handle.

Continuing to brood following his afternoon meeting with Farsuk, Warnach spoke little during dinner at home that evening. Both Sandra and Araman had observed his distant demeanor and had directed neutral conversation toward redecorating ideas to update some of the guest suites.

Once evening prayers ended, Araman left her deeply contemplative son inside the Brisajai alongside his still kneeling ki'mirsah.

Gentle pressure against the center of his back increased, rousing him from the course of ponderous thoughts. Blinking several times, heavily lashed eyelids opened. His head twisted. His mouth lost its grim line. "You're always here."

Her smile imparted comfort. "Constant worry will accomplish nothing, Warnach. You must let this rest in God's hands. He will guide our steps. In the meantime, we must cherish the life He has given us."

Rising, he took her hand and helped her stand. Lovingly, he stroked his fingers along her cheek. "I am ever grateful that the Great Spirit guided our steps onto the same path."

Cherish the life He gave us. In bed that night, her words repeatedly saturated his mind as he frantically made love to her. The assassination attempt on Tarmantrua could have easily ended her life as well as his. The events had generated explosive awareness of just how precious and transitory life could be. His own life meant more to him than ever. Sandra's life he valued above all others. Lost in the aftermath of loving her, he clung to her tightly while desperately burying fears of ever losing her.

Only weeks later, they again boarded the ministry vessel Rahpliknar. This time, they accompanied Rodan Khalijar on-mission to Simartis Major. There, in a tranquil, neutral environment, Warnach would lend his support to Rodan's intensive negotiations between the worlds of Lethamori and Ishwani.

~

"More coffee?"

Bright blue eyes glittered playfully above the rim of the raised, empty cup. "Are you really allowed to bring your own stash with you?"

"As much as I want, and it's a good thing. You'll need the caffeine. I hear Rodan has you swamped."

Rueful laughter lit Peter's fair features. "Drowning is more like it. No complaints, though. I still count my lucky stars that he accepted me to replace Advocate Carmandy."

"Rodan is outstanding. I can't tell you how glad I am for you, even though I know he'll work you to the bone." Grinning mischievously, Sandra said, "So, tell me, and don't lie to me. Are the rumors true?"

"Rumors? What rumors?" Peter asked in a tone of exaggerated innocence.

"Don't play coy with me. You know my connections and networking are solid."

"Yeah, yeah. I also heard you had lunch with Emilio before he took off for Chimparius."

"Well?"

"Yes, it's true."

"I knew it!" she exclaimed delightedly. "You and Druska! A match made in heaven!"

"Heaven? Sorry, haven't been there yet. The match was made on Chikondra."

"C'mon. Admit it. Chikondra is heaven!"

"Whatever," Peter laughed before pausing and assuming a more serious expression. "It's tough leaving her behind. Still, I'm glad she opted to continue working with Minister Tirasam at Ministry Headquarters."

"Druska's great at what she does. Get ready, though. With Tirasam planning to retire in a year or so, Druska should have no trouble securing a field ministry advocacy."

"I'm hoping she changes her mind about pursuing field ministry."

"Why?" Sandra asked curiously. "She excelled at the academy, and there's no denying we need every competent mind we can get out here."

Pursing his lips, Peter shrugged. "Can't help myself. I know her work would be impeccable. She's just such a tiny thing. I'd be worried all the time."

Disapprovingly, Sandra shook her head. "I'm practically an Amazon, but that doesn't make Warnach worry any less. Think of it this way. Druska makes a smaller target."

"You are nuts. The good thing is that Druska doesn't have your penchant for getting herself into one scrape after another."

"Ouch. Low blow, my friend."

"Do I detect the stimulating aroma of my lifemate's coffee?"

Twisting in her chair at the interruption, Sandra smiled broadly. "That you do, my dear Minister Sirinoya. May I offer you a cup?"

Approaching the lounge table where she sat, Warnach leaned forward and kissed her left temple just above Kitak. "I would love some coffee." Sitting down, he smiled at Peter. "Have you unraveled her secret of taking over one of the ship's lounges and converting it into her own private café?"

"Minister Sirinoya, I stopped asking questions a long time ago about how she does what she does. I decided that it's probably safer if I don't know."

Smiling, Warnach watched rich brown fluid fill the porcelain mug now in front of him. "Your approach is likely the wisest. So, tell me. Are you ready for tomorrow?"

Meeting the minister's gaze, Peter nodded. "This is my first major mission with Minister Khalijar. I'd be lying if I said I'm not nervous. On the other hand, I can't deny a sense of excitement. I'm also open to any and all advice about maintaining my sanity while keeping my responsibilities rolling."

From behind, a hand firmly grasped Peter's shoulder. "If you continue working as you have since you joined my staff, I am confident that you will deliver an outstanding performance, Advocate Collins." Stepping to the side, Rodan joined them at the table. "Do I smell genuine coffee from Earth?"

"I take it the good Minister Khalijar would also like some coffee?"

"I fear visits to the Sirinoya home are addicting me."

An hour later, Warnach followed Sandra into their quarters. "I am so glad for a chance to relax a while. Watching your friend reminds me of my first mission."

While removing the hip-length scarf draped around her neck, she smiled thoughtfully. "I can't imagine you ever being quite so nervous."

Warnach's expression grew sheepish. "I was terrified of making a stupid mistake. Minister Rahmansinar had me totally in awe and thoroughly intimidated."

Walking toward him and wrapping her arms around his neck, Sandra grinned. "My dear Minister Sirinoya, I can't imagine you being intimidated by anyone."

"My dear Advocate Sirinoya," Warnach toyed with her habit of formal address, "whether or not you believe, I once was young, inexperienced, and in great need of confidence."

"You're still young," she countered with a gleam in her eye. "And now, your experience and confidence are nothing short of inspiring."

"You always refuse to allow me to win any dispute," he teased.

"What I refuse is to allow you to berate my lifemate in any way."

"I do not berate him. I voice only his observations. However, your lifemate does appreciate your loyal confidence."

Meeting Captain Trifehrian that evening for dinner, the two advocates and their ministers observed longstanding tradition. No matter how frequently diplomatic teams departed from mission vessels, risks were never more prominent than the night before a mission. Neither was there a more appropriate time to enjoy safe haven and the unique camaraderie shared by mission teams and the military forces that transported and protected them.

Twisting a stemmed glass from side to side, Captain Trifehrian absently watched the resulting swish of golden liqueur. "Simartis Major is an excellent site. Facilities are exceptional, and Simartis neutrality will certainly alleviate worries for delegates from both Ishwani and Lethamori."

"Not only for them. Less stressful conditions should facilitate the entire process." Rodan leaned back and sipped from his own glass of liqueur.

"Undoubtedly," Warnach commented. "I cannot deny looking forward to working in an environment not strained by years of war."

"Peter," Rodan said with a quick upward lift of his head, "despite the exceptional hospitality we shall enjoy on Simartis, I promise you will discover how complicated life on-mission can be."

First casting a brief glance toward Sandra, Peter responded to Rodan's friendly warning. "Minister Khalijar, although I hold no illusions that all will go smoothly, I am optimistic. After all, I do have the privilege of serving this mission with the two best field ministers the Alliance has ever known. On the other hand, I think my hardest challenge might be survival for that very same reason."

With a grin hidden behind her hand, Sandra's eyes darted from face to face. Amusement and appreciation for Peter's honest candor were evident in three approving sets of brown eyes.

"Rodan, my friend, perhaps I owe you an apology."

"An apology?" Rodan shot back at Warnach. "For what?"

Warnach replied with a wickedly humorous smirk, "I believe I may have allowed my advocate to spend too much time coaching yours. Peter's remark sounds hauntingly familiar."

Recalling hilarious exchanges at home following the Frehataran summit on Chikondra, Rodan laughed out loud. "No apologies necessary. Considering the successes you have enjoyed with your advocate, I think all ministry advocates could use her coaching."

Amusement shone from Sandra's eyes. "Gentlemen, this advocate thinks this is a perfect time for her to retreat. She expects a very busy day tomorrow, and an early bedtime seems quite in order."

Warnach's black brows arched high. "Advocate Sirinoya, I've never known you to retreat so easily."

Rising from her chair, Sandra turned slightly. "Captain Trifehrian, thank you for a lovely dinner. For now, I think I shall say goodnight while I can still make a gracious escape before getting myself into trouble with two Alliance field ministers and an advocate who has known me far too long."

Smiling broadly, Warnach also stood. "I may regret letting her go so easily, but I think I shall also retire. Captain, I also thank you for dinner. Goodnight, gentlemen."

Returning to their suite, Warnach and Sandra quickly readied themselves for bed before pausing for night prayers. Leaning sideways against his arm, she breathed deeply of the fragrant incense that wafted around her. How serene she always felt whenever she listened to the low, soothing tones of his voice while he prayed. Feeling his lips press against her head, she smiled. If only the entire galaxy could experience such peace just once.

Three days later, Peter and she waited side by side while watching the fanfare accompanying the arrival of the Ishwani and Lethamori ambassadors and their respective entourages. Ahead of them, the president of Simartis Major presented an elegant figure as she graciously welcomed the newest visitors to her planet. Flanked by the senior field service ministers who would direct the meetings, President Kirimaris conducted introductions with style and flair.

While arrival formalities continued, the two advocates discreetly disappeared for a final inspection of the conference chamber where all parties would converge to receive the formal agenda and other information before the beginning of actual talks the next day.

"Peter, my compliments," she told him while slightly adjusting the angle of a monitor to better align with the table edge. "I read your prep work yesterday. That and your set-up are outstanding."

He smiled appreciatively. "Coming from you, that means a lot."

"Arrival ceremonies should be winding down. Ready to make a mad dash back out there?"

"Right behind you!" he answered as he matched her rapid pace out of the guarded room and down the corridor.

Outside, they quickly resumed their places. The juggling act had begun. Advocates would provide organizational support, emergency research, and oversight of amenities while experienced diplomats danced the delicate ballet of coaxing, charming, coercing, and convincing hostile parties to consider alternatives to war.

Weeks later, the process ground on. Taking advantage of a holiday observed by both the Ishwani and Lethamori, President Kirimaris hosted a dinner at her private residence for members of the Alliance's diplomatic party. Her accomplishments in fostering diplomacy met serious rivalry in the face of her hospitality. Delicious wines produced in the Simartis-Talriga quadrant perfectly complimented the wide variety of both meat and vegetarian offerings. A quartet of musicians blended together a tapestry of melodies that created a soothing background for the much-needed respite from the rigors of negotiations.

Following the leisurely dinner, everyone retired to a spacious sitting room decorated predominantly in warm shades of browns and reds. Attendants carried silver trays around and offered crystal glasses containing after-dinner cordials. Subdued lighting and a ring of comfortable, velour covered loveseats created an intimate ambiance where conversation assumed less animated and more relaxed tones than over dinner.

"Warnach," Nolj Kirimaris began with an impish grin, "despite some rather high profile missions these past few years, you show none of the signs of excess strain one might expect. If anything, you look more relaxed and more handsome than ever."

Gleaming eyes and a slightly discomfited smile acknowledged his longtime friend's remarks. "Nolj, I shall take that as a compliment." Firmly grasping Sandra's hand, he continued, "Unification has yielded a wealth of benefits."

"Sandra, indulge me. I have a question for you. What is it like working with our Alliance's renowned and notorious Minister Sirinoya while simultaneously sharing your personal life with him?"

Green eyes sparkled almost as brightly as the smile that lit her face when she glanced at Warnach's confounded expression and Rodan's look of utter amusement when he diverted his stare toward his glass of icy blue liqueur. How funny, Peter thought, as he sympathized with the two ministers who had included him in the night's invitation.

Opting for a diplomatic response that would surely confuse her lifemate, Sandra answered the president's inquiry. "Working with Warnach is extremely challenging. His assignments always seem fraught with unexpected events. Maintaining his pace while fulfilling his demands on-mission can be daunting at best. On the other hand, I believe our personal empathies allow me a unique comprehension of how best to accomplish what he needs and expects."

Swiftly picking up Sandra's intent, Nolj went on, "I admire your grit. Warnach is a dear friend but one who has earned his formidable reputation. I think I should find it very difficult to work with such a man. It would be impossible if I were married to that man."

Before Warnach could say anything, Sandra said, "I never expected life with him to be easy. His character is far too dynamic. However, in all honesty, I'm not always as timid and reserved as you might think." Her eyes darted sideways to assess her lifemate's reaction. "I can assure you. He encounters his fair share of complications just having me at his side."

Clearly expecting her more typical teasing, Warnach felt unsure how to respond or even if he dared say anything. Finally, taking a fortifying sip from his glass, he tilted his head. "Nolj, there's no denying that Sandra has completely changed my life. My work has never been more satisfying despite recent events. Her support is invaluable, and she never fails to surprise me. Perhaps that's the reason behind your observation. I now live my life in constant anticipation of what will happen next whenever she's around."

Sharing one of those moments of unspoken, intuitive, feminine communication, both Nolj and Sandra laughed. In self-defense, the men utilized years of finely tuned diplomatic skills to head the conversation in a different, less confusing direction.

The following week, Warnach and Rodan prepared to enter the latest joint meeting with leaders from Ishwani and Lethamori. Earlier, Rodan had focused his efforts on the Lethamori negotiators who had brought more strident complaints to the negotiating table. Warnach had spent hours reviewing the widely varied perceptions and issues presented by the Ishwani. Meeting until late several nights in a row, the Chikondran ministers had compared results and developed strategies that finally served to open strongly promising dialogue. If all went well, this morning could well present a turning point in negotiations.

Standing inside the stylishly decorated room reserved for operations of the mission's support services, Sandra completed a last-minute revision Warnach had requested. Inserting the shielded data rod safely into her portfolio, she remarked wryly, "The life of ministry advocates. Always a revision. Always an urgent, last-minute search for some detail the minister thinks he remembers from something he read only God knows where or when."

Peter laughed. "I know what you mean. One thing about it. These two ministers keep us hopping."

"That's for sure. Now, we'd better get hopping into that conference room."

Striding across the first floor of the conference center's reception gallery, they stopped to clear the first of several security checkpoints leading to the second-floor conference salon. Since the incident on Tarmantrua, Sandra had found it impossible to rely solely on what she knew were exceptional security practices. Despite more stringent scrutiny ordered by Captain Taplinchna, her eyes never stopped moving. She never let down her own guard.

As security specialists verified their identities, she noted Peter's wary expression as his line of vision swiftly traveled from one side of the gallery to the other. Saying nothing, she waited until they were well on their way to the final security station at the foot of escalators leading up to a short hallway where Warnach and Rodan were already greeting Ishwani and Lethamori officials. Pausing, she grasped his arm. "Tell me."

His face revealed no trace of surprise. Hair prickled and stood up straight along the back of his neck. "We've both talked about not liking the layout here. I don't care how famous Simartis is for providing neutral ground for negotiations. I almost feel like we're in a shooting gallery with that open area running around the third floor above."

"Did you notice all the new faces of Simartis guards on duty?"

"I did. Is it just me, or does something not feel quite right?"

Momentarily, she chewed at the inside of her lip. Breathing in, she yielded to her inner senses of intuition. "Here." She handed him her portfolio. "Clear that last security checkpoint and give these to Warnach when you deliver your updates to Rodan. Then, get back down here."

Noting urgency in her tone, Peter nodded and hurried toward the conference room. Returning quickly, he found her in quiet discussion with two Chikondran security officers. All the while, her eyes roamed the perimeter of the upper platform encircling them. Suddenly, her posture stiffened. Following the upward angle of her face, he felt an instantaneous surge of adrenalin shoot through his body.

"Code Red!" Sandra shouted and lunged sideways, propelling Peter and herself past the protective polymer railing of the escalator. Falling to the floor, they saw one security guard shove the other just as a flash shot past them, searing the wall behind them. Smoky plumes rising from the first guard's coat were accompanied by the acrid stench of burned flesh.

"Lieutenant Mehdazh! Quick! Toss me that rifle!"

Trapped behind the security counter with the downed comrade who had saved his life, the lieutenant grabbed the lazon weapon and kicked it toward Sandra. Lifting her head slightly, she snatched up the rifle as it clattered across the floor. Grabbing her, Peter heaved her toward him and away from killing rays following the noise of the gun.

Rapidly, while the remaining Chikondran swiftly freed his security comm, the two Terrans scrambled around the edge of the escalator rail. Sandra fired the lazon rifle upward, striking a shooter on the floor above before she dropped and huddled low on the moving steps at Peter's feet.

Reaching the second floor and jumping up, they raced down the protected corridor toward the conference room. Careening around the corner, the two advocates shouted at the six guards standing outside the entrance. "Code Red, gentlemen! Inside! Now!" Sandra cried out.

Warnach and Rodan instantly jerked their heads upward in alarm as their advocates and security officers barged into the conference room. President Kirimaris raised stunned eyes that mirrored the shock of her guest dignitaries.

Peter shouted, "Everyone! Down! On the floor! Next to the wall and away from windows!"

"Guards!" Sandra ordered security with shouted commands. "Protect your ministers! Drop the tables! Keep everyone between them and the walls! Brace the doors! No one in or out until you're absolutely sure the situation is secure!"

"Sandra!" Warnach's voice called out as a guard and Rodan physically held him back.

For only a fraction of a second, her eyes met her lifemate's before she repeated her orders. "Guards! At all costs! Protect your ministers!"

Glancing at Peter, she nodded toward the door. "Brafmand! Come with us!"

Darting a swift look outside the double doors, she saw that the hallway remained clear but heard the distinctive piercing screeches of ray guns from the central gallery beyond the far corner of the corridor. Lieutenant Brafmand pressed a hand weapon into Peter's grasp just before the three bolted through the doorway and across the hall. Pressing themselves tightly against the walls, they listened to the sounds of heavy furniture banging against the doors inside the conference room.

Tense excursions with the group on Earth had honed instincts and developed a knack for communicating with few words. Peter and Sandra had walked every foot of the Simartis facility. They had memorized locations of doors, windows, and storage rooms. Behind them, they had left mission leaders and alien dignitaries as protected as possible under critical emergency circumstances. What worried them most was what lay beyond the corner only a dozen feet ahead of them.

"Brafmand, around the corner. There's a door to a stairwell. I checked inside locks upstairs and down earlier. They were secure, but I want you to stand guard at the stairs. If you hear anyone coming through, signal us immediately. Come back in, lock that door, and shoot anyone who comes through it."

"Peter, we'll cover Brafmand first. Then, we'll see if we can make our way back to the escalator."

Eyes met, and everyone nodded. Reaching the door, Brafmand eased it open. Silence in the stairwell. Curtly nodding, he slid through the opening.

Just as the door closed, she felt the vibrations in her security com. Quickly, she lifted her wrist close to her face. "Lieutenant!" she hissed into the slim, silver-colored bracelet. "This is Advocate Sirinoya. Report."

"Dakahln is critically injured. Reports from the main gallery indicate five down, condition unknown. Eight are shielded behind reinforced polymer barriers. We've spotted at least four attackers on the upper level. No idea how many on lower level. All enemy wearing Simartis uniforms. Taplinchna is on his way with reinforcements."

"Mehdazh, hold your position. We're coming."

Peter cocked his head to one side. "Is this what they call a mission complication?"

Letting go of a breath fraught with stress, Sandra answered, "Not the kind of complication I banked on. This isn't supposed to happen. Especially not here on Simartis."

Peter grinned ironically. "Great first mission. Ready?"

"Ready."

Low to the floor, they scurried toward the top of the escalator. On the lower level, Mehdazh pointed his weapon around the edge of the counter platform and fired. Sounds of crossfire reached their ears. Alliance security intended to force any attackers on the lower level to run a fiery gauntlet of deadly lazon rays.

"Peter, watch the upper level while I go down."

"Careful!" he responded.

Dragging the silk scarf she wore from around her neck and over her head, she flung it aside and rolled onto one of the wide, grooved, escalator steps. Clutching the rifle, she began the nerve-wracking descent while using one hand to prevent her clothing from catching in the interlocking grooves of the steps. Just as her step rolled toward the floor, she cringed. Fortunately, spotting an attacker above her, Peter fired his pistol. Tucking into a tight ball, she rolled off the escalator and behind the wide counter with Mehdazh.

Agony contorted Lieutenant Dakahln's youthful features. One glance confirmed the worst. He was dying. Ignoring continuous fire, Sandra tenderly pulled his head onto her lap. "Dakahln, I won't leave you."

"Advocate Sirinoya," he murmured weakly. "Prayers?"

"I know. I will take them for you."

Her heart fluttered. Chikondrans traveled galactic expanses in unceasing efforts to promote peace. Only a guarded few outsiders knew of their deep, secret fears of dying alone, away from Chikondra. According to traditional beliefs, if someone could be trusted to carry final sacred prayers to loved ones, the departed soul would not endure sorrowful delay in reaching peaceful repose. Warnach, Araman, and Badrik had patiently taught her the prayers in the hope she would never need to bear them.

Lifting her eyes for only a moment, she sighed in relief. Peter had safely made his way down the escalator. Her eyes dropped to the ashen face lying on her lap. She listened carefully to pain-broken utterances. From memory stored more in her heart than in her brain, she repeated the phrases that evoked faith and comfort. Somberly, she then slid eyelids down over eyes that no longer held the light of life.

"Sandra?"

Looking upward, she gently placed Dakahln's head on the floor. "Is Taplinchna here yet?"

"Outside. Securing the outer perimeter. The assault squad inside must be scattered throughout the building. Two are holding support service staffers hostage. We figure there must be six or more on the third level. Thankfully, the escalator serving that floor is in full view of our people in the main gallery."

"Okay. Quick. What are their options to get to the conference room?"

"All-out attack against security in the lobby or via the stairwells. That's it unless they have air attack capability."

"That's Taplinchna's problem." Twisting her head, she watched Mehdazh duck a shot that struck just inches away from the curved end of the counter. "You're our only hope here until Taplinchna gets his people in."

Without speaking, all three understood the dangerous tasks awaiting them. Once more, Peter and Sandra launched themselves onto the escalator. Swiftly, they retraced their steps back to the stairwell door.

"Brafmand! Status!" she barked into her comm.

"Watch out! Coming in! Sounds like the door upstairs is ready to give!"

"Open now!"

As the door opened, Peter and Sandra both bolted through, dropped to their knees beneath the door frame, and raised their weapons. Their vantage point provided perfect aim. Waiting until the last possible second, they fired. Bodies rolled down steps or fell over stair railings to the floor below them. Desperately, they scrambled back into the corridor and slammed the heavy door.

Crouching with his back against the opposite wall, Brafmand positioned himself directly across from the door and ordered Peter and Sandra to flank him about five feet on either side. Quarters were tight. They would have no choice but to fire their weapons.

Suddenly, the floor shuddered beneath them. Explosions. Pungent fumes reached their noses. Clouds of smoke rolled up the escalator and seeped beneath the stairwell door. Brafmand's eyes closed thankfully. "Taplinchna! That smell is udrimanone! He's coming after the attackers!"

Pandemonium sounded just beyond the door in front of them. Shouting. No English. No Chikondran. Desperately furious blue eyes darted up and down the hallway. "They're after the mission team. Hurry!"

"Now! The table! They get to my minister over my dead body!" Sandra cried out.

Leaping to their feet, the three ran and whipped around the reception table outside the conference room doors. Flipping it onto its side and falling to their knees behind what little cover it offered, each hardly breathed. Furious pounding. The resounding bang of the door flying open and crashing against the wall. Pale blue uniforms. Wildly flying lazon rays. Angry shouts. A scream. A furious curse.

Total confusion rapidly transformed into highly orchestrated training in practice. Security tactical leaders assessing surroundings and securing premises. Clipped communications efficiently transmitting status reports while simultaneously determining the condition of the mission team. Instructions for immediate dispatch of medical technicians.

Impatiently, Taplinchna waited as security inside the conference room responded to his commands to clear and open the doors. Forcefully entering the room, he questioned guards who had been ordered to protect ministry personnel and alien dignitaries alike. Obviously relieved that the negotiators and diplomats were all safe, the security chief consulted yet again via com with his officers throughout the building. Control had been regained, and security was reestablished.

Professional composure failed to conceal dread in Taplinchna's dark eyes as he met demanding gazes from Ministers Khalijar and Sirinoya. "Minister Sirinoya, please. We need you outside."

Watching the instantaneous drain of color from his colleague's face, Rodan gripped Warnach's arm. "I am right behind you, my friend."

Fear marked the rushed steps that carried Warnach over tables and around chairs toppled onto the floor. Reaching opened doors, he halted abruptly. His heart leapt into his throat, and his breath escaped in a soul-emptying gasp. Across the hall, one paramedic hurriedly produced a life scanner while two others set up emergency medical equipment. On his knees, Peter's tense profile conveyed abject fear.

Launching himself across the broad corridor, Warnach dropped to the floor next to Peter. "Sandra," he gasped hoarsely as frightened black-brown eyes flinched at the sight of the scorched fabric of her nashavri. "Sandra?"

"Minister Sirinoya, please. Step back for just a moment," the lead paramedic instructed. Passing the scanner back and forth over her still body, the medic noted vital signs. Twisting his head, he barked orders to his colleagues. "Farmenobene infusion. Quickly. Start removing scorched fabric from that shoulder."

Immediately, the requested medication was slapped into his hands, and he administered the drug. Waiting thirty interminable seconds, he scanned again. Looking into Warnach's worried face, the medic almost smiled as he stood up. "Minister Sirinoya, her injury isn't life-threatening. The medication I just gave her will take a few moments to enter her system, but it should relieve most of the pain until we can get her in for HAU treatment. Obviously, we must transport the most severely wounded first. We'll take her as soon as possible."

Swallowing repeatedly, Warnach swayed drunkenly before falling again to his knees. Grateful to be on her uninjured side, he took her right hand and lifted it to trembling lips. "Sandra? Can you hear me? Sandra?"

As pain-glazed eyes fluttered and then opened, she turned her head toward his voice. The ever-so-slight motion resulted in an agonized moan and a flood of involuntary tears. The sound of his name emerged from her lips as a strangled whisper.

"Shi'níyah, be still," he told her tenderly as he leaned forward to kiss her forehead.

"Stay with me?"

"Of course, I'll stay with you. Just be still, Shi'níyah."

Her tiny nod in response produced another pained grimace. "Rodan? Peter? Nolj?"

Rolling his eyes, he sought to master raging emotions. "All safe, Sandra. Now, please, be quiet."

Again, a slight nod that was followed by the closing of her eyes. For a moment, Warnach found himself fending off terror. The paramedic attending her smiled reassuringly. "Sir, the medication is taking effect. Perhaps you could remove her Kitak before we place her on the stretcher."

Warnach's chest contracted to the point he questioned if his pounding heart might not erupt from his body. Sliding forward, he tenderly removed the engraved ring circling her head. He clutched the precious band against his chest and then clung to the limp fingers of her right hand until medical personnel came to evacuate her.

He wondered when he had ever had more difficulty standing up. Gratitude seeped through him for the strength of Rodan's firm grasp. "I must go with her."

"Of course, you must. I will come as soon as things are settled here."

Grimly, Warnach met his friend's concerned eyes. "Tell Taplinchna I want a full report the minute he figures out what happened here and how."

"He already knows. Go now. They're leaving."

Thankfully, Simartis Major's large Terran population necessitated the presence of HAU's specifically calibrated to human biological patterns. Insistent upon not leaving her, Warnach had spent two hours on a hard chair outside the HAU. Glancing through the transparent polymer pane above her, he grimaced at ugly burns marring her left shoulder. Medication would alleviate pain. Additional HAU sessions would not only heal injured tissue and bone; the treatments would eliminate scarring. Nothing the doctors could do would ever erase the terror that had inundated him that morning.

Gray shadows of evening filled the hospital room. The door slid open and closed with a smooth, quiet swish. Warnach looked upward and forced a grim smile. "How glad I am that you've come, my friend. How bad was it?"

"Very," Rodan answered honestly. "Twenty Simartis guards murdered with poison. Seven members of our security team are dead. Three support staff and five security guards were injured. Two fight for their lives."

Warnach's chest expanded with the mighty breath he inhaled and expelled. "Plus Sandra."

Rodan nodded. "Plus Sandra. Peter told me that several intruders made a final advance in an attempted assault on the negotiators. Sandra and Lieutenant Brafmand were both hurt, but the three of them slowed the assault squad until Taplinchna's men reached the corridor."

Strain carved tense, worried lines into both faces. "Advocates are supposed to be the last line of defense for their ministers. Ours should have stayed in that conference room with us."

Quiet steps carried Rodan across the room. Crouching, he stared upward at Warnach's weary expression. "Our advocates possess rare courage. Lieutenant Mehdazh informed me that they sensed a problem before the onset of the attack. He had just cautioned forward security when the first shots were fired. Without Peter and Sandra, things would have likely been much worse."

Warnach's eyes searched his friend's face for answers. "What do I do, Rodan? How can I possibly expose her to risk like this again?"

Rodan's jaw clenched. He forced back the lump in his throat. "You and I have faced these risks for years. No matter what, we know we do the right thing for the right reasons. We continue because we also understand that our work makes a difference. What you must do is talk to her after all the facts are established and ask her what she wants to do. Then, you must decide together how you will continue."

Sharp, side-to-side movement of his jaw reflected inner chaos. "Rodan, I nearly lost my ki'mirsah today. If she had died, my life would have lost all meaning."

In a low voice, Rodan disagreed. "No, Warnach. I know you. You would have grieved, undoubtedly for the remainder of your life. However, I believe your resolve would have strengthened. If you lose her on-mission, you could never let that loss be in vain."

Nervously, Warnach fingered her half of Kitak he still held on his lap. "I wish I could believe that."

A muted moan interrupted the resultant silence. Quickly standing, Warnach placed her Kitak on the bed by her side. Bending forward, he stroked her hair. "Shi'níyah?" Tenderness in his voice prompted a weak smile.

"I thought I heard your voice."

"Rodan is here with me. I can safely say we are both relieved to see you awake again." He watched her lips draw into another faint smile. "How do you feel?"

"Groggy. Glad to be alive, but my shoulder hurts like hell."

The hint of humor in her voice heartened him. "No one is happier than I that you survived today."

The following morning, accompanied by a heavy security entourage, he returned to the hospital just as she was being taken for additional treatment. Despite neuro-sedation, she was still awake enough to cast him a reassuring smile. Outside the HAU, he waited again with ponderous thoughts as company.

Rodan's words had haunted him throughout a sleepless night. Looking back on a long career, Warnach recalled other incidents that had placed his life at risk. Reflecting on those moments, he remembered anger more than anything else. That fury had been aimed directly at those committed to killing and destruction. Staunchly, he had done what Rodan and hundreds of others in their profession had done. He had consciously dismissed nightmarish memories and turned his focus to the future. As a result, entire worlds had moved out of the chaotic hell of war. Lives had been spared. Until now, he had always believed results justified the risks.

Ever since he had met Sandra on Earth, his entire life had transformed. Her dreams were shared vision between them. Her gentle presence provided calm for his soul. Her dynamic character inspired him to awaken and face each new day with optimism. The day before, his chosen career had threatened her life for the third time. Reluctantly, he faced an uncertain future as he recognized an urgent need for time to reassess the direction of his profession and his life.

Later, she smiled wanly as she slowly chewed a bite of fresh fruit. "My ki'medsah, I told you already. Constant worry will change nothing. The Zeterons are growing bolder because diplomatic efforts are successfully holding them at bay. Now is when we need to forge ahead and be stronger than ever."

His jaw ached from constant, tense grinding of his back teeth. "Sandra, I'm not sure I can go on this way. Placing my own life at risk was one thing. Allowing you to put your life in constant danger terrifies me as nothing ever has."

Gradually finishing her light meal, she thoughtfully listened while he poured out the innermost thoughts and feelings troubling him so much. Bederand. Tarmantrua. Now, Simartis Major. Each incident had literally threatened her life. That she could not deny. Intellectually and empathetically, she suddenly realized how fully she comprehended the intensity of his turmoil.

Finally, when his words slowed and stopped, wisdom reflected from the depths of her being. With a quiet chink, she rested her fork on her plate. "Warnach, look at me."

Raggedly breathing in, he met her serious gaze. Unable to utter a single word, he waited for her to speak.

"My ki'medsah, you must know that I understand exactly how you feel. You seem to forget that the incident on Bederand plus these recent, back-to-back attacks on Tarmantrua and Simartis also brought me painfully close to losing you. I won't pretend anything. I'm scared. What scares me most is that I don't know if I could ever pick up the pieces of my life if I would ever lose you. I just don't know if that's possible.

"In the meantime, I do know that we can't simply turn away because of what might happen. We have to try, Warnach. We have to keep doing what we believe is right. I want you to remember what I told you years ago on Earth. If I die, I will die filled with thanks for every single moment we've ever shared and for the treasures wrapped up in every second of our life together. We need to cling tightly to what we have and cherish every memory because tomorrow holds precious few guarantees."

In silence, his mind rambled. Her eyes commanded his attention. Her wisdom inched its way throughout his body, mind, and soul. Her steadfast courage inspired him. Of its own volition, his right hand raised, and his fingertips traced circles at his temple. No smile crossed his face, but deeply etched lines eased. "Are you ready for your Kitak?"

# Chapter Seventeen

L ush greenery lavished the enormous hospital atrium. Brilliant reds, sunny yellows, and cheerful oranges crowned broad and slender stems alike. From the spotlessly clean, domed skylight above, sunlight spilled inside on brilliant beams intent on driving away shadows and gloom. Dressed in mauve robe and seated at a scrolled table, Sandra stared blankly beyond Rodan's shoulder.

"I, too, am worried. In all the years I've known him, never have I seen Warnach so distressed."

Forcing herself to face Rodan, she sadly shook her head. "We talked again this morning. He's always known the risks."

"Sandra, knowing that danger exists is far different from seeing someone you love nearly killed," Nolj Kirimaris stated contemplatively.

Green eyes drifted momentarily to a huge scarlet blossom. "Even though my initial commitment is nearly over, I don't want to leave field ministry. Not yet, although I will if he insists. I just don't want him to leave like this. He excels in field diplomacy, and the impact he has affects so many lives."

Clasping hands together on the table, Rodan gazed into the face of his best friend's lifemate. So young, he thought. So dedicated. So attuned to the man she loved. "Sandra, Nolj and I have both talked with him but to no avail. You're the only one who can influence him into changing his mind."

Tears glistened in her eyes when she looked up. "I was so wrong last night when I thought I'd already gotten through to him. If he resigns, he'll regret the decision sooner or later. With everything he can still accomplish, how can I possibly face being the cause of such monumental regret when he finally realizes what he's left behind? How do I reach him before it's too late?"

Rodan leaned forward over the round tabletop and took her right hand as Nolj responded, "Perhaps that's your best argument. Point out dramatic progress on Frehatar and even Bederand. Discuss the key roles he played on those worlds and many others. Express your feelings. Emphasize your fears."

Sandra's face dropped, and teardrops splashed into carved designs on the white table. "Pray for me," she whispered pleadingly. "Pray that I'm not wrong about this and that I can help him make the right decision." Tightly squeezing Rodan's hand, she sought both comfort and encouragement.

A day later, Warnach carefully helped her dress. Although still sore, her wounded shoulder had responded remarkably well to HAU treatments, enabling quick release from hospital care. When he finished fastening the back of her nashavri, he grasped her uninjured arm and gently spun her around. He looked down at her and closely examined her face. Relieved by how well she looked, he smiled before bestowing a lingering cerea-semi'ittá.

With a dreamy expression, she gazed at him as he backed away. "Ci'ittá mi'ittá, my Warnach."

"Ci'ittá mi'ittá, me'u Shi'níyah." Love shone from solemn eyes. "Are you ready to leave?"

"Absolutely."

Grateful for Rodan's continuing professional support, Warnach excused himself from a day of meetings to dedicate time to making her comfortable in a suite at the Simartis presidential palace. Whisking her into bed for doctor-ordered rest, he shed formal coat and shoes before reclining by her side into a mountain of pillows. In his hand, he held the antique book Sandra had received as a graduation gift. "I hope you don't mind that I packed this. I always think that someday I may find time to read to you again."

"That's a promise I'd nearly forgotten," she remarked delightedly. "You're really going to read to me?"

Fleeting but nevertheless evident fear flashed across olive features. "I must make more time to keep my promises to you." Then, placing the large book atop a cushion on his lap, he escaped into one of his world's oldest tales.

*Fresh, so clean and bright, arriving light would step upon precious ground and into the sacred waters of Mamehr Chikondra. In joy would holy guardians of Meichasa acknowledge the arrival of the new child of light. Into joy had this helping soul come to deliver from darkness Chikondra's steadfast warrior.*

*Upon their love would Yahvanta smile. Upon their hearts would the Great Spirit bestow precious blessings. Bound they would be to one another. Bearing holy vows and sacred intent, afar would their paths carry them, afar from Chikondra's loving embrace.*

*For respite, they would always yearn. Seeking renewal and revival, to Meichasa's spirits would they return. Always waiting, always listening, Meichasa's guardians would welcome their new light and her valiant warrior.*

*In joy again, with inner purpose restored, the two spirits joined by Yahvanta would venture anew. Passing the stars of the Great Spirit's universe, touching the hearts of His many peoples, His chosen defender would journey with the light of his soul. In purpose combined, they would continue their duty, fulfilling the mission decreed at the coming of Meichasa.*

*Bearing faith and filled with their love, still, the great lights felt an empty chill. Longing did they know, but they continued their quest. Neither cried in the cold. Neither complained of empty arms. Their spirits chose to be thankful for the love granted to them.*

*Always watching, always listening, Meichasa's spirits bore silent message unto the Great Spirit. These faithful lights deserved never the dark when into shadows they must surely go.*

*Wise in heart, the Great Spirit did hearken unto Chikondra's guardians. Indeed, those guardians did understand. Besides, Mamehr Chikondra's defender spirit and his helping light would need much aid.*

"Warnach?" Her hand came to rest on his thigh, interrupting him. Thoroughly relaxed from listening to wonderfully rich tones in his voice, she could hardly stay awake.

Noting her expression, he smiled affectionately. "I can read more later if you like."

"Promise?" she murmured.

"I promise." Setting aside the antique volume, he turned and kissed her. "Sleep, me'u Shi'níyah. I shall be right here when you awaken."

Watching until healing sleep descended upon her, Warnach settled back with a sigh. Velvety shadows caressed the crystal blues and mint greens of the room's interior. Rounded lines defined edges of ivory finished furnishings. Framed, oval paintings elegantly punctuated walls wearing the muted glow of shining paper stripes. Cool. Clean. Smooth. Peacefully, he drifted into a light sleep.

～

Onboard the Rahpliknar, she curled into the corner of a sofa inside a secluded reading lounge. Sighing, she set aside her book, its old text still too difficult for her. Besides, she thought, he read so beautifully. Someday, they might actually finish the story. Her thoughts then sadly strayed to their final days on Simartis Major.

Tall and impossibly slender, the ambassador from Ishwani had congratulated Rodan Khalijar and Warnach Sirinoya for wise counsel. He had also praised the bravery of the Alliance's mission team. The Ishwani leader had faced death alongside his enemy under circumstances where both had been defended by another people. The alien diplomat had confronted unique, unexpected reality. Perspective entered transition, prompting initial steps onto the road toward negotiated peace.

Chimes signaled the opening of the door, and she looked up. Her smile faded. "I wish you would smile, my ki'medsah."

"I will. As soon as I deliver you safely home," he replied before depositing himself beside her.

"What will you tell Baadihm Farsuk?"

Thoughtfully, he shook his head. "The truth. The time has come for my direction to change."

"Oh, Warnach, how I wish you'd reconsider."

Twisting toward her, he reached out to touch her Kitak. "You know how I feel."

Dropping her face, she stared at the Mashana on her finger. "Do my feelings matter in this?"

"Of course," he responded tautly.

Daring directness, she met his questioning gaze. "There are things you forget."

"Such as?"

"Such as the seven months left on my service commitment. Your resignation means I'll have to seek another advocacy post."

"Another post! What does that mean? I thought you said…"

"I said I would follow you if you insist on resignation. However, you obviously shut out what I said about leaving after I meet my obligations."

His eyes narrowed in disbelief. "Sandra, you can't be serious."

Firmly, she set her jaw. "I am. Completely. You know how seriously I view commitments. I worked hard to earn this advocacy position, and I think I deserve to finish it honorably. Then, despite how much I thrive on our work, I'll join you because you're my most important commitment."

Frustration defined itself in his expression. "If you worry about reimbursement for your studies…"

"Warnach, I don't give a damn about the money. I know you have plenty enough to repay the academy for my grants. That's not the point. My self-respect is at stake here. I accepted the grant. I agreed to three years of service in exchange. You need to understand. I have every intention of fulfilling my part of the agreement."

Jerking to his feet, he stormed across the lounge before spinning around to glare at her. "Sandra, I don't want you back out here! Conditions are worsening! Who knows where Zeterons will strike next or with how much force? I will not face that risk where you're concerned!"

Rising too quickly, she winced at pain shafting through her arm, but she refused to yield. "The choice isn't yours to make! I don't want to leave field ministry! Because I love you, I will. However, you'll have to wait until I complete my service agreement." She paused, her eyes flashing stubbornly. "My next HAU treatment is in fifteen minutes. I have to go."

Quiet opposition marked the remainder of their voyage home. Avoiding him, she concentrated on therapy for her injured arm and shoulder. Long hours aboard ship were also spent on laborious efforts detailing the deadly altercation on Simartis and assisting Peter as he compiled Rodan's final summaries related to the negotiations. Meanwhile, finding it impossible to cope with her obstinacy, Warnach withdrew into depressive isolation.

~

Rodan looked up. "Peter, your draft is excellent. I noted only a few minor changes. Read through them, and let me know if you have any questions. Beyond that, you can prepare the finals."

"Thank you, sir. I'll have everything completed before we reach Chikondra." Appreciation gleamed in Peter's eyes, and he started to leave.

"Peter, before you go, may I talk to you? About something personal?"

Seeing Peter's nod, Rodan continued, "I know that you and Sandra have been close friends for many years. Has she mentioned anything about…"

Peter instantly recognized his minister's discomfort. Chikondrans normally hated to pry, even where friends and family were concerned. He smiled reassuringly. "She told me that Minister Sirinoya plans to leave the ministry. She also insists that she has every intention of staying with the ministry until she finishes her service commitment."

Thoughtfully, Rodan bit into his lower lip. "I wondered what direction she would take."

Surmising details Rodan declined to reveal, Peter mused aloud. "She's convinced that Minister Sirinoya is making a serious mistake. Knowing her, she's likely terrified that he might blame her for his leaving."

"Warnach and I have been friends for many years. Field diplomacy is ingrained in the very way he breathes. I also believe he's making a grave error, but he would never blame her. He loves her too much. That's why it pains me to see them so at odds. Her safety is his sole reason behind the decision to resign. However, I do admire her for standing up to him so she can meet her obligations. That can't be easy." Pausing, Rodan looked embarrassed. "I apologize."

"Sir, there's no need for an apology. I probably think the same as you. We hate seeing them in conflict. I suggest you look at things this way. She knows how much he'll eventually regret this. We both know she's the only one who can change his mind. Personally, sir, I wouldn't worry so much. I know all the stories about how tenacious Minister Sirinoya can be. I also know Sandra, and my bet is on her. Once she sets her mind, even he can't outlast her."

Staring at the closed door after Peter left, Rodan mulled over his advocate's words. Memories of another near-tragedy prompted sudden optimism that made him smile. After all, Sandra had survived more than Zeterons. She had conquered Ku'saá.

~

Holding the towel high, she let light breezes ripple the fabric straight before smoothing it out on the beach. Firmly, she thrust the striped umbrella into the sand and set a jaunty angle against the afternoon sun. Lying backwards, she rested her head on an inflated pillow and closed her eyes. Azure skies. Fresh, sea-kissed air. Whispering tides.

Beneath protective shade, rest eluded her. How she had hated the expression on Araman's face when Warnach had announced his plans to resign from field service ministry. Even worse, she had overheard his heated discussion with Badrik. Tired and irritated, she had gone to bed without dinner, without entering the Brisajai. Rising before dawn, she had shoved some things into a bag and hastily left the house. As if sensing her need, the seashore had summoned her.

Reluctantly, she opened her eyes and grimaced. Black eyes peering down at her sparked with anger. Impatiently, she rolled over. "Go away."

Refusing to move, he crouched beside her and talked to her back. "Do you know how many people I called looking for you?" When she refused to answer, he reached out, inadvertently grasping her left shoulder. Her cry of pain shocked him onto his knees. "Sandra, are you all right? I'm sorry. I didn't mean...."

Bolting upward and pressing her hand against her shoulder, she glared at him. "I came here to get some peace, Warnach! Just go away! I'll come home when I'm ready."

Uncertainty carved deeper lines into his tired face. "Shi'níyah, I'm really sorry. Sandra," he paused to draw in a sustaining breath, "please, listen to me. I love you. I cannot bear having you so angry with me."

Without a word, she impatiently rose to her feet. Gathering her things into a haphazard bundle, she rapidly strode back to the house. Tossing everything into a heap beside the kitchen door, she leaned over the sink and splashed cool water on her face. Looking sideways, she watched his hesitation before he slowly came inside. How sad he looked. Feeling her heart lurch with guilt, she moved into his arms.

Holding her for the first time in almost two weeks, he savored the sense of reconnection that seeped throughout his being. "Sandra," his whisper pleaded, "don't be angry with me anymore. I only want to keep you safe."

For the second time since the assault on Simartis, she cried. She wanted to forget the pain. She wanted to escape memories of Dakahln's death and then delivering his final prayers to grief-stricken parents. She wanted to erase the unusual conflict that had divided her and Warnach. She wanted to ease her ki'medsah's mind. She wanted her life back. Her words muffled against his shirt. "I love you, Warnach, but I'm so afraid of how this could come between us."

The swelling knot in his throat prevented speech. Instead, he guided her to the lounge and sat with her on a sofa. Tender fingers brushed tears from her cheeks. Full lips tautened with regret. "I can't forget, Shi'níyah. Every time I close my eyes, I choke with fear."

Now. If not now, she instinctively realized she would lose. Lovingly, she rested her hand against his cheek. "I know. How I wish I could promise nothing will ever happen, but I can't. Warnach, we both know how much your work has always meant to you. No one exceeds your diplomatic skill. Not even Rodan. The choice you're making right now could affect entire worlds for centuries. Can you begin to imagine the guilt that makes me feel?"

His eyes squeezed closed. "You should feel no guilt. The decision is mine."

Countering, she continued, "Long before I ever met you, I decided on my own to enter field ministry. I was there because of my own free will. You didn't fire that lazon rifle, but that doesn't stop you from assuming blame because I got hurt." The look in his eyes spurred her on. "Warnach, we're both rational, capable adults. We both know the risks inherent in field diplomacy. We also understand gains accomplished by that work, especially when you do it."

With his chin wedged into an open hand, he nervously stroked his beard between thumb and forefinger. "I can't lose you."

"If you go through with this, I know I'll lose you. Warnach, I remember something you said on our honeymoon. You told me how you felt that you'd lost part of yourself when Lashira demanded you leave active mission work. You still aren't ready to sacrifice the part of your life that is field diplomacy. Neither am I. Think, my ki'medsah. You can't let fear decide for you. If you do, you'll never forgive yourself, and you'll condemn me to a lifetime of guilt."

Time crawled. His stomach churned. His head ached. All the while, with eyes closed, he relished the light weight of her hand upon his chest. How well she understood. What could he do? What could he say? Finally, he breathed out a sigh. "Shi'níyah, you went to bed last night without prayers. Neither were you home this morning."

Too surprised to muster a smile, she dropped her forehead against his arm. His voice alone conveyed decision. Without a word, she let him help her up and guide her into the Brisajai.

~

Voices called her from sated sleep. She resisted waking. How sweet and gentle his lovemaking had been. How much she had needed him. How good she had felt with him sleeping beside her.

Suddenly, her eyes flew open. Shaking off drowsiness, she sat up. Responding to urgency, she rolled out of bed and ran. With long hair whipping in the wind, she scanned the open sea. Tides noisily unfurled upon the shore. Again, she heard urgent voices. Without regard for churning waters, she raced into the swirling foam. Within moments, she saw them.

The adult male made repeated shallow dives. The female's distressed cries pierced her brain. Struggling to stay on her feet, Sandra hurried toward them. Finally reaching them, she gasped. The adults were desperately trying to prevent one of the younger Quazon from sinking. The youngster flailed helplessly, trapped in netting used to protect ocean harvests from schools of hungry fish.

Adrenalin overcame weakness in her shoulder. Reaching out, she bounced with waves while supporting the panicked youngster. Desperately, she assessed the tangled netting. She could never free the Quazon without help, but neither could she desert her friends.

A wave tossed her backward. "Hold him! Just a moment longer!" Doggedly moving forward, she rubbed her temple. "Warnach," she begged, praying he might sense her desperate thoughts. "I need you! Help me!" Then, she grabbed onto the Quazon and held him to allow the adults a moment of rest.

"Sandra!" Having awakened to the plea heard inside his mind, he now shouted her name as he rounded the corner of the bungalow. Spotting her just as a wave rolled over her head, he raced toward shore and dived into the water. Dragging her backward, he felt weighted resistance.

Sputtering, she coughed and spat salty seawater but refused to let go of the ensnared Quazon. "Warnach! I'm okay! Hurry! Go find something that'll cut through this netting!"

Staggering out of the water, he stumbled toward the bungalow. Banging open the lid of a toolbox, he snatched up a cutter used for garden fencing. Reaching shore again, he reentered the water. "Sandra! Pull him in!"

Twisting her head, she kicked strong legs against the sandy bottom, continuously propelling herself toward the beach. With the young one securely held by bloody hands tangled into the netting, she gave a final heave and fell backward with the heavy Quazon across her legs. Despite her voice growing hoarse from swallowing salty seawater, she initiated a cooing monologue to soothe the frightened creature.

Warnach frantically tugged at the net. Finally creating a little slack, he slid the cutters between silver skin and strong filaments. Working rapidly, he carefully snipped clinging wires. With the net quickly loosening, Sandra was able to help free the Quazon from the deadly fabric. Then, Warnach helped her slide the helpless creature from her legs. Using the incoming tide for buoyancy, they turned the youngster. Supporting him from opposite sides, they slowly moved toward deeper water until the exhausted youth floated on its own.

Breathless, Warnach stared in dismay at Sandra's cut and bleeding hands. "Shi'níyah, we must go inside. I need to take care of your hands."

Nodding, she smiled weakly. "Go. I'll just be a minute."

Pausing after reaching shore, he watched as the great creatures surrounded her. Tears flooded his eyes. Never in ten lifetimes could he have ever imagined waking to rescue a sacred Quazon.

Calming seas rushed around her. Despite sea salt burning into cut hands, she reached out and offered soothing caresses to weary friends. She smiled at their thoughts invading her mind. "I'm glad we were here when you needed us. You've always been here for me."

Soft laughter erupted. With the amazing resiliency of youth, the small Quazon had revived and wriggled close to her. Stroking his narrow snout, she shook her head and gazed affectionately toward the smiling female. "I suppose you're right. Even young angel spirits have much to learn."

Her arms wrapped around the small Quazon and drew it tightly to her breast. Swiftly, her mind dismissed thoughts of children she wished she could have with Warnach. Aloud, she spoke to the adults. "My friends, some advice. I suggest you watch over this mischievous fellow more closely. We don't want to lose him."

Within minutes, broad tails curled around her legs in fond farewell. Watching until they disappeared, she smiled and returned to the house and the man waiting within.

~

"Little sister," Badrik told her days later over lunch, "my brother had me seriously worried when you returned from Simartis Major. He's quite strong enough to live with any decision he makes, but he is more than fortunate for the way you understand him."

"We both know how much he loves his work. I shudder to think if…"

Badrik smiled and reached across the table for her hand. "My sister, you never fail where Warnach is concerned."

Hesitantly, she gazed into Badrik's handsome, bearded face. How well he had picked up on her thoughts. "Badrik, I trust your advice. Tell me. Have I done the right thing? I love my work, too, and I don't want to quit the ministry. At the same time, I never want to face something like this again. Still, the Alliance needs him."

Leaning back in his chair, Badrik drank from a cup of tea. Gazing into troubled eyes, he understood underlying implications. Work sent her around the galaxy to unstable locations. Already proving herself a strong asset to the ministry of field diplomacy, she had also gained admiration for her abilities to react quickly and definitively in the face of volatile situations. As Warnach Sirinoya's advocate, she supported one of the busiest and most successful diplomatic ministers in history. As that minister's lifemate, her brush with death had nearly frightened him into leaving his vocation. Professional responsibility was one thing. Potential to end a career credited with saving millions of lives loomed as great burden.

Obsidian eyes reflected the depths of his thoughts. "Sandra," he began, "the fear both of you just faced is completely understandable. On the other hand, Warnach fully recognizes the value of diplomacy. He pursues diplomacy not only as a profession. The quest for peace is defined as purpose for our people. You comprehend that on a higher plane than do many Chikondrans."

He paused, choosing words carefully. "I have no way to express my admiration for your obvious willingness to advocate so strongly in favor of my brother's vocation. Your decision to continue is easy for neither of you. Although I do expect time to alter your careers, I firmly believe that, for now, you take exactly the right steps for both you and Warnach."

Needing reassurance, she smiled. "Thank you, big brother. My head tells me I'm right, but my heart wants to get in the way."

"Because you love him." Grinning, Badrik reached again for her hand. "I must return to base for a briefing, but remember. Your big brother is always prepared to listen whenever you need."

# Chapter Eighteen

Five months later, Sandra waited anxiously to disembark from the crowded shuttle. Gone for more than three months, she had substituted when Alliance Council Master Devorius' senior advocate had requested leave to be with an elderly parent. The goodwill sweep through the MemRa-Jopring Sector had lasted ten weeks and had carried them through five solar systems with stops on nine planets. Completing the mission, she had submitted quickly approved final reports and headed for a brief visit to Earth. All the while, she had maintained regular communication with Warnach, who had remained on Chikondra to attend meetings of the Chikondra High Council. Still, she missed him terribly and could hardly wait for their reunion.

The public arrival concourse bustled with peoples of dozens of races from around the Alliance. Diplomatic identification allowed swift bypass of slower-moving lines. Cleared to enter the concourse, her eyes swept a sea of faces. None were familiar. With disappointment darkening her eyes, she gripped the portfolio strap over her shoulder and briskly headed toward the main corridor.

"Patience might erase frustration from that step!"

Stopping, she sharply pivoted. Handsomely attired in a tailored, knee-length coat, Warnach hurried toward her. A glowing smile instantly banished shadows from green eyes. Within seconds, his arms surrounded her. Ignoring the throngs around them, they held tightly to one another. When he dared ease their embrace, his hands framed her face.

"Me'u Shi'níyah, your ki'medsah welcomes you home." With that, he escorted her through the busy shuttleport, collected her belongings, and whisked her outside to a waiting transport. With a private chauffeur piloting them home, he clung to her hands while peppering her with questions about her family, the Edwards, and her experiences on-mission with Master Devorius.

With Araman visiting Nadana in Tichtika, they were able to savor a leisurely afternoon and evening together. Shoving packed luggage into her closet, they surrendered to need spawned by separation. Deft fingers undressed her while ravenous lips devoured kisses she offered. Hands reacquainted themselves with smooth skin and firm contours of bodies clamoring to reestablish the physical connections manifesting their love. Noon sunlight, peeking through windows, transformed into late afternoon shadows as they loved one another.

Having ordered in a gourmet meal to mark her return, Warnach suggested a walk before dinner. Fresh autumn air delighted her senses following the voyage from Earth. Back at the house, laughter punctuated conversation over supper. Hours passed quickly. Soon, they knelt inside the Brisajai. Serenity vibrated within the deep voice offering prayers thankful for her safe arrival home.

Warmer than usual fall weather found them outside again the following day. Their walk led them far from the house. Sun washed their world with golden light. Dancing brooks, rich soil, and evergreen foliage combined to fill the air with aromatic fragrance. Leaves had begun their descent, creating colorful piles that invited high spirits to leap into colorful, crunchy depths.

Unusually lighthearted, Warnach grinned wickedly as he shoved stacks of fallen leaves into a huge mountain. Gay laughter filled the air as she watched him. Shrugging out of his coat, he carefully spread it atop the leaves. With ebony eyes gleaming, he beckoned her closer.

Her face was alight when she reached him. "My dear Minister Sirinoya, am I to believe such boldness?"

Planting a deep, stirring kiss on her smiling mouth, he groaned softly. Dragging his lips away, he snugly gripped her waist. "There's no one but us. Where better to make love than here, Shi'níyah, surrounded by such total splendor?"

Soon, cooler air on her skin failed to compete with his fiery touch. Coaxing tiny moans from her, his mouth teased erotically sensitive lines along her neck and shoulder. His hands cupped beneath her hips, drawing her toward full union with him. With trees standing sentinel around them, they loved until neither could withstand consuming forces so powerful that both were completely awestruck.

When they were finally capable of coherent thought, he helped her up. With trembling hands, each helped the other with the task of straightening clothes. Enchanted by their divine afternoon interlude, speech eluded them. Instead, sharing caresses and kisses in silence, they savored their love and one another.

Approaching the house, Warnach looked up and emitted an exaggerated groan. "Badrik! It's the middle of the day. What are you doing here?"

Green eyes glittering in a flushed face shifted from one man to the other. "Big brother, that expression of yours is far too serious. If you two gentlemen will kindly excuse me, I have something to do inside. Let me know when it's safe to reappear."

Once Sandra disappeared, humorous lights sparkled in Badrik's eyes as he inspected Warnach's somewhat disheveled appearance. "You, dear brother, are a mess. You shall only have to clean the leaves she carried inside if we brush you off out here."

Disregarding the mocking tone in Badrik's voice, Warnach pulled off his jacket and shook it. "Not a word," he warned as he noted broken shards of red, orange, and yellow also clinging to his shirt and trousers.

Feigned innocence flashed across Badrik's amused face and quickly fled. "Baadihm asked me to stop when he couldn't contact you. Parliament leaders from Alphamiya have requested urgent mediation assistance. They've reached an impasse in resolving the dispute there. There are fears that all-out civil war may be days away."

Casting his eyes heavenward, Warnach impatiently shook his head. "Can people in this galaxy do nothing better than seek excuses to kill one another?"

"I know it must be hard to think about going on-mission when the two of you have been apart so long. She's entitled to four weeks of home duty. Remind Baadihm. I'll tell him that I stopped but had to leave a message." Badrik continued with a teasing note in his voice. "In the meantime, enjoy yourself."

Appreciation filled Warnach's eyes. "Believe me, Badrik. I intend to do exactly that."

Eight days later, Warnach sat beside Sandra on board the Rahpliknar. They had spent hours viewing recordings of failed negotiations on Alphamiya. Rebellious Meryites claimed that the majority Alphimidian party had launched destructive attacks against defenseless communities. Vehemently denying the accusations, Alphimidian leaders railed against sniper assaults aimed at civilians on city streets. Video evidence supported furious complaints and flaming rhetoric from both sides as the situation rapidly deteriorated. With both factions grudgingly willing to discuss issues, slim possibilities existed to avert war. Poring over fine details, the Sirinoyas discussed current and historical data while planning strategy before reaching Alphamiya.

Two weeks following their arrival, strenuous days were already well defined. Rising at dawn, Warnach and Sandra scheduled time for exercise, prayers, and breakfast together. Arduous meetings followed and frequently lasted as many as twelve hours with brief breaks and meals worked into the day. As mission advocate, Sandra supervised support services, recorded meeting summaries, and submitted reports to the orbiting Rahpliknar for transmission to Ministry Headquarters on Chikondra. She also spent long hours sitting through conferences by her lifemate's side. Returning to heavily guarded quarters each evening, the couple devoted at least an hour to discussing personalities and continuing stratagem before exhaustion led to hasty prayers and bedtime.

After five intensely emotional weeks, Alphamiyans postured and threatened. Both sides claimed truce violations. Each faction accused the other of staging attacks designed to blame the opposition and stall mediations. Frustrated, Warnach forcefully demanded a three-day moratorium on meetings and warned about consequences should the violence continue. He sought time to regroup and reassess failing tactics.

"Me'u ki'medsah, what you need is rest so you can clear your mind. Perhaps then you can think of fresh alternatives."

Looking up from a monitor displaying Alphamiyan cultural analyses, he studied her expression. "I think you look more tired than I feel. Are you all right?"

A wry smile crossed her face. "I haven't been sleeping well. Over the past week, someone has kept me awake every single night with all of his tossing and turning."

"That I don't doubt." Expelling a frustrated sigh, Warnach leaned far back into his chair and stared thoughtfully into his lifemate's face. "Tell me. What are we going to do here?"

She had begun to ask herself the same question. After nearly six months on-mission with barely any downtime, fatigue fogged her thought processes. "Warnach," she ventured at last, "personally, I think we need a miracle. No one from either side intends to budge."

"Least of all the Alphimidians." Noting her drooping eyelids, he pressed in a command that darkened the monitor and closed the slim computer with a muted whir. "Let's say prayers early tonight and try to get some sleep. You're right. If we're more rested, maybe we can see things in different light tomorrow."

Five days later, he insisted that she not join him until afternoon meetings. Two nights in a row, they had stayed up until the wee hours of the morning, repeatedly covering dialogue and arguments exchanged between Alphimidian and Meryite representatives. Both agreed. If they could not neutralize some of the personality clashes, there could be no hope for steering negotiations toward common ground.

Rising an hour and a half after Warnach had left, she dragged herself into the shower and then dried her hair and dressed for the day. Looking into the mirror, she flinched. No wonder Warnach had sounded concerned. She looked wrung out. Sternly, she lectured herself. Noting the resulting familiar gleam in stubborn eyes, she grinned and called security to transport her to the Alphamiya Parliament complex.

"Advocate Sirinoya! Hold on!" The pilot shouted in warning as he sharply banked his sleek, heavily shielded transport to the right.

Her head struck the polymer window with a thud. Shaking off stars, she shot a glance toward the left. Three speeding attack pods had barely missed them while firing volleys directly at scattering pedestrians on streets below. Clutching tightly to padded rods inside the transport, she choked back a burning surge of vomit when her pilot maneuvered the agile transport into a steeply spiked climb and backward roll while evading shots from the attack pods.

Screaming past them flew Alliance pilots assigned to protect mission personnel en route between residence quarters and meeting sites. First one explosion, then a second. Two pods were struck and destroyed. The third dived, aimed fire at people on the street, and then climbed straight up toward the sky.

"Drummond! Take us down! There! To the right! In front of that blue building!"

"I can't! Not until that pod is stopped!"

"I said, get us down there!"

Muttering a curse, the pilot veered left and upward, slicing a wide circle above street level. Angling the transport, he decreased speed and descended, all the while barking commands at fighters pursuing the evasive pod and a fourth that had suddenly appeared. "Now what?" he cried over his shoulder.

"Open the damned door!" she yelled back. "Stay inside and keep your shields up! Look!"

With his line of vision following her leap through the rising door, he watched her race across the broad sidewalk. His heart missed a beat. Two women huddled together next to a wall on steps in front of shattered windows. With fighters and attack pods screeching overhead, Drummond sucked in his breath. Disregarding instructions, he released his harnesses and scrambled out to help her. Trusting the skills of his comrades and racing a zigzag pattern, he reached the three women.

Gratitude flashed in Sandra's eyes. "Drummond, get the women inside! Hurry!"

Carrying a petite female over his shoulder and dragging a young woman by the hand, he ran back to the transport. His heart raced as he secured them inside. Another explosion. Relief. Another pod spiraled downward from the skies. He twisted around. "Advocate Sirinoya!"

"Get inside! And get us out of here!"

Fiery bolts spat across concrete. Broken bits of stone rose upward within billowing dust clouds. Another fiery round sounded just as she ducked into the back seat. "Go! There's a hospital behind us."

"Secure yourself!" An anxious glance showed Alliance fighters in pursuit of the last pod. Engaging engines, he launched his transport off the ground and turned toward a medical center near their quarters. Silently, he shuddered. If only she knew how pitifully hideous she looked, drenched with blood and clutching a small child tightly to her breast.

Forty-five minutes later, nurses paused while guiding a gurney through crowded corridors. On the way to surgery, their patient grasped Sandra's hand. "Don't hesitate. Tell him. If my daughter dies, I'll never forgive him. I swear. I will hate him for the rest of my life."

Flanked by six security officers, Sandra watched the nurses disappear beyond sliding doors. Wondering for a moment if her heart would ever cease its erratic beat, she turned around and headed toward the exit.

Covered bodies lined the hallway, awaiting removal. Busy doctors afforded her a curious glance before resuming emergency treatment of injured victims. The alien woman's face bore unspeakable fury as she informed her escort that they would leave immediately for the conference site.

"Advocate Sirinoya," Drummond protested, "you can't go inside Parliament like that."

Anger flared in her eyes. "Like hell I can't. They're sequestered and probably have no idea what just happened. My appearance may be just the shock treatment some of those war-mongers need. Now, if you won't pilot this transport, I'll damned well do it myself."

Arguing was useless. Ordering security guards to stay on either side of her, he helped her inside. Within half an hour, with his own uniform soiled and stained, the captain strode past armed guards while leading a ghastly parade dominated by Advocate Sandra Sirinoya.

Reaching the isolated floor where negotiations continued uninterrupted, Alphamiyan eyes stared. Alliance personnel and security officers alike exchanged stunned looks. Acknowledging no one, Sandra stormed toward conference room doors and furiously thrust them open. Directing an icy gaze toward her frozen lifemate, she spoke in a commanding voice, "I apologize for my late arrival, Minister Sirinoya. I encountered an unexpected delay."

Pushing himself up from the table, he visibly shook. "Advocate Sirinoya?"

President Omeen, the primary obstacle to progress in the mediations, also stood. Florid features flushed brighter red as he glared in response to her startling appearance. "What is the meaning of this?" he demanded.

Her shoulders squared. She spared a downward glance at her blood-stiffened attire before glaring back at him. "I assume you refer to my unfortunate appearance."

Relief instantly flooded Warnach when he realized she was unhurt. Sensing angry intent but fully trusting her, he nodded approval for her to assume dramatic control.

Omeen looked toward Warnach. "I believe your advocate is out of line."

The response was calm. "I believe my advocate has valuable information for the members of this meeting. She has my approval to address the conference."

Sandra paced toward a window. Stopping for a prolonged moment, she slowly turned around. "Mr. President, en route to this meeting, my transport was forced to avoid fire from several attack pods. Those pods bore Meryite insignia. Curiously, the ships were of Alphimidian design."

"Are you suggesting…?"

"I suggest nothing, Mr. President. I state facts that you may later verify," she boldly interrupted. "You assured us numerous times that all your craft were secured and accounted for. Therefore, we have our first dilemma, one which I believe is quite obvious, especially considering that the Meryite leadership has been fully cooperative in providing our inspectors with open access to their war materiel.

"Now, that subject aside for the moment, I will offer further explanation to your first question. During the unfortunate attack I witnessed on my way here, attack pods brutally and mercilessly fired at defenseless civilians on the streets of this city. Statistics have yet to be compiled, but I am quite certain numbers of dead and injured will climb into the hundreds."

Meryite representatives appeared sickened but remained in shocked silence. In contrast, the Alphimidian president's attitude grew adamant. "I have no obligation to listen to another word. As far as I'm concerned, this meeting is ended."

Before Warnach could utter a word, Sandra's voice lowered with frightening warning. "You may end this meeting, Mr. President, but you will not leave this room until I finish." A sharp jerk of her head resulted in Drummond slamming the doors shut and physically barring the exit.

"Now," she continued, "let's discuss those statistics. Men. Women. Children. No way to run fast enough to escape lazon fire. Perhaps we should also include in those statistics the number of severed limbs. Perhaps we could calculate the volume of blood shed onto the streets. Perhaps we should list victims, name by name, so every person in this room might possibly begin to comprehend that every number in those statistics is a life, not a damned numeral."

Her jaw set, and her voice strengthened in response to the president's vulgar expletive. "Not good enough, Mr. President? Don't worry. I'm nearly done. Then, you're free to leave.

"First, I promised to deliver a personal message to you from one of those statistics. Captain Drummond, who blocks the door, bravely risked his life and mine landing his transport. While Alliance pilots blew those pods from the sky, he and I jumped out and dragged three of those statistics into our transport and flew them to hospital for medical treatment.

"The youngest statistic is a five-year-old girl with beautiful red curls. When I left, surgeons were fighting to save her life. Her mother stopped me on the way into surgery for injuries of her own. She sent you this message. She told me that she has begged you for weeks to end this madness. She also asked me to tell her father that if her little girl dies, she will hate him until the day she dies."

President Omeen collapsed onto his chair. Veins in his face protruded and began to throb. "My granddaughter? My Kima?"

"Your daughter. Your little Silya. It is her blood that is soaked into my clothes."

The gray-haired man's body shook violently. His breathing quickened. For several moments, he looked faint. Aides offered him water, but he shoved them away. Gulping in several breaths, he finally met Sandra's waiting gaze. "I swear to you. My commanders will be required to provide full explanation. Please. I must go now."

By the time Warnach guided her inside their quarters, her adrenalin rush had subsided. With it, infuriated bravado ebbed, and delayed emotional shock set in. She staggered as he led her into the bath. Standing mutely until he stripped away her clothing, she entered the shower and sobbed pitifully beneath the cleansing spray. Meanwhile, he instructed a security officer to discard ruined garments so she wouldn't see them again.

Sitting at her bedside later, he tenderly stroked her pale face. Admiring eyes watched her. "What you did today was the most unorthodox piece of field diplomacy I've ever witnessed. It was also courageous and brilliantly executed."

Weakly, she smiled. "I'm hoping I'll wake up to find it was all a nightmare."

"Unfortunately, me'u Shi'níyah, war turns the worst nightmares into reality. You have an ugly bump on your head. Get some rest. We can discuss this later." Leaning over her, he calmed her with cerea-semi'ittá and then watched protectively until she fell asleep.

Three weeks later, the mission team entered the diplomatic concourse at the Kadranas shuttleport. True to his word, Omeen had investigated the attack that had necessitated amputation of his daughter's legs and nearly killed the granddaughter he adored. Resulting inquiries had yielded suspicious details, and several high-ranking officers had been arrested. Following whirlwind negotiations, a truce had been implemented. Further consultations were already being planned in hopes of achieving a more permanent accord. In the meantime, Warnach needed the respite almost as much as his lifemate.

A few days after their return home, she dragged herself into Ministry Headquarters. Chancellor Edsaka had been especially charming and insistent on meeting with her. Inside his office, she was surprised by the intensity of Farsuk's welcoming embrace, considering the presence of Masters Barishta and Devorius. Acknowledging the Alliance masters with a bow and a smile, she turned an inquiring expression to Farsuk.

"Please, Sandra, sit down. I promised to take only a little of your time. How are you?"

Graciously, she shook her head. "Still tired, I'm afraid."

"Rightfully so." His smile held compassion. "My dear, I shall come directly to the purpose of this meeting. After your departure to Alphamiya, Master Devorius and I extensively discussed the recent mission on which you accompanied him. He expressed tremendous appreciation for your professionalism and work on that trip."

Curious and somewhat nervous, she smiled at the distinguished Kurulian master before returning attention to the chancellor.

"Master Barishta and I have also closely reviewed your performance records. You have made outstanding contributions during your advocacy – contributions evidenced by your minister's remarkable successes and reinforced by recognition from experienced officers and dignitaries. Following serious consideration, Master Barishta and I have concurred and accepted Master Devorius' recommendation. You will continue to report to Minister Sirinoya but no longer as Ministry Advocate. We're proud to be the first to congratulate you, Deputy Minister Sirinoya."

Half an hour later, she clutched a small velvet case in her hand and entered Warnach's office suite. Zara looked up. "Sandra, I didn't expect you today."

Smiling a shaky greeting, Sandra answered, "I wasn't expecting to come in today. Is Minister Sirinoya in his office?"

"He just returned. He mentioned something about submitting some approvals before going home for a few days." Receiving only a nod as Sandra walked past her, Zara shook her head in puzzlement before resuming mission staff appraisals.

The sound of his door opening and closing caused Warnach to look up. "Shi'níyah, what are you doing here?"

Leaning back against polished wood, she stared into dark eyes. "I… Did they really not tell you?"

"Excuse me? Did who not tell me what?"

"You really don't know?"

Standing, he rounded his desk and approached her. "If you intend to confuse me, you are succeeding. Come. Sit down and explain."

Minutes later, he cradled the velvet case in his hand and stared at the ruby-encrusted pin signifying her new status. "Sandra, this is excellent news. This provides so many more possibilities for our continued collaboration. I had considered broaching the possibility with Farsuk, but I wanted to avoid any impression of nepotistic impropriety. How very proud I am. You truly deserve this."

"Warnach, I never expected… It seems too soon."

"Sandra," he told her, "especially with recent developments, we need to strengthen diplomatic ranks. Although certainly not a precedent, you've earned a rare honor." Lost for anything more to say, he then congratulated her with a kiss.

After more than a week, Sandra found herself still unable to escape the slump that had begun on Alphamiya. Even a few days of shopping in Nalichtaka had failed to relieve her doldrums. Worried about starting to feel sick as well as depressed, she finally called Dr. Barrett and scheduled an appointment for the following morning. Then, resting aching head on her hands, she sighed and started to read through details of upcoming procedural changes.

"Have you considered seeing a doctor?" Warnach frowned as he deposited himself on a chair in her office.

Looking up, she grimaced. "Yes. I already have an appointment at the clinic tomorrow morning."

"Now I'm really worried. You haven't been yourself since the attack on Alphamiya. How much weight have you lost?"

"Complaining, are we?"

"Not complaining. Worrying. Besides, Badrik called today and threatened me if I didn't make you go in for a check-up."

"My ever-watchful big brother," she chuckled. "Well, if it makes you feel any better, I'm starving. Can we leave early and stop for something to eat?"

In Dr. Barrett's office the next morning, she responded to a battery of questions. Home again, her returning appetite should offset the eight pounds she'd lost. Despite the fact she was also sleeping well again, her worst complaint was excessive fatigue and overall weakness. For whatever reason, she described feeling like every ounce of energy was being sucked right out of her body.

Carefully studying her appearance, Dr. Barrett's eyes shadowed with concern. Her movements were slow and lethargic. Her voice was weak, as if she couldn't breathe well. Dark circles rimmed her eyes, and even her hair lacked healthy luster. Combined with her pallor, something in her overall posture did not look right for a woman he knew to be strong and healthy. With all her recent travels to so many planets, he ordered immediate scans in hopes of identifying any malady before it could reach a crisis.

Referring other patients to colleagues on duty, Dr. Barrett decided to personally supervise extensive exams. Methodically, he read computerized displays as skilled technicians operated sophisticated scanning devices. Data compilations were troubling. Blood analyses revealed seriously depleted levels of oxygen and key nutrients. Blood pressure was low. Heart and lungs performed sluggishly, and other vital organs showed signs of severe overwork. Suddenly, he stopped the technicians. Shaking his head, he reread the data.

Uncertain of his interpretation, he stopped the scans and asked Sandra to relax for a while until they could repeat the exams to assure accuracy of results. Hurrying to his office, he contacted two specialists in the clinic. After explaining preliminary findings, he waited.

Both doctors reached his office within fifteen minutes. Accessing data from her scans, Dr. Barrett pointed out various readings that had caught him off guard. The two specialists stared at him, then at one another. Heading toward the examination room, they discussed the urgency of confirming the data. If their preliminary diagnosis was correct, they had little time to develop appropriate treatment in the slim hope of averting disaster.

# Chapter Nineteen

"Zara? Has Minister Sirinoya returned from his meeting?"
Hearing breathy weakness in the voice on the opposite end of the com, Zara's mature features tightened into a frown. "I'm afraid not. He checked in a while ago and said the meeting would likely last until late. I did inform him that you had called and would be longer than expected. Sandra, is everything all right?" A prolonged pause and a deep sigh followed her question.

"Medical exams just tire me out. If Warnach checks in again, will you tell him I won't be coming to work today? Also, I'd really appreciate it if you'd ask him to come home as soon as he's free."

The call ended. Zara stared at her lighted desk console. Throughout her many years of service, rarely had she interrupted either Morcai Sirinoya or his son from meetings for personal reasons. Troubled by something in Sandra's voice, she resolutely stood, smoothed her nashavri, and left.

Reaching the conference floor at the chancellery, she spoke with aides outside a secure meeting salon. Yielding to her commanding insistence, one aide courteously opened a door. Executing a graceful bow to faces noting her unexpected arrival, she directed her gaze toward Warnach.

Confident that Zara would never disrupt any meeting without justification, Warnach excused himself and escorted her outside the conference room. Detecting genuine concern as she urged him to leave immediately for home, he experienced an almost nauseating hollowness within. Assuring Zara she had been right to interrupt the meeting, he then returned long enough to advise Farsuk that he needed to leave.

Clear afternoon skies shone brilliantly blue overhead as Sandra slowly strolled across a broad stretch of faded grass. Winters in the Kadranas region of Chikondra were rarely as cold as those she had known on Earth. Still, she had wrapped herself in a coat over layered sweaters. Fatigue draped like a heavy cloak around her even though infusions of therapeutic nutrients had already begun to soften sharp edges of exhaustion.

Dr. Barrett had vehemently protested her refusal to check in for hospital care. Despite compelling arguments from three physicians, she had desperately craved the kind of refuge that existed only at home. Stubbornly maintaining her stance while the doctors' repeated warnings echoed in her ears, she had left after promising to return the next morning for additional scans and treatment.

Her sigh fell with a rush upon her adopted world. Light breezes stirred leafless tree branches. Soaring evergreens leaned against silent heavens. A deer-like pira'amisa bounded through the trees. Icy cold waters crossed rocky courses and lifted crystalline notes into crisp air. Absorbing the beauty of her lifemate's ancestral home, she paused. Wrapped in its peaceful embrace, never had she more appreciated this land, this place, this world.

Resuming her random stroll, her thoughts rambled. So far, her life had far exceeded her little girl's noble and adventurous aspirations. Such unbelievable changes in her life since that fortuitous encounter in John's office more than six years earlier. So many tears, both sad and happy. So much work. So much love. Memories of her most recent visit to Earth invaded her contemplation. Both of her parents had actually shown their affection. Images of Araman and Badrik drifted across her mental line of vision. Warnach's beloved smile. What would they say? How would they react? How would any of them, herself especially, confront the immediate future and decisions it would demand?

Her feet carried her toward a stand of trees, but she only walked along the heavily wooded edge. Earlier, listening to Dr. Barrett, disbelief had filled her eyes. Impossible! The thought had exploded inside her mind. Her unification with Warnach, though still relatively new, provided unparalleled personal joy and satisfaction. Her dream career had already reached a summit with higher pinnacles yet to conquer. Now, the life she had so determinedly undertaken lurched precariously before her. Her spirit churned. Her mind boggled.

Long strides quickly carried Warnach from the garage into the quiet house. Taking two steps at a time, he rushed upstairs and ran into the master suite. Greeted by dark shadows and silence, he swiftly spun around and headed through the hallway and back downstairs. He called out her name. No response. Breath snagged somewhere between lungs and throat.

Creeping worry swelled fearfully as he turned down the hall and entered her office. Crossing the room, he glanced at her portfolio resting on the desk. Open draperies admitted sunlight to bathe the room with its cheerful glow. Looking outside, he nearly choked. Relief at finally spotting her dissolved upon watching her motionless figure cast a solitary shadow across the meadow.

Anxiety-driven steps carried him rapidly through the house, outside, and down steps. Breaking into a run, he swiftly covered the yards separating them. Nearly reaching her, something totally indiscernible in her expression brought him to an abrupt halt.

"Warnach?"

He hardly realized she had moved when he felt her arms encircle his waist. "Shi'níyah," he whispered, drawing her tightly against him. "You're shivering. Come. Let me take you inside."

Reaching the broad patio where they had danced on the day of their unification, she walked away from him and stopped. Gripping carved railings with gloved hands, she stared out at lengthening shadows. "I think you have no idea how much I love being here."

Willing calm, he resisted going to her. "Sandra, what happened this morning at the clinic?"

"What happened?" The repeated question was a disconcerting echo. Her shoulders rose with the deep breath she inhaled. "Sometimes, I find it hard to believe how quickly one's entire life can change."

"Shi'níyah, that says nothing to ease my worry. What did Dr. Barrett say today?"

"Dr. Barrett? He called in two specialists. They ran two full series of scans. Of the three, I'm not sure which doctor was angrier when I refused hospital admission."

"*What?* They wanted to admit you? Sandra, what's wrong?" Apprehension saturated his voice, especially when she kept her back to him.

"Warnach," her voice finally interrupted burgeoning tension, "it's all so unbelievable. This can't be happening. It just can't."

Feeling paralyzed, he could hardly breathe. "Shi'níyah, please, just tell me."

"Warnach, they ordered immediate oxygen treatments and a vitamin infusion. I promised Dr. Barrett that I'd rest today and be back at the clinic early tomorrow morning. Before I left, he gave me a second vitamin infusion. Tomorrow, more of the same plus a special vitamin and dietary regimen they're hoping will restore my body's normal functionality. My system is so weak right now because of the constant drain on oxygen and nutrients."

Finally, as she turned around, he saw tears streaming down her face. His voice quaked. "Shi'níyah?"

"Warnach," she murmured, "I've spent this entire afternoon contemplating a future that today is totally different from anything I imagined only yesterday. My career, my life - the life you and I share. Expectations, beliefs - everything changing in the face of incalculable odds."

His patience threatened to evaporate. "Shi'níyah, one thing that nothing can ever change is my love for you. We shall face whatever it is together. Just tell me."

Pupils widened within their evergreen frames. Long lashes fluttered a moment. She forced a wan smile. "How do I tell you?" Pausing, she searched for words. Then, swallowing hard, she softly said, "It seems, my dear Minister Sirinoya, you've accomplished the impossible. You've made me pregnant."

Lucid thought failed. Surely, he had misunderstood. He remained speechless as his black eyes stared without comprehension.

"Warnach? Please," she choked on a muted sob, "please, don't be angry with me."

The very tone of her voice snapped him from shock. A sudden rush of tears overflowed his eyes. Unsteady steps carried him forward until he could hold her in a protective embrace. Her name was the only word he was capable of uttering.

Sensing weakness nearly matching her own, she managed to ease away. Gazing into his tear-stained face, she smiled. "I'm really tired. Can we go inside?"

Nestled into the corner of the sofa, she wearily leaned sideways against the sofa back with her legs stretched across his lap. Twisting slightly, his arm stretched over the back of the sofa, and he stroked her hair as he gazed earnestly into her face. "Help me understand. According to the specialists, fetal development related to the baby's Chikondran genetics has caused your weight loss and exhaustion."

Her eyebrows lifted, and she nodded. "That's what they think. Even in a typical pregnancy, it's not unusual for human women to feel tired and moody. However, initial development of cerea-nervos plus other biological differences in Chikondrans require more nutrients and higher oxygen absorption than in human fetuses. My body's response was to supply the baby's needs while dangerously weakening me. Dr. Barrett's most pressing concern was that I might collapse and miscarry. Or worse."

Blood drained involuntarily from Warnach's face. "How could he then allow you to leave the hospital?"

Her breasts rose and fell. "They had already dosed me with therapeutic vitamins. I also underwent two oxygen treatments. Physically, I was actually starting to feel a little better. Mentally and emotionally, I was in shock. I needed to come home. This is my haven, the place where I feel most at peace. Besides…"

Her mind wandered. She had blamed menstrual irregularity on stress and fatigue. Later, contrary to her normal resistance, she had sought medical care. Then, unimagined truth settled in as the obstetrician and pediatric specialist allowed her to view scans of her unborn child. As the baby's steady heartbeat filled one Chikondran and three humans with awe, gentle voices echoed inside her mind. Whether she remained in hospital or went home, it would make no difference. The child she had conceived with Warnach was meant to be.

Firmly, he squeezed her hand. "Finish the thought."

"If you go with me to the clinic tomorrow, you'll understand the same as I did. Our baby is meant to live."

With the passage of several minutes in contemplative silence, Warnach rediscovered speech. "Me'u Shi'níyah, you said something outside that we must settle. Right now. I cannot imagine why you thought I would be angry with you over what is surely a miracle."

When her eyes dropped, he insisted that she meet his gaze before he continued. "Sandra, you're right. This baby will change the entire course of our lives. I've never said anything before because there were times when I could hardly bear my own sadness. However, the truth is that I've wanted a child with you for a very long time."

When dinnertime came, he made certain that she ate well and took supplements the doctors had given her. Following especially fervent night prayers, he had helped her upstairs and into bed. Watching her quickly fall asleep, he lay close by her side as moonlight shafted over his shoulder and softly illuminated her face.

Having long ago resigned himself to never having children of his own, he comprehended the many levels of change now confronting them both. Physically, she would submit to intense scrutiny to avoid health problems for her sake and the wellbeing of their baby. Her condition would necessitate major adjustments in demanding professional schedules. Should the Great Spirit indeed deliver this child into their lives, Warnach would not hesitate nor would he waver. Despite inevitable objections, he would acknowledge the blessing by serving home duty for the first year of his child's life.

She turned over. As he snuggled closer to her back, his left arm snaked around her. His long fingers rested over her abdomen. Beneath his hand, secure within her body, beat the tiny heart of a fragile new life. Tears swam behind closed eyelids. Breathing silent prayers, he cherished the resurrection of his secret dream of having a child with his beloved ki'mirsah.

～

"So, Minister Sirinoya, are you ready? Scans will even determine the baby's sex."

Warnach's trembling hand clutched Sandra's as a nervous grin lit his face. "She said this morning that she thinks we have a son." Loving eyes glanced into hers. "Let's see how accurate her prediction."

Dr. Walters, head of the clinic's obstetrics department, exercised his best bedside manner and laughed. The mood of earlier conversations had been far more serious. Both he and Dr. Nimartlal, a Chikondran specializing in prenatal and neonatal pediatrics, had recommended extreme caution. There existed not a single benchmark by which they could gauge this pregnancy. Unpredictable factors could easily cause spontaneous abortion. Frequent scans would be necessary to monitor any changes that might signal trouble.

Sandra had simply smiled at well-intended warnings. Once initial shock subsided, certainty had seeped into her consciousness. While Warnach listened intently to the doctors, her mind had drifted seaward. A life created for a life saved. Searching her memory, she had finally recalled the wish of which they had reminded her the day before. In truth, she had wished nothing in their presence. Instead, she had merely remembered a wish surrendered and appreciated even more the life of the young Quazon she had helped to save.

Increased pressure around her fingers drew her from momentary regression. Shifting her glance to the side, she saw that Warnach's eyes were fixed on a large overhead monitor revealing life suspended within a watery world. Dr. Nimartlal's voice pointed out narrow, distinctive bands across the baby's forehead. With fluttering motions, the fetus moved. Along with more detailed readings, visual confirmation came into view. The Sirinoyas had conceived a son.

Left in privacy so she could dress, Warnach kissed the side of her neck as he fastened the back of her nashavri. In the face of his deep-rooted concern, her optimism was a welcome contagion. With faith in her instincts never failing, he looked toward the future with newfound excitement.

Seated again inside Dr. Walters' office, Warnach and Sandra listened carefully. Scans clearly showed that, although human characteristics were present, Chikondran genes were dominant in the eleven-week-old fetus. Weekly scans would monitor maternal health and the effectiveness of nutritional supplements geared toward development patterns typical of a Chikondran baby. Both physicians recommended continuing caution in everything she did.

Returning home, Warnach checked in with Zara and, after much reassurance, advised her that he would not be in the office for the remainder of the week. Insisting that Sandra rest according to doctors' orders, he prepared and served lunch. Afterward, he sent her to bed for a nap while he cleaned up.

Availing himself of afternoon quiet, Warnach decided to take a walk. Sunshine brightened azure skies. Wintry breezes, nipping at his cheeks, failed to dispel the warmth enveloping him. He couldn't avoid smiling as he remembered startled expressions on the doctors' faces. After listening to all their warnings and all their plans for prenatal care, Sandra had issued a warning of her own. While she immensely appreciated their concern and would respect their medical advice, she had reminded them that she was pregnant, not terminally ill. She had also stated that she would not tolerate anyone treating her baby as a science project. Oxygen treatments and nutritional therapy were rapidly restoring her mentally as well as physically.

Thoughts and feelings filled him with appreciation. Lifting his face skyward, Warnach savored cool, fresh air as prayer escaped his lips. "My praise and my thanks do I send to you, most sacred Yahvanta. I trust your wisdom and your love in giving us this child. I ask only that you protect my ki'mirsah and my son, and guide me so that I may be worthy as badehr and lifemate."

～

Medical intervention worked wonders. When her pregnancy passed fourteen weeks, even her physicians grew more optimistic. Her energy had returned, and her spirits soared. The baby's development progressed at what could only be described as normal expectations. Scans performed twice weekly revealed no problems. Every sign indicated that both mother and child were healthy.

Warnach gladly assumed the role of loving taskmaster. At home, he ensured that she took daily supplements and got moderate exercise and plenty of rest. At the ministry in Kadranas, he shielded her from anything that might create unnecessary stress. If anyone questioned his protective attitude, no one, not even Sandra, dared voice any comment or protest.

～

Warnach decided that observance of her Thanksgiving merited a special family gathering. Beyond gratitude for their personal miracle, Warnach reasoned that a family announcement was in order, especially considering that changes in her figure, visible only to him for the moment, would soon be apparent to everyone.

Supervising her efforts in the kitchen as she prepared dinner, a sternly cocked eyebrow was all that he needed to remind her to avoid lifting things he thought too heavy or to sit down for frequent breaks. Finally, with help from everyone, the dining room table was laden with typical foods imported from Earth. Golden corn on the cob steamed beneath melting butter. Fluffy mashed potatoes sat beside a bowl of yams lightly sweetened with brown sugar. Green beans and cranberry-orange relish contributed bright, contrasting colors.

Biting her lower lip to avoid laughter, Sandra watched as Warnach set down a huge platter edged with dressing that yielded mouthwatering aromas of sage and onion. The stuffing surrounded seasoned feshbi, which she had molded into something that almost resembled a golden brown turkey and then garnished with a large, two-sided picture of a real roasted turkey.

With the feast set before them, Warnach ceremoniously rose from his chair at the head of the table. "Everyone, please." When all eyes turned in his direction, he smiled. "I hope not to ruin this delicious dinner after all the effort my ki'mirsah has put into it; however, I do have an announcement."

Warnach smiled at her blushing grin before resuming his speech. "Quiet now. This is important. The Chancellery will issue official notice next week, but I wanted you to know first. Please, join me in congratulating my colleague, Deputy Minister Sirinoya."

"Congratulations, little sister!" Leaning sideways in his chair, Badrik hugged Sandra tightly as excitement erupted around the table.

"Everyone! Please!" Warnach again interrupted his family's excited chatter. "Please," he said seriously. With quiet restored, he said, "As you know, Thanksgiving is one of the Earth holidays observed throughout much of the Alliance. We know how special it is to Sandra. For me today, her Thanksgiving is especially significant. Let us pray thanks for all our blessings."

Following their feast on foods rare to Chikondra, the entire family participated in clearing the table and cleaning the kitchen. Laughter and conversation subsided as Warnach, whose features once again grew serious, requested everyone to join him inside the Brisajai.

Eyes narrowed and fixed on his expression. Araman glanced curiously at Nadana. Badrik shrugged his shoulders at the odd request but, with a grin, gripped Farisa's hand and led the way with gregarious comments about the joys of coping with eccentric older brothers.

Inside the home's prayer sanctuary, Warnach silently lit candles for each member of his family, including one for his unborn son. Holding tightly to his ki'mirsah's hand, he carefully guided her down onto thick cushions.

Turning attention to his family, he spoke softly. "I appreciate your patience tonight. I find Sandra's Thanksgiving holiday especially appropriate for another announcement, one that I never in my life expected to make."

Questions glinted from dark Chikondran eyes gazing back at him. Observing growing inquisitiveness, he knelt on the floor beside his lifemate. "May I ask that we all kneel and join hands?"

Although no one spoke, they responded to his request and waited until, trembling with emotion, Warnach began to pray. "Great Spirit, we gathered at dinner to offer gratitude for the many blessings our family shares. As we continue celebrating Your gifts, I also ask my family to join me in praying Your most special blessings upon my ki'mirsah. The miracle she now bears reflects great joy upon our unified lives. Great Spirit, I humbly ask both Your guidance and protection as I offer deepest thanks for the child she now carries to perpetuate the family Sirinoya. Eyach'hamá eu Yahvanta."

Obsidian eyes opened and shifted to gaze adoringly upon ivory features before moving from one stunned face to the next. Shock held Badrik and Farisa suspended in motionless silence. Questions marked Nadana's astonished expression.

Only Araman moved. Rising very slowly and approaching Warnach, she whispered while lifting small hands to cradle his bearded face. "My son, is such news truly possible?"

Still on bended knees, Warnach tilted his head backward to receive her tender cerea-semi'ittá. He then stood and leaned forward to draw Sandra from the floor and wrap his arm around her back. "Mamehr, the Great Spirit blesses us with a son."

Teardrops sparkled in gleaming eyes. Araman embraced both Warnach and Sandra. "How can I possibly express my happiness for you? My children, your son is a blessing to our entire family. "

∼

"My brother, I will gladly accompany you if you really decide to go."

A cocked brow and nearly imperceptible lift of his head indicated Warnach's appreciation. "The journey can be very difficult."

Badrik's gaze across the restaurant table was direct. "We went in our youth when we had little genuine comprehension regarding the significance of such a pilgrimage. With all the blessings we each now have, I believe the effort would hold lasting meaning for us both."

For a moment, Warnach stared into his nearly empty teacup. "My only reluctance is leaving her, even for just two weeks."

Badrik smiled. "She'll understand your need to do this. Besides, Mamehr and Farisa will watch over her."

"That I know," Warnach remarked with a grin. "I've never seen Mamehr so excited about anything in my life."

"Nor I," Badrik chuckled. "So, when do you think to go? I need to schedule leave."

"Sandra wants to visit Earth before the pregnancy advances too far. If we leave in four weeks, by the time we return, we'll have about fourteen weeks before the baby comes. I'll wait to make certain she's settled after the trip. Then, we can go."

Two weeks later, Warnach strolled back to his office following a grueling lunchtime match of pafla with Rodan, who had jokingly warned that pafla would provide excellent conditioning for impending pilgrimages and fatherhood. Energized and refreshed after exercise and a shower, Warnach's thoughts were happy ones. Badrik had been right about Sandra. Not only had she quickly grasped his jumbled explanation of reasons for wanting to make the trip to Efi'yimasé Meichasa, but she had also actually encouraged him to pursue the reaffirmation of his faith.

Upon reaching the office suite, Drajash quickly informed him that Zara and Sandra had taken a late lunch but should return shortly. Crossing his private office, Warnach paused for several moments. Gazing out the window, he smiled at the odd sensation of not wearing his Kitak, which he had earlier tucked into the top drawer of his credenza before going to meet Rodan at the pafla court.

"No man alive is as handsome as you, Warnach."

Startled from private thought, he swung around. Too surprised to move, he stared as she approached and wrapped him in a tight embrace. Rich fragrance filled his nostrils. Firm breasts sensually pressed against his chest. Heaving in a deep breath, he grasped her upper arms and pushed her away. Staring into eyes framed by lush lashes, he shivered involuntarily.

"I wanted to surprise you."

Muscles tautened, drawing his face into a dark mask. "Surprise is hardly the word I'd use. What are you possibly thinking?"

"What I've always thought, of course. How much I love you." Beautifully shaped and colored lips spread into a dazzling smile. Suddenly, as she rose on tiptoe, her seductive mouth welded to his in a passionate kiss as her arms locked desperately around his neck to resist his attempts to disengage himself from her hold.

"Warnach, are you ready..." The question died abruptly. Shocked evergreen eyes met his as he finally succeeded in freeing himself. "I...I...I'm sorry. I didn't know you had a - visitor. I...I can come back."

Pain in her expression fueled the searing rise of nausea. "Sandra! No! Stay." With a sharp jerk, he threw off the manicured hands that gripped his arms. "Sandra, please…"

Mutely, Sandra stared as the most exotically beautiful woman she had ever seen turned around.

"Sandra? That is your name? I'm sure you'll be kind enough to excuse Warnach and me."

Warnach's heart lurched as he saw shaking hands spread protectively over the slightly swollen mound of her abdomen. "Sandra, stay. Please…"

"Warnach?" Sensuality dripped like honey around his name. "We need to talk privately. I'm certain whatever work she has can wait."

Fearful eyes begged her to stay as words emerged in a stiff voice from a choked throat. "Sandra, this is Lashira Ehmedrad."

# Chapter Twenty

Gleaming black tresses fell into long waves hugging her shoulders. Firm breasts tilted upward from the body that curved inward to a dramatically narrow waist and then outward into perfectly proportioned hips accented by clinging fabric. Her face was an artist's dream with wide eyes, high cheekbones, and exquisitely shaped lips that currently held a slightly confused smile. The femininity she exuded was saturated with sexual overtones expressly cultivated to command constant admiration.

Her black eyes, barely concealing impatience, lifted to his. "Me'u Warnach, tell your little assistant here she can leave. You and I have so much to discuss, my love." Boldly, Lashira looked over her shoulder. "Sandra, you may go now."

Marshaling her senses required tremendous effort, but Sandra drew in a sustaining breath. "Miryah Ehmedrad, I'm afraid I must stay. Minister Sirinoya and I have much to do because we shall soon leave Chikondra for a few weeks. Perhaps you can schedule an appointment with Zara on your way out."

"Excuse me?" Lashira's expression held honest astonishment when she looked from Sandra to Warnach. "My love, your assistant has a strange sense of humor if she thinks I need to make an appointment to be with you."

Straightening beneath the weight of dread and infused by anger over Lashira's audacity, Warnach responded to the lifeline extended by his lifemate.

"Actually, Lashira, Sandra is correct. You may leave. However, there is no need to schedule an appointment. You know as well as I we have nothing left to discuss."

Dark eyes snapped as Lashira ignored Warnach for a moment. "Sandra, whoever-you-are, would you please be kind enough to leave us? I just returned to Chikondra last night so that Warnach and I can discuss some very personal matters."

"Lashira," Warnach began as he firmly grasped her left arm, "I told you. We have nothing to discuss. Is that so impossible for you to understand?"

As if his words had been a dramatic cue, tears glazed black eyes, and she looked pitifully toward Sandra. "We had a terrible lover's quarrel. I must find a way to make it up to him. I'm certain you can understand our need for privacy to talk." Then, turning her charm toward Warnach, she smiled tremulously. "You know that my heart has always belonged to you. Please, don't make this so difficult."

"Lashira, I have no idea what scheme you have in mind, but it's useless. Lover's quarrels don't last ten years."

"But, Warnach, I love you! I do!"

"Love? Do you even know the meaning of the word?" Sandra blurted out unexpectedly.

Sudden anger sparked in Lashira's eyes as she twisted around. "Damn you! How dare you speak to me with such disrespect? Who do you think you are?"

Warnach's voice regained stridency. "Lashira, whatever I tolerated from you years ago will not be repeated. More than that, you will not speak to Sandra that way. Do you understand?"

Switching from English that had begun upon Sandra's arrival, Lashira cried out in Chikondran, "I understand nothing! Why do you refuse to send her away? For God's sake, she's only a nosy, pregnant Terran."

"Perhaps I should leave so you can sort things out."

Warnach looked past Lashira and observed ivory features pulled into an expression impossible to read. "Shi'níyah, you belong here with me. Lashira is the one who will be leaving."

Lashira's eyes narrowed in a pointed stare. "Warnach? Did you just…"

Coldly, he returned her stare. "Yes, I just addressed my ki'mirsah as *Shi'níyah*. Sandra and I are unified in Nivela-Ku'saá. As you can also see, we are expecting our first child."

"Impossible!" she spat out. "You're lying! Morcai Sirinoya would shudder in his grave at the very thought of your being unified with a Terran!"

Warnach's left brow raised sharply as anger flared in his eyes. "Respect is something you still haven't learned, Lashira. Badehr may be gone, but Mamehr has graced us with her blessing for both our unification and our child."

"How dare you lie to me this way? You know as well as I that Araman Sirinoya would be aghast at the idea of a Sirinoya in unification with a Terran." Her voice verged on hysteria. "Why are you doing this to me? I came to apologize…to make things right with you."

He responded with a short, incredulous laugh. "Make things right? Lashira, things were never right with you and never will be. Now, I will appreciate it if you leave and not return."

Stubbornly, she cast a brief, disdainful glance toward Sandra and refused to move. "I will understand what has happened here. You told me a long time ago that you would always love me. I won't let you go back on that promise. I made a terrible mistake, but I love you, and I will not give you up! I know you still love me!"

Selfish, spoiled, and stubborn as always, he thought. Her way or no way. "Lashira, if I once thought I loved you, I was seriously mistaken. My life with Sandra has revealed to me what real love truly is. Go." Firmly, he took hold of her arm and started pushing her toward the door.

Obstinately, Lashira jerked her arm free. Hatefully, she glared directly at Sandra, noticing for the first time the diamond-adorned Kitak. "Terrans!"

she pronounced as if the word left a filthy taste in her mouth. "You're the ones who know nothing of respect. I tell you now. Warnach loves me. He always has. You will not keep him."

Brown eyebrows spiked high. Patience dwindled. "I have no intention of arguing with you, Miryah Ehmedrad. However, a lesson might well be in order. I don't *keep* Warnach, as you put it. He is with me because he wants to be. I agree with my ki'medsah. It's time for you to leave."

Furiously, Lashira bristled. "Don't presume to tell me what to do, you…"

"Lashira!" Warnach's voice crackled with exasperation. "Stop it immediately! You walk out of this office now, or I'll have you escorted out."

Pivoting on her heel, disbelief mingled with the disdainful anger in Lashira's expression, and her voice rose insultingly. "How could you do this? Warnach, how? Sirinoya blood represents the continuity of ancient nobility! Look at her! She's Terran, for God's sake! Not only are you consorting with this – this - woman! You've actually defiled noble Chikondran blood by having your baby tainted with Terran blood! What's wrong with you? Have you gone mad?"

"Minister Sirinoya, it seems you require assistance." A uniformed security officer, flanked by two guards, had entered Warnach's office.

Swallowing fury that made him want to slap Lashira full in the face, Warnach responded tersely to the officer, "Miryah Ehmedrad entered my office uninvited and has since engaged in malicious defamation directed toward Deputy Minister Sirinoya."

Curtly, the officer nodded his head. "Yes, sir. We heard her last comments. Your instructions, sir?"

Warnach's jaw shifted sharply from side to side. Blazing obsidian eyes failed to conceal utter disgust. "Take her to Central Security. I want her identity processed immediately. Then, I want her banned from all future access to Ministry Headquarters."

"Warnach!"

"Not another word, Lashira! I warned you. Sandra is my ki'mirsah, and I honor her. I will not tolerate your lack of respect or your unforgivable abuse directed toward her or our baby." His eyes met those of the security officer. "Please, allow me half an hour. I shall then meet you at Central Security."

Tears streamed down Lashira's face as she tried to free herself from the restraining grasp of security guards on either side of her. "Warnach, don't do this to me! Please! I love you! You know that!"

Crossing the short distance to Sandra, Warnach placed a protective arm around her shoulders and felt faint trembling in her body. Ignoring Lashira's theatrical pleas, he addressed the security officers. "Remove her at once."

Quiet. Desperate to drive pained shadows from eyes he adored, Warnach pulled Sandra against him. Her abrupt withdrawal knifed into his heart. "Shi'níyah? Please. Let me hold you."

Shimmering tears brimmed in her eyes but did not fall. Her chin quivered as words sputtered. "I - I can't."

Stung, he winced. "I had no idea she had returned to Chikondra. I'd just come back from playing pafla with Rodan when she caught me totally by surprise. Shi'níyah, you must believe me. I didn't…"

Shaking fingers reached out to stroke the tense line of his jaw. "I know it wasn't your fault…"

Reaching for her, he pleaded. "Then, let me hold you."

Shaking her head, she stepped further back. "No. You - your coat. You smell like her perfume."

Dragging in a ragged breath, he reached for her hand and led her to the sofa. Through the window, he saw that rain clouds had chased away afternoon sunshine, darkening his office. Ironic, he thought. Like a storm, Lashira had blown into his office, leaving happy thoughts and his ki'mirsah's smile tumbling in her wake.

"Sandra," he murmured in a low, soothing tone, "finish whatever you're working on. In the meantime, I'll go to security to address formalities with Lashira. When I come back, I'm taking you home."

Staring at the beige carpet, her head shook slightly from side to side. "Warnach, I don't give a damn about anything she says or thinks about me, but our baby is totally, completely innocent. He didn't deserve her insults. I wanted to pick something up and hit her as hard as I could. I honestly wanted to hurt her for what she said." Her voice dropped to a tense whisper. "I still do."

Gently, Warnach leaned toward her and kissed her temple, allowing his lips to touch the rafizhaq ring. "As do I. Unfortunately, we both know that would accomplish nothing. I learned long ago that Lashira will never change. The person who does not bend to her will faces the vileness of her temper through both insult and revenge."

Sandra's voice choked. "Why attack an innocent baby, though? Why? I just don't understand."

"Shi'níyah, she was attacking you and me. She is quite adept at turning the most emotional subjects into barbed weapons." He paused. "If you won't let me hold you, will you at least let me look at you?"

Prolonged seconds passed before she finally faced him. Grimly, he smiled. "Shi'níyah, I refuse to let her ruin my life again. What I have with you is far too precious. That's why we go home after I put on my Kitak and go to security. These clothes come off, and I intend to wash away every trace of her touch. Then, I intend to hold you very, very close."

Taking a deep breath, Sandra managed a feeble smile and murmured, "I like that idea."

Fifteen minutes later, Warnach swiftly strode into the ultra-contemporary office of Central Security. His severe expression and rigid posture clearly conveyed seething fury as Security Chief Jaflishta greeted him and accompanied him to a private office. There, with a security officer standing behind her, Lashira sat at a bare, rectangular, white table.

Standing, she faced Warnach with a hesitant smile. "How glad I am that you've come. Perhaps we can now sort through this terrible misunderstanding."

Chief Jaflishta said, "Miryah Ehmedrad, it is my duty to inform you that my officers witnessed enough of today's incident to fully justify Minister Sirinoya's request to prohibit you from ever returning to this ministry. Such conduct, especially from a Chikondran, is intolerable."

Warnach watched with almost detached curiosity while Lashira's expression and body language transformed as she aimed a wounded, helpless expression meant to gain sympathy from the security chief. Thinking he had never seen such an accomplished actress, he started upon hearing his name a second time. "Excuse me?"

"Miryah Ehmedrad wishes to speak with you privately. I can allow that if you wish."

"Chief Jaflishta, there's no need. I authorize full prohibition of Miryah Ehmedrad's access to Ministry Headquarters."

Lashira sobbed quietly. "Warnach, why? I only want to talk to you."

"Lashira, the time for talking is long past. Sandra more than fulfills every dream I ever had. The only role you have left in my life is that of a nightmare best forgotten."

"But I need you. I love you."

"The likelihood is that you need money again. Go back to your extravagant games and debauchery, Lashira. I never want anything to do with you. Ever." Cutting short whatever she had intended to say, Warnach spun on his heel and left.

Outside, the security chief joined him, and the two men went to Jaflishta's office to finalize codes and records that would effectively ban Lashira from the ministry complex. When they were finished and Warnach had thanked the chief for his quick assistance and discretion, the security officer smiled encouragingly. "Minister Sirinoya," he said, "my officers confirmed your statements. I want you to know that they were appalled by what Miryah

Ehmedrad told you and Deputy Minister Sirinoya. What she said does not reflect what most Chikondrans think."

Unable to respond verbally, Warnach responded thankfully with a nod and a bow before he left to take Sandra home.

Warnach disrobed. Sniffing, his nose wrinkled in disgust. Sandra had been right. Lashira's heavy perfume had permeated the fabric of his coat. Sliding aside glass doors, he stepped inside the steaming shower. Opening his mouth, he imagined the hot, stinging spray washing away every remnant of a kiss he cursed. Wondering if he might ever cleanse himself of her revolting touch, he stopped the water and left the shower.

After drying long, tousled hair, he drew on a robe and securely tied the wide belt at his waist. Emerging from the bath, his eyes swept the spacious elegance of the master suite. Open draperies exposed windows. Outside, rain coursed downward along the glass. On the loveseat placed in front of the window, Sandra's legs were drawn toward her chest, and her head rested on her knees.

Rounding the end of the loveseat, he knelt on the floor and reached out to caress her hair. "Shi'níyah, I wish for you not to look so sad."

Lifting her head slightly, she sighed and forced a smile. "I'm sorry. It sounds so ridiculous, but I can't quite discard the shock of seeing her kissing you."

"May I sit with you?" Receiving a weak nod for a yes, he rose and, sitting down, waited until she rearranged herself beside him. Gently, he guided her face to rest against his chest. Grinning was impossible as he heard her sniff. "Better?"

Pressing her cheek more tightly against him, she knew she must be blushing. "You smell like my ki'medsah again."

"For which I am very glad." Gazing at gray rivers of water slithering down the window, he breathed in deeply. "Sandra, I can't imagine how you felt this afternoon. I wish it were possible that I could turn back time or erase the memory. What I can tell you is that I was thoroughly sickened by her presence alone. As for the rest…"

Words emerged from a tight throat. "You don't have to explain. After the initial shock, I saw the look in your eyes. I just didn't know what to do or say."

Soon, Warnach rose and lit pillar candles atop tables and columns scattered around the room. Then, grasping her hands, he guided her toward their bed. First, he took her Kitak and placed it on the nightstand. Gentle fingers unfastened and removed her clothing. Untying his belt, he opened his robe and let it drop from his shoulders to the floor. When he finally felt her skin warm against his, he sighed. "Me'u Shi'níyah, may I love you?"

Within minutes, he had joined with her. Lips feverishly baptized her skin with damp kisses. Hands molded themselves beneath her hips for firm support. Careful of her rounded abdomen, he positioned them both to fully partake of the sensual ecstasy drawn from their union. Shuddering from an explosion of pleasure, he clutched her body close.

Finally, reluctantly, they parted. Kissing her lightly, he smiled. "You are my life, Shi'níyah. No one could ever compare with you. I promise never to let you forget."

Resting her lips against the hollow at the base of his throat, she also smiled. Restored by his loving, she closed her eyes. When he realized she had fallen asleep, he breathed several slow, measured breaths. Despite the strength everyone associated with her, no one knew her hidden insecurities better than he. Especially now, he vowed to shield her from any doubts or fears.

Hunger drove him directly from bed to the kitchen. Thinking to have a snack and start dinner, he was surprised to find Mamehr already there. "I thought you were dining tonight with Nahtouman."

"Nahtouman wasn't feeling very well, so I decided to come home early." Leaning forward, Araman placed a baking dish inside the oven. When she straightened and turned to face Warnach, her expression held worry that her son noted immediately.

"Is her illness serious?" he asked.

"Not nearly as serious as the com call I just took."

Warnach's heart sank. "Lashira?"

Araman nodded. Minutes later, seated at the table, her expression grew progressively more concerned as he related details from the afternoon encounter in his office. "Warnach, I don't trust her. Beyond vile insults, she sounded irrational to me. I wouldn't worry so much except that Sandra's pregnancy makes her vulnerable."

Tense lines etched around Warnach's eyes and creased his forehead. Cerea-nervos pulsated erratically. "Mamehr, I think you may be right. Experience tells me she's in serious trouble and hoping to persuade me to help her. Whatever the case, Sandra doesn't need further exposure to such behavior."

"Talking about me?"

Twisting around in his chair, Warnach forced a smile. "Shi'níyah, I expected you to sleep a little longer."

Leaning forward, Sandra placed a kiss against Araman's cheek before replying, "I didn't mean to fall asleep in the first place. So, am I the topic of this discussion, or is it really Lashira?"

"Both," Araman answered honestly, reaching across the table to take Sandra's hand. "Lashira called earlier, and she wasn't pleasant. We don't trust her, especially where you're concerned."

Gazing blankly at tiny flowerets woven into the blue tablecloth, Sandra sighed and murmured, "I won't let her hurt my baby."

Leaning across the table, Warnach reached out to stroke his lifemate's cheek. "It is my intention that she hurts neither you nor the baby. We were fortunate today you'd left the door open. Zara heard and realized what was happening. Security officers are always moments away at the ministry. That might not be the case if you're out somewhere on your own."

"Do you honestly think she would physically attack me?"

Warnach smiled reassuringly. "I think not, Shi'níyah. However, I prefer taking no risks where my lifemate and my son are involved."

Awake well into the night, Sandra stared into darkness with her hands over her stomach. Her anger seethed. Lashira's words had spewed the venom of blind hatred. Had those words been aimed at Warnach or herself, Sandra could have borne the assault with relative calm. Still, uncomfortable fears assailed her. Though certainly few, others would surely harbor the same prejudices. How would she react? How could she possibly insulate her child from unjustified hurt?

The bed shifted as Warnach turned onto his side. His arm snaked across her body. "Shi'níyah," he mumbled thickly, "your thoughts keep me awake. Remember what you said. Our baby is meant to be. Go to sleep."

Grasping his hand, she lifted it to her lips and whispered, "Are my thoughts really so loud?"

"Mmhmm."

Smiling as he fell silent, she breathed a prayer. She hadn't wanted to admit, even to herself, how her confidence had been shaken in the face of Lashira's stunning beauty. Warnach's lovemaking that afternoon had been perfection. Within his touch, she had felt love and reassurance. Her thoughts stilled. Sighing softly, she drifted off to sleep.

~

Framed by sleek, golden lines, the photograph conjured memories of times that couldn't possibly be so long ago. How handsome Warnach had always been, then and now. Like her badehr, he had been doting and generous, lavishing her with beautiful clothes and feminine gifts. Surrounded by the luxuries they had shared, she had felt gay and carefree, adored, beautiful, and desirable.

Shining black irises rose, momentarily observing the perfect features staring back at her. Despite the years that had passed and the life she had lived, the mirror remained her friend. Smooth skin, the color of light cinnamon, was flawless and showed no sign of aging. The beauty reflected by the glass demanded repeated, hungry looks from every man she had ever met. The thought provoked a bitter sigh. Earlier that day, Warnach had not looked at her even once with that expression of desire.

Unable to put his picture down, she carried it across the room to her bed. Reclining against a stack of cushions, her mind reverted to those early days when she had first moved in with him. In the beginning, their relationship had been filled with fire and passion. No man she'd ever known could rival him as a lover. However, he had been especially selfish when it came to his career. Young and vibrant, she had thought his attention should have been concentrated on her instead of faceless people from planets she couldn't begin to name.

Only weeks after they began living together, boredom had quickly descended. He was often far too serious and intellectual. She couldn't begin to converse with him on subjects that interested him. He showed little desire for gaming or entertainment that sparked her limited imagination and delighted her fanciful attitude toward life. Arguments sparked easily. Often, she cried, knowing he would relent and buy her something expensive to placate her wounded feelings.

Still, his attentions insufficiently satisfied her ego. With a wandering eye, she had sought other lovers when his work merited more importance in his life than she did. Never had she dreamed he might return that night. Naked, she had deserted her newest lover and chased Warnach downstairs. He had never turned around, never said a word. All she had seen was his back as he stormed out of the house.

Mistakes of youth. Surely, she had thought, enough time had elapsed that Warnach would listen and forgive her. He would understand her reluctance to tell her badehr about debts she had incurred that exceeded the generous allowance provided since her teens. Warnach would not only forgive her; he would remind her of how many times he had promised always to love her, and he would help her. In return, she would force herself to settle down and be more patient with his life.

How impossible it seemed that she had been away from Chikondra for most of ten years. Following her breakup with Warnach, she had returned for a few brief visits with Badehr. Over the past several years, she had made up excuses to avoid coming home. Instead, Badehr had visited her on the worlds she frequented for extravagant entertainment.

As unbelievable as it now seemed, she had missed news of Warnach's unification. Completely disinterested in anything political or historical, neither had she seen stories regarding his recent diplomatic accomplishments while accompanied by an advocate who was also his lifemate.

Hot tears scorched her eyelids. Shapely lips thinned into a line she would have considered ugly. How could he have gone back on his promises? How was it possible he had unified with anyone else, especially an alien? Unable to believe that he could have forgotten her, her stomach churned. As teardrops created silent trails along her cheeks, Lashira convinced herself that, although he refused to admit it, Warnach would always belong to her.

≈

Two weeks later, while getting ready for a morning appointment with her doctors, Sandra shook her head in frustration. Her patience had been tested daily. Within the ministry complex or at home, she maintained a relatively normal routine. However, every time she ventured beyond, someone was always with her. Growing aggravated, she had sneaked away from the office twice. Twice, Badrik had greeted her with an expression of innocent surprise and stayed with her until she returned to work.

Downstairs, she greeted Araman with a wry grin. "Are we ready?"

"You don't look so happy that I shall accompany you."

Guilt flitted across her expression. "It isn't that, Mamehr. I just hate dragging you all the way to Kadranas just because Warnach is meeting with Baadihm Farsuk and insists that I not go anywhere by myself."

Araman's features reflected understanding. "I know that you're accustomed to your independence. You know that my son only considers your safety and that of your baby."

Nodding, Sandra's face grew serious. "I'll be glad when we leave for Earth. I can use the break. I imagine Badrik and you might also appreciate some relief from being my constant guardians."

Araman laughed. "We never tire of being with you. Besides, I'm excited today. I finally get the chance to see my grandson."

Waiting while three doctors administered a battery of scans and exams took nearly three hours. Displeased by her plans to travel to Earth, her doctors and the pediatric specialist had insisted on reviewing every possible shred of information related to her condition. While the physicians were forced to acknowledge the pregnancy continued to progress well, Sandra and Araman exchanged pride-filled grins at glimpses of a very healthy fetus.

By the time they left the clinic, Sandra complained about a growling stomach that threatened to deafen her. The baby must certainly be frightened by so much noise. Laughing, Araman linked her arm with her daughter's, and the two women strolled toward a swank café for lunch.

They arrived just after the lunchtime rush, and an elegantly uniformed man seated them. Within minutes, a server appeared at their table with the classic chibitl, a small brazier platform used to keep pottery pots of herbal teas bubbling hot. Looking slightly chagrined, Sandra excused herself with a humorous quip about pottery pots filled with liquid being dangerously suggestive to pregnant women.

Smiling happily to herself upon exiting the ladies' room, Sandra headed toward their table. Abruptly, she stopped. Hovering ominously over Mamehr's left side stood Lashira Ehmedrad. Araman's face held anger she'd never seen before.

Trained eyes recorded even the smallest details of their surroundings. For days, she had been convinced that Warnach had overreacted to Lashira's unexpected reappearance. Instinct instantly altered her thinking as, swallowing and unconsciously floating one hand over her stomach, she slowly neared the table. Firmly grasping the back of her chair, she pulled it toward her and made her presence known. "Miryah Ehmedrad, such a surprise seeing you again."

"You will excuse me. I am speaking with Mirsah Sirinoya."

Boldly, Sandra refused to be dismissed. "I, too, am Mirsah Sirinoya." She then shifted her gaze to Araman's tense face. "Mamehr, are you all right?"

Lashira's face jerked to the side. "You dare allow this Terran to address you as Mamehr?"

Fury blazed on Araman's face. "According to ancient ways, Sandra is my daughter. Not only is she entitled to call me Mamehr, I feel happy and honored when she does so."

"You always hated me, didn't you?" Lashira hissed. Then, without waiting for a response, she faced Sandra again. "You and your diamond Kitak. You're a fool if you really think he'll stay with you."

"Lashira, go back to whatever you were doing. Mamehr and I are here to have lunch. Privately."

Arrogant challenge saturated Lashira's sneer. "I will go when I so please. I warn you. Warnach belongs to me, and he always will."

Impatient, Sandra attempted to signal the restaurant manager while smiling cynically. "Warnach is not a possession. He belongs to no one."

"I tell you, he's mine! He can't love you because he loves me!"

369

In contrast to the rising volume of Lashira's voice, Sandra spoke in quieter tones. "I believe you deceive yourself, Miryah Ehmedrad. I remind you. Warnach shares Kitak with me."

Noting growing disruption, the manager finally responded to a hand signal from Araman. "Ladies, is there a problem?"

Lashira began to shake with rage. "Yes, Medsah Neyfrahliz. I would like to have this Terran escorted from my badehr's restaurant."

Medsah Neyfrahliz gave her a confused look. "Miryah Ehmedrad, I cannot ask patrons to leave without a valid reason."

Araman stood up. "There's no need to ask. My daughter and I will gladly leave."

Lashira's face flushed. "Idiot! Stop calling her your daughter! She has no claim to Warnach! I'm the one who loves him!"

Anger stiffened Sandra's features, but she remained outwardly calm. "Mamehr, shall we go?"

"Excellent suggestion. Go! Go back to Earth, where you belong. Warnach belongs here, among his own people. Here, I will make him happy."

"The same way you did before?" Her sarcastic question that slipped out surprised even Sandra.

Lashira's eyes narrowed threateningly. "What happened before was a misunderstanding. Things are different now. Warnach will soon appreciate how much I really love him."

"Lashira," Sandra addressed her coldly by her given name, "you know nothing of what it is to love anyone except yourself. You may be the most beautiful woman I've ever seen, but your kind of beauty is nothing more than a fragile shell. On the inside, you're as cold and empty as the ice caves on Vagba. When the ice breaks on the outside, there'll be nothing left except harsh, bitter loneliness."

Fury flared in a woman accustomed only to flourishing compliments. "You see, Mirsah Sirinoya? This Terran isn't as sweet and harmless as she seems. Listen to her insults."

For a matter of seconds, Araman glanced at Sandra before turning flashing brown eyes to Lashira. "In my opinion, my daughter's comments hold more kindness than a dezhrashth like you deserves. Daughter, let us leave now."

"How dare you?" Incensed, Lashira grabbed Araman's arm, twisting it painfully.

"Lashira! Let her go! Now!"

Furious and verging on hysteria, Lashira spat in Sandra's direction. "And who will make me? You're nothing more than Terran trash, pregnant with a half-breed child."

"Miryah Ehmedrad! Stop! The ladies wish to leave. Please, you're disturbing our other guests." Stunned by actions foreign to his culture and his experience, Medsah Neyfrahliz was unable to move.

"Neyfrahliz, get away from me and mind your own business!"

Fiery temper snapped in Sandra's eyes. "Lashira, I'm warning you. Release Mamehr now so we can leave."

Digging in sharp nails while twisting Araman's arm, Lashira ignored Sandra's warning. "This old woman needs to learn a lesson."

Suddenly, with lightning speed, Sandra snatched a cup from the table and hurled it. Lashira screamed as the cup bounced off her cheekbone and landed on the floor, shattering into pieces. Freed, Araman jumped backward out of Lashira's reach.

"You pregnant bitch!" Lashira cried out as she pulled bloody fingers from her face. "You will pay for that!"

"Stay away from me while you have the chance. If you force me to defend myself, I swear! You'll live to regret it!"

When Lashira would have lunged forward, Sandra forcefully shoved the chair over. Agilely, Lashira avoided the chair by stepping backward. Infuriated, she advanced again. Adrenalin shot through Sandra's body as the only clear thought in her mind was to protect her baby. Within the span of mere seconds, Sandra leapt sideways and toppled the heavy table toward her attacker. Crashing tableware mingled with agonized shrieks.

Frozen in place and facing the doorway, Sandra stared blankly at police officers who had arrived at the restaurant but had been unable to negotiate their way around tables and onlookers fast enough to reach Lashira and restrain her. An arm reached around her, and she heard the comforting voices of two colleagues from the ministry.

Mentally, her brain was paralyzed. Without protest, she allowed herself to be guided to the manager's private office. Someone offered her a glass of water, but her hands trembled too violently to take it. Her heart pounded. Her head throbbed. She felt as if she might either throw up or pass out.

Paramedics entered the office. One examined Araman's slender, bruised arm. Just as a second knelt in front of Sandra with a scanner, the door flew open, and Warnach swept in like a whirlwind. Practically on his heels, Badrik followed and rushed to Araman's side. "Mamehr! Are you hurt?"

"Sandra! Deputy Minister Prag contacted me. I came immediately." Warnach dropped heavily to his knees beside the arm of the chair where Sandra sat, leaning forward. Apprehensive eyes questioned the medic.

Despite instantaneous recognition of the famous diplomat, the young paramedic's face remained coolly professional. "Minister Sirinoya, your lifemate is uninjured. However, I am concerned that her blood pressure is seriously elevated. I wish to monitor her a while longer."

Warnach only nodded in response. His gaze was locked on Sandra's ashen face. Reaching out, he tenderly stroked her cheek. "Shi'níyah, I'm so sorry. I never should have let this happen."

Unable to contain raging emotions a moment longer, she burst into sobs. Instantly, Warnach perched on the broad arm of the chair and gathered her close to him. Her body quaked as she released anger, fear, and indignation. Helpless to stem her crying, Warnach shuddered as he tenderly cooed words of comfort. Both Araman and Badrik joined his attempts to console her. It seemed the more they tried, the harder she cried. Even the paramedic tried to quiet her by pointing out the need to calm herself for the sake of her baby. Every effort proved ineffectual as she clung to her ki'medsah and buried her face against his coat.

Minutes passed. Hiccupping and still shaking, her sobs slowly subsided. Refusing to budge from the haven of Warnach's embrace, she continued to hide her face. The sound of his voice and even his masculine scent penetrated her weary mind with the sense that she was safe. All the while, he rested his cheek against the top of her head and murmured gently. Finally, she quieted.

"Deputy Minister Sirinoya, may I please perform another scan? I want to recheck your vital signs and those of your baby."

Raising her blotched, sodden face, she forced a hoarse whisper. "What do you want me to do?"

The medic smiled reassuringly. "I want you to sit back. Try to relax and breathe deeply but regularly." Shifting her gaze downward, the woman intently reviewed scan data.

Swollen eyes opened and sought Araman's face. "Mamehr? Did she hurt you?"

Araman smiled through a glaze of tears. "I'm all right, child. Just sore and bruised. Mostly afraid for you. We must take care of my grandson and his mamehr."

When the paramedic completed the scan, her face still held concern. "Deputy Minister, your vital signs are strong, but your blood pressure remains elevated. I think it best for you to go to hospital for a more thorough evaluation. I prefer the safer, more conservative approach, just to be certain blood pressure readings can be attributed to circumstances."

Fresh tears overflowed Sandra's eyes. "My baby. I just want my baby to be all right."

"Shi'níyah," Warnach interrupted, "that's why we shall follow the paramedic's advice. You know I could never bear for anything to happen to either of you."

Her weak smile quickly faded. Exhausted, she leaned once more against the solid support of his body. Too tired to speak, she heard the paramedic excuse herself to arrange medical transport. Unsuccessfully, she tried to block out Mamehr's quietly spoken account of the confrontation with Lashira. The voice of the restaurant manager interrupted to express concern and apology. With the earlier adrenalin rush subsiding, exhaustion set in as she rested within her lifemate's protective embrace.

A hand gently grasped her arm. "Deputy Minister, the medical transport is here. Do you think you can walk?"

Reluctantly, Sandra forced herself away from Warnach and twisted to face the female paramedic. Her speech remained thick from crying. "I think so."

The medic smiled comfortingly. "Come. Let's get you to the transport."

Her legs felt nearly numb with weakness as she stood and swayed a moment. The paramedic was quick to steady her, and Warnach's strong arm held her securely. "Are you certain you're all right?"

"I...I think so."

Fortunately, Badrik was standing nearly in front of her. With her first step, sudden dizziness caused her to pitch drunkenly forward. Reacting quickly, he swept her into his arms. "Little sister!"

"Badrik!" she whispered before turning her eyes toward her frightened lifemate. "I'm so sorry. I'm all right. Honestly. I just feel a little dizzy."

Badrik winked at Warnach. "Don't be sorry, little sister. You haven't let me play my hero role for a while."

She couldn't help but grin. "You'll always be my hero, big brother. Just the way your big brother will always be the love of my life."

Badrik smiled his approval and carried her outside to a waiting ambulance.

Promising that he would leave right away to join her at the hospital, Warnach caressed her face while medical attendants secured her to a gurney and guided the hovering stretcher into the emergency medical transport. Anxiety carved deep lines into his face as he watched the doors close. Swallowing hard, he waited for the vehicle to lift and ascend for the short trip to the Kadranas Medical Center.

"My brother, she's in good hands. Shall we leave? I want Farisa to check Mamehr's arm."

"Of course..." Warnach's words stopped short as another team of paramedics maneuvered a stretcher toward the second waiting transport. Rolling her head toward him, he saw Lashira's swollen, blackened eye and cheek. Overcome with contempt, he felt not a shred of sympathy.

"Warnach," she called out in a thin, pitiful voice as she reached for him. "I knew you'd come. Warnach..."

"Brother, we must go. Sandra will be waiting for you."

Glaring at Lashira, Warnach had no time to utter the bitter curses erupting inside his mind. He would deal with her later. Without a word, he followed Badrik for the brief trip to be at Sandra's side.

Badrik smoothly descended his transport and stopped. Glancing around, he noted the severe expression still drawing his brother's face taut. "Are you sure?"

Reclining in the passenger seat with his head back and his eyes shut, Warnach nodded grimly. "I have no choice. This must end now. I can't allow Sandra or my baby to be exposed to any more of Lashira's bizarre behavior."

"Warnach, you have my full support. Even though the doctors decided to keep her overnight for observation, I'm certain she'll be fine tomorrow. We might not be so fortunate if Lashira should provoke another confrontation."

When the door to Amlal Ehmedrad's house opened, they were greeted by Lashira's older brother, Daltrehm. Once, Warnach and Daltrehm had been friends. Following the split with Lashira, Daltrehm had distanced himself from a man he respected and admired. At that moment, his eyes showed no hint of surprise at the unannounced visit. Bowing formally, he invited Warnach and Badrik into the house.

Once inside the foyer, Warnach was first to speak. "Daltrehm, I apologize for disturbing you. However, I must speak with your badehr. Is he home?"

Daltrehm flinched, then nodded. "I suspected you might come. Warnach, I can't tell you how ashamed I…"

Compassionately, Warnach reached out and firmly grasped the arm of his one-time friend. "You bear no guilt in this matter. We both know how willful and volatile she can be."

Daltrehm's head shook back and forth. "I know, but this exceeds anything I ever heard about her. Your ki'mirsah and your mamehr. How are they?"

"Mamehr's arm is bruised, scratched, and sore. The doctors kept my ki'mirsah in hospital for observation. Her blood pressure rose quite high for a while, probably due to emotional stress. She had stabilized and was feeling better by the time I left."

"For that, I am glad. Come. I shall take you to Badehr."

Inside the living room, Amlal Ehmedrad stood by a massive stone fireplace and gazed morosely at a portrait hung above an ornately sculpted mantle of white marble. Hauntingly beautiful, the image of his deceased wife looked strikingly like the daughter she had delivered at the scene of a transport crash, only minutes before she had died. Her final words had been a plea for her lifemate to take care of their newborn baby.

"Medsah Ehmedrad," Warnach spoke. He and Badrik both bowed respectfully when the white-haired man turned around.

Amlal gestured with age-spotted hands for his guests to be seated. Sad eyes looked upon his son before he sighed and sat directly across from the Sirinoyas. "You wish to discuss this afternoon's unfortunate incident involving my daughter."

"Sir, what happened this afternoon is much more than unfortunate. It is inexcusable. There was no reason for her to attack and hurt Mamehr. Further, my ki'mirsah is pregnant. Her encounter with Lashira has resulted in hospitalization."

Resistance flared in the old man's eyes. "Warnach, my daughter was also hurt today. She was released from hospital only after emergency treatment and an hour of HAU treatment. Additional treatments will be required to treat the injuries she received after your lifemate intentionally turned a table over on her. She suffered serious burns from scalding tea and coals from a chibitl. She'll be fortunate if she isn't permanently scarred. Add the injury to her face…"

"Badehr…"

Amlal Ehmedrad impatiently glanced at his son. "I will deal with this."

Placing a restraining hand on his brother's shoulder, Badrik stood. His height and powerful build combined with his angry expression to create an intimidating image. "Medsah Ehmedrad, we have spoken with police authorities who have already interviewed many witnesses, including the restaurant manager. All gave consistent reports. Your daughter insisted on confrontation with my mamehr and my sister, and she deliberately prevented them from leaving peacefully. Lashira also grabbed and twisted Mamehr's arm. My sister had little choice but to act forcefully."

"There was no cause to hurt my daughter that way. She was simply upset and meant no harm."

"Medsah Ehmedrad," Warnach spoke out, "I had hoped for a respectful discussion of this matter. However, I see that nothing has changed in the years since last I saw you. No matter what Lashira ever does, you defend her. Today, she crossed the line beyond merely immoral conduct. She resorted to violence against an elderly woman, and you have the audacity to say she meant no harm."

"I tell you. My daughter meant to hurt no one. Warnach, what do you really want?"

Giving his brother no chance to respond, Badrik angrily addressed Medsah Ehmedrad. "Sir, quite frankly, your attitude is deplorable in a man otherwise known for honorable integrity. What we want is for Lashira never again to come near any member of our family."

Medsah Ehmedrad's face harshly tensed. Somehow, he thought, he must change the mood of the discussion. "Gentlemen, please, let us attempt a more calm resolution here. As it is, authorities already shamed Lashira with an arrest. They also informed us that she will be required to face a magistrate. If you request dismissal for humanitarian purposes, perhaps citing her injuries already sustained, I will discuss your request with Lashira."

Warnach's eyes burned furiously. "You misunderstand. Deliberately, I believe. We did not come to negotiate. We came with a warning, not a request. Your daughter's unwarranted attack today against our mamehr will not be excused. Neither will we tolerate another sordid incident of hate slurs directed against my ki'mirsah because of her Terran origin or against our baby for being what Lashira called a half-breed with tainted blood. If you do not agree to stop Lashira's harassment, we will demand the most severe punishment allowable by law."

Amlal Ehmedrad's face blanched. Chikondran law maintained high regard for justice. Although crime was a rarity, lawbreakers were treated to a sympathetic system of rehabilitation. However, because of lofty ideals related to Chikondra's mission of promoting peace, there was no tolerance for those harassing others based on ethnicity. Violators could look forward to long periods of incarceration and re-education under humane but austere conditions. Lashira would never survive such punishment.

"Warnach, Lashira was understandably upset today. Whether or not you believe me, she really does love you. Are you certain this isn't means to gain revenge for your breakup years ago?"

"Badehr!" Daltrehm exclaimed. "I will be quiet no longer! This is absurd! I spoke with Neyfrahliz myself. Lashira clearly antagonized those two women today. It's time for you to face reality. My sister is a spoiled, selfish, and obnoxious tramp!"

"You will not speak of your sister in such insulting terms!"

"I speak only the truth from which you hide! This must end, Badehr. Your money and your influence cannot buy her out of this predicament. Do you think I don't know about all the times you paid her debts and moved her from one planet to another to save her from facing either legal prosecution or bilked lovers? Yes, I know all about it, and I'm sick of it!"

"Your jealousy does not justify your speaking of private family matters in front of guests, especially unfriendly ones."

"Badehr, you're right. I am jealous. I'm jealous because you ignore your son, who has never asked more from you than your time and affection. Instead, you lavish all your resources on a daughter who cannot even visit you unless she's in some sort of trouble. Badehr, Eyalá Ehmedrad was my mamehr, too, and I believe she loved me as much as she loved Lashira. Why don't you?"

"Daltrehm, I demand that you stop now. We must help your sister."

"No, Badehr. Not we. You. If you can. This time, she went too far. I honestly hope you haven't ruined her life completely. If the magistrate rules that she must face the consequences for her behavior, maybe she can learn a lesson and salvage something of her life.

"On the other hand, since your daughter seems to be the only child who merits your attention, you do what you can on your own. When I walk out of this house tonight, you'll not see me again, nor will you ever again see my mate or your grandchildren. I want my children to live honorable lives, not just talk hypocritically about them to others."

Shocked, Amlal stared at his son. "You would risk your inheritance over this?"

"Badehr, even if you haven't spent my inheritance paying for years of my sister's misdeeds, it means nothing to me. I have lived the life of honor you always said you valued. I have done everything to earn your respect and some measure of your affection. I've also prospered. Your wealth is not what I want. What I want and need is my badehr."

Warnach got up and, standing beside Badrik, added his voice. "Medsah Ehmedrad, I warned you many years ago that Lashira's greatest problem was your refusal to insist that she accept responsibility for her actions. It's obvious that you're as much to blame for what she did today as she is herself. I pray that when my own son is born, I will recall your example as one to be avoided at all costs.

"In the meantime, my greatest concern is for the safety of my ki'mirsah until we meet with witnesses before the magistrate. Out of respect for an old, respectable family and for Daltrehm, whom I know to be a man of the highest integrity, I advise you to keep Lashira away from my family. Is that very clear?"

"Warnach, is it possible that you have no compassion at all for my daughter? Can you remember nothing about how you once loved her?"

Warnach's jaw set firmly. "What I remember is the pain caused by that love when I came home and found her having sex with another man in the house I bought to share with her. Did she tell you that truth, or did you believe another of her lies?"

Receiving only a look of dismay, Warnach continued, "Any compassion I might have had ceased when she attacked my ki'mirsah and my mamehr. Her future now lies in the hands of the courts. I agree with Daltrehm. If you really love her and want her to have any chance for a future, I suggest you insist that she finally assume responsibility for herself."

Defeat was defined in the slump of his shoulders. Still, he could not avoid a final attempt. "Warnach, will you please reconsider and enter a request for clement judgment?"

Badrik responded coldly, "He will not. Neither will our mamehr. Especially not after what has been said tonight. My brother and I will leave now with a reminder. Do not let your daughter near our family again."

Daltrehm nodded and rose to walk out with them. His gaze rested upon his badehr's face that suddenly looked infinitely older. "Badehr, I bid you well. Goodbye."

Just as they reached the arched doorway of the living room, Lashira appeared. Clad in loose-fitting robe and slippers, she looked tired and dejected. HAU treatment had concentrated on her burns, leaving swelling and purplish-black bruising around her eye. The moment she saw Warnach, she forgot her pain and rushed to embrace him. "Oh, Warnach! I knew it! I knew you still cared. Just seeing you makes the pain better."

Roughly grabbing her arms, Warnach shoved her away in disgust. "Don't touch me!"

Tears instantly brimmed in her eyes. "Warnach? I don't understand."

Pivoting on his heel, he started to leave, but she clutched his sleeve. "Don't go. I have so much I need to tell you."

Jerking free of her, he turned. "I told you that day at the ministry. Time for discussion passed long ago, Lashira. I came to ask your badehr to convey a message that I now deliver personally. Don't approach my mamehr again, and never go near Sandra or our child. Is that very clear?"

Tears spilled down her cheeks. "Warnach, I know I made terrible mistakes, but you didn't have to punish me by unifying with a Terran. We can find some way to work things out. Badehr is so wise, and he knows everyone. He'll help us."

"Lashira, what does it take for you to understand? Your badehr can't find enough wealth on the entire planet of Chikondra to change the fact that Sandra is my life. I love her."

"You must love me, Warnach. You said you always would."

"I did say that, but whatever love I felt for you, you brutally and shamelessly destroyed. I don't love you, Lashira. I haven't for years. I'm leaving now, but I remind you again. Stay away from Sandra. Do you understand? Stay away!"

Casting a sharp, furious glance toward Amlal Ehmedrad, he scowled and rapidly strode toward the front door. Ignoring pain from her burns, Lashira ran after him. "Warnach! Don't go! If you do, you'll regret it! You know you will!"

Arriving home that evening, Warnach wearily climbed the stairs to check on Araman. Knocking on her bedroom door, he went in and sat beside her. Briefly, he described the visit with Amlal Ehmedrad. Then, after giving her an affectionate cerea-semi'ittá, he headed to the Brisajai. From there, he dejectedly went to his own rooms.

How empty the master suite felt without his ki'mirsah's sunny presence. Checking the clock, he decided she must be asleep already. Touching his Kitak, he smiled thoughtfully. He then removed the golden band and joined it with hers that he'd brought home for safekeeping. Climbing into bed, he rolled onto his side and buried his face into her pillow.

For several moments, he wondered how he could have become entangled with Lashira in the first place. How could he have ever descended into such a hole as to have been rendered oblivious to her true character? That period of his life would always remain a series of unfathomable, unanswerable questions. He could only remind himself to be thankful that he had escaped Lashira's destructive grasp.

Turning restlessly in the dark, he finally smiled. The Great Spirit had understood his remorse. Considering Sandra to be living symbol of Yahvanta's forgiveness and love, Warnach breathed in on a comforting thought. He would go the next morning for his ki'mirsah, and home would feel like home again.

~

Two days later, Sandra knelt beside a flowerbed while inspecting a tiny speck of green peeking through the ground. Springtime was coming to Kadranas. Just in time for her to visit Earth entering the throes of winter cold, she wryly thought to herself. Smiling at the thought of reaching Earth in time to spend her first Christmas back home since she had come to Chikondra to live, it took her several moments to realize that a transport was skimming just above the approach lane to the house.

She stood and watched as the unfamiliar transport eased to a stop. Two well-dressed men exited the vehicle. The younger of the two smiled and approached her. His expression was serious as he greeted her with a formal bow, which she returned in kind.

"You are Mirsah Sirinoya?"

She noted the elegance in his accent. He must have studied at the finest schools on Chikondra. "I am Mirsah Sirinoya. May I help you?"

The man's smile was polite and almost nervous. "I hope you will forgive me for arriving without advance notice. I am Daltrehm Ehmedrad. I have come with my badehr. We hoped that we might speak to Warnach. Is he home?"

Showing little reaction, Sandra nodded. "My ki'medsah is home. You may follow me inside."

Inviting the two men to be seated inside a formal lounge, she excused herself and announced visitors to Warnach. After the two came from his office, she then disappeared and quickly prepared a large pot of tea. Carrying a tray weighted with tea service, she earned a frown of disapproval from Warnach, who immediately went to her and took the heavy tray from her and placed it on a large coffee table.

"Mirsah Sirinoya," Daltrehm began with an odd smile, "you show gracious hospitality to guests who, under similar circumstances in other homes, would not be welcomed."

Uncertain of his intent but recalling complimentary comments from Warnach about Lashira's older brother, Sandra smiled back. "It's my understanding of Chikondran customs that anyone worthy of being invited into a home should always be treated with courtesy and respect. I take pride in honoring generations of tradition carried out in my ki'medsah's ancestral home."

Puzzled by her response and its perfect wording according to tradition, Amlal Ehmedrad studied the Terran more closely. Her mastery of the

Chikondran language was rare. Her respectful reference to ancestral tradition had been sincerely delivered. What amazed him most was the sparkling diamond set in her Kitak. Glancing from her face to Warnach's, he noted the invisible connection between them. Weight descended upon his heart. Lashira had waited far too many years before recognizing her love for Warnach.

"Badehr?"

Shaking off the lapse of attention, Amlal met Warnach's waiting gaze. "I apologize. These last days have been difficult for an old man. As you can appreciate, I face an even more difficult future for my daughter. However, she understands that she must acknowledge her guilt when she faces the magistrate."

Warnach released a thoughtful sigh. "Acceptance of responsibility will likely lighten her sentence."

In a voice saturated with regret, Amlal said, "That is my hope. It has been painful for me to face what happened. You were right when you accused me of defending her every action. I wanted to protect her. Instead, I... Suffice it to say that the prospect of losing my son and my grandchildren has finally forced me to examine Lashira and myself in new light. That is why I asked Daltrehm to bring me. I came to offer my personal apology and to ask your forgiveness."

A prolonged silence ensued. With her left hand, Sandra reached out and touched Warnach's arm. She sensed his suspicions and felt his doubts. Raising her right hand, her fingertips lightly stroked her Kitak. Intuition told her that Lashira's badehr continued to struggle but was sincere in expressing his regrets.

Ebony eyes turned toward her. Although he wasn't sure it was definition-perfect telepathy, understanding of her thoughts astonished him. Broad shoulders lifted with the deep breath he took. According to ancient tradition, Warnach stood and approached Amlal. First bowing, he offered both hands.

In response, Amlal rose, bowed, and joined hands with Warnach. Without speaking, the men departed the lounge and went to the Brisajai.

There, they would each light two cones of incense and recite ancient prayers. The smoke from the first cone each had lit would dispatch their enmity to the Great Spirit for complete dissolution. The second cones would carry prayers for lasting peace between them.

While waiting for them to return, Daltrehm turned a more confident smile to Sandra. "You make him very happy."

Her smile was radiant. "I love him. Seeing him happy is very important to me."

"So I noticed. Your Kitak is beautiful and, in these days, rare. The Warnach I always respected and admired needed someone like you to fulfill his dreams. I say this not as any kind of insult, but how amazing it seems that he would have found that love and comprehension of our ways in a Terran."

Detecting no malice in his remark, she smilingly replied, "I've been just as amazed as you. I've long since decided that I was born to love him."

From behind, she received a kiss over her temple. "As I was born to love this incredible lady."

That evening, they quietly discussed with Araman the unexpected visit. There had been no mention of any request for leniency in Lashira's favor. There had been only calm discussion of the incidents at the ministry and the restaurant. In fact, Warnach felt encouraged. Years earlier, he had valued Daltrehm's friendship. Optimistically, he looked forward to reviving the relationship that had suffered a brother's personal embarrassment regarding his sister's behavior.

Days later, the incident was presented to a magistrate in Kadranas. True to his word, for the first time in his life, Amlal Ehmedrad had demanded that his daughter accept full accountability for her actions. During the hearing, the magistrate listened to testimony from various witnesses. She questioned Araman and Warnach. Gently and with compassion, she discussed details of the incident with Sandra.

Following a brief recess, the magistrate ordered Lashira into four months of detention at a women's facility. With proper behavior, she would be released for six months into her badehr's custody while under constant court supervision. In exchange for the light sentence, Lashira would also be required to receive court-mandated counseling for one additional year and agree never again to intentionally approach Araman Sirinoya, Sandra Sirinoya, or any children she might have.

Following the judge's decision and the court's dismissal, Sandra turned to face her ki'medsah. Slowly, she moved into the security of his arms. Tenderly, he kissed her hair before resting his cheek against her head. For both, Lashira's long-lingering shadow had been cast away.

Across the court chamber, as a uniformed officer escorted her to secure quarters pending transfer to the reformatory, Lashira paused at the door. Tormented eyes observed a true lover's embrace. Turning away, she wanted to die. As the guard led her out, she swallowed tears that would flood her nights for years to come. Of all the men she had ever taken as lovers, only Warnach had won her heart. He should belong to her. For the remainder of her life, she would ask herself how it could have taken her so long to realize how much she loved him.

# Chapter Twenty-One

Sandra strained to peer through dense cloud cover as they approached Earth and the shuttleport just outside Washington. Finally, she spied the first glimpse of blue oceans and white-blanketed shores and cities. The grin she turned toward Warnach lit her entire face. "Almost there!"

When he shook his head in laughing response, dark waves brushed back and forth across the shoulders of his coat. His lifemate, a deputy minister of the Dil-Terra Interplanetary Alliance, acted more like an excited little girl as she laughed happily and turned to stare toward her home planet.

Half an hour later, he adjusted the collar of the royal blue cape he had bought for her. No finer, smoother wool was to be found anywhere in the known galaxy. Artistic Chikondran hands had applied exquisite embroidery along with traditionally intricate designs in white piping. The cape would serve well to keep her warm and satisfy her mischievous intent to hide her newly obvious pregnancy from John and Angela until the moment that struck her as just right.

Clinging to her hand, he practically ran down the sloped ramp leading to the waiting salon inside Washington's colossal shuttleport. "Shi'níyah! Slow down! You might trip and fall!"

"I'm fine!" she exclaimed, excitedly picking up her pace. Passing through a shimmering air curtain, she entered the immaculately clean waiting concourse. Instantly, she spotted two brilliant, welcoming smiles. "Angela! John!"

Surrendering any ideas of keeping up with her, he slowed his pace and watched as she greeted both with effusive hugs. Reaching them, he also received warm embraces from both John and Angela. While exchanging amiable comments with them, his thoughts briefly strayed. If only she could look forward to such a wonderful greeting from her parents. The notion swiftly evaporated. Her enthusiasm claimed his attention as they marched through the shuttleport to retrieve belongings and leave for the Edwards' home.

Upon reaching the house, Warnach's expression was stern. Insisting he would carry in their luggage, he grudgingly accepted his lifemate's assistance with some of the lighter packages they had brought. Shrugging and comically rolling her eyes at Angela's humorously questioning expression, Sandra laughed. "He's afraid I'll break. By the way, I haven't seen so much snow in years! Did you order the white Christmas just for me?"

"Just for you," John said with a hearty laugh. "Day after Christmas, this stuff goes away."

Once inside the house, John offered to take Sandra's coat. Raising her hands, she held the elaborate closure of the blue cape while sparkles danced merrily in her eyes. Amusement shone on his face while Warnach watched her slowly undo the row of clasps. From behind, John lifted the woolen cloak from her shoulders. In front, Angela gasped. "Oh, my God! Sandra!"

Startled, John's blue eyes fixed on his wife's shocked face. "Angela? What's wrong?"

"My God!" Angela exclaimed again. Launching herself forward, she wrapped Sandra in an excited embrace. "You didn't tell me! Oh, my God! Oh, my God!"

With Sandra's cape still dangling from his hands, John stared. "What am I missing this time?"

Grinning broadly, Warnach quickly reached out and removed the cloak from John's grasp. "Perhaps you'll understand if your wife will turn my lifemate around."

Loosening her embrace, Angela gently spun Sandra around to face John, whose eyes bulged. "Sandra?"

Smiling as she rested her hands on her slightly expanded middle, Sandra laughed softly. "I thought I'd surprise you."

"S...sur...surprise? More like shock! I thought you couldn't...that Terrans and Chikondrans..."

"So we thought ourselves," Warnach said, effectively rescuing the tongue-tied John. After a brief pause, he said, "We're both very happy that the Great Spirit has proven us wrong."

It was John's turn to hug Sandra tightly. His voice quivered as he whispered, "You look wonderful! I'm so happy for you!"

Afternoon's wintry cold shadows might as well have been worlds away. Bedecked with lights and scented with fresh evergreen, the Edwards home surrounded the two couples in comfortable warmth. Inevitable questions arose regarding the unexpected pregnancy, and humorous quips marked lighthearted discussion. As evening brought more snow to blanket the world outside, discussion grew reflective over dinner. Later, affectionate understanding showed in approving eyes when Warnach excused himself to make sure his lifemate went to bed early.

Arising the next morning, everyone chatted over an early breakfast before departing for a day of last-minute shopping. Tears of laughter trickled down Sandra's cheeks at Warnach's insistence on donning a traditional Santa cap to camouflage his cerea-nervos. Always prepared, John produced hygiene sheets to mop up happy teardrops.

The day sped by. When they finally returned home, Sandra reluctantly admitted to fatigue and need for a nap. While she slept, Warnach joined John and Angela in the kitchen. Over meal preparation, the Edwards openly expressed joy regarding the baby and concerns about how Sandra's father would react. Warnach shared his own feelings of relief that, when she called to advise them of her sudden trip to Earth, her parents had already committed to visiting elderly relatives at Christmas. She had insisted that they follow through with their plans, telling them that she and Warnach would come to spend the New Year holiday with the Warner family. In truth, both had preferred spending Christmas with the Edwards, free from the tension so common in her parents' house.

~

Christmas Eve. The brief note she left on the kitchen table had said only that she wouldn't be gone long. The store clerk had complimented the unusual design of her blue cape and had glanced curiously at her golden Kitak. With two bundles of roses in hand, Sandra had then returned to a waiting taxi for the trip to the cemetery.

Large, black, wrought iron hands in an antique clock tower marked eight-thirty. Banks of clouds crept across the sky, replacing morning azure with dull gray, blotting out teasing sunlight, and promising a fresh snowfall. Light winds brushed her face with arctic chill. Crooked fingers pointed heavenward from stocky tree trunks. Marble and granite carved lonesome profiles rising from frozen ground carpeted by deep snow.

She went first to Diana's grave. Stretching out a gloved hand, she brushed mounded piles of snow from the tombstone. Red and white roses adorned the grave of the friend whose smile would forever reside in Sandra's memory.

Trudging through the snow, she reached Derek's grave. Again, although it made little sense, she brushed snow from carved stone even though heavy flakes were already descending from the heavens. Bending forward, she laid a bouquet of yellow roses across a ledge running around the marker. Straightening, she pressed her hands against her stomach, making her pregnancy more obvious despite flowing folds of her cape.

"Derek," she spoke softly, "I brought yellow roses. Just like always."

A chill breeze tugged the lined hood off her head. Ignoring wind-ruffled hair, she gazed down at frosty layers of snow covering the gravesite. In her mind, she saw piercing blue eyes, golden hair, and an optimistic grin.

"Derek, this isn't really easy. You know I'll always care about you and that I'll always miss you. At the same time, my life grows richer every day. Warnach and I are expecting a baby. This wasn't supposed to happen, Derek, but I love this baby so much. I also love his father with every ounce of my being."

She breathed out a heavy sigh. "Derek, I've also kept a promise to myself by finding ways to keep your memory alive. Diana's, too. Now, at long last, I finally feel like my life is mine. Today is Christmas Eve. For me, it's time to bid farewell to the past and embrace the happiness I've found with Warnach. I just needed to tell you what I've never really been able to say before." Pausing, she smiled. "Goodbye, Derek."

She murmured a prayer, crossed herself, and turned to leave. Startled, she stared into bitterly accusing eyes. "Mrs. McKenzie. I didn't expect…" Nervously, she glanced over Stella McKenzie's shoulder and into the surprised face of Derek's sister. "Mary Elizabeth. Hello."

"Sandra, how good to see you."

"Mary Elizabeth, quiet!" Sharply, Mrs. McKenzie rebuked her daughter and glared again at Sandra. "A fine way to remember a young man who died because of you."

"Mom!"

"Mary Elizabeth, I said, be quiet!" scolded Mrs. McKenzie, her gaze never leaving Sandra's face. She again addressed Sandra in an even harsher voice. "I once believed in how much you cared for my son, but now I see that you're just like everyone else."

Not wanting to argue with the older woman, Sandra smiled grimly. "Excuse me. I must go now."

Stella McKenzie stepped in front of Sandra and blocked the way. "Just like everyone else, you betrayed Derek. My son is dead, lying underneath this frozen ground. Look at you. Fine way to show respect for the young man who sacrificed his life for yours. Coming here with your fancy jewelry and clothes and with your belly swollen with some alien's child."

"Mom, that's enough," Mary Elizabeth gasped. "Sandra has a right to live her life."

"And betray my son like you and your dad?" Stella cried out in a voice verging on hysteria. "Everyone has forgotten your brother except me! And just look at this one! She comes here to torture Derek's spirit by talking about how much she loves that damned alien and this brat she carries! She has no compassion! No shame!"

Fire flashed from Sandra's eyes. "You're wrong, Mrs. McKenzie, and you know it. You also have no right to criticize me or insult my baby. If anyone is in the wrong here, you are. I've heard how you've mired yourself in unending grief to the point of alienating everyone who ever cared about you. The way you've hurt Mr. McKenzie, Mary Elizabeth, and all your friends is bad enough, but you're the one who should be ashamed. You stand here over Derek's grave and shame his memory by saying things that contradict everything he ever believed in."

"How dare you…"

"How dare I? I loved Derek! I've also done everything possible to perpetuate his memory so that the good he lived and died for isn't forgotten! Can you say the same? Absolutely not!" Sandra's voice rose shrilly in anger. "Derek's spirit is likely cringing in horrific pain at hearing his own mother utter the kind of cruel insults that infuriated him in life! Out of ugly bitterness, you call down insults on an innocent, unborn child because you want to punish me for not dying that night. Well, I love my baby, and I defy you or anyone else to hurt him with your nasty bigotry! Your son defended the innocent, like my baby, and anyone else needing help to find his way. You're the one betraying his memory, not me! Derek deserves better than such disgrace from the mother he loved. A spirit like his returns to life with God. If anyone really is dead, Mrs. McKenzie, it's you."

Forcing her way past Stella McKenzie, Sandra stormed off, her boots crunching atop ice on the stone path. Short, quick breaths froze into cloudy puffs. Her heart pounded. Blood throbbed inside her temples. Scarlet color flushed her cheeks, and anger snapped in her eyes.

"Ma'am? Are you all right?" The elderly taxi pilot worriedly glanced over his shoulder at the obviously distressed passenger inside his transport.

Closing her eyes, Sandra breathed in and out. She felt her baby shift positions. Life, she thought. Life is mine. Gratefully, she smiled at the man's genuine concern. "I'm fine. Thank you. Could we fly around a few minutes before you take me home?"

By the time she stepped through the front door, her fury had abated. She had argued herself in and out of feeling sorry for Mrs. McKenzie. Despite losing their only child, John and Angela had clung to one another in abject sorrow before focusing on living as tribute to their fallen daughter. Mr. McKenzie had concentrated on Mary Elizabeth and her family while dedicating his energies toward building other lives in honor of his dead son. The incident at the cemetery had certainly been regrettable, but Stella McKenzie's outburst, coming so soon after Lashira's attack, had stoked fires of righteous indignation. Sandra refused to feel guilty about lashing back.

"Where in the world have you been?"

As if the morning's encounter had been non-existent, Sandra smiled brightly and handed her coat to Angela. "Took care of an errand and talked with some people I used to know."

Coming around the corner from the family room, Warnach appeared. Frowning as he grasped her shoulders, he stared into her face. "The weather outside is awful, and snow and ice are treacherous. Where were you?"

Pulling her features into a comically petulant expression, she stared back. "Out. I had things to do. I'm all grown up, my dear minister, and quite capable of navigating in the snow. Besides, I left you a note."

Anxiety had exasperated him. "What if you'd fallen? Remember, young lady, you're pregnant. You need to be careful."

Pursed lips added to her exaggerated look of rebelliousness. "My dear Minister Sirinoya, I know I'm pregnant. However, pregnancy doesn't equate to physically disabled. I was careful, and I'm safely back now. End of story."

"Warnach, how about some hot cocoa to soothe your jangled nerves and warm a chilly guest?" Angela suggested cheerily.

Sandra welcomed Angela's timely rescue with a grateful grin. "Do you have marshmallows?"

Late in the afternoon, Warnach sat on the edge of the bed. Despite the affectionate way he stroked her hair, he still looked annoyed. "How long do you want to sleep?"

"A couple of hours. Hopefully, that'll be enough for me to stay awake through midnight mass." She paused. "You don't know how much I look forward to celebrating Christmas mass here with you beside me."

His expression gentled. "I know. Shi'níyah…"

"Yes?"

He hesitated as he tucked a velvety blanket around her shoulders. "You were upset this morning. Angry, I think. I felt it. Are you sure everything is all right?"

She responded with a drowsy nod. "I'm fine, my ki'medsah."

"But something did happen?"

Rosy lips formed a gentle smile. His perceptive question evoked no sign of surprise. "Yes, something happened, but it's over now. There's no need for you to worry."

As her eyelids slid closed, he gazed thoughtfully at her. The pregnancy had gradually enhanced and strengthened bonds forged during Ku'saá. As each week passed, he grew increasingly aware of her emotions. She had been more than angry that morning. Outrage more aptly described sensations that had vibrated within his Kitak. Sighing, he felt thankful that tranquility now marked her sleeping face. Leaning over, he kissed her lightly and left.

~

Following her example, he knelt a moment before sliding into the well-worn oaken pew. After lifting the blue cape from her shoulders, he watched with an indulgent smile as, with rosary in hand, she dropped to her knees on the padded kneeler and bowed her head. Folding her cape onto the seat between Angela and him, Warnach then joined her in prayer.

When finally they stood, he lost himself within the magic of her Christmas Eve. The great church, nearly dark when they had entered, began to awaken as enormous ivory candles on the altar were lit. Their flames then passed from candle to candle held by those who had braved the wintry night to celebrate the remembrance of Christ's holy birth. Exuberant voices swelled, filling the vast cathedral. Their majestic hymn, accompanied by organ and brass instruments, stirred both heart and spirit.

As the symbolic service continued, Warnach firmly held Sandra's hand. Glancing several times from the corner of his eye, he noted the peaceful glow that embraced her like a clinging aura. How beautiful he saw her. How significant this service, he thought, as he contemplated the coming gift of his own son. Totally absorbed in contemplative reverie, he was late responding to cues to stand or kneel. For his troubles, he sheepishly smiled back into green eyes shining beneath curiously cocked eyebrows.

Rising for the stirring recessional, he added his voice to the glorious outpouring of song. So many times had he heard her at home singing *Joy to the World*. Now, hearing it for the first time with full chorus and brass instruments, he suddenly comprehended why it was her favorite Christmas carol. Music and lyrics perfectly suited her personality. Leaning sideways, he kissed her temple. *Joy to the World* perfectly suited the way she made him feel.

"So, what did you think?" she asked while he buttoned the front of her soft flannel nightgown.

Dark eyes shone in soft lamplight. "I think, my noble Terran lifemate, that your Christmas is indeed magnificent. I also think it's late, and we could both use some sleep. I still haven't quite figured how this Santa Claus person fits into the story, but it would be a shame to be passed over because you were too excited to go to bed."

Giggling, she dived toward the bed. "Last one in is a rotten egg!"

Hurriedly climbing in beside her, Warnach tugged the blankets over them and dragged her into his arms. "Rotten egg?"

Grazing his mouth with her lips, she laughed lightly. "A positively ancient children's taunt. Never made sense to me either."

Having her close felt so satisfying. Lying beside her, he stroked her rounded abdomen while she quietly hummed a Christmas carol they had heard that evening. Suddenly, he felt a faint yet distinct bounce beneath his fingertips. "Sandra, what? Are you all right? What was that?"

She shook with subdued laughter. "That, my dear Minister Sirinoya, was your son wishing you merry Christmas!"

"My son? Are you sure?" Disbelief sounded in his voice as he sat upright.

Grasping his arm, she pulled him down again. "Shsh. He's grown to the point that now you can feel him move. Lie still and let just your fingertips rest on me." Again, she began to hum.

Following two more bumps beneath sensitive fingers, a single tear slid from the corner of his eyes. Her humming grew quieter, fading into a peaceful night. Awake for some time, Warnach prayed in thanks on Christmas morning for the personal miracle of the baby his beloved Shi'níyah carried.

～

Offering her his hand, Warnach helped Sandra rise from the floor. Brushing away clinging bits of ribbon and wrapping paper, she smiled questioningly. "Mr. McKenzie, what a surprise. Merry Christmas."

Outstretched arms invited her forward. Those arms wound around her in a tight embrace. "Sandra, how can I thank you for the Christmas present of a lifetime?"

When she backed away, his earnest expression perplexed her. "What Christmas present? I haven't yet delivered yours."

Half an hour later, Mr. McKenzie departed. Leaning back against the sofa, Sandra closed her eyes in pensive contemplation. The confrontation at the cemetery had left Stella McKenzie in shock. In righteous anger, Sandra had voiced what no one else had dared to say. Sharp, hurt-filled words had successfully penetrated the steely shroud of mourning. Derek's mother had finally looked beyond her own sorrow to see how her pain had compounded the grief her family suffered. Engulfed by tears of regret, she had called her estranged husband on Christmas Eve. Promising to seek additional counseling, she had apologized profusely and begged him to come home. At Mary Elizabeth's house, the reunited couple had spent their first Christmas morning together in three years.

Deep in thought that afternoon, Sandra's eyes opened, and she accepted a mug of hot cocoa from Angela.

"Today has convinced me of one thing," Angela remarked as she settled herself in a chair across from her guest and sipped from her own cup of sweet, fragrant chocolate.

"What's that?"

"Christmas miracles still occur."

Glancing downward and thinking of the precious child within, Sandra smilingly nodded in full agreement.

# Chapter Twenty-Two

Perusing Warnach's schedule of upcoming meetings, Sandra's mind drifted. Her visit with her family had gone surprisingly well. Of course, her father had retained his aloof attitude with Warnach and had expressed dismay over risks related to her being pregnant with the child of an alien species. However, there had been no arguments. The result was that her time with her mother, her brothers, and even her sister had been unusually pleasant.

"Daydreaming?"

No guilt showed in her expression. "A bit. Thinking about the visit home."

"You enjoyed yourself, didn't you?"

She sighed. "Yes, I did. Even Daddy was on his best behavior."

"Perhaps he finally realized what a protective lifemate you have." Behind Warnach's laugh lurked the secret he hoped she would never learn. With this being her first Christmas on Earth since their unification, he had been determined to avoid any potentially upsetting confrontations. Literally resorting to threats, he had warned her father against uttering a single word that might cause her unnecessary distress.

For several seconds, Sandra stared at him. Deciding to ignore odd perceptions niggling her mind, she grinned. "I think I like the idea of you being my protector."

Lifting his left brow impossibly high, he smiled back. "Good. That way, I can expect no disagreement when I tell you it's time to leave remaining reviews for tomorrow so we can go home."

With some difficulty, she stifled the urge to protest and grinned sheepishly. "As you wish, my dear Minister Sirinoya."

Outside Ministry Headquarters, brilliant sunshine bathed tree-lined walkways with golden light. Greening grasses framed floral beds lavished with white and pastel blossoms. Gentle breezes promised the imminent kiss of summer warmth. Hand in hand, lost in themselves and the splendor of spring, the Sirinoyas strolled toward the docking tower reserved for diplomatic ministers.

Two weeks later, summer had unfurled its velvet influence all across the city of Kadranas. Days had grown quite warm, although rarely humid or sultry as was so common where she had lived on Earth. Summery blooms released sweet perfumes into the air and spread blankets of vivid color across carefully tended flowerbeds. Large birds, donning glossy feathers in shades of ruby, emerald, and sapphire, swept across the skies in grand dances. Trees fully attired in rustling, leafy finery swayed to melodies arranged by dancing birds.

"Chilled mirmaja for you, Shi'níyah."

Accepting the tall glass of magenta-colored liquid, she tucked his image safely into a corner of her mind. No summer heat or sunshine could compare to the light shining in his eyes. "Thank you, my good minister."

Seating himself at her side, he leaned precariously sideways and kissed her cheek. "We can leave after breakfast."

Sipping tangy-sweet mirmaja, she smiled. "I haven't seen them in quite some time. I can hardly wait."

Gazing pointedly at her expanding figure, he cocked his head far to the right. "Waiting seems to be an unavoidable fact of life for us right now."

So comical was his expression that she burst into laughter. "Warnach!" she exclaimed as she pressed her hands atop the generously curved mound that had replaced her once-flat middle. "You should try waiting on my side of this equation!"

Good-natured teasing drew Araman into the fun that marked the remainder of breakfast and followed throughout the trip to the seashore.

Reaching the beach house, combined efforts quickly accomplished restocking the kitchen and unpacking for a long weekend. Delighted to be included in her son's weekend getaway plans, Araman shooed him and Sandra off to change into swimwear and relax.

Following a leisurely lunch, Warnach helped Sandra carefully climb into a hammock. Joining her, he settled himself for a welcome afternoon snooze. Lying in the swaying hammock with his eyes closed, his mind meandered through the day's tapestry of thoughts and sensations.

During the trip to the seashore, Mamehr and he had cajoled and pleaded with her to reveal her choice of names for the baby. Teasingly, he had threatened to withdraw his consent for her to choose the baby's first name. Ideas and techniques related to child-rearing had filled luncheon conversation. Mamehr's eyes had sparkled in response to Sandra's requests for parenting advice. His lifemate's face had shone with the rosy glow of a happy, healthy pregnancy.

Waves unrolled swishing rhythms on the shore. Light pressure from her hand, resting on his side, evoked deep, satisfying happiness. His body curved to accommodate her enlarged abdomen. Feeling the rounded hardness created by his unborn son, Warnach smiled. Breathing in, he fell asleep while thinking how awesome the changes she had wrought in his life since their unification.

~

Gigantic orbs reflected their silver faces on the sea's shimmering surface. Foamy seawater lapped onto the shore, leaving beautiful ripples to linger as evidence of kisses from an ageless romance. Summer air wafted the tangy fragrance of the ocean upon caressing breezes.

With Warnach inside preparing the vitamin shake his lifemate drank every evening, Araman appreciated the chance to study her daughter without distraction. Leaning against the corner wall of the bungalow, she had watched Sandra stroll along the deserted shore. The younger woman's image, illuminated by glimmering moonbeams, had been one of peaceful contemplation. Remembering final weeks of her own first pregnancy, Araman understood well the odd mixture of emotions. Anxiety. Anticipation. Fear. Excitement. Worry. Joy.

Strong arms wrapped around her slim shoulders. A low voice whispered tenderly. "What are you thinking, Mamehr?"

Reflective and content, Araman sighed. "Recalling the way I felt when I was pregnant with you. Your badehr often brought me here because the sea was so calming. He would be so proud of you, Warnach. He would also be very happy over how much you love your Sandra."

For once, Warnach's heart wasn't heavy at thoughts of his badehr. Still embracing Araman from behind, he also sighed. "How I wish he could have met her."

"My son, he certainly would have loved her. After you left Lashira, I remember how hard he prayed that you'd find someone who would love and understand you. I think no one ever prayed harder for anything, and I always believed the Great Spirit would hear his prayers."

"Did you ever expect the answer we received?"

Araman laughed softly. "A Terran lifemate? I think none of us expected the answer He sent. However..." She stopped. "Look. What is she doing?"

Focusing more clearly on his ki'mirsah's pregnant silhouette, Warnach watched as she leaned forward and removed golden strapped sandals. With her back to them, she stared out toward the moonlit horizon. Noting her motionless stance, he released his mamehr and straightened. His left eyebrow swept upward, and the timbre of his voice dropped. "She hears them."

Araman's eyes closed to hold back tears. Her jaw tightened for a moment, and her chin quivered. "How can this be, Warnach? How?"

Swallowing hard, he shook his head. "I have no answer, Mamehr. She brings one miracle after another to my life. I can do nothing beyond accepting."

After several minutes, Araman turned and looked into her son's watchful face. Stretching upward, she caressed the smooth skin of his cheek. "I think I shall go say night prayers. Why don't you go to her?"

Appreciation shone from obsidian-colored eyes. Leaning forward, Warnach saluted his mamehr with cerea-semi'ittá. Moments later, his bare feet walked through warm, finely-grained sand. Stopping, he stood completely still to avoid disturbing her.

Long moments passed before she turned to face him. Illuminated by the soft glow of moonbeams, her image transfixed him. Her hair, a little longer than his, curved around her cheeks and shoulders. Near enough to discern her features, he noted gleaming eyes and tranquil smile in features that appeared to have been carved from the finest ivory. Her loosely fashioned dress was made from delicate fabric woven into a swirling pattern of pastel orchids and blues. Its wispy layers, fluttering in the breeze, enhanced the rounded beauty of her pregnant figure.

"Shi'níyah?"

Wordlessly, she approached him. How soothing - how comforting his arms felt as they surrounded her. Resting her head against him, she peacefully smiled into velvet darkness. "Tomorrow morning. They're coming tomorrow morning."

$\approx$

Sitting on a bright red towel, Warnach reached up for a covered mug of coffee Araman had carried outside. A broad smile beamed on his face. "Seven o'clock seems to have become our magic hour."

Araman chuckled and joined her son on the towel. "I see she's already in the water. Has she heard them yet?"

"I think not," he replied. Sipping his coffee, he gazed at Sandra's back. Then, watching as her head suddenly tilted to one side, he lifted his. "Look,

Mamehr. I think they approach." Quickly, he set his cup aside and stood, drawing Araman up with him.

Slowly, Sandra moved ahead, steadily advancing until the sea swirled up to her waist. Turning to face Warnach, she grinned. "They're almost here!" she called out just as a silvery projectile hurtled out of the water and arced behind her.

Despite their latent concern, laughter was unavoidable. Patiently, at the line where aqua seas kissed white sands, Warnach and Araman waited. Watching, both realized how carefully the Quazon conducted themselves with Sandra. The Quazon obviously delighted in splashing her with playful slaps of wide tails. Pleasure shone on her face as she stroked and hugged them. Finally, responding to his lifemate's beckoning, Warnach led his mamehr into the water to join her.

Waves rolled toward shore. Occasionally, Warnach reached out to steady his ki'mirsah when incoming tides threatened to push her over. As before, the magnificent creatures showed exceptional gentleness with Araman. Even with him, they behaved more calmly. Their typical joviality had been tempered, and tranquility marked smiling Quazon faces. Finally, Meichasa's angel spirits departed, creating showers of diamond-like droplets to spray their admirers.

"Shi'níyah?" Warnach's voice sounded against the hushed roll of waves headed toward shore. Gently, his hand tightened around hers. "Is something wrong?"

Glancing around, she drew in a deep breath. "No. I just can't help wondering about them."

From the opposite side, Araman reached out and caressed her daughter's face. "As does our entire family, child. You were right all along. The best any of us can do is to accept the gift of their presence in our lives."

That evening, inside the Brisajai, Warnach studied his ki'mirsah closely. With head bowed and eyes closed, her image was one of pious faith. As she prayed, he again recognized the signs.

In her mind, she was listening to their words. Minutes passed. She stilled and then formed the sign of the cross over her chest. Looking up and meeting his curious gaze, she smiled. "They were reminding me to cherish our love and always to have faith. Then, they laughed because of my round belly."

Jagged rocks protruded upward like fearsome gargoyles perched around the base of the mountain. The mount itself was shrouded in billowing clouds failing to rise high enough to obscure the time-worn peak. Ahead lay the most difficult and perilous approach to the sacred caves.

Badrik closely studied rugged terrain as light mist saturated morning air. Reaching up and behind his head, he tightened the band securing long hair away from his face. "We must be especially careful once we get closer to the base. The paths are smooth stone, and I suspect they'll be dangerously slippery after last night's rain."

With full lips tightly pursed, Warnach tightened straps around the wrists of black, fingerless gloves. "Are you sure you want to go ahead with this?"

Badrik's eyes roved once again across the forbidding landscape. Turning back to Warnach, his eyebrows rose and fell. "I feel as you, my brother. Uneasy peace rests upon the Alliance. Despite all the uncertainty, you and I are blessed. We must demonstrate our faith and offer gratitude for our gifts."

Warnach's smile held no humor as he firmly grasped Badrik's shoulder. "Before we start, Badrik, I want you to know that no man could have a brother finer than you."

The corner of Badrik's mouth lifted in the slightest of smiles. "A feeling that is shared, my brother."

Three hours later, after winding their way through narrow, rugged passages and over moss-slick stones, they decided to rest on a relatively dry, flattened boulder. Munching light wafers packed with nutrients and drinking small amounts of water, they spoke little. The trek they had undertaken would require more than physical strength. Each man's thoughts turned inward, seeking substance within their souls from which they would draw perseverance to complete their pilgrimage.

By nightfall, they reached a level area sheltered by a broad overhang. Weary, they arranged sleeping bags and ate the modest meal traditional for pilgrims to Efi'yimasé Meichasa. Crispy wafers, a cheese spread, and thin, dried slices of fruits and vegetables provided sufficient nutrition without bulk. After the meal was consumed in contemplative silence, they organized packs and supplies before preparing for night prayers.

Badrik lit a tiny cone of Efobé. Its fiery tip glowed orange-red in the dark. Undulating fingers of smoke danced upward into the night. As elder of the two, Warnach initiated the chant that would carry both men into a reflective state of meditative prayer. Seeking the Great Spirit's unseen presence, they began the initial stage of releasing personal burdens that might hamper the cleansing and renewal they believed was possible if they could successfully reach the caves of Efi'yimasé Meichasa. Drawn toward infinite space, each dispatched the disappointments, sorrows, and fears of their respective lifetimes.

Sleep followed exhaustive days of trekking across paths strewn with large, loose stones and climbing over rocky obstacles seemingly intent on blocking their way. Long, chilly nights were spent on hard beds distant from the loving caresses of the ki'mirsahs whom they so loved. Gray mornings dawned too soon for the weary sojourners.

By early afternoon of the fifth day, strong, well-conditioned bodies had grown sore and tired from their slow, steady ascent along the obstacle-strewn mount. Fingers, backs, knees, and toes felt stiff. Rations that provided energy were far less satisfying than the delicious foods they enjoyed at home. Despite their physical discomfort, they exchanged relieved looks. The sacred cave opened above a broad ledge no more than fifty yards away.

Cautiously, with bodies pressed against the rough, craggy face of the mountain, they clung to rocky handholds and sidestepped along the narrow path leading to the protruding table of stone commonly called Ti'ichari'i. From there, they would enter caves that had received pilgrims for millennia.

Drawing on willpower and patience, they finally reached their goal and stood beneath the edge of Ti'ichari'i. Warnach braced himself and boosted Badrik upward. Secure on the ledge, Badrik removed his backpack and lay down on cold rock. Each brother tightly grasped the other's wrists. With a groan, Badrik dragged his brother up. Shoving backpacks aside, they sat and collapsed backward to rest against the mighty mountain. They had arrived.

Despite all the blessings promised, in recent times, few ventured to the sacred natural altar of Efi'yimasé Meichasa. The majority of Chikondrans clung to faith and continued to observe old ways. However, the necessities of modern life and influences from other worlds detracted from the tradition of pilgrimages. Such journeys required a commitment of time and dedication to self-reflection.

As young men, Warnach and Badrik had completed the trip to Efi'yimasé Meichasa. Seated on the edge of the precipice with legs dangling over its steep edge, both realized their previous conquest had been more of an adventurous confirmation of manhood than an affirmation of faith. Exchanging glances, each smiled at their shared thought of how the years had changed both perspective and purpose.

After a solemn night spent just inside the cave's mouth, the two brothers knelt above a single candle and two cones of incense. Wispy plumes of smoke carried prayers to the Great Spirit. Soon, they would advance into the mammoth cavern. They planned to penetrate the cave from the right side, which was the more demanding approach taken by those seeking the original route taken by Perazhan.

If all went well, they would reach the chamber called Ka'atrifan. There, they would encounter two Luradrani committed to a lifetime of retreat at the holy site. Before the pilgrims could progress toward the final altar of Efi'yimasé Meichasa, they would join the Luradrani in prayer as preparation for meditation at the location where Yahvanta had first revealed Quazon to Perazhan.

Hours passed. From the far side of the cave, dampness from open ocean penetrated chambers and passages carved by forces of time and nature. Perilous drops required constant vigilance as they progressed over slick, slimy stone. By the time they reached the chamber of the Luradrani, both had scrapes and bruises from slips and falls along the way.

Natural shafts permitted the influx of fresh air. Carved into solid rock, tiers held rows of lighted candles. About a dozen cots lined the left wall. On the right, a plank table was lined with five chairs per side and one chair at each end. The far end of the table was set for four.

"Welcome." Attired in black robes cinched at the waist with gold rope, a middle-aged man greeted them with the formal Chikondran bow.

Warnach and Badrik returned the bow and responded in unison, "Esteemed Luradrani, we greet you on this sacred day granted by the Great Spirit."

The second Luradrani appeared, carrying a large tureen. Little puffs of steam escaped from between lid and bowl as he set it on the table. He then turned and saluted the pilgrims with a bow. "We have awaited your arrival. You will share our meal with us."

Grace was offered over fresh, warm, crusty bread and thick, savory stew. In tranquil silence, they consumed their lunch. Afterward, the Sirinoya brothers were invited to rest on clean cots while the Luradrani cleared remnants of the shared meal.

When morning came, Warnach awoke first. Stretching stiff, aching limbs, he sat up. The two Luradrani sat on a cushioned bench. Each held a worn and tattered prayer book in his hands. While Badrik continued dozing, Warnach approached the holy men. Slowly, almost childlike, he sat on a padded mat in front of them. Raising his face, he gazed at them, waiting, though he knew not why.

A slight smile crossed the face of the older man. "Honor and encouragement have you and your brother brought to us."

"We are the ones honored that you receive us into this holy place."

"The holy ones themselves advised us of your coming." This time, the younger one spoke.

Warnach's brow creased in question. "I don't understand, Esteemed Luradrani."

Both men smiled, but only the elder continued. "You, perpetuators of the honorable Sirinoya, carry within your veins the blood of Perazhan. Few know this fact.

"The great chieftain himself was the first Chikondran to be granted revelation of the Great Spirit's gift of Meichasa. As told in the ancient chronicles, he was drawn by angels to the sacred chamber now called Efi'yimasé Meichasa. It was there that Yahvanta Himself spoke to Perazhan and blessed his eyes with the vision of angel spirits incarnated as sacred Quazon. It was to this same place that faithful Perazhan returned five years later to witness the moment when Quazon delivered Mehrashahm from the ocean itself."

Fascination shone from dark eyes that shifted to note his brother joining him on the mat. Badrik had apparently heard all. "Esteemed Luradrani, is our ancestral link to Perazhan reason for the holy ones advising you to expect our arrival?"

The priests smiled enigmatically. The younger of the two replied, "In part. The rest, we are not certain we understand. During our meditation, they communicated many words. Their messages, even to us, remain indiscernible."

Only with eyes closed did Warnach dare further questions. "Esteemed Luradrani, are you free to share those words?"

A solemn hush descended upon the four men. When the elder Luradrani again spoke, his voice dropped to a lower tone. "Children of Perazhan, you must yourselves ask your questions of the angel spirits who dwell here at Efi'yimasé Meichasa."

Late morning. Sunlight would be abundant until evening. The time was upon them. Leaving their gear in the care of the holy men, Warnach and Badrik took lanterns in hand and began their descent of steep, carved stone steps leading to the Efi'yimasé Meichasa.

One painfully slow step followed the other. With the rock stairway almost as perilous as the first section of the cavern, they made sure that each foot was planted flat and secure before allowing their weight to move forward. Still, nearly an hour passed before they clearly heard the roar of the ocean and smelled its salty aroma. Subduing any urge to hurry, they continued their painstaking path toward Efi'yimasé Meichasa.

Finally, they were able to gaze out the wide opening through which Perazhan had first glimpsed Quazon and then, five years afterward, his beloved Mehrashahm. Outside, late afternoon sunshine dappled ocean waters with sparkling highlights. Fresh breezes cooled sweat-drenched faces. To the right, natural sunlight bathed a wide stone altar in golden light.

Crossing the chamber, each brother pulled from his pockets a candle and an Efobé cone. Solemnly, they lit candles and incense. Badrik and Warnach then knelt on hard rock to offer brief prayers of thanks. Rising, they went to the edge of the great window over the ocean and settled themselves into indentations that had been worn into smooth, curved seating by centuries of meditating pilgrims. Closing their eyes, they began chanting traditional hymns of faith-filled visitors.

Prayer carried them into trance. Trance carried them into the shadowy depths where Quazon dwelled. Unfamiliar voices spoke words of both warning and encouragement. As foretold in ancient writings, dreadful darkness approached. They must cling to courage and purpose. They must not surrender their sacred mission. They must never submit to evil's onslaught. The angels of Meichasa assured them that perseverance and faith would bring blessed rewards. The Great Spirit would not fail to send His light to dispel the darkness.

Released from the cocoon woven around them by Meichasa's angelic spirits, Warnach and Badrik gazed at one another. Their minds sought to grasp full significance of the mystical journey from which they had just returned. Deep, private contemplation filled hearts and souls. By the time they returned to the Luradrani, neither brother had spoken a word.

A week later, Sandra arrived home early from Kadranas. Tired after days of continuous meetings with political leaders visiting from Earth, she wanted to rest. Reclining on her lifemate's lounge in the music room, she smiled into peaceful solitude as her thoughts rambled.

After returning from their holiday visit to Earth, Warnach had delayed his pilgrimage from the original plan. Indeed, he had been reluctant to leave her at all and had even considered canceling his plans. Following their most recent encounter with the Quazon, she had spent several days convincing him that she would be all right. Intuition told her he needed to go, and Quazon had affirmed her instincts. Despite knowing she had done the right thing, the separation had grown more difficult with each passing day.

As her left hand rubbed circles over her protruding stomach, her right hand lifted to her Kitak. Suddenly, her eyes flew open. Awkwardly, she lurched off the curved lounge and hurried outside. With eyes skyward, she watched Badrik's transport descend and skim over the entry lane until it reached a smooth landing. Happy that he was finally home, she could hardly wait for Warnach to release safety restraints and exit the transport.

The moment he stood on solid ground, she raced into waiting arms. His dashing smile quickly disappeared as she connected her mouth to his in a wildly enthusiastic kiss. Hearty laughter interrupted their reunion when Badrik exclaimed, "And to think! People actually wonder how a Chikondran and a Terran managed to conceive a child!"

Giggling, Sandra shook her head. "And to think! Terrans actually think Chikondrans are dour, straight-laced, and humorless!"

Tossing his head backward, Warnach laughed. "Ah, me'u Shi'níyah, Terrans are right. At least they were until you decided to make your home on Chikondra."

While Sandra clung tightly to her lifemate's arm, Badrik quickly helped carry Warnach's things inside. Then, claiming the need for a long, relaxing, hot shower before welcoming Farisa home from the clinic, Badrik left for home.

While Warnach disappeared upstairs for his own shower and change, Sandra prepared a light snack and fruit tea, which she served outside. Settled into a chair, she paused mid-sip when she felt his warm face nuzzle lovingly against her neck. "Ci'ittá mi'ittá, me'u Shi'níyah. I missed you."

Watching as he slowly sat across from her, she smiled. "I'm so glad you're home."

His features were thoughtful as he served himself several slices of dark yellow cheese on toasted crackers. Studying her intently, he sipped icy tea before finally returning her smile. "You were waiting outside. How did you know we were coming?"

Her shoulders lifted in a slight shrug. "I felt you through Kitak."

Leaning forward, his long fingers stroked across engraved metal. "You feel more through Kitak than practically every Chikondran I've ever known. How is that so?"

Tranquility marked her expression. "I think perhaps no Chikondran has ever known the magnitude of love I feel for you."

Thick black lashes fell as he drew in a deep breath. Years together in unification had not dampened or diminished the power of her words to move him to the very depths of his soul.

~

Araman glanced up with inquisitive eyes. "How was the pafla match?"

"Invigorating!" Warnach exclaimed as he leaned forward to kiss her cheek.

"You beat Rodan again?"

Boyish sparkles glinted from dark eyes. "That I did. He has to continue paying court dues for another quarter." Perusing the contents of a crystal candy dish, he selected a wrapped piece of chocolate from Earth and peeled away golden foil. Slowly, he bit away half the confection and savored its delicious smoothness melting onto his tongue before popping the remainder into his mouth. "Where's Sandra?"

"I don't think she's been still all day. She said she was going outside for a short walk."

Warnach grinned wryly. "She can't be comfortable. I'm not sure how you women manage."

"That's considering she isn't big compared to most women. You should have seen me in the final stages of pregnancy."

Several quick shakes caused black waves to ripple. "Remembering Mirah, I think it best I didn't see you."

Araman chuckled. "Typical male response. While I go inform your lifemate that her pafla champion has returned home, why don't you go change before dinner?"

Afternoon sun lengthened velvety shadows across lush green grasses. Towering puffs of white clouds dotted blue skies. Soft breezes whispered through leaf-laden treetops. As Araman strolled onto the path Sandra had taken, she thought of how often her daughter had poetically verbalized images of Chikondran nature. Smiling at the thought, Araman turned a corner. Looking ahead, she saw Sandra leaning with her back against an enormous tree and her hands locked tightly around her stomach.

"Sandra?" Hurried steps carried Araman forward. "What's wrong, child?"

Relief clearly shone from green eyes. "Mamehr! I had to stop. I needed to catch my breath," she answered breathlessly. "Contractions. Strong ones. I think the baby's coming."

Araman stroked Sandra's cheek comfortingly. "Stay calm, daughter. I'll help you."

"Don't worry, Mamehr. I'm all right. The contractions. They're just so strong."

Halfway back to the house, Sandra felt another powerful wave move across her pregnant abdomen. Thankfully, they were close to one of the many benches dotting the estate. Gripping the back tightly, she lowered herself onto carved stone and then grinned into Araman's concerned face. "Let me rest a minute?"

"Do you think you'll be all right here long enough for me to go get Warnach?"

Still grinning, Sandra nodded. "That's probably a good idea. Don't worry, Mamehr. I won't go anywhere. Promise."

Araman rushed through the house just as Warnach was trotting down the broad staircase. "Warnach! Sandra needs your help. The baby!"

Running forward and grasping her slim shoulders, he stared into his mamehr's flushed, excited face. "Where is she?"

"The first bench on the path to the old tower. Go. I'll notify the doctor and the hospital."

Tiredness evaporated as Warnach's long legs stretched into a full run. Anxiety quickened his pace. Reaching her quickly, he dropped onto the seat beside her and kissed her forehead. "Shi'níyah," he gasped.

Her lips formed a regretful line. "Don't look so frightened. I needed help, and Mamehr is so tiny."

"Don't look frightened? The baby isn't due for two weeks yet! Let me help you back to the house. We can call for an ambulance."

Her response was a breathy chuckle. "Me'u ki'medsah, first babies have a knack for coming a little early or a little late. I don't think we'll need an ambulance unless you're too nervous to transport me yourself."

Ten minutes later, Warnach tossed her bags into the rear of his transport while she begged a final trip to the bathroom. Standing outside the door, he heard her loud gasp. "Sandra? Sandra!"

"It's okay," she called out shakily. "Just a huge contraction. Maybe you should grab some towels in case my water breaks!"

Soon, hospital attendants helped her from the transport and onto a hoverbed. Leaving the transport to a valet, Warnach clutched her hand as attendants guided their patient through doors that swung open automatically. Within minutes, a nurse was helping her change into a loose gown and trying to make her more comfortable.

Hoping to ease her lifemate's anxiety, she smiled after taking several measured breaths through a contraction. "Warnach," she whispered, "everything will be okay. You'll see."

A little later, earlier optimism vanished as her patience swiftly ebbed. Dr. Walters, her obstetrician, seemed not to comprehend that his battery of questions was growing impossible to answer. The pediatric specialist, Dr. Nimartlal, had brought an entourage of colleagues who constantly adjusted scan sensors and screens monitoring the baby's condition. Nurses were on every side, and constant noise was distracting her ability to concentrate on her breathing. Finally, following a particularly difficult contraction and tightly squeezing Warnach's hand, she forced a hoarse shout. "Stop it! Get out! Get out!"

Not knowing what to do, near panic crossed Warnach's face. "Shi'níyah, calm down."

With time between contractions quickly decreasing, her speech grew more difficult. "Farisa! Call Farisa!"

"Sandra, I know…" He glared impatiently at doctors oblivious to his earlier request for a calmer setting. Disappearing for only moments, he returned and bent forward. "Farisa is coming. She'll get this sorted out," he whispered against her ear.

A Terran nurse approached her. "Mirsah Sirinoya, let me apply these sedation electrodes. They'll help with the pain."

Reaching out, Sandra batted expensive medical equipment to the floor. "It's not the pain, damn it! Warnach! I'm trying to have a baby! Make… them…go away!"

Unexpectedly but with great gentleness, a tall, slender nurse grasped Sandra's free hand. The nurse, a black woman from Earth's African continent, smiled compassionately before sternly addressing the doctors. "She's right. This is more like a circus than a birthing. Get some of these people out of here! And move some of that equipment aside where we can reach it quickly if we need it! She deserves respect, and so does her baby!"

Grateful tears filled Sandra's eyes as the woman tenderly stroked her hair. "Everything will be all right, sweetheart." Glancing upward, the lead maternity nurse nodded. "Dr. Sirinoya, I'm so glad you're here."

Farisa placed a firm hand on Warnach's shoulder and then glared impatiently at Dr. Walters. "I warned you this could get out of hand." Switching to Chikondran, she angrily scolded Dr. Nimartlal for his lack of sensitivity and ordered his team out of the birthing room. Quickly, a quiet, more peaceful state replaced earlier confusion.

Leaning over Sandra, Farisa smiled. "Better?"

Tremulously, Sandra murmured, "Thank you."

Soothing background music dampened the hum of necessary medical equipment. Bright lights were dimmed. Her nurse, Busara, showed Warnach how to massage his lifemate's shoulders to ease her tension. Able to focus her mind at last, Sandra listened to Warnach's comforting voice. She concentrated on breathing through contractions while absorbing the many sensations and images of one of the most significant days in her life.

Puffing rapidly, she was no longer able to resist primal urges to push.

Her doctor signaled Dr. Nimartlal and a pair of pediatric nurses to get ready. Holding Warnach's hand in a painful, vise-like grip while Farisa supported her shoulders, she followed Busara's coaching and pushed. Within minutes, a baby's cry filled the room. Perspiration glistened on her skin as her eyes followed the source of continuing cries.

Swiftly, Dr. Nimartlal performed initial scans before allowing attending nurses to wrap the perfectly developed baby boy in pastel blue swaddling. One of the nurses then made certain the wailing infant was snug in his father's arms before allowing parents to introduce themselves to their newborn son.

Smiling through a glaze of tears, Sandra marveled at her ki'medsah's expression. Black-brown eyes gleamed as they fixed upon the face of his tiny son. Full lips quivered as they formed a shaky smile. His glance continually shifted toward his lifemate and back again to the new life cradled securely in his arms.

Reaching out, she tenderly stroked the velvety cheek of her crying infant. "I love you, sweet baby," she whispered.

Visibly overwhelmed, Warnach looked toward Sandra. "He's wonderful, me'u Shi'níyah. I never knew - I could feel this way." His voice thickened with swelling emotion. Cerea-nervos pulsated in patterns new to her.

"Warnach," Farisa interrupted quietly, "I think he needs one thing Sandra cannot give him."

Weakly smiling, Sandra nodded. "I think you might need the same thing, my good minister."

Warnach lifted his son and ever-so-gently bestowed upon him the first cerea-semi'ittá of his life. As seconds passed, crying subsided and was replaced by a soft humming sound. Bonded to his newborn baby according to Chikondran ways, Warnach's soul felt awash in feelings impossible to name or define.

A pediatric nurse approached Warnach. Reluctantly, the new badehr released his son into her care and turned pleading eyes to Farisa.

"Don't worry. I know how Sandra feels, and I've talked with Busara. She won't let them treat him like a science project."

The nurse paused, allowing Sandra time for a parting kiss and caress before disappearing with the child. Another nurse advised the new mother that the doctors had finished tending to her. They would soon transfer her from delivery to a regular room.

Fatigue set in as soon as she slid onto the bed inside the elegantly decorated hospital room. Affectionately, Warnach tucked covers around her shoulders. "Me'u Shi'níyah," he murmured, "each time I think it impossible to love you more, you always find some way to carry me to a new plateau higher than the last." Receiving a sleepy smile in response, he continued, "Rest. I must go tell Mamehr and check our son once more before I go home for the night."

"Warnach?" Her whisper was barely audible.

"What, my beautiful Shi'níyah?"

Tugging slightly at his hand until he bent forward, she whispered into his ear. Seeing astonishment on his face, she smiled and whispered again. "Ci'ittá mi'ittá, me'u Warnach. Ci'ittá mi'ittá."

Walking from a corridor into the waiting area, his memory listened to that whisper over and over again. Reaching the plush waiting room, he watched Badrik jump to his feet and offer his hand to Mamehr. "They're fine. Sandra's resting and my son - Mamehr, he's - perfect."

Relieved and happy, Araman crossed the room and embraced her elder son. When she finally found herself able to meet his gaze, she saw his image through a blur of tears. "How glad I am, Warnach. Can we see him?"

Badrik tightly gripped Warnach's upper arm. "Yes, can we see this son of yours?"

Arrangements had been made to keep the baby in a private room away from eyes that might be too curious over the first child born of a mixed Chikondran and Terran union. Busara noted their approach and, with a smile, offered them surgical robes before leading them to where a nurse watched over the now quiet infant.

Gazing down, Warnach once again felt incredible fullness inside his chest. All the science related to reproduction was reduced to total insignificance when compared to the miracle of his sleeping child.

"I felt the same way about each one of you when you were born." Araman's voice was sweetly reflective.

Even Badrik found speech elusive. "He... My brother, I am so happy for you."

Delicate fingertips tenderly touched tiny, balled fists. "He is beautiful," Araman remarked without taking her eyes off the peaceful little face that reminded her of another newborn. "Has Sandra told you his name yet?"

"Finally," Warnach replied with a slight nod.

"Are you going to tell us?" Badrik asked.

Reaching outward, Warnach placed his palm against Araman's cheek. "I think I never loved you so much as tonight, Mamehr. I also think Sandra expected that and anticipated what we would all miss most. Somehow, she found a way to fill that void." Dark eyes beheld once again the tiny baby as Warnach nearly choked. "She has named our son Morcai."

Involuntary tears spilled onto Araman's cheeks. Throughout the evening, she had dismissed as wishful imagination the sense of her late ki'medsah's presence. No longer did she doubt. His spirit had joined them, watching and waiting with them until the child had been born. His grandson would perpetuate the noble Sirinoya line and the name of the badehr who once had collapsed after nightlong prayers that the Great Spirit would one day grant peace and love to his own firstborn son.

Drawn into her elder son's embrace, she wept with joy. Echoing within Araman's heart were words she now felt certain her ki'medsah's spirit would hear. "Ci'ittá mi'ittá, me'u Morcai. Ci'ittá mi'ittá."

~

Shining eyes studied every shadow and every color, every angle and every motion. Intent ears listened closely, hearing fresh, new tones in a beloved voice. Never in his lifetime had he seen anything so sweetly tender as his lifemate that morning, holding their son to nurse at her breast.

"Me'u Shi'níyah. Good morning."

Hushed words claimed her attention. "Warnach, good morning," she responded with a glorious smile. Within moments, she raised her face to receive his kiss and then watched as he dropped a second kiss atop Morcai's thick, dark hair. "He's beautiful, isn't he?"

Before long, Warnach cuddled his infant son. After fastening the top of her gown and sliding her legs to the side and off the edge of the bed, Sandra earned her lifemate's disapproving smile.

"What do you think you're doing? You aren't supposed to be out of bed!"

Laughing at the worried demand in his voice, she kissed his cheek and retrieved the baby. "I'm preparing to give you your first live demonstration of what fatherhood is all about. Your son needs a diaper change. Oh, and by the way, I am allowed out of bed."

Late in the afternoon, Araman arrived with Nadana. Soon afterward, Badrik and Farisa joined them. While the new grandmother and uncle admired an alert and curious Morcai, Farisa talked with Warnach and Sandra about medical exams that, so far, indicated a strong, healthy baby.

Meanwhile, Nadana quietly observed. Spiritually, she prepared to accompany the family to a reserved, consecrated chapel inside the private hospital. As was Chikondran custom, on the first full day of life, the baby would be presented to the Great Spirit in a ceremony called Ohmtra'ame eu Si'im. Placed upon a hammock-shaped altar beneath a skylight, the religious presider would offer thanks for the blessing of new life. Prayers would also be offered for health, joy, and honor on the lives of the child and new parents.

From a different perspective, Nadana faced a renewed, disconcerting tide of questions. Research into ancient religious writings and prophecies haunted her. Were prophecies mere fairy tales told to enchant children during olden times? Was she reading far too much into the old legends because of the intensity of her own faith?

Affectionately, she suddenly smiled. Joy brightened her sister's face. Beyond any doubt, the birth of Warnach's son had already revitalized a woman who had never stopped mourning her lost ki'medsah. When Araman had called just after midnight, even her voice had sounded rejuvenated. Now holding her new grandson in her arms, she beamed with newfound happiness.

For a few moments longer, Nadana pondered the name that had stolen her breath in that morning's wee hours. An ancient name rarely heard in modern times. Morcai. He who leads in faith. Coincidence? Perhaps. However, as godparents arrived and the aging Simlani joined the infant boy's growing circle of admirers, a single question echoed throughout her spirit. How many coincidences were required to build a prophecy fulfilled?

# About the Author

Sandra Valencia has lived her entire life in the state of Ohio. Growing up in a modest home with two brothers and two sisters, she always loved books. When classmates groaned over writing assignments, she relished new chances to put pencil to paper. Also captivated by studies of foreign languages, she has studied several languages and enjoys added zest in her life by traveling abroad to meet new people and personally experiencing the wealth of different ideas and cultures.

From early childhood, she encountered a dramatic range of experiences commonly grouped into a category called paranormal activity. Dreams, visions, precognition, and telekinesis are among only a few of the things that have sometimes frightened her, sometimes inspired her, and always fascinated her. Those experiences have become a treasure chest of ideas and concepts that are often included in her writing.

Ms. Valencia consolidated two decades of dreams into the series, Legends from Turand. She has been both surprised and gratified to be contacted by readers from around the world, including Colombia, England, Italy, Mexico, The Netherlands, and Portugal. Descriptions from readers of Song of Turand and Return to Turand include comments such as:

"Use of vivid imagery makes the novel a joy to read."
"One reading is not enough!"
"Truly inspirational…"
"So vividly described, one feels a part [of the story]."

Married for more than four decades, she is the mother of two dynamic sons who challenge her intellectually and spiritually. Besides writing and travel, she greatly enjoys classical and Latin music. Favorite hobbies include entertaining friends and family, camping, gardening, and exploring the many aspects of esoteric phenomena.

www.sandravalencia.net

CPSIA information can be obtained
at www.ICGtesting.com
Printed in the USA
BVHW030028030720
582423BV00008B/102/J

9 781633 373655